PLAYER MANAGER

4

PLAYER MANAGER 4

TED STEEL

Podium

Podium

THE STORY SO FAR

Max Best has convinced the board at Chester Football Club to create a director of football position for him. He is focused on making long-term decisions: improving the club's culture, bringing in talented youngsters, prioritising the pathway from the youth team to the first eleven, and creating a women's team. But under the management of Ian Evans, the club is flirting with relegation and Max cannot currently play. The signing of left back Jack Litherland has given the entire club a much-needed lift as the transfer deadline approaches.

PLAYER MANAGER 4

SLAM DUNK

*Football glossary: To Slam Shut. Opposite of "to open."
According to the Sky Sports in-house style guide, the transfer
window must always slam shut. In the real world, there are
many ways to close a window. Slowly and one-handed from
a crouching position so your neighbours don't notice that
you've been spying on them. Quickly, because you just threw
an insect out. Or passive aggressively, because someone has
started smoking just outside. But in the world of football,
windows can only slam shut.*

Tuesday, January 31, 2023. Last day of the transfer window. Last chance for clubs to trade players.

"And breaking news from Portugal is that Benfica have *rejected* an improved bid from Chelsea for World Cup star Enzo Fernandez, said to be in the region of eighty million pounds. Benfica are *adamant* they won't negotiate. The player has a one-hundred-million-pound buyout clause, but Chelsea insist they won't improve their offer. Brian, what do you make of it?"

"I think he's a good player, but is he an eighty-million-pound player? I'm not so sure."

"Thanks, Brian. More on that story as it develops. Now over to Nottingham Forest, who seem to have forgotten they signed twenty players in the summer because they're *linked* with about twenty more."

Someone in the breakroom spoke to me. "Mad, isn't it? All this transfer stuff."

It was the left back from the credit card company who I'd taken the piss out of after he'd started sledging me. I'd seen him around a few times and we were on friendly terms. "Yeah, bonkers."

"You going to sign anyone else?" He was asking in my capacity as Chester FC's director of football. It was my job to decide which players to buy and sell.

"We're done," I said. "Unless you want to sponsor us."

"Nah. I'm a Palace fan." He grinned and got on with making his coffee. I took one last look at the TV, muted it, and went on a tour of my domain.

I started by checking out the first team's training, where I spent far too long laughing and joking with the world's greatest living human being, professional footballer and professional Scouser Jack Litherland. While I was at Das Tournament, our loanee left back had made his debut for Chester in a team that also featured a strong start from James Wise. The new signings gelled into the team perfectly, and propelled Chester to a 3-0 win. Litherland sent in two delicious crosses that my good mate Henri Lyons headed home. Three points for the team, two goals for my client, and one big, long text message from a deliriously happy MD.

That had been part of the reason I'd let Spectrum see out the remaining games of Das Tournament. Yes, it was the right thing to do and all that, but also, Chester Men's first-team manager Ian Evans wasn't going anywhere. Two signings and Chester were back on course for a mid-table finish. With my chances of taking over Chester's first team currently at zero, I could relax and get back to some long-term planning.

Vimsy blew his whistle to start the next drill, and Jack was keen to "get a sweat on," as he put it. So I let him rejoin the main group and popped into the medical room to see what was up. And to check out Livia's latest ponytail variation.

Ah! How nice to be surrounded by bare, white walls while I brushed my hand along those hard, flaky massage tables. I wondered, *But this is shit. Why do I like this?* That's when I realised what was different.

"What *is* that smell?" I asked.

Livia smiled. What a smile it was, too. It really suited her ponytail. Today's version had a little scorpion kick just before the end. Very dramatic. "That's the diffuser."

"The what now?"

She was rubbing a guy's leg, and now she switched to the other one. "Dean went with Magnus to a, what was it called? Holistic therapy centre. And they chose an essential oil that conveyed the desired, er, spirit and tenor of the workplace."

I bent to see who was getting the treatment. It was D-Day, the winger who Evans was using as a striker. He was malingering, but I didn't care. He'd be out of the club in a few months. All the pricks would. "Smells nice."

"Yeah. I think it's orange blossom and honeycomb."

"Huh." I closed my eyes and imagined I was in the Shaolin Temple or somewhere like that. "Really does a lot to make it nicer in here. So he's trying, is he?"

"He" meant Dean, our head physio. I'd suggested to him that his future with Chester FC depended on him making the medical room warm and inviting. Livia repressed a smile. "Yes."

"That's it? No goss?"

"No. He's trying."

I slapped my hands together. "Good enough! Can't ask for more than that, can I?"

"Not really."

"Well, I'm going to." I waited for her to roll her eyes; she didn't. "But not today. Today is already top. It's the best day ever."

"No more transfers to do, then?"

"We are skint. The squad's the squad." I caught myself giving D-Day a dirty look, but cut it out right away. No culture wars today! Today was a good day.

"You missed a great match on Saturday. So dynamic! Positive! That's the best they've played since..." She stopped rubbing D-Day's obnoxious calf while she thought.

"Since Oldham," I suggested. That was the match where I'd decided I would have to become a player so that I could become a manager.

"Yeah. Yeah!"

"A lot more of that to come, I reckon. Big finish to the season. New contracts for all the important players." I did a rude gesture behind D-Day's head that Livia found shocking and funny. "Nice solid foundation for the next manager to build on." I waggled my eyebrows because the main candidate for the job was her boyfriend, Jackie Reaper. She didn't take the bait. "Be like that. I'm off to say something nice to Ian Evans for the first time ever! Wish me luck!"

On my way, I checked my phone. There were tons of messages from unknown numbers and emails from randos. I'd check them out over a hearty brek (which is what we call breakfast in Manchester). I was feeling so good I was even tempted to try a vegan option. Oats in oat milk. A bit cannibalistic, in my opinion, but when you were on top of the world you had to take the chance to see things from a new perspective.

Evans was in his customary position on the side of the pitch, stock still. The hair, as always, quivered in the breeze.

"Ian! Big win. Amazing, congrats. New lads were right at it, I heard."

He smiled. "They were. I knew all about James, course, but Jack? Mmm." Hard to describe that "mmm." It seemed like Evans's version of a chef's kiss. For a guy like Evans, hard work and doing the hard yards was nine-tenths of football, but there was still room in his heart for beauty, and the kind of cross that Litherland could hit was as beautiful as it got, especially with a thunderous Henri Lyons header at the end. The Frenchman was the pot of goal at the end of Litherland's rainbow.

I rubbed my hands together, both from cold and excitement. "Ah, well, top all round. Top all round. And you were right."

"'Bout what?"

"At Shona's party. I was doing that online coaching course and had questions to answer about the World Cup matches. One question was: Who's the Argie player with the highest transfer value? Your guess was Enzo Fernandez. I couldn't choose him because he wasn't in the first eleven, but I don't think I'd have gone for him, anyway. And now Chelsea have bid eighty million for him. Insane, but you saw it coming. Maybe you know a bit about this game after all!"

It sounds like a dickish thing to say, but I was in such a good mood Evans took it for what it was—a bit of fun. He smiled and almost looked sheepish. "Yeah, well, been doing it long enough."

"And for another five months, fingers crossed!" I was tempted to grip him by the shoulder and give him a friendly shake, but there was the risk of him punching me. That, despite his age, would hurt.

I turned, ready for my world premiere vegan breakfast.

"Best," said Evans.

"Yes," I said, spinning like a soldier on parade.

"We could use a proper right mid."

He wanted more signings? I'd got him two great ones. I sagged, just a fraction. "Ah. Sorry, mate, really, but the piggy bank's empty. I honestly would if I could."

He shook his head at my stupidity. "I meant you, you twat."

I beamed. The best day ever just got better! "Ah! Two weeks till my hearing. But sure, fuck it, why not? I'll burnish your late-stage CV with a few ten–nil wins. Count me in. Don't expect me to shuffle and slide, though."

He scoffed. "I won't."

I skipped away, feet barely touching the ground. What had made him warm to me? The new signings? Beating Wolves? Turning Tyson into a player? Whatever. We'd have five harmonious months, he'd fuck off to grow vegetable marrows, and once the door finished slamming behind him, I'd be able to run my club exactly as I wanted. In the meantime, playing a game or two sounded like fun. I wanted to tell more stories. A lot more stories.

The deluge of texts was mostly from agents about possible players we could sign, but it wasn't very interesting. Or timely; we had no money left. I replied to most because it seemed like a good idea to have good relationships with all those guys. I ended up scrolling back all the way to Sunday's texts.

Spectrum: I fucked up. We lost 5–4. They scored in the last minute because I went men behind ball. Tried to get to penalties. I feel sick.

Me: When you're in charge, you're in charge. I know you went as attacking as you felt comfortable with.

Spectrum: Were you here? I didn't see you.

Me: I'm always there. I'm like the spirit of Baby Yoda watching over you.

Spectrum: I messed up the tournament.

Me: Nope. You scored four goals against Stoke. What would you have said, on Saturday morning, if I said you'd be slugging it out in the semifinal with a Championship team?

Spectrum: But that was our best chance to win it. Probably ever.

Me: Nope. That was our worst chance to win. Every year we'll get stronger. Also: I'm behind you. I'm about to touch you on the shoulder.

Me: Made you look.

So we lost the semifinal, and we lost the third place playoff. The kids were shot, for that last one. They'd put a lot of effort into the matches, and the other teams were generally fitter. It wasn't just physical fitness; it was experience. Most of Chester's matches were easy wins or huge defeats. They weren't used to actual contests. As we improved the squad, we'd have to find new ways to challenge them. Maybe we'd enter them into under-sixteens tournaments! Fourth place in Das Tournament, though. It wasn't bad.

And Tyson. Wow. He'd really come through. He was a player now. Teamwork 7 and rising. Plus 2 CA points. On pitch? Tick. Off pitch? Well, he'd warned me that Beth had been asking about Dani (a deaf superstar I'd found), and he'd stolen a lunchbox from Notts Forest (so I could learn how big teams fed their young players). He'd turned into an asset. Someone who was starting to believe in the Chester story. That had been a long, exhausting process that had begun on my second day in Chester, when I'd managed the under-fourteens and subbed him off. All that time spent fixing him. Time I could have spent doing hundreds of other things. Yeah. Wouldn't change a second. Worth it.

That penalty? Yes, mate! Beyond the *obvious* benefits that came from Tyson passing to Benny, it was a moment everyone was talking about. Even Dani asked me about it. *Is it true that Tyson passed from a penno?* For a young man who wants recognition to be given more of that sweet, sweet sauce for a *pass* than he could ever get from any shot . . . Yes. I couldn't have planned a better outcome.

The kids I'd yoinked from Hope Farm Juniors? They were staying. Spectrum? He lost his nerve near the end of the semi, but he'd really had a go until then. I was weirdly proud of him.

Das Tournament had been *such* a win. I loved the (mostly) friendly vibe, the constant stream of matches, the absolute cornucopia of young talent. When I wasn't picking up XP from managing, I was getting it from scouting. And I'd already bolstered our ranks with a new signing.

Saturday's Playdar had come through. After I'd scouted all the kids, I'd got in my car and pinged. But I didn't need to drive; the perk led me to a kid on the touchlines of a Crewe match, playing Heads and Volleys with some subs. He didn't have a club—he'd only come to watch his mate play. His name was Dan Badford, he was a fourteen-year-old central midfielder (CM), and he had a PA of −1.

Potential Ability −1! I'd found another Magnus type!

Magnus had PA −2. It stood to reason that −1 was better. Right? Or not? Anyway, it was intriguing. A player's PA was always out of 200. Having negative values made no sense, but it didn't seem to be doing Magnus any harm.

I invited Dan to my demo match and he was happy to play, even if he kept his puffy jacket on the whole time.

I got him to nag his parents to drive him to Chester a few times a month so he could start training. At the end of the season, I'd see if he'd caught up to the other kids, and then I'd make a decision on signing him properly.

On Sunday, I'd hit Playdar again after I'd handed the reins to Spectrum. But it took me to a kid playing for Shrewsbury whom I somehow hadn't scouted in all my time circling the area. Annoying! He wasn't even that good.

Still, with the transfer window closing, the only real urgency to my scouting was finding enough players to field a women's team in their first match, which was scheduled for February 17. Three days after the FA hearing that would decide if I was allowed to play football again this season.

Ugh. Why did I have to go and ruin my mood? Positive. Positive. Hadn't something else good happened?

Oh! The demo matches. You know how some video gets, like, a thousand hits and some garbage website says "This video BROKE THE INTERNET"? Well, I broke the curse. I'd gathered loads of little kids—when I first went round chatting to the other managers, they were all a bit "errr nah," but when I started crushing Premier League teams and being all *legitimate*, they changed their tune. I got a five percent discount code for the first match (the code was the word *CHEAT*), which had two five-minute halves. And I got a ten percent discount code for the second (the word *BOOHISS*), which I let go on longer so the kids could run up the score.

The curse paid up, but it got mad at me for, like, bending the rules or whatever, just because I sent Benny, Tyson, Captain, and Bomber off on some errand while the randos I'd gathered smashed what was left of the team. And what was left of the team was under strict orders from Spectrum to not tire themselves out.

So yeah, I got the coupon codes, but then I got a message saying the perk was finishing early owing to "unforeseen use cases."

I was equal parts annoyed and relieved. One less opportunity to progress; one less thing to manage.

After training, I spotted Jack Litherland and his agent walking towards the latter's car.

"Richard," I said, smiling at the guy who'd proposed this deal. "Nice to see you. Everyone's buzzing about Jack."

"I heard!" he said. "I knew this would work out great. Listen, just so you know, we're off to see a specialist. Jack had ankle surgery a while back. We're going to get it looked at."

"Are you in pain?" I said, worried.

"No, Max," said Jack reassuringly. "It's good as new. Been doing my Pilates and all that. It's a routine check. Personally, I'd rather skip it. Don't like hozzies. I've never felt better." He wasn't the first footballer I'd met who disliked hospitals.

"Are you available for tonight?" We were at home to Alfreton, the team I'd dumped out of the cup in my first competitive match as a player.

"Course! Wouldn't miss it. I read your scouting report. Four-five-one, hit them on breaks from corners. And that's exactly what you did. Amazing, man. You're absolute bosh."

I loved this guy so much. How had he found my scouting report? He was probably only the fourth person to ever read it. The glow I felt around him was unreal. "Right, that time you said *bosh*. Admit it." I often got the feeling Scousers exaggerated their accents to wind me up.

"No boss, I said bosh. Where are you off to?"

"Vegan cafe, and if that doesn't work out, pub."

There were a few people gathered round the outside of the pub, staring at a telly. "What's going on?" I said.

"Just Chelsea being Chelsea," said one dude, as the crowd dispersed. The chevron on the TV read: *Chelsea refuse to increase bid for Enzo*.

I popped inside and stood under one of the TVs listening to the host explain the story. "And if you've just joined us, breaking news from Cobham where Chelsea have announced they will not, repeat not, increase their bid for Enzo Fernandez."

Someone had come up behind me at the TV, which was odd because there were plenty of others she could have gone to. She made a faintly disgusted noise. "How is *that* a story?" she said.

"I know, right?" I had a quick look. Generic older woman, and when I say old, I don't mean, like, thirty-one. I mean sixty. She had that haircut that some women of that age have, where they look like goalkeepers from the 80s. Really nice smile, though. Made you think she'd do a proper cup of tea and cut your sandwiches diagonal to make them taste better. I turned back to the screen. What *were* Chelsea doing? In the summer they'd signed twelve players and if they signed Enzo, that would be another eight in January, for a combined cost in the region of £600,000,000. They already had a massive, bloated squad. This might be a good time to remind you that football teams comprise *eleven* players.

"Do you know why they're doing it?" said the woman, apparently reading my mind.

"Partly," I said. "They're signing these guys on eight-year contracts so they can spread the cost of the payments across eight years of accounts. But players they *sell*, they can book *all* the income in that year. It's a bit of financial wizardry to quickly rebuild the team before UEFA or the Premier League changes the accounting rules."

"Are you making that up?"

I laughed. "I do make things up sometimes. But my flights of fancy aren't normally about amortisation. No, the eight-year contracts are a massive risk, but they have a *bit* of logic behind them. And they're signing twenty-two-year-olds. So that's good. I like young players. Give them a good coach, let them get on with it."

"But?"

"But you're paying prime Ronaldo money for baby Ronaldo. Do you know what I mean? Enzo Fernandez is really good, but he's not worth a hundred million. They're assuming he will reach his potential, but it's not a guarantee he'll continue to improve. And the first rule of football is don't buy a player who had a good World Cup. People always overrate World Cup performances. For a hundred million, you might as well buy the twenty-six-year-old who *is* the best in his position. Twenty new players. I heard rumours that they're spilling out of the changing rooms into the corridors. You've got an eleven v eleven training game on pitch one, and a nine v nine game on pitch two. And *everyone* is in the first team! Yeah, it's bonkers. It's fun to watch. Fun to learn what not to do." I grinned. "What if it works, though? What if the secret to football management is being absolutely ridiculous and really committing to it? Wouldn't that be fun? I know a guy who'd be fucking *incredible* if those were the rules."

She smiled. "Can I buy you a drink?"

"None of my nine girlfriends would like that."

"I know you only have one, Max Best."

Huh. "Why do I feel like I'm about to get told off?"

The nice, warm smile faded for a moment. "I'm dead nervous. I need a drink. If you won't have one, will you promise not to run off while I get one for meself?"

I smirked. "I don't make promises I can't keep."

Different parts of her face each did a different expression. I don't think she met many people like me. "Ha," she said. Then she turned tail and almost literally ran off. I looked at the TV again, then followed the weirdo to the bar.

The weirdo eventually told me her name was Jill Stocks. When I decided she wasn't a maniac, I ordered a pie with extra gravy and listened to her story.

She had played football for Chester City's women's team, back in the old days. Of course, when the men's team went bust, so did hers.

"It was awful, sickening, a real gut punch, but for me the timing wasn't too bad. I was at the end of me playing career, and I was just starting out doing some coaching. Just helping the young girls out with sessions, a few drills, teaching them some things I'd learned. It wasn't much, but they said they liked it. My husband pushed me to do more, and that was surprising."

"Why?"

"He was never much into the women's football. Didn't have an awful lot of respect for it."

"He sounds charming."

"Well," she said. She obviously didn't want to say anything bad about him. "He'll always admit when he's wrong. He said he was wrong about you."

"Oh, shit. Where's this going? Who is he? Your name is Stocks? Stocks . . . Stocks . . ."

"Never mind that. That's my name, not his. No, he wasn't very supportive, but when I told him the girls liked my sessions, he got frustrated with me. *'Then do it more! Don't you realise you have a talent? Do you know how often players go up to a coach and say wow, that was good? Never! If you're getting that, you must have something. Come on, Jill, wake up. Put yourself forward.'* Well, coming from my husband, you can imagine. Really made me think. But then came the crash, and that was that."

"More wasted talent," I mumbled, though I was mostly trying to work out who she was married to.

"Maybe. I thought I'd never know. But you're here now. And you've made a women's team. And you don't have a coach yet."

Oh! I laughed. "Lucky for you I popped into this pub. Have you been here since the start of January, waiting for me to come in?"

She looked down. "I was too much a coward to write or call. I've been tormenting myself. Trying to pluck up the courage. And then—then you just walk in off the street while I'm waiting for my mate." News of a transfer came through on the curse news feed—one of the screens to which I had always-on access simply by willing it. I frowned. Jill took it wrong. "I'm sorry. I shouldn't have bothered you. I know you're busy, especially on a day like today. It's your busiest day, right?"

I jerked a thumb at the TV behind me. "Did you hear that just now? Joao Cancelo from Man City to Bayern on loan. What the shit? He's been one of their best players for, like, three years. He's incredible. And they let him go?"

"Problems with the manager," said Jill.

"Problems with the manager," I repeated slowly. "Listen. Everyone says I'm a prick. There's no smoke without fire. I'm probably *awful*. I strongly advise you against working with me. You think you can do some good sessions? Fine. Come and do them. If that's all you've got, I'll kick you to the curb. I'm not interested in having a tier-seven women's team. I want to go to the top. The actual top. I'm out there, scouting, bringing in top talent. I need top coaches. I don't have a coach right now, so you'd be an upgrade. But if I find a better one and I can afford her, you're out. I can't afford to be sentimental. I literally don't have the money for it." I stared at her and couldn't read her face, so I ploughed ahead. "The new Chester is no place for gammons. I don't care if a player is gay, fat, weird, or even, yes, even French. All that matters is talent and team spirit. Our best player is deaf. How are you going to coach a deaf player? We have a little bit of money for year one. What are you going to spend it on? Entering a tournament, or buying equipment? Why? Answer in eight hundred words, ask the invigilator for more paper if you so require. Should I go on?"

"Yes."

"Football. No offence, but it's changed since you played. Long ball is dead. Unless *I'm* doing it," I added with attractive smugness. I had used archaic long-ball tactics in Das Tournament to ruffle the feathers of some pampered princes. "Now the game's all about letting pressure come onto your goalkeeper and passing through the lines. Pressing. Gegenpressing. Can you coach it? When do we use an underlapping fullback? I want a double pivot. Can you give it to me? Oops, I've changed my mind. Now I want a single pivot as part of a two-six-two."

"Two-six-two!" she exclaimed. "That's mad."

"Is it, now?" I nodded a few times, then pointed at her. "Ian Evans."

"What?"

"Your husband."

"Please," she said. "As if I'd marry a defender." Huh. That narrowed it down slightly. Jackie Reaper was out. Jill sipped on her Bailey's. "Just so you know, I watched your recruitment video." I had made a video all about Chester FC's new welcoming atmosphere, set to a Harry Styles song. It was pretty phenomenal but hadn't gone as viral as I'd hoped. "It made me cry. That's another reason I was scared to talk to you. You've got the guts to do what I always wanted. We had some girls who didn't quite fit in, back in those days. They needed someone strong to take their side, and I didn't. I regret that so much." She lost about ten decibels. "I just wanted to say that."

"Yeah, yeah, yeah I'm fantastic," I said, though acknowledging a weakness was a point in her favour. She'd be motivated to do better next time. "What about *coaching*?"

"I can't do *all* those things you said," she admitted. "I can do some of it. And I can learn some of it. And the rest, you don't need the rest. Not yet. I can help you get going, I think."

"Can you, now?" I said, with a hint of a challenge.

"Yes," she said, but she wasn't responding on an emotional level. It was a simple statement of fact. I think she was wondering where her limit was. Underlapping fullbacks was my guess.

And she was right about one thing: I didn't need the full package right away. Jill was a former Chester player who'd had good feedback and was willing to learn. This was a slam dunk. "The women train Mondays and Fridays right now, and we'll expand that as we get the numbers in. There's, like, seven players so far. If you can come to those sessions and help out for a couple of weeks, I'll take a look at you. Then we'll take it from there. Minimum wage, by the way. What do you say?"

"I say yes."

I reached out and shook her hand. "Welcome to the Thunderdome."

Richard Carling: Max, specialist is worried about a shadow on the X-ray. Advises to rest a couple of days, rescan. Jack could play tonight if you insist.

Me: No. Tell him to rest up.

There were loads of messages coming in from increasingly desperate agents. I wondered what it would be like once we were in a higher league and had some money in the bank. There was a rumour that Man United, who had about as much left in the transfer budget as I did, had tried to sign a fairly mediocre player just to get an extra body in. And when people heard about it, every agent in Europe got on the phone. If *he* can play for United, so can my client! I imagined whoever was on the end of those calls turning his phone off for an hour, lying down in a darkened room.

It was a crazy sport run by idiots.

In my quest to do better, I checked how much I had in the bank.

XP balance: 509

Debt repaid: 610/3,000

I earned experience points for watching football matches—the rate doubled if I was managing one of the teams—and there was a shop in my head where I could buy perks to add to my powers.

Had my priorities changed since I'd last thought about it? Next on my wish list was Morale, costing 2,000 XP. Injuries was after that at 3,000.

Maybe learning more about injuries needed to be a higher priority—it could have told me that something was wrong with Jack. I had enough cash to instantly unlock 4-5-1, but formations had to wait, sadly. I'd try to have a couple more before the next tournament. There were a few youth tournaments scheduled for Easter weekend, about nine weeks away. Plenty of time.

I was fairly sure my XP growth would accelerate once the transfer window had slammed shut. There was a trade-off between using Playdar and attending matches that I would probably shift in favour of the latter. If I found one new player a week, that would be fifty a year. Plenty. Especially if I kept poaching talent from rival teams.

My brain detected that something interesting was happening and tuned into the Sky TV coverage I was streaming. "And we have . . . breaking news. We are hearing reports that Chelsea have made a new bid for Enzo Fernandez. The new bid is thought to be . . ." The host touched his ear as if to say, can you repeat that, mate? "Ninety-four *million* pounds. That's Chelsea's final bid, take it or leave it."

"Jesus Christ," I said, laughing. They'd end up paying the release clause, I was sure of it. Why embarrass yourself with all this final offer shit? I put my laptop away, popped out my earphones, and went for a walk.

I saw a bunch of kids playing in the park. It was just after school, so there probably wasn't much footy going on. I felt sure Playdar would direct me to those kids and reveal their profiles. I hit the ping, but the column of light appeared way off in the distance. Ah, well.

A delivery driver whizzed past me on a scooter. Scooter! That's what I needed if I hit Playdar in the city. Whizz to my destination just as fast as a car, and sometimes even faster. On a scooter I could take shortcuts and get closer to the pitch without worrying so much about parking.

Yeah. Maybe I could use this idea to spend some time with Henri. He didn't like watching shitty matches with me, but he liked riding around. Yeah, we could try that, after I'd had a day or two off. I'd overexerted myself since becoming DoF. I needed a break. I needed to do something absolutely bonkers like go to watch rugby. Or go see my mum and watch *FBoy Island* for a few mindless hours.

I took one last look at the column of light and watched it fade away.

A gust of wind blew just then, and it was an unusually cold one. The back of my neck responded like I'd just seen a corpse.

We were in the director's box at Deva Stadium. Me, MD (the only person close to being my boss), Smasho and Nice One (former players), Ruth (a board member who had financed the women's team), and a few bigwigs. The number of VIPs interested in attending Chester matches had dwindled. The dour football, the bad results, the lack of atmosphere in the stadium. It wasn't the place to be.

But I was still in a pretty good mood. The kind of mood that Steam, the online store where you buy PC games like *Jade Empire 2*, *Half-Life 3*, and *Paradroid Infinity*, calls "overwhelmingly positive."

My friends and I joked about the transfer window and the bad deals that were going on. Everyone was very interested in my take on Das Tournament—they'd heard something amazing had happened. I regaled them with stories and got quite a lot of laughs as I told the tales. I kept an eye on MD. He was impressed, but I knew the real work would be done when he confirmed the details with Spectrum. I could just see it: *Oh, wait, he really did that? He wasn't joking?* And Spectrum would be forced to admit, *No, he wasn't joking. He really did sub off his entire forward line after a minute. He really did use a semifinal to turn Tyson into a legend.*

Nice One kept asking me to repeat the bits about Benny, but Ruth was only interested in one aspect of the story.

"So we got Dani?"

"We did!" I beamed.

"I hope that means what you think it means." I think after meeting Emma, Ruth had got a bit light-headed about working with me, but now that her £200K had flown away from her bank account, her enthusiasm had come right back down to earth and she was back to wondering if I was just a handsome idiot.

I tried to reassure her. "It does. She's our Michael Jordan. The one from *Space Jam*, not the baseball one."

"Tell us about the women's coach you hired," said Smasho.

"Yeah, well, she's experienced, she's got good qualities, and—wait. I haven't told anyone." I realised what it meant. "You! You're the husband."

Smasho was a happy bunny. "She bumped into Max in the pub, and now she's got the job! That simple."

Ruth crossed her arms. "Do I want Smasho's wife coaching our team, Max?" She asked me, but she was staring at the former striker. Poor guy.

I said, "I think you do, yeah. It's just a feeling. You can't tell until you're on the pitch."

Ruth was still eyeing Smasho, who was looking more like a naughty schoolboy by the second. "Is she here?"

"Course, yeah." He was third on Chester's all-time top scorers list, but that didn't impress Ruth and he knew it. "Comes to every game."

"In the cheap seats, while you're up here drinking champers. What a charmer."

Smasho flushed. "She knows I'm working. This is work. Legends Night. I'm a legend?" The question mark on his statement very nearly made me spit out my drink.

Ruth took a step forward and jabbed him on the chest. "Go and get her. I want to meet my latest investment."

For some reason, he looked at me for help. I flicked my head towards the stands. *Better hurry!* He put his beer down and did a walky-run towards the nearest exit.

"Fun," I said.

But I was next in line for Ruth's ire. "When I signed off on this loan, I didn't expect you to pick up our first-team coach in a pub!"

"In a pub at *lunchtime*," said MD, who was an annoyingly good listener sometimes.

"They have good pies," I said. "And it's all tourists, so I don't get recognised. Except today."

"Max," said Ruth, "I expected you to follow your nose when it comes to finding players. You're the expert there. But when it comes to hiring staff, I expect you to follow best practice. That means open applications. Interviews. Following up references. Not just tucking into a pie and offering a job to the nearest blonde. Who happens to be married to a man who is, famously, a bloke."

MD winced at the word *bloke*. I assumed it was bad, but to me it just meant a man.

"We had no coach. Now we do. That's progress. I'll be able to see if she's doing a good job."

Ruth glanced at MD. Obviously they shared certain, highly specific doubts about me. The same kind of doubts Shona had. That I was amateur. Immature. Flighty and capricious. The fact that they were right did slightly sour my mood. I could afford to be *a bit* sloppy because I'd see how good a coach was via the greens and reds on the player profiles. No, I didn't know how to conduct an interview. But I could see, better than anyone in human history, how effective a coach was. And my skills would only improve. Maybe the Staff Search perk should be my new priority? It had been seventh on my list until I'd bought Playdar. But getting good employees was incredibly important. More important than knowing what was bothering Henri? Surely not; he was my friend and he needed me. Argh! Why was this so hard? I hadn't needed to think this hard to crush Das Tournament.

Jill came in, and over the next ten minutes was very politely grilled by Ruth. So politely that Jill didn't even realise it was happening. Smasho understood that Ruth was giving the job interview that Ruth felt I should have done, and he was a nervous wreck while it was going on.

He needn't have worried. Jill's good nature and work ethic was obvious, as was her passion for the sport and for developing young talent.

MD intervened; in his time he'd interviewed thousands of potential new employees and had seen enough. "We're very pleased to have you on board, Jill. I think a lot of people still remember your name. It'll give Max's team a bit of cachet, if you ask me." That last comment was aimed at Ruth.

Ruth said, "Well, it was great meeting you. Why don't you get another drink while MD and I talk shop with Max?" A very relieved Smasho boinged over to the bar. "Okay, Max. I approve. But can we please be more normal from now on?"

"In situations where I don't know best, yes."

"Impossible boy," she said, but she was being very provocative with her drink's straw.

"Max, transfer window is about to close," said MD, oblivious to the fact that his dream woman was mooning at me.

"Slam shut," I said.

He ignored me. "Are we sure we've done everything we can?"

"Have we got any more money?"

"No."

"Then what? What? Sorry, I don't understand what there is to talk about."

Ruth leaned forward. "You know there's the big Fans Forum coming up? We want to review the transfer window with you so we know what you'll say. Has it been a success?"

"Oh. Sure." I took ten seconds or so to think through the players I'd signed since I started. "So Jack is a massive win."

Ruth turned to look at the pitch behind her. The match was still 0–0, and it was garbage. I was keeping an eye on it for the XP, but I wished I didn't have to. "Is he playing? I didn't hear his name."

"He's got a minor ankle prob. No biggie. He's obviously a good player, balances the team, hits great crosses, which is fucking electric when you've got Henri on the end of them, but it's his whole vibe. He's lifted the place. I sometimes think I'm a bit dead inside or whatever because I don't seem to process the world like normal people, but holy shit, Jack is really something. Makes you laugh, makes you think, is interesting, is interested. He's just the best thing ever. Don't tell Emma I said that. Our other big signing, James Wise, not so much. He is good, though." Wise was on 7 out of 10 for the match, along with Sam Topps. "He and Sam are a very decent combination. That's one of the best pairings in the division now. I think that was money well spent."

"We committed a lot of resource to Pascal Bochum," said MD.

I shrugged. Pascal was a tiny German with a high ceiling. "He's cheap for what he is. Unique opportunity. We'll make good money from him."

"As long as we don't get relegated," said Ruth, using another word that made MD wince. He preferred to call it Scenario B.

"If we'd used that five hundred a week to bring in another first teamer on loan, it could have made a difference. Maybe. But then we'd still have no assets. We'd be locked into this cycle. We have to break out of poverty!"

"Okay, fine," said MD. "It makes me nervous, but okay. Then there's Youngster."

"Yeah. He's basically free, though. For now. He's doing okay, from what the coaches have told me. And he's going to be massive. Sometimes I forget how epic he is because he's all like, 'Max can I put Bible quotes in the toilets' and 'Max, God told me you'll be unhappy soon and I must be there for you.' Mad shit like that. The eighteens don't *look* much stronger yet but those two are really the only good players in the squad. Add a couple more talents and Pascal and James will really stand out. Who else? Vivek, Dan Badford, Mark Nelson. Very happy with those. We signed a few others who've raised the average level but probably won't get through to the first team. On the women's side, Dani, obvs, she's huge, and Pippa."

MD frowned. "Pippa, Max. She's fairly old to be just starting."

"She's an experiment. She's got bags of talent. If it's too late for her, fine. Didn't cost us anything. If she can only reach *half* her potential, that's still a really, really good player for us. If she can still get to the hilltop or whatever the phrase is, that opens up a whole 'nother line of scouting."

MD smiled. "I love the ambition. Not sure we're at the stage where we can afford to be doing experiments, though."

"I don't think we can afford not to." I pointed to the pitch, where Alfreton had just scored.

Apart from the CMs, almost every Chester player was on 6 out of 10. It wasn't a bad performance, really; it was just lifeless. Morale had dropped. All the energy Jack had brought, he'd taken with him to the specialist's clinic. We'd have him for sixteen more matches, though. Look on the bright side, Max!

So Morale, then. That was the priority. Trying to find ways to get inside the players' heads, to get more out of them for the rest of the season.

"This is bad," said MD. He was on his phone. He showed me the current scores from the other games. Two of our rivals at the bottom of the league were winning. We wouldn't drop into the relegation zone, but we'd be using the bottom four teams as a pillow. The Princess and the Scenario B, by Hans Christian Andersen.

MD and Ruth went back to mingling with the guests, while I sat alone, as far from everyone else as I could get. There was some strange draft in the room that was blowing around and landing on my neck wherever I went. That sensation I'd had when I hadn't pursued the

Playdar target. Was I being reprimanded for not chasing the opportunity? It felt like it. I mentally shook a fist at Old Nick, the demon who had cursed me. *Fuck* you, Nick. I've been busy. I'm tired. All right?

We equalised with a half-decent finish from D-Day after some good work from Henri. But then Alfreton were right back on top of us, and it seemed inevitable we'd lose.

The goal came late, so the team didn't have time to respond. All things considered, it was a pretty joyless performance. The sense of acceleration was gone. Losing Jack had slammed on the brakes.

As the VIPs started leaving, MD and I went down into the Blues Bar. It was usually pretty busy with home and away fans, players and their families, and sometimes even Ian Evans. I thought that was one of the ways he kept the crowd onside—a guy he bought a pint for once was much less likely to call for his head. With its cheerful blue paint and cheap booze, it was normally a jolly sort of place, even after a defeat. This time, I felt that same ill wind blowing, to the point that I went round checking all the windows were shut.

MD and I had done all we could to safeguard the future of the club; we watched the rest of the transfer window play out on Sky Sports.

A transfer was announced. I'd never heard of the player. How was someone paying £24,000,000 for him? "This would have been me," I told MD, as I drank mineral water.

He was on something a lot harder. "What d'you mean?"

"My plan was to play ten games for Darlo so I'd get a winner's medal if they won the league. Then come to Chester."

"Really?" he said, cheeks flushed. Couldn't hold his drink, despite how much he practised. "That was really your plan? Get Ian sacked and come here? I don't know if I should slap you or kiss you."

"Yeah. Either. Both. Henri loved it, but he was mad at me, too. Said you can't play a match for Darlo and make the phone call to leave just before you hop in the shower."

"He's right! That's awful! You're such a brat. You can't do that!"

I stuck out my bottom lip. "I probably could. It was better this way, though. I'm glad I didn't have to burn all those bridges."

"You went out on a high!" he said, very nearly spilling his drink on me as he thrust it forward. "Top of league! Darlo are fucked, though. I think they only won one match since you left."

"Yeah," I said, rubbing my chin. "It's pretty weird."

"Not weird," he said. "They had a taste of caviar and now they've gone back to . . . What do they eat there?"

"Same as here. Nando's and Weetabix. Oh, what the shit?"

Up on the screen, the chevron had changed, and the general hubbub in the room quieted enough so we could hear the presenter.

"Breaking news! Chelsea have signed World Cup winner Enzo Fernandez for a British record fee of one hundred and six point eight *million* pounds."

The hubbub was back with a vengeance. British record! For a guy who had played half a season in European football.

"Fuck me," I said. "It's so chaotic. Imagine being that bad at transfer windows. All those agents have been taking the absolute piss out of them and they don't even know it."

"Hundred million," said MD, almost tearful. "I'd love some of that, Max. Do you really think we can get some of that with Pascal? And Youngster?"

"Deffo. Youngster's a slam dunk. Pascal's in off the backboard. Got to stick with them. Got to get them chances in the first team. But yes, I'm sure of it."

Random voice: "Are you Max Best?"

I was getting used to that. "Yes."

It was a pretty drunk guy. Friendly, but I wouldn't like to meet him in a dark alley. There was one just outside the Blues Bar that always made me feel weird. "Can I get a selfie?"

"Quick one."

He snapped. "Oh, mint! Ace. Hey, is it true about Jack Liverpool?"

"Litherland. What about him?"

That was the moment the Chester guy went prehistoric. I barely understood a word. "I seed on Twitter he wore on Southend. Ye can't let him garn to Southend, thick, we needs him. He's sound. Cranny lad; he's in good buckle."

"Southend?" I said, focusing on one of the two words I was sure I'd heard. The guy fumbled with his phone for a bit and showed me a tweet. It was a photo of Jack and his agent Richard Carling going into Southend's Roots Hall stadium. Didn't prove anything—could have been taken anytime. But the tweet was from some local journalist, timestamped an hour ago. The text read, *New signing? Anyone know who this guy is?*

I grabbed MD and we raced up into the boardroom. He texted our club secretary, Joe, and our admin lady, Inga, and soon the four of us were there, hitting the phones, checking the news. I was pacing around, trying to get in touch with Carling, or Jack, or anyone from Jack's club.

"Fuck!" I said. "What the shit is going on?"

I bit my nails for a while. "MD, see if you can do a deal for that guy Ian Evans liked. Thickes."

"We don't have the budget!"

"We do if Jack's gone."

"He can't," whined MD. "He's already played for two teams. It's the same situation as you. He can't play for a third. What are Southend going to do, sign him and not use him?"

"He could play," said Joe. "It's *not* the same situation. This loan doesn't count if he's sold in the window."

"It makes no sense," I said. "We're a good club for him. He'll play. He likes it here. He must be the best liar of all time if he was faking it. What the shit?"

Three things happened at the same time.

First, my phone rang. It was Richard Carling. I waved at everyone to shush. I accepted the call.

Second, MD came over and thrust his phone in my face. I read a text from a guy at Swindon. Thickes was back in the first-team squad. Not available for loan.

"Maxy boy!" said Richard. He was the cat who'd got the cream, all right.

"Richard," I said. "How's Jack's ankle?"

"Ooh," he said, voice dripping with *something*, "bit sore." He laughed, long and loud.

The third thing: the latest curse news.

Southend United have signed Jack Litherland from Solihull Moors for £10,000. The 26-year-old was thought to be on Chester's wish list.

"Ten thousand pounds?" I said. An unbelievably small amount of money. That's what Chelsea spent on essential oils. Per week.

Richard's laughter died. "How could you possibly know that? Who've you been talking to?"

"Why have you done this? Jack would have been happy here."

"In tier six? The *bottom* of tier six? Give me a break. And you know why I did it."

"I have no fucking clue, mate."

"I've been asked to pass on a message. One you'll understand. Hang on, I wrote it down." Sounds of him putting on glasses and unfolding some paper. "Here we go. Are you sitting comfortably?" Another awful laugh.

"Go on."

Carling cleared his throat, laughed at his own joke, then cleared his throat again. Finally, he got to the fucking point. His big, dramatic message was five tiny words. "*'Bradley Rymarquis sends his regards.'*"

JUDGEMENT DAY

Excerpt from the transcript of the Chester Fans Trust Mid-Season Forum, dated Wednesday, February 1.

Those present include DoF, MD, first-team manager, board members (Bulldog, Sean, Ollie, Barnesy, Ruth), club secretary.

NOT for distribution.

Club Secretary: Moving on . . . Item two: review of transfer dealings.

Sean: On a point of order, Mister Chairman.

Club Secretary: Go ahead, Sean.

Sean: I call for a vote of no confidence in Director of Football Max Best.

Ollie: I second the motion.

Ruth: This isn't a board meeting.

Sean: We can't wait that long. Most of the board are here. Let's bin him off before he finishes wrecking the club.

MD: Sean, sit down. This is a place for discussion.

Sean: I vote we discuss binning him before he finishes wrecking the club.

Ollie: I second the motion.

Ruth: Oh, do grow up.

Club Secretary: He's right. Most of the board are here. We could form a quorum.

MD: Joe!

Club Secretary: It's the statutes!

MD: You just like saying "quorum."

Max Best: All right, guys. Take your best shot. Get a majority of people here to agree with you and I'll walk out right now.

MD: Max!

Best: I always said, if I can't even persuade half the fans, it's not going to work. Let's just check the rules. Sean, can women vote in this?

Sean: Of course.

Best: Ooh, Sean's gone woke, everyone! [Laughs.]

MD: Max, this is serious.

Best: Yep.

Club Secretary: A full vote? This is most irregular. I don't have ballot slips. We need pencils. Dozens and dozens of pencils.

MD: Don't worry about it. It won't come to that. Sean, what's on your mind?

Sean: Since Max Best came to the club, we've won one game. One game in the whole of January.

Best: Your honour, I would like many other defeats to be taken into consideration.

MD: What?

Best: Every match Chester City and Chester FC lost since the day I was born. I'm to blame for those, too.

Sean: That's not . . . that's not what I'm saying. Don't try to make me look stupid. I'm saying he was brought in to make things better. But it's worse. You all know he's got his clients here. You can't be in charge of a club and be an agent to some of the players. That's what killed Oldham. And his clients aren't that good. Not worth having this drama about. He tells us Lyons is the best striker in the league, but he's scored, what, three goals? Two of those were easy headers from perfect crosses from a player who played one game and left because Max has shit relationships with agents. He wants to turn us into some kind of vegan club. That video he made! It was all over the Wrexham fan boards. They were pissing themselves. We're a laughingstock. Okay, maybe we'd put up with a load of snowflake shit if he was scoring goals, but he isn't. He promised to play, but he hasn't played a minute. Last I heard, he was training with the goalkeepers! We all read the article—he chickened out of the match against our main rivals!

Best: Article? What article?

Sean: That article is full of shameful stuff. Not letting players shoot? Not letting parents attend games? I happen to know he released a good young player for playing sensible passes. In that piece it says, there's an actual football expert there who said, yeah Best has some tricks but he'll get found out and won't win another game. And he was right! They didn't. So even this so-called success of his was just smoke and mirrors, like the writer said. He promised us local signings, but he's brought in a German dwarf, a Bible Basher who is also—shock—his client, and a deaf girl. Yell all you want, but she's deaf. She can't play to a high level.

Ollie: I agree with that.

Best: There's nothing on the Manchester Evening News website.

Sean: Everyone I talk to tells me he's erratic and nothing he does makes any sense. He winds people up. Employees are quitting or thinking about it. He has no sense of priority. He barely watches the first team, but he's off at youth tournaments, which, I'm sorry, aren't that important. They're just not. And a couple of weeks ago he was watching Burnley instead of us! He's acting like the son of a billionaire who's bought a football team. He doesn't seem to realise we're in a hole and he's doing most of the digging.

Ollie: I second everything Sean said.

Best: And you do it very well.

Ollie: You think you're funny but you're not.

Best: I'd like to hear more about my bad relationships with agents, please.

Sean: Jack Litherland got himself a transfer to Solihull and the agent made sure it happened late in the day so that we couldn't get a replacement. See? Look at his face! He doesn't even deny it.

Best: The timing was certainly unfortunate, but I can't believe an agent would deliberately make himself unpopular with an entire club just to annoy one little guy.

Sean: Maybe he thinks you won't be around long.

Best: Ah, is that it?

MD: What do you mean, Max?

Best: Nothing.

Sean: So are we going to vote or what?

Ruth: We haven't heard the other side, you cretin. And we're going to be a vegan club? What are you blabbing on about?

MD: Max made a joke about it. We're not becoming a vegan club. Sean, if you'd like a serious discussion, can we stick to things that are real?

Best: To be fair, I did have oats for breakfast yesterday. It was quite filling.

MD: We could address the real points one at a time, maybe? Ian, you're in charge of the first team. Do you assign any blame to Max for performances since he arrived?

Ian Evans: I think Best does his job the way he plays. Very fast, takes big shots, somewhat indisciplined.

Sean: See?

Evans: But why would he be to blame for anything I do, Sean? The first team's my responsibility. End of.

Sean: I heard he made a substitution from up in the director's box.

Evans: What? What are you saying? That I'm not in charge of my team? Watch your mouth.

Best: He means when Trick Williams was hobbling on the other side of the pitch from you and I told Dean to check him out.

Evans: He'd done his quad! He'd done his quad, Sean! Is that what you talk about? That Ian Evans isn't in charge of his own team? That Ian Evans doesn't pick his own team? Is that what you tell each other?

Best: Ian, who's the best striker in this division?

Evans: Henri Lyons by a country mile.

Best: It's actually me, but you're close enough.

Unknown Fan 1: Then why don't you play?

Best: Problem with my registration. Paperwork stuff. We're going to London on Valentine's Day to sort it out.

Fan 1: Why haven't you told us?

Best: I wouldn't have played anyway. I've been working pretty hard.

Sean: Going to Burnley.

Best: Yes. And Rotherham. And Anglesey. And Swindon.

Unknown Fan 2: Can I say something?

MD: Please do.

Fan 2: My son is the goalkeeper for the Chester Knights. The disabled team. Max stayed with us the first weekend he was here, and he was a lovely boy. He told all kinds of crazy stories and my son was very charmed. But I've been finding out those stories were true! That article confirmed he was the manager of a women's team in Manchester. They beat Manchester City! The writer of the article was the captain. I even emailed her to check!

Best: What's this article? Beth's article is out? Someone send it to me.

Fan 2: Anyway, we went to the tournament in Crewe. I'm sure you've seen clips of Max coaching that deaf girl. You can't believe what it was like in there. Talk about goose bumps! The atmosphere was like nothing else. He took a nobody and turned her into a superstar in ten minutes! And that's our director of football. I'm so proud when I think our head of football takes time to come and see my little boy play . . . I'm sorry, just give me a moment. I can tell you all now, we're the envy of the rest. Terry says everyone wants to come and play for us now. Parents who turned us down before have done a one-eighty. People are calling from Ellesmere, from Warrington. So no, Sean, we're not a laughingstock. We're the opposite.

Best: *The Wizard of Oz* had eleven writers? When did I say that? [Laughs.] She's shameless.

Bulldog: Me next, I suppose. The things I do . . . My son, T, is in the youth system. He's the one from the article everyone except Max Best has read. I think I've suffered from Max's craziness more than anyone here. I've had sleepless nights from being so stressed and angry. He's denied me one of the biggest joys in my life—watching my son play football and play it well. If this is a vote about wanting to slap Max Best in the face, I'm in. If this is a vote about cracking his head open in the alley outside, I'm probably still in. If this is a vote about football, what the hell are we even doing? With all due respect to Ian, when it comes to football the guy's on another level to anyone else here. Yeah, one coach quit because of him. And guess who's his biggest fan now? The same coach. He thinks Max should be the next first-team manager. Sean, you were trying to make training with the goalies seem like a bad thing. He's a winger. What does he know about goalies? Nothing. So he's learning. He wants to be better at his job. It's dim, even for you, to try to use that against him.

Best: The Munchkins! Don't tell me the whole thing is . . . It is! This is amazing.

MD: Max, can you read that later?

Best: Fine. Guys, listen. I appreciate the defence and everything, but Sean's problem seems to be that other fans are laughing at us. I don't give a shit what other fans think. I only care what you think. It's just us. This time yesterday I was really happy. I thought I'd had a five-star January. We found a few little gems for the youth teams, we did well in two youth tournaments, we signed two big talents, we got the women's team financed and started, Jack and James had improved the first team.

MD: The sponsors loved the video.

Best: Right. Generally, there was a feeling that the numbers were going up, across the board. I'll be honest, now, the Jack Litherland fiasco was a gut punch. I felt sick. I've been curled up in a ball the whole day. And it's worse because we still had just enough time to fix it. If I'd been in the game longer, had more contacts, had a list of six left backs who could come in and do a job for us, six clubs we could call late in the window . . . but I don't. Not yet. So yeah, not a good end to my day. But that's the last time anyone's going to do that to us. This time next year, we'll have talented young players in every position, in every age group. Agents can try to pull our pants down. Other clubs can try to take our players. We won't win every battle. But we'll always have a plan B. Plan B isn't loans and scrambling around to fill holes in the squad. Plan B is talent. We signed a nine-year-old. When's he going to make his debut? Ten years. That's the horizon now. He's going to be a right back, but I've told the coaches I want him to play twenty percent of his matches at left back. Because a decade from now we might need him to fill in.

Unknown Fan 3: I play five-a-side and Sunday League and I've seen Max scouting at three of my matches. He said he'd scour Cheshire and he's doing that. He didn't sign me, so maybe he's not as good a scout as he thinks, but he's fucking grinding like he said he would.

Best: Are you Jed Fry?

Fan 3: Yes.

Best: [Laughs.] You're not a striker, mate. Give it up.

Audience: [Jeers.]

Fan 3: I am. No, really!

Best: Come on, be serious now. Drop to left mid. There's that guy Rory. Let him go up front.

Fan 3: Rory's our best centre back!

Best: Put Rick and Lucas at CB.

MD: Max, maybe we could get back to the topic.

Best: The topic was, what, the way Sean and Ollie know way more about football than me?

Audience: [Laughs.]

Best: All right, listen up. I'm not going anywhere. I just started. And it's been a good start, with one bump in the road. Sean and Ollie, I've been poking fun at you tonight but here's the thing: I plan to be here for years, but you'll still be Chester fans long after I'm gone. You can support your team any way you want, even if that means making weird allies and trying to get me out. I can take it. And Pascal and Youngster can take it, too. Your hate will inspire them. But I made a promise to the deaf player. I promised her that the Chester FC community would be right behind her, all the way. I promised her that in this stadium, in this city, she'd never have to defend her right to exist. So if you don't think this amazingly talented young girl deserves a chance to show what she can do, same as Tyson, same as Benny, then you need to step down from the board.

Audience: [Cheers and yells.]

Best: Ian Evans Blue and White Army! Ian Evans Blue and White Army!

Audience: [Ear-splitting chanting.]

Audience: [Applauds itself.]

Club Secretary: Item three on the agenda: bathrooms in the Harry McNally Terrace not cleaned often enough.

The Fans Forum cost me. I was already drained and exhausted when the Jack Litherland hammer blow fell. That pushed me into something like despair. Turning up at the Forum, smiling, wearing the mask of the uncaring, aloof boy genius, *that* pushed me over the edge into burnout. Being attacked by the morons didn't affect me much, but being defended by Chesterkid's mum and Bulldog was more than I could take. Why was that? No clue, but their interventions helped me find some reserve of resolve, one last reload, and I gave Sean and Ollie, the pricks, both barrels.

Chanting for Ian Evans was the natural extension of my emotional state and my whole "We Are Us" mania, possibly influenced by the fact I was teamwork 20. Or maybe the whole thing was pure self-defence, and my scarred, scabbed psyche was simply lashing out in a crowd-friendly way. The plot Sean and Bradley Rymarquis had hatched had one big flaw—I was fucking incredible at crowd dynamics. Influence 20, bitch.

But it all came at a price. I was a natural introvert. I'd spent years alone, and while I couldn't help but get myself into conflict, I hated it. I hated every second of it. Since I'd become a player, my release valve had been playing. Running fast, smashing shots, winding up crowds. Brad had taken that away from me. Add in a large dollop of financial stress, the humiliation of being tricked, and our slide towards relegation, and I was really struggling.

So I spent a few days in Henri's house in Darlington, only leaving to attend matches—solo—to grind for XP in case I ever felt like doing my job again.

Thursday morning I watched a season of *BoJack Horseman*. Depressing as fuck, hit the spot. In the afternoon I finally started *Catch-22*—incredible, a masterpiece, depressing as fuck, would read again. And that night I started going through *Rolling Stone*'s top 500 albums, hoping to find new music to get enthusiastic about, mostly while lying flat on the floor, eating cheese slices. Nothing really spoke to me.

I tormented myself with worries. Was I so unlikeable that everyone would always turn against me? Was I so naive that the unscrupulous would always try to exploit me? Was there something wrong with me in my very core? Some fatal flaw that meant everything would always turn to shit?

It was this thought that stopped me scouting. What was the point bringing more talent to Chester if I got sacked and the Seans and the Ollies took over? If I wasn't there to stop the bullying and the banter, people like Trick Williams and D-Day would make my signings' lives miserable until they quit. I knew I should have used Playdar anyway, just in case, but I didn't feel like chasing beams of light. The tool had to serve me, not I the tool.

On Friday evening, I put on my cleanest hoodie and drove to Birmingham to watch West Bromwich Albion host Coventry City in the Championship.

The match was interesting in some ways, most notably because Coventry played a 3-4-2-1 formation I was sure I'd never seen before. I could imagine some use cases for having two CAMs, especially if the other team were heavily into man marking. But even as I picked up a good chunk of XP, I was mostly thinking about the National League North league table.

	TEAM	P	GD	PTS
19	Blyth Spartans	29	-24	35
20	Chester	30	-11	33
21	Leamington	28	-12	31
22	Bradford	29	-21	29
23	Kettering	30	-23	26
24	AFC Telford	31	-34	18

The bottom four teams would be relegated. Every team would finish the season having played forty-six matches, so we had sixteen left to go. Our goal difference was not so bad, thanks to Ian Evans's defensive nous. If Leamington drew their two games in hand, we'd still be above them on goal difference. Of course, if they won even one of their games in hand, we'd drop into the relegation zone outright.

Ian Evans . . . He'd been fairly supportive, all things considered, at the Forum. There was a moment he seemed to turn, though. That was when Bulldog had said that Spectrum thought I should be the next manager. Evans had glowered at me and folded his arms. I'm fairly sure they stayed that way the rest of the night, even as I led the entire room in a rousing rendition of his chant.

God, trying to work out how everyone was thinking and feeling was all so exhausting.

But what my black mood boiled down to was the simple fact that I was powerless. I couldn't change the squad, and I couldn't influence the tactics. If I found another Raffi or another Youngster, it'd be a year before they were ready to play. So the squad was the squad and Ian Evans was Ian Evans.

The crowd noise picked up: West Brom had a fast break. Exciting, but it came to nothing.

I brought the table up on my phone again. Telford, there, languishing at the bottom, were doomed. If I'd gone to Telford as player-manager, this whole mess never would have happened. Right? Even if my enemies had pulled the same registration trick, I'd have been managing the team. We'd have won a few more, drawn a few more. We'd have been creeping up on Chester, starting to climb above the very worst teams. No chance Telford would have gone down under my management. No chance.

Maybe the worst thing of all was that I knew another big defeat was coming at the FA hearing. It was a fight I couldn't win—it was a fight I couldn't fight. I'd been fighting for so long, and I didn't have it in me to fight anymore. Four randos and one imp would get some free shots at me, and I'd have to take the blows. Then I'd gather my strength and fucking destroy all comers, starting the summer.

The best thing to come out of the Forum had been getting the link to Beth's article. Apart from a few outright lies, which I had to admit tied the narrative together in an interesting way, it was really quite truthful. She'd always dumbed herself down, tried to make herself seem like a real girl. But the article proved she was whip-smart, observant, and hardworking. She must have interviewed everybody there, unless she made half of it up. Somehow I didn't think she'd invented any quotes except for mine. She felt that I owed her, so she could take a liberty or two. Or maybe she thought I'd appreciate the storytelling craftsmanship.

Regardless, I thought it was a wonderful piece of writing. Maybe it was only because I was in it, but I found it incredibly addictive. When the Forum was over and I'd shaken enough hands, I slipped out. As soon as I got to my freezing-cold office in the bowels of the stadium, I read the article five times in a row, and I'd read it another five times since.

The *Daily Mail*, though. Ugh. Beth was ambitious, tough, and ruthless. Basically a good person but if someone charismatic told her to do something slightly unscrupulous for the greater good, she'd do it. I knew that from experience. Why had she always pretended to be a bit dim? Odd. On the subject of hiding one's true nature, I needed to be even more careful with the whole wizard thing. Beth had spotted me trying to literally tap my screens. I wasn't aware I sometimes did that. Hands in pockets for the next match!

Back in the present day, West Brom scored and continued to have the edge in a chaotic match. Good fun, but not enough to take my mind off my troubles.

The next day, I travelled to Swansea to watch them play Birmingham while Chester were losing 2–1 at home to Spennymoor. I watched the highlights later. Doug Walker filled in at left back, which he was capable of doing when Aff was around to help him out. With Aff injured, the role was a bit too much for the guy. Both Spennymoor goals came from our weak left-hand side, and the storm over Jack Litherland whipped itself up again. No one mentioned the avoidable injuries to Aff and Trick that were the *real* issue.

The next week I did even less. On Tuesday I watched Port Vale against Accrington Stanley, but mostly I tried to ignore football. I went on little day trips. Cheap dates that didn't pound my dwindling bank account too much. I went to Barnard Castle to test my eyesight, then took Emma to Grassholme Observatory, where we had our minds expanded by gazing into the ever-expanding universe. The next day, we went to Durham Falconry and walked around learning about birds of prey. One evening, we were just pottering when we saw some kids playing rugby. Emma asked me to explain the rules to her, which I did by way of invention, since I'd never played the game or even liked it much. "That guy is called the Big Bird. He's the only one who's allowed to stick the ball up his shirt and run with it. The guy with the ball now, he's the bishop. He can only move diagonally. The referees aren't called referees, they're called judges. They're allowed to change five rules every match, and the players and spectators have to work out which."

It was awesome spending time with Emma, but it also cost me energy. A few times, my mask slipped and she caught me being catatonic, but she knew I'd overexerted myself in January and didn't make a big deal of it. And best of all, apart from a few very specific questions, she almost never asked about my upcoming hearing.

MD was good, too. A few journalists had found Beth's article and wanted to do follow-ups or their own versions, and he sent the requests to me. I kicked them all into touch. Not interested. But he gave me space and didn't ask why I wasn't showing up.

Then on Saturday the 11th, I walked into Mordor, right up to the Eye of Sauron, which as you know is conveniently located near a tram stop in Beswick, North Manchester.

Mordor was also known as The Campus and everything was named after various climate criminals and painted a gross shade of blue.

If I'd been alone, I would have left a trail of vomit, like a handsome slug. I wasn't alone; Kisi was my tour guide, and she'd invited her coach, Sandra, and her new friend, the Butcher of Burnage, Meghan. My meteoric rise in the world of football had not gone unnoticed in one small corner of The Campus.

"You lied to me, Max" was one of the first things Sandra said to me.

"Yeah, probably. Which bit in particular?"

"You said I was way ahead of you in our careers. Now you're a director of football and causing chaos at tournaments." Kisi must have passed the article around her team. Again, I had that strange feeling of being totally unknown in the world, except in certain very specific circles where I was very, very famous.

I tried to remember the incident she was talking about. "You mean when I was inhaling painkillers and reorganised your team?"

"Oh, was that it? I thought you'd been huffing glue."

Kisi made us stop. Her version of a tour guide had the elegant, precise movements of a flight attendant. "To your left, across the road, you can see the world-famous Climate Crisis Stadium." I think that's what she said, anyway. I was dizzy from being surrounded by Manchester City players and staff. They were everywhere, millions of them. And I'm not exaggerating when I say millions.

"I've been to a match there," I said. "It's got great acoustics. You can hear a pin drop."

Meghan started to respond, but Kisi stopped her. "Max is teasing. Really, Megs, you can't let him wind you up all the time. He'll only do it more. That's something my brother is yet to learn."

"Kisi says you think her brother will be a great player," said Sandra.

"Top. Top talent."

"And he's cute," said Meghan, causing Kisi to slap her on the arm.

Kisi fell back into tour-guide mode. "Straight ahead, the Academy Stadium, where Max will be our guest of honour today. To the right, the Performance Centre."

"What's this shit?" I said, jabbing at a series of pitches behind me.

"Junior Academy pitches."

"Yeah and that little half-pitch thing?"

"That's for goalkeepers."

"Fuck me," I said, both impressed and disgusted.

"As I said, that's for the little kids. Over there," she pointed to loads more pitches, "is where the older youth teams train. That includes us. Behind the Performance Centre are more pitches. They're for the first team. And the Performance Centre, obviously, has a grass pitch and an artificial one."

"Where's the escape rocket?" I said.

"What?"

"One of these pitches slides apart and then the top brass fly off to Mars."

"That's secret," said Meghan, giving me a friendly middle finger that Sandra didn't spot.

It was all depressing, obviously. The facilities were beyond perfect. All this cost hundreds of millions of pounds. They'd thought of everything—there was a nice space for parents to chill while their kids were training. It had bedrooms so kids or even first-team players could sleep overnight. The gyms were pristine and fully equipped. The boot rooms had columns of pegs for every player, and they were full. Eight pairs of boots per player; even the young guns here had better gear than me. The dressing rooms were vast, luxurious, and welcoming.

Meanwhile I was burning through my meagre savings sending our teams to tournaments and bribing kids to bring their mates to training.

Through every set of doors was another cog in the machine: kids on training bikes, office workers in soothing open-plan spaces, physios helping players bend and stretch. One thing was conspicuous by its absence: gammon. City wanted excellence, and that meant diversity and a good working environment.

Outside, half the pitches were occupied. Warmups, drills, friendly but serious little games.

I stopped by one pitch, chosen at random. I needed a break; it was so overwhelming. By the time I'd spent £200,000,000 catching up to this, City would have bought another thousand hectares and installed another hundred swimming pools. I couldn't beat them financially—they were owned by an oil state. I couldn't beat them on talent, on tactics, or even on culture. Every aspect of the football club was ten out of ten.

Sandra misunderstood what I was thinking. "Good, isn't he?"

"Who?"

"Patricio."

I looked around until I saw a player profile that matched the name. It was a seventeen-year-old with high PA and technique 20 who was taking free kicks at an empty net while a bunch of other kids acted like every shot was bending through space-time.

"He's all right," I said.

"Max is jealous," said Meghan.

"Meghan," said Sandra, slipping back into teacher mode.

"Max is the best at free kicks," said Kisi, not heeding her own advice about being easily wound up. "He's, like, the actual best."

"Prove it," said Meghan, pointing to the pitch.

I had no energy for showing off. "Patrick is better at free kicks than me. Okay? Can we go now?"

But Meghan wouldn't have it. She grabbed my wrist and pulled me onto the pitch. I was worried I'd crumble to dust when I crossed the cursed boundary, but I didn't. It was just some grass in Manchester.

"Oi, lads," announced Meghan, who had changed when we crossed the white line. She'd become gobby. "This guy thinks he's better at free kicks than Patricio."

The group as a whole reacted with disbelief, disdain, almost dismay. Some of them were so saddened by my delusion they suggested I get my head checked. Kisi quietly fumed behind me, but she didn't have a "boy mode" like Meghan, so she kept her thoughts to herself.

Patricio, though, the handsome little git, was all, like, magnanimous or whatever. He came over and proposed a challenge. "Take shots, see who misses first."

I took a long look at him. Seemed like a nice kid. They all did. My beef wasn't with them, or anyone who was there that day. Everyone here was just doing their job, trying to have a good career. And the pitch was gorgeous, like a snooker table. Being in the middle, having a bit of an audience. It stirred me.

And who knew—maybe this would be the closest I ever got to playing in the Premier League.

"Nah, boring," I said. "Take another shot. Let me see you up close."

He shrugged, went back to his favourite spot, and went through his motion. I kept an eye on the ball as it curled into the top-left corner.

"Yeah," I said, "Good spin. Good arc. Gorgeous technique. You like that, don't you, Megs?" I gave her a knowing little smile, which annoyed her. She asked for it! "Dude," I said to one of the other kids. "Ball." He threw it over and I rolled it around and did a few kick-ups. "Fuck me that's a nice ball. Holy shit. Do you have any without—never mind." It would have been classless to finish the sentence, even for me. So it had a Man City logo on it. So what? As long as it obeyed me. I dragged it a few metres to the side. "Amigo," I said, "Do that again."

"You're going to shoot, too? What are the rules?"

"The rules are, don't be a baby about it."

"About what?"

"Try to score, bro."

He gave me another sun-kissed smile and looked at the top-left corner of the goal. He started his striking motion, and a split-second later, so did I.

His ball arced slowly, gently, perfectly towards the top-left corner.

Mine slammed into his, sending it flying towards the main road, while mine deflected down into the goal.

"Holy shit!" was the only thing anyone said.

I turned to walk away and noticed Kisi blazing with pride. Sandra was giving me an odd look, while Meghan was . . . I have no idea.

"Wait!" said Patricio. I turned again. "But who are juu?"

"I'm Max Best. Director of football at Chester FC. We need talented players. If any of you guys don't make it here, look me up. I can't offer you any of this," I said, waving my finger around. "But I can offer you a fuck-ton of that." I pointed to the spot where my ball was resting in the back of the net.

While Chester's first team were losing away to league leaders King's Lynn (no real surprise there) I watched Man City Women beat Arsenal Women 2–1.

"Don't you think it's a bit lame all the teams are called 'Women'?" I said, during the entertaining first half.

"No," said Meghan.

"These are almost all new teams, really. This could be the Man City Cheaters versus the Arsenal Supernovas."

"Cheaters?" said Meghan.

"You know, the big cats."

"Oh."

"You're thinking of names for your new Chester team?" said Sandra.

"Yeah. Want to give me some feedback on some ideas?"

"Sure."

I whipped out my phone to make it seem I had a list prepared. "The Chester Warrior Princesses."

"No."

"The Chester Contesters. Your face says no. Chester Megalodons. Why not? Think of the branding."

"I think there's a reason most of the team names are as bland as they are. But why did you suddenly ask to come and watch a game? It's been ages since Kisi started. Honestly, I thought you'd come knocking for a favour ages ago. And I thought it'd be something bigger."

"I've started my women's team. First match is soon. It's way past time to scout the opposition, yeah?"

Meghan scoffed. "We're not your opposition, Max. What league will you start in?"

"I'm hoping the North West Women's Regional Football League. Division One, probably, but if we impress in our friendlies, I'm hoping they might pop us straight into the Premier League. Worst case is tier seven, Cheshire Women and Youth."

"See, I don't even understand any of the words you just said," said Meghan. "We're a Women's Super League team. You'll never play us."

"*Tsch*. With me as manager? We're getting promoted every year. The farther down they put us, the more leagues we're going to slap. We've already got a player better than anyone here."

"Really?" said Kisi.

"Almost," I said. And it was true. I had several reasons for inviting myself to see this match. One, to check the levels. In terms of PA, it was more or less what I expected. Similar to the men's Premier League but with more variation. The two best players at Arsenal were injured, so that dropped the average. The best player on the pitch was Arsenal's Leah Williamson, the England captain. She had PA 181. The worst in the starting line ups had PA 138, and a few of the subs were under 100. Clubs had only recently started taking women's football seriously, so I expected standards to improve rapidly in the next few years.

Two, to see how much XP I'd get. To my surprise, I got 7 per minute, same as for the men's leagues. When I thought about it, it made sense. Old Nick wanted me to grind so he could power up. And the tactical battle between the managers was pretty intense. They were on the sidelines, yelling and gesticulating.

And three, to put what I'd done so far into a long-term context. What I'd learned was that if I found ten more Danis, we could challenge for this league. But to get me out of my starting league, I'd surely only need a few Pippas.

"What's happening now, Max?" This was Kisi, getting me to show off by pointing out tactical tweaks the managers were making.

I shook my head, but my reluctance wasn't very serious. Taking that one free kick had improved my mood tenfold. "Wubben-Moy is having a mare. Four out of ten. If you're playing three-four-three and the central centre back is making those kinds of mistakes, you're in for a bad time. It looks like he's asking his CMs to drop and cover, but that's making it way too easy for City's midfield."

"What would you do?"

"I'd sub Wubben-Moy off right now. Sometimes it isn't your day. People make such a big deal about early substitutions. You played shit, get off the pitch. No big deal. Do better next week and we're all good. But I don't want to lose this game just to spare your feelings."

It turned out to be one of those "Max is a Witch" moments that are really just coincidences. A mistake from the same defender I'd pinpointed gave the ball to City, who pushed forward and scored an easy goal. Sandra gave me another odd look. That was, I think, number twenty for the day.

We went to queue for some halftime refreshments. Kisi and Meghan went in front so that I'd have more time to look at the options.

Sandra pulled at my arm and whispered, "Max, were you serious about giving those boys a second chance?"

Why was she being secretive? "Er, yes? They're bound to be good. I doubt any of them would make such a huge step down, but if one of them does and we turn him into a player, that's win-win." I laughed. "Maybe it'll do him good to learn to clean his own boots."

"They clean their own boots, Max."

"Do they?"

"I don't know, actually. My girls do. Listen . . ." She glanced around her. I was all ears—maybe she was about to say something blasphemous like "This club should be owned by its fans" or "This club should follow the same financial rules as everyone else." "I've coached loads of girls over the past few years. Most get released. Maybe some of them would be interested in dropping a few levels knowing you'd be coming straight up. I know a couple who'd see it as a big challenge. Would you want some ex-Man City players?"

Unexpected. "Of course I would."

"I'll make some calls . . ."

The queue moved forward, but Meghan was stuck in place. I pushed forward and stood next to Kisi so no one else could cut in. But for the first time since I'd yelled at her for trying to cripple one of my players, she looked like a little girl instead of a tough defender. "If I don't make it," she mumbled, not looking at me, "will you give *me* a second chance?"

"No," I said, and left a tiny pause. "You're going to make it."

"You don't know that."

I scoffed. "Don't I? Nah. If you end up playing for Chester it's because we bought you." I grinned. "Or you could make sure you're out of contract in the summer of, let's say, 2028."

"Max!" complained Sandra.

"What?" I said. "I'm just saying we'd be delighted to sign her. And maybe she'd like to play at the same club as James Yalley."

I was saying it to tease Kisi the way Meghan had done, but to my surprise, it was Meghan who turned bright red.

The trip to Manchester was restorative. Really lifted my mood. I'm not sure what it was—maybe spending a few hours with cool people, or the tantalising prospect that one day, half a dozen high-PA Man City–trained women would show up at my doorstep. Or maybe it was my quick pop in to see mum and Anna, thankfully now bored of *Soccer Supremo.*

But when I got home, there was more shit to deal with. More shit to knock me back, sap my spirit. During the Chester match, people had started texting me about an incident on the pitch. D-Day had missed a penalty. I was shocked that Evans had let D-Day get anywhere near taking such an important set piece, but I assumed he had a good reason. The texts and voice notes kept coming. It was unusual for so many people to get so animated about a single incident.

So I loaded up MD's Wyscout account and watched the footage. With the score at 0–0 and with us apparently battering the league leaders, we'd got a penalty. D-Day decided to take it, even though Henri Lyons had picked up the ball. Clearly, Henri was the designated taker. But D-Day made such a fuss that he ended up with the ball in his hands. He then strolled up to the ball and passed it, very slowly, into the goalkeeper's hands. There was some aftermath, but that first time I was so blinded by rage that I literally couldn't see it.

You can guess the rest: The team's bright start was wasted, King's Lynn scored soon after, game over.

I stayed in Darlington on Sunday, trying to chill with Emma. I didn't have to work so hard to seem normal, and we read books in cosy silence, went for walks, had a quiet dinner. But while I spent most of the time being cool and charming, my mind kept returning to the footage of the missed penalty. Outsiders were trying to sabotage our season; now insiders were as well. Was it all part of the same plot? Had Ian Evans deliberately played two injured players? Was he in on it?

While I was thinking that, something unprecedented happened.

Spectrum: Ian Evans came to watch the under-14s today.

Why now, suddenly? The news put me right back on edge, and I was relieved when Emma's train left the station. I was free to go from *simmer* to *boil*.

On Monday, with the FA hearing only a day away, I decided we needed to have another talk about culture.

I drove to Chester bright and early, and I was waiting on the training pitch when the players finished their team meeting. As they approached the pitch, I walked over and put my arm around D-Day's shoulders. I encouraged him to follow me. He said he didn't want to, maybe. I think I suggested his opinions weren't all that germane.

D-Day's version, incidentally, just for balance, was that I dragged him all the way across the pitch and dumped him in front of the penalty spot. Which, come on, be serious.

"Take a penno, mate," I said, calmly, with no flecks of spit flying anywhere.

"What the fuck?"

"Take a penno, and you'd better blinking score, my good friend."

"You've cracked."

"Score or you're finished here."

"Max!" said a few people, but in the end, D-Day had to take the penalty while half the first team watched and the other half raced forward to see what they were missing.

He hit it about a metre high, just inside the post. I launched myself to my left and pawed it away. In a real match it would have gone for a corner.

"Shit!" I said. "Try again."

I went back to the middle, and as he struck the ball, I exploded to the right and extended my arms. He'd aimed a bit higher, but I got a good hand to it. Not even a corner this time.

"Dogshit!" I said.

"That's enough," said Vimsy, standing in front of D-Day, putting a stop to the special drill I had dreamed up on my commute. Annoying, because I had a lot more planned.

I stormed past a lot of horrified players, took a stance near Ian Evans, and pointed backwards in the direction of D-Day, the worm. "*That* guy doesn't take *any* more set pieces for *this* club," I suggested.

Then Raffi was on me, and he bounced me off the pitch before I could finish my presentation.

The drive to London was awful. Heavy traffic, weird junctions, crazy drivers. Exorbitant parking and the air in the entire city smelled of burnt metal.

I walked to the building and while the decor was super snooty—it could have been an interior from a *Jeeves and Wooster* episode—the staff who worked there were friendly. It didn't really cheer me up, and neither did seeing MD there, waiting for me in his best suit.

"Ah, the hoodie," he said, looking me up and down.

"I'm a footballer. I have to dress for the job I want to get, or whatever the phrase is."

"Before we get into all this, can we talk about yesterday?"

"Yep."

He looked at me and hesitated. "Maybe it should wait."

"I'm fine. Hit me."

He sighed. "Is it true you embarrassed one of our players before training yesterday, forcing him to take penalties against you, which you saved?"

"Yes."

"That player was D-Day?"

"Yes."

"And you know I have to tell you off for that?"

"Definitely."

"Yeah, well," he said. He took his phone out and brought up a text he'd got from Ollie, the prick. It read: *Heard Max Best took piss off of that twat D-Day. Maybe I was wrong about him.* "D-Day is currently the least popular person in Chester. People hate him more than our last member of parliament. That penalty, wow. I really struggle to remember being that angry at one of our players. People are saying you showed more passion going after him than the team did on the pitch. But we both know you did it because you're burned out and you can't think straight. And look, you shouldn't ever disrupt training. And you definitely, definitely shouldn't tell Ian Evans how to run the team."

My head sank. "I know."

"You should probably apologise."

"To whom?"

"To Ian."

"End of list?"

"I would have thought so."

I screwed up my eyes. "Playing football is my vent. I can take out my frustrations on some hapless goalie. I need to run around and kick a ball."

"I get it. That's what we're here to fix." He grabbed my shoulder. "It's going to be all right." He got a text and read it. "Great. So listen. You are what experienced executives like me call *going batshit crazy*. You've worked too hard and now it's catching up. I've seen it a hundred times. It's good you went to the castle with your girl. That kind of thing? Big thumbs-up from me. Do more of that. Decompress. I heard about you turning up to those casual games. That's good, too. There are ways out of the red zone. But right now, Chester Football Club can't trust you to open your mouth in that room. This is me formally and officially telling you to keep your flappy Manc gob shut."

"No way. I've been daydreaming about this. I've got stories. I've got overlapping and underlapping narrative arcs. I've got a backup, too, if that one doesn't seem like it'll go down well. The backup is based, get this, on the *Wizard of Oz*. I'm going to call them munchkins and rip the curtains down."

MD rubbed his eyebrow. "Yeah. Just shut up. I'm really serious."

I was too frail to argue. I gave him a tiny thumbs-up. "If there's anyone who I'd trust to speak for me, it's you."

"That's cute, Max, but you have more people in your corner than you think."

The lift pinged. Emma and her dad emerged and walked towards us. They were both wheeling airline suitcases. Had they flown in from Newcastle? What was that, a seventeen-minute flight?

"So," I said. "It's a conspiracy."

"You're right it is," said MD, as he stood to shake Sebastian's hand. With a huge effort, I pushed myself upright and shook hands, too.

"Unexpected," I said.

"You've got the most persuasive lawyer in Newcastle on your side," said Sebastian Weaver, the smug git.

"I know, thanks."

"I meant Emma."

I grinned. "Ah. Right."

He took a step back and looked me up and down. "Max, you look like shit."

"You know how Superman gets his energy from the sun? I get mine from football pitches." It was a joke, but it almost felt true. The little free kick session at Man City had given me a huge energy boost.

"Let's go get you back playing, then."

The FA panel had five members. Our hearing was at 11 o'clock and once they were done with us, they'd go to have a seven-course lunch at one of those stuffy clubs where women aren't allowed. Four of them would, anyway. The other would take off his clothes and turn back into a literal sub-demon.

Proceedings started with a bland retelling of the sequence of events. Namely, that I ended my contract with Darlington in order to sign for Sheffield Wednesday. That my registration was held by Sheffield Wednesday, and that I was disputing having signed the forms. The panel would listen to my case and decide what to do.

I'll just say now that MD sat to my left and Emma to my right, and every time I stirred or inhaled like I'd say something, one or both of them would pull me back or jab me in the ribs.

So after the preliminaries, Sebastian showed why people paid him hundreds of pounds per hour. He started with a long string of legal gobbledegook to establish dominance. The only parts I understood were references to prior cases, Wigan Athletic FC versus Heart of Midlothian and, of course, Fleetwood Town versus AFC Fylde.

After that barrage, Emma unzipped the suitcases—MD became extra wary since he was briefly guarding me solo—and Sebastian began slapping documents onto the panel's table.

"Signed, sworn, and witnessed affidavits from the Sheffield Wednesday manager stating that he never had any intention to sign Max Best and had only brief, exploratory talks. Signed, sworn, and witnessed affidavits from the Sheffield Wednesday club secretary stating that these forms were never filled in under his watch. Signed, sworn, and witnessed affidavits from their equivalents at Darlington Football Club, saying they never sent the forms from their side. Both clubs deny that this ever happened!"

The guy in the middle was the most senior, the most gammony, and the most hostile to me. But why? I didn't know him. Did fucking Bradley Rymarquis have an army of agents like a James Bond villain? He couldn't, surely—he was grinding in the lower leagues. Judge Gammon cleared his throat and offered up a slight smile. "The facts of the case support the conclusion that Mr. Best sent the forms himself."

I was struck in the ribs from both sides.

Sebastian seemed perplexed, as though he'd never even considered the possibility that I'd done this myself. "There could be no conceivable motive for the act, nor would his so doing become proof of registration." He spouted off a few more precedents and a mouthful of Latin. "However, even the most cursory look at the timeline of events shows Max could not have sent the faxes." Emma moved to the second briefcase and opened it, neatly stacking some documents into little piles. Her dad picked up the first one. "At the time the first fax was sent, these twenty people swear, affidavits, et cetera, that he was in the away team dressing room in Scarborough, asking to be allowed to go see . . ." He flipped through the pages. "Some local flamingos." He slid the pages next to the other piles. Emma handed him the next batch. "Affidavits proving that at the time the second fax was sent, Max was getting, quote, massively hammered, unquote, in the Eastbourne training centre."

"He could have slipped out of the party," said the FA prick.

"Could he, indeed? These witness statements swear he didn't. Nevertheless," said Sebastian, using one of my favourite lines. I briefly wondered if he'd heard Emma say it and added it to his own lexicon, or if it was more common than I thought. He picked up the next pile. "Plans and layouts of the Eastbourne training centre . . . Please note the location of the party, marked with a red dot here. For Max to send the fax, he would have had to go down this corridor, then here, then slip out here . . ." He came over to get yet another piece of paper, brought it over to the front and slammed it down two metres away from the rest. "And get in his car and travel across the city to Blackwell Meadows stadium, where the fax machine is."

The main gammon gave the imp a filthy look, and for the first time, I felt something like hope. Sebastian was fucking killing this. He'd worked it all out, and then gone and got the receipts. The guy was to law what I was to free kicks and being annoying.

"One more thing," said Sebastian, the greatest living Englishman. He rummaged in the suitcase and came up holding a printer. He placed it in front of me. Then another one, then another one. "Max. You are twenty-two years old, a digital native. Could you please identify which one of these can be used to send faxes?"

"Oh," I said, laughing. "What? Did you raid a museum for these? What on earth?" The three devices were broadly similar. Beige rectangles with buttons. "This is for covering paper with hot plastic. Right? Henri has one. And this is a printer. Scanner. Printer-scanner. This must be a fax machine. It's got the phone bit. I know faxes use phone lines."

"Could you please fax this document for me, Max?"

The machine wasn't plugged in, but I got what he was trying to say: that I was too stupid to use a fax machine. Making fun of me while winning the case—genius. He handed me a piece of paper. Where did it go? There was a thin hole on the bottom, and a paper tray at the top. I tried pushing the paper into the bottom, but that didn't go well. I tried putting it in the paper tray.

"Very good, Max. Then what do we do?"

I lifted the phone receiver and brought it to my ear. But that made no sense. Who would I talk to? I laughed again. It was like trying to use a loom or something. "Er . . . the paper's in. I . . . shit. Type the phone number, press the green button. Something like that?"

"Something like that." Sebastian smiled. "But you've put the paper in the wrong way round. You just sent a blank fax."

"A wonderful performance," said the gammon. "Most entertaining and, as you know, Mr. Weaver, legally worthless." He looked at the spread of documents in front of him, then at the two men to his left and the two to his right. "Someone did something and it is most improper."

Someone did something, indeed. *Bradley*. But hang on. He might have been able to send the first fax, the one from Sheffield. But as Sebastian's investigation had proven, he couldn't have sent the second one. He was at the party with us, in the wrong building in the wrong *postcode*.

This wasn't Brad.

It had never been Brad.

Fuuuuck.

Sebastian continued, "We have proven that Mr. Best did nothing, let alone something improper. He has been unable to pursue his career for two months, and a footballer's career is short enough. Restraint of trade is not trivial, and many organisations have been sued into oblivion for playing fast and loose with that area of law. I respectfully but *strongly* recommend you lift all restrictions on Mr. Best and allow him to commence playing for the club that did, in fact, sign him in the correct way: Chester Football Club."

Judge Gammon had a hard, calculating look in his eye; it had all been done in subtext, but Sebastian had implied that *he* had been the one suing firms into oblivion and he would love a go at the FA. Gammon looked at me and said, "Do you wish to add anything?"

I looked at Sebastian. He shook his head. I copied the gesture. Emma gave my knee a little squeeze to show I'd done the right thing.

We had to fuck off while the FA guys debated what to do.

Outside in the corridor, MD was ecstatic. He raved about Sebastian, claiming he was "better than Columbo," whatever that meant. Sebastian took some of the praise but claimed that when he started looking into the case, the more fishy it became. He said, and I quote, that something stank and he couldn't sit back and do nothing.

We were called back in.

The panel had decided that, on the balance of probabilities, the registration with Sheffield Wednesday had probably been some kind of prank. Emma and MD celebrated.

"But," said the dude. "The move *was* registered with UEFA and FIFA. Mr. Best has also played for Darlington this season. He cannot, therefore, be registered with Chester."

Emma was pissed, to say the least. "So he can go back to Darlington."

"He cannot."

"Write to FIFA and tell them it was a mistake," demanded Emma.

"Even if we had the resources, the process would take months. He can register for a new club in the next transfer window. Not before."

"This is restraint of trade," said Sebastian, genuinely happy. "You don't have a leg to stand on. I will destroy you! By the time I'm finished with this, I'll own Wembley Stadium!"

"Max will," said Emma.

"Right. Max, my fee is ten percent. I'll take the West stand."

Everyone waited for him to get the go-ahead. So when it didn't come, attention turned to me. But nothing was going to change. Their case had been smashed to pieces by a lawyer who had run rings around them once and would do so again. These empty suits weren't risking their careers for Bradley Rymarquis. No way. I'd assumed Brad was in cahoots with Old Nick, but now I knew that Brad had nothing to do with it.

I'd gone round slagging him off, and when he'd found out, he'd lost his shit the way I would have done. He'd stitched me up with the Jack Litherland deal, and presumably he'd keep trying to land blows on me. But getting the Football Association to stop me playing, come hell or high water? It was Old Nick. And if I wasn't careful, Old Nick would start lashing out at everyone else here. Emma. MD. Even Sebastian, who didn't deserve it. Maybe a little? No, not even a little.

I had this strange feeling inside me—peace.

The worst had happened. I couldn't play professional football for the rest of the season. But the curse had given me the body of an elite athlete. If I couldn't find a way to keep fit, make money, and annoy Nick, then I wasn't trying hard enough. I felt the grin come back.

I got up and swaggered over to the table where the five guys were sitting down. I sat on the edge of the table facing the imp, uncomfortably close to him. He did not like that. "So you can stop me playing football for a few months. What about in Scotland?"

"You can't play anywhere in FIFA jurisdiction," said the imp.

I nodded. "Great. Well done. What about tennis?"

The imp blinked. "Huh?"

"Can't stop me playing tennis, can you?"

"What?"

"Don't you think there are things someone as fast, strong, and smart as me can do? For money? As a career, even?"

"No, that's . . . that's not the . . ."

"MD," I said, looking over my shoulder. "Are you going to sack me for not being able to play?"

"No, Max. This is a travesty. I'll support you all the way."

"I need cash. I've got an idea for how I can blow off steam and make some money on the side. It might be a little bit . . . insane. I don't think Sean and Ollie will like it."

"What you do in your spare time is up to you, Max, but I think you'll find tennis is harder than it looks."

I leaned in to the imp and whispered into his right ear, the one farthest away from everyone else. "And you, you little scamp. You tell your boss I'm cutting him off. I'm done with football. Okay? I'm cutting off my nose to spite his face. Ho-kay?" For some reason I was talking to him like you talk to a baby. "We good? We good, bro? Yeah, you tell him that."

"But you need to get experience points," he whispered. "You haven't even found Wibwob."

"I'll do what I want," I said. "And what I want is to slap your boss pink. What's coming next is going to be a lot more fucking embarrassing for him than me playing a few games of football, let me promise you that. All right? And if you ever do anything like this again, make sure it doesn't involve coming to fucking *London*. Or I'll rip your head clean off."

The four of us left, with the Weavers rolling their empty suitcases behind them. They left the museum pieces in the room, along with all the papers. I think the idea was to give the FA guys some extra work to do, but I knew it would be the normal employees who'd have to do it.

In the lift and out on the street, MD and Sebastian got each other worked up about how unfair that all was. How absurd. Sebastian begged me to let him start legal action. MD turned pale at the idea.

"I don't want to get Chester involved," I said. "MD, we'll survive this season. We'll find a way. And next season, the golden age begins."

That evening, I went to where Darlington's first team were warming up before their session. I walked over and blew my whistle. There was a fair bit of annoyance but then a few players recognised me. "That's Max Best!" "Course it isn't, don't talk rot." "Max! What are you doing here?"

I waved at everyone to come over. "Apologies to the coaches! Yes, everyone, it is I, superstar football star Max Best. Currently Chester's director of football. I've decided I want to play for you for a couple of matches."

"Play for us?" said one of the guys. They were a very mixed bag, physically. Some tall and powerful, some short and squat.

"Yep." I mimed that I was anointing them with holy water. "You have been chosen."

"Why?"

"My plan is, play a couple of matches for you. Score loads of free kicks. Then get a move to a bigger club and rinse them for cash. What do you reckon?"

"Why don't you play for Chester?"

"Football Association is being a dick. If I play, they might deduct points. We'd smash them in court, but it's not worth the hassle. No, not worth it. I can play for *you*, though."

The main coach guy had tolerated my appearance since some of his players seemed to recognise me. He'd been tapping on his phone. "Is this what you mean by taking a free kick?" He held up his screen. I recognised the footage of me scoring that free kick against Alfreton. A few guys crowded round to check it out.

"Yeah. I can demonstrate if you want."

Another coach threw a ball to me that I caught just in front of my face. Careful, bro! He gave me a sly grin. "Go ahead."

The guys shuffled aside and watched as I placed the ball where I wanted it. I eyed the posts, then stepped up and scuffed the shot sideways. There were loads of laughs. I grinned. "Out of practice. Try again!"

I went through my routine with a little more care. I decided to hit through the dead centre of the ball, aiming to hit it in a straight line like a cannonball.

Poof.

The ball sailed pure and true, this time, the contact expressing itself as a soft, powdery exhale, like a book closing.

"There we go!" I laughed. "No goalie is saving *that*."

"Can you do that again?"

"Absolutely. Do you want me to bounce it in off the post or something like that? It's pretty boring without a goalkeeper."

"No, through the middle's fine."

I shrugged and repeated the strike.

There was a murmur of excitement now. It wasn't just me turning up to their session and adding some energy. They were starting to dream—what if I really *did* play for them?

The head coach guy was going through some calculations. "Have you ever played before?"

"Nah. I like kicking balls through sticks though. And being paid for it."

"We don't really pay what you're used to."

"Don't worry about it. I only need a thousand pounds or so. You'll double your money. Imagine the ticket sales when the people of Darlington realise Max Best is back." I visualised the posters that could adorn the town. I filled in the headline and the tag. "Max Best is back! And this time, it's rugby."

PUDDINGTON PIRATES

From a marketing point of view, I'd chosen an incredible week to become a professional rugby player. On Sunday, my beloved Darlington RFC were due to play at home to their fiercest rivals, Hartlepool, known as Pools.

Of course, if we consider this little adventure's impact on my *football* career . . . the timing wasn't great. But then again, I'm pretty sure everything that happened only happened *because* instead of grinding and using Playdar, I spent three and a half days trying to learn the basics of rugby. Suffice to say that there were three and a half days where Old Nick saw I was serious about not giving him XP and it freaked him out.

Sunday, February 19. Darlo versus Pools.

I pottered around, waiting for someone to tell me where to stand. Rugby looks organised on TV, but if you wander onto a pitch, it's absolute mayhem. There were players everywhere.

"Max," called my captain.

I jogged in his direction. We were wearing black shirts, black shorts. Pools were in red. Most players were strong, but slow. "Yes, boss?"

"You're the kick-boy. Take the kickoff."

"Right." He threw the ball to me and wandered away. I had to drop-kick it from kickoffs and restarts. "Where do you want me to put it?"

"Over there somewhere. At least ten metres. See the line?"

"I could score from here. Just saying."

He smiled. "You know those onside kicks in the NFL? Think like that. Chip it up so we can try to get it before they have control of it."

"Oh, cool, that's fun."

So I did that, and then fourteen blacks and fifteen reds bumped into each other like dodgems. After ten seconds almost everyone was covered in mud. I hovered twenty yards from the action. Trying to contribute to what was called "open play" wasn't really going to work—there were so many arcane rules that when I tried to help in practice, I was told I'd just given away a penalty. So I'd announced my intention to be a kick-boy and nothing else, and everyone was cool with that. I had two jobs: scoring penalties and booting the ball away when we were under pressure.

After spotting some infraction, the referee blew his whistle and pointed in our direction. "Aw," I said.

"It's good when he points at us," said our fullback. His normal job was to clean up any long kicks the other team made, and he had the added job today of keeping me out of trouble. "That's our penalty."

"Oh, top," I said. So the refs pointed the wrong way in this sport. No one had told me that. I went to the spot the penalty had been given, waited for the ball, and placed it. I was allowed to use a little ring to hold the ball in place. I'd seen other rugby dudes take bloody ages getting their kicks lined up and going through their little rituals. My process was a lot more straightforward, but I didn't want to get in trouble for taking the kick too fast, which sometimes happened in football. "Can I kick it now, ref?"

"If you're ready, Best."

Penalties in rugby followed the rules of a free kick in football; you took the kick from the spot where the foul happened. This one was halfway between the middle of the pitch and the edge, so the angle wasn't hard. It was only the shots from the very edge that were tricky. There wasn't a defensive wall, there wasn't a goalkeeper, and you had to kick the ball *over* the crossbar! I supposed it would be hard on a windy day, but otherwise?

"Ref, what do you reckon? Seven iron?"

"You don't know the first thing about golf, either, do you Best?"

"Not really, no."

I kicked the ball through the posts, the linesmen held their flags aloft, and we were three points ahead.

The crowd cheered.

The ref turned to me. "There's no bonus points for style," he said, smiling.

I wandered around for a bit. I had no feel for the game and no curse to help me. So I waited, patiently, until someone told me to take a penalty. I stepped up, scored, 6–0. The Pools players watched as I eased the ball through the posts with extreme nonchalance, and despite their evident bravery, their hearts sank a little bit. It was clear that every single tiny mistake they made would be punished.

It's fair to say I knew the feeling.

Friday, February 17—two days earlier.

My first drive to Chester since the incident with D-Day was clear roads all the way. The universe was rewarding me for standing up to Old Nick. I arrived at 4 p.m., checked if anyone was at the Deva, had some food, then went to the King George V Sports Hub where most of our women's and youth training sessions and matches were held.

I was supremely early, but this was going to be the first ever match played by my team and I didn't want any insane things to go wrong. I put out the corner flags, I put up the nets, I brought out the warm-up balls and the match balls.

By the time Spectrum and Jill turned up, the grunt work was done and they could focus on the warm-ups and all that stuff. I let them take over for a bit while I turned into a cheerleader. I welcomed the players, said hi to the first few parents and fans who'd come to watch, and then made a big fuss over our opposition.

The Puddington Pirates were a team from a small village in Cheshire. Inga had chosen them as our first opponents based on the progression principle I'd explained to her: Our matches should get slightly harder each time until by the end we were playing some really good teams, but we'd never be completely outmatched. And early signs were good—the Pirates were not physically imposing, they didn't all wear the exact same kit, and there was a very amateur feel to their whole operation. Inga had nailed it.

Still, Puddington were doing us a massive favour playing this game, and they were also lending us a left back because I hadn't found one yet. So I turned the charm all the way up. Their manager was a small, bookish type wearing round glasses. During the match she kept quite still, and only her head rotated. In my head, I called her The Owl.

The referee arrived, and again I dished out the charm, not to get an advantage but because no ref, no game. If I didn't have good relationships with referees, it'd be harder to arrange matches.

And then that was that. I'd done pretty much everything I could. I'd scouted *most* of a first eleven and borrowed a few randos from local clubs to make up the numbers.

When the warm-ups started, I had my first shock. The Pirates were way better than they had any right to be. Half the team were PA 1, but others ranged from PA 7, same as Beth, to PA 22. And they were almost all maxed out on CA. They'd trained, seriously. Their average CA was 8.

We had a very healthy average PA of 45, but that was massively distorted by Dani. Our average CA was 2.5.

Ten minutes before kickoff, my screens kicked in. I didn't use Bench Boost or Triple Captain because our most important games would be near the end of the season when we were trying to show we were worthy of being placed in a higher division.

The Pirates were using 4-4-2. The curse had assigned us the default tactic, 4-4-2, with the players in the right spots, and I left it like that.

We had a goalie. The left back was on loan from our opposition. The rest of the defence was mediocre, to be honest. The best was a PA 21 centre back. Two of our midfielders were at that level, too. But we also had Pippa and Dani, by far the best players on the pitch. I put Pippa as the right-sided central midfielder so she'd be able to combine with Dani. If they could turn into a good partnership, that'd be a source of strength in the future.

Up front we had a rando to make up the numbers, plus Beatrice Pearce, the girl I'd found training in the dark. The one who thought Max Best was fit. She was PA 36, so she'd be the third best player—eventually.

We also had a motley crew of subs, whom I would throw on near the end as a thanks for coming.

"What's up, Max?" Spectrum knew me far better than Jill.

I said, "It's going to be a long match."

"What's the special plan? One-eight-one? Three-seven-oh?"

"Four-four-two, keep things tight first five."

"Ha ha, but really."

"No, really," I said.

"Oh," said Spectrum.

"Listen," I said, scratching the back of my neck. "Let's be positive, yeah? Focus on the good things we do."

"Max," said Jill. "You're talking like we're going to lose. The Pirates are a village team."

"Must be a hell of a village. Er . . . Pippa's captain today. Tell me if you see leadership qualities in anyone else."

The match kicked off and we enjoyed a nice spell of possession. The ladies hadn't had many training sessions, but it was clear they'd had some coaching. When the ball got to Dani, there was a nice buzz from the crowd.

The crowd! Quite a few people had turned up to watch. Lots of curious Chester fans, with a high proportion of women and girls. Plenty of fathers and sons, too, it looked like. One turned and pointed something out to the man next to him and I realised it was Tyson and Bulldog. Ah! That whole section was the under-fourteens. It looked like most of the squad. And there was Vivek, his sister, his mother. Over there was Ruth with some guy. I was too far to get a proper look, but he seemed overly handsome. To my left, MD, Joe, Inga, some of MD's rich friends. And look at that! Henri, Raffi, Shona, and a bunch of first-team players. Physio Dean and Magnus were nearby—spectators, but ready to help if someone was badly hurt. Our other physio, Livia, turned up about twenty-five minutes in, holding hands with her boyfriend, FC United's third most important coach. He'd probably decided to come late to make sure I wouldn't mistake his head for a rugby ball and practice dropkicks on it.

Ah! And, even more fashionably late, making a dramatic entrance, my assistant manager. We kissed. "How's it going?"

"Okay for now but we are *about* to get smashed," I said. The ratings said as much. Lots of 4 out of 10s. Pippa was on 5. Our best player was the left back the other team had lent us.

Emma slapped my arm. "Don't talk like that! Fearless football. Do you know how shit the trains are in winter?"

"Not worse than in summer, I don't think."

Emma scanned the pitch. "Four-four-two?" It's fair to say she'd learned a lot about football in the past few months. "I didn't trav-el three hours to see four-four-two, Max. What happened to *The*

Wizard?" Her calling me The Wizard in a sarcastic voice had taken over from intoning "*the board*" as her favourite way to tease me.

I smiled. "Losing a match might be good for my reputation."

"That makes no sense."

"Wizards don't lose matches. If I lose, I'm not a wizard. *Cogito ergo sum*." Dropping Latin phrases into conversations was *my* new favourite way of teasing *her*. While I was grateful to her dad for his help, and while he was incredible at his job, dropping hand grenades in a dead language was pretty pompous.

"How's Dani doing?"

"Shit," I said. The curse was sort of forcing her to stay at her post, like it did with all the players. So our shape was fine, and when the Pirates got the ball we were rarely *badly* exposed. But when Dani got the ball, her inexperience showed. She wasn't alone, but since I'd made such a big fuss over her, her indecision was the most public. "Almost everyone is having a shocker. It's fine. You can't just turn up never having played a match and expect to be good."

Unless it's me and the sport rewards players who can kick far and with accuracy. I'd scored four penalties out of four. The other team's kick-boy had scored one out of two. One of the worst teams in the league was beating one of the best, 12–3.

And scoring penalties wasn't the only unfair advantage I brought. My second job was, when someone threw the ball to me, to kick it miles down the field. Our team would be under pressure near our goal and would work really hard to get the ball. But in rugby, having the ball near your own goal was almost as bad as the other team having it. You were still at risk—one mistake would lead to a goal, also known as a "try"—so instead of attempting the whole pass-and-run thing that the All Blacks did, most teams kicked the ball away and tried to rush up the pitch to get away from the danger zone.

What our coaches had worked out with admirable speed was that I could kick the ball almost anywhere they wanted. The balls were stupid egg-shaped nuisances, so there was always a big random factor about how they would bounce. But I could kick it over to the left, miles down the middle, or to the right, and if they wanted, I could make it so the ball was likely to go out of bounds. That was good, apparently, as long as it bounced first.

So the fullback would throw me the ball and yell, "Long left, touch!" or "Middle, long!" or whatever. And I'd follow his instructions like a robot. And Hartlepool would trudge backwards forty or fifty yards and have to rebuild their attack from scratch. And because throw-ins were contested, we always had the chance to recover the ball.

All my teammates had to do was defend hard, let me get them out of trouble, then scrabble around doing rugby things until we got a penalty.

Dani gathers the ball. She has a little bit of space. She passes inside to Pippa.

Pippa holds onto the ball, evades a challenge, and dinks the ball forward.

That's a nice touch from Dani. She's striding forward.

Dani drops her shoulder left and accelerates right.

She's clear!

She looks up and finds Bea Pea with a crisp pass.

Bea Pea takes a touch and shoots!

But it's blocked.

The ball comes loose. Pippa is beaten to it.

It's played out to the right. Great tackle!

But Puddington are first to the ball. They play it left.

The winger goes on a run.

That's a nice-looking cross.

The striker has evaded her marker!

GOOOOAAAALLLL!!!!

Lovely football from Puddington.

A great team move.

"Max, you're right," said Spectrum, shaking his head. "They're a really good team."

"They know each other really well," said Jill. "We look like a bunch of strangers."

"That's fine," I said. "That's what we are, really. To get to there we have to start here. Remember, be positive. At halftime, think of some upbeat things to say, yeah?"

"Yes, Max."

"Great half, lads!" said Dan, the Darlo manager and head coach. "Wow! Max, incredible. The looks on their faces when you hit that one from the touchline." That provoked general merriment. The rest of the team was grafting and putting a shift in, and for once it was paying dividends. They were buzzing.

"That was fifty-fifty," I said. "That's really hard, that angle." I could have made it easier for myself by striking the ball left-footed, but I was stubbornly hiding the extent of my two-footedness.

"Dan!" called one of the players. "Let Max do the halftime team talk! The football lads call him Tommy Tactics."

"All right," laughed Dan. "Come on, Max."

I stood and went next to him. "Right. They're playing offside trap, men behind ball. Flat back ten, with five sweepers. I say we switch to a dynamic four-three-three and hit them through the middle." Plenty of laughs. "Seriously, though, I'm getting bored. Your sport is really boring. I want to do something cool in the second half."

Dan frowned. "You said you didn't want to, and I quote, spend the rest of your life in traction, eating through a straw."

"Yeah, well, I've seen it up close now. It's mental, obviously, the way you smash into each other. But it's not like footy where guys are trying to snap my ankle off. I think I can take a couple of hits."

Dan nodded. We had a pretty good connection. I was helping him win and had quadrupled the attendance. In return, he accepted that I wasn't fully reverential about the sport. "How about you try a Garryowen?"

"Yes, perfect."

"Do you know what that is?"

"No clue."

Halfway through the second half, Puddington were winning 2–0. We had a few nice moments, and generally looked like a team with more technical quality, which is what we were. But we were also unfit, in-experienced, and young. Puddington started to overwhelm us, and I had no answers for it.

"We could go men behind ball for a couple of minutes," I suggested. "Then go more attacking. Surprise them."

"In a game like this," said Jill, "when you go defensive, you stay defensive."

"Long ball?" suggested Spectrum.

"Their centre backs would eat Bea Pea alive."

"Yeah," I agreed. "Look, we can't fix this in-match. We fix this with recruitment, with training, with more matches." My coaches nodded. "Spectrum, do you think you can get some of the boys to play against the women sometime? Maybe some short matches against the credit card company guys. Just whatever we can do for every little drop of match experience we can squeeze into them." I had a little think. "And we need a special move."

"What like?"

"When I play, there's free kicks and corners. Or that little kid from Notts who was doing all those through-balls. Or Ja—or that player who was good at crossing. We need a special move that's going to get us a goal every now and then."

Hartlepool reorganised at halftime and came out a bit more prepared for my barrage. I didn't know the names of the positions, but even I could work out they were attacking with fewer men and leaving more sweepers back to collect my punts. There was some rule that meant if they got to the ball fast enough, they didn't have to wait for us to get there before taking the throw-in—they could just restart quickly.

Their attacks were weaker then, but they were more solid defensively, which meant their attacks were more relentless. Good manager!

We were way ahead on the scoreboard, 24–13, but Pools had recently scored a try and if we didn't change something, they'd probably overhaul us.

So at the next defensive turnover, the captain yelled, "Garryowen!"

That was my cue to take a couple of slow, slow steps and absolutely wallop the ball as high as I could. Then I had to chase my own kick and try to get it before the guy catching it could gain control. I hit it so high the ball came down like a snowflake—there was no way the guy was going to catch it cleanly. I had handling 20 and even I found catching the egg-shaped "ball" hard. As was normal in the Garryowen situation, the guy jumped and reached up just before I got to him. The ball hit his hand and bounced away. I didn't have the same instincts I had when playing football, but I reacted fastest anyway. I plucked the ball from the air and started towards the far side of the pitch.

But I'd hit the ball too high, and many other defenders had come to the area. One threw himself at me—I hurdled him. Another two were zoomed from the left—I put my head down and accelerated with all my might. One of them, incredibly, was fast enough to get a big chunk of my shirt. He tried to pull me down. It was like being hit by a baseball bat, but reflex took over. I snorted and took short, powerful strides like a bull, adding in a hand-off as well. Then I was clear of the guy, and I powered forward to the halfway line. I couldn't risk turning to check how far they were, so I kept at full pace until I was in the end-zone. Only then did I look round to see how close the nearest players were—absolutely nowhere.

So I jogged across to the middle, behind the goalposts. If you've got the choice, you score the touchdown from there because then the extra points are easier for the kick-boy. But I was the kicker, and I wanted a bit more action. So I jogged towards the edge so I'd have a harder shot. When the crowd realised what I was doing, they went bonkers. They all knew more about rugby than I did. If I missed the kick and we lost, it wouldn't be a good story. So I popped the ball down, leaving myself an easy kick to add two points to the five I'd just earned.

"Perfect, Max!" said the captain. "Think you can do that again?"

"Yeah."

"You might want to change your shirt first."

"Why?" I looked down. "Huh." My shirt had been ripped almost in half. "That's annoying. I was going to put that on eBay."

"I think you might get more with it like that."

At about the same stage of the match when my new move messed up Hartlepool's plans, Puddington put their foot on the accelerator. Goals three and four came close together. We held out for a while before conceding goal five. And then goals six and seven came in a manic final minute where they realised we had nothing left in the tank and our substitutes were even worse than our first eleven.

The great Chester Women project had begun with a 7–0 defeat.

With two minutes remaining in Darlo versus Pools, I was subbed off so that I'd get a round of applause from the fans. My first one! The applause turned into a standing ovation, which I milked shamelessly.

I pulled on a coat and sat in the dugout. The manager turned to me and said, "Man of the Match on your debut. So how much are you going to charge for the next match?"

I smiled and nodded towards the pitch. "See that? I'm pretty sure . . ." I considered what I was about to say, and decided it was almost certainly true. "I'm pretty sure that was my entire rugby career."

I said thanks to The Owl and praised her for the way she'd coached her team. She didn't give much away, but I think she was pleased. I wished I had the staff profiles unlocked, because she was really impressive.

Then I gathered our team for the post-match team talk. MD had come over to listen, as had a lot of people, but he got a phone call and moved away.

"Ladies," I said, with Dani's father translating beside me. He wouldn't be able to come every match, but he wasn't going to miss her debut. "I've never said this before, and I doubt I'll ever say it again. But losing that one? That's fine."

I was just getting into my flow, but I spotted MD doing a walky-run. He was so unathletic!

"You are good. That's a fact. But some of you have never played an eleven-a-side match before. Some of you have never played with a *referee* before! You have an idea what's needed now. The levels. You've played a really good team there. No weaknesses, not letting you get settled, not letting up. Remember that, because we'll be doing what they did to us, to other teams."

I paused. MD had run towards Jackie Reaper and was whispering in his ear. What sort of news would MD get that Jackie would need to hear about? A bomb in Liverpool would do it. I briefly felt sick. That's why I tried not to read the news—I always feared the worst. I told myself to try to stay positive.

"Okay. Jill and Spectrum were watching closely. We saw a few nice moves that we liked. We'll see about repeating those and adding to them in your next sessions. We're not going to focus on your mistakes, but if you've got questions about things you did wrong, you can ask. All right? Next week, we've got another friendly. It's supposed to be a little bit harder, but I think it's going to be a little bit easier. Any questions?" MD and Jackie had vanished, but Livia was standing there, looking lost. For some reason, she looked right at me.

Dani was the first to ask, through her dad. "Are you sure we're good?"

That broke the tension. Everyone laughed. "I'm sure. Go get your showers. Sorry it's cold."

"Er . . . it's hot showers for the women," said Spectrum.

"What?"

"Ruth said. There's like five club hairdryers, too."

"That's coming out of my budget, is it?"

"Yes. She says you don't need three goalkeepers, but her team does need to do their hair nice."

"*Her* team?"

"She said, 'She who pays the Pippa calls the tune.'"

"Very funny," I said, but I was only half paying attention. All around me, phones were blowing up. Parents, fans, Chester players, our staff—everyone was glued to their screens. I took mine out. Nothing. "Er . . . what's going on?"

Spectrum reached into his pocket and pulled out his phone. I saw he had seventeen unread messages. He angled his phone away and gave me a "Do you mind?" face. That expression didn't last long. "Fuck me," he said. "Ian Evans has quit."

The curse news feed confirmed it. I shoved my hands as far into my pockets as they'd go, then read and reread the message.

Ian Evans resigns from his position as manager at Chester FC. Chester will now be looking for a new manager.

What the fuuuuuun. I realised I was walking around like a headless chicken, and when I turned back towards where I'd last seen MD, a gaggle of my closest friends were coming at me in a semicircle. I joined them and we formed a conspiratorial huddle.

"Max," said Henri. "Is it true?"

"Apparently so," I confirmed.

"Wow," said Raffi. This wasn't necessarily good news for him; Evans had shown a fair amount of faith in Raffi, even if he hadn't played much recently. The next manager might not. Shona leaned against him, looking worried.

"Why are you out here and not in there?" said Emma.

"In where?"

"In wherever MD is."

I pondered that. Good question. "Obviously he's trying to talk Evans out of quitting. And when that fails, he'll offer me the job." There was a lot more laughter than I expected, since I was expecting one hundred percent agreement. "What's the problem?" I demanded.

"One," said Emma, incredibly disloyal. "You just got slapped seven–nil by Puddington."

"Two," said Raffi. "You was fighting one of our main goalscorers this week."

"Three," said Henri. "Chester might not want their next manager to come from the playing staff of Darlington Rugby Club."

"It's Darlington Rugby *Football* Club," I snapped back. "Shit. I can't believe this." The timing was shocking. Unbelievable. That fossilised prick had chosen the absolute worst conceivable moment to quit.

A call came through. MD asking where I was, telling me to go to the car park.

I looked at my so-called friends and pointed a finger at them. "Don't go anywhere!"

"Oh, we won't," said Henri.

MD was with Jackie Reaper by one of those bins dog owners are supposed to fill with poop. I'd never seen anyone empty such a bin. What was the deal with that? Did it just dissolve?

I went over and pretended to be out of the loop. "Is it true?"

"Yes," said MD. "He called me, said he was going to put it on Twitter when he hung up."

That was almost as shocking as the news. "Ian Evans is on Twitter?"

"Yeah, mostly it's just one-word reactions to TV shows. There's a group of fans who try to guess what he's watching."

Awkward silence.

"MD," I said. "Do you think we should talk alone, briefly?"

"About what, Max?"

"About our next steps."

"Our next steps? You're looking at him." MD smiled in the direction of Jackie.

"The other day I got told off for not following the proper process. The proper process here is we discuss who the next manager should be."

"Yes. Next time. This time, it's already decided."

Jackie had been quiet. Not much going on facially. Now he grinned. "Am I not your first choice, Max?"

"Of course you're my first choice, you prick. But MD needs to know I'm ready to step in as caretaker manager for tomorrow's game and I can't say that when you're here looming over the area like a ghoul. Evans's body isn't even cold yet and you're here, trying on his boots."

Both men rubbed their mouths with the sides of their palms. Like my friends, they found the idea of me taking over after a 7–0 defeat *amusing*.

After a few seconds, MD said, "Fortunately, Jackie's contract allows him to leave FC United for a management position. He'll be in his post in time for tomorrow's match."

"Right," I said, slapping my hips a few times. "Right. So this is all good news. This is . . . good . . . news. Is this good news?"

"It's good for me," said Jackie, with a smug smile.

My thoughts turned away from trying to insert myself into the manager's dugout somehow, even if it was only for one match, towards practicalities. "What do we do? Announce Jackie right away? Or let people, er, mourn or whatever?"

"It's unseemly to announce right away. We'll wait until breakfast."

"I was planning to go back to Darlo tonight, but I can stay overnight if you need me around in the morning."

"You're fine, Max," said Jackie. "I've got it."

"You've got it? Tommy Tactics, right here. At your disposal."

"I've got it."

"So . . . what do I do?"

Jackie put his hand on my shoulder. "You make sure you're nice and rested for your big debut on Sunday."

MD rubbed his mouth again. They were taking the piss.

I nodded a few times while I got my annoyance under control. "Thanks, man. That's very kind of you." I realised they were trying to not look at each other because that would set them off laughing. And it really hit me then, the simple fact that they'd known each other for years. MD trusted Jackie more than he trusted anyone, especially about football. My opinions had suddenly become a lot less important. My voice had become diminished. And my role had been squashed into a pea-sized blob.

It was going to take some getting used to.

"One thing," I said, as I half-turned to leave. "Why did he resign?"

MD frowned. "He wouldn't say. He simply . . . resigned. Said it was the right time."

"Huh," I said.

I walked away, leaving Chester's managing director and the new first-team manager behind.

Saturday, February 18.

I kept a low profile and snuck into the director's box without being spotted. The box was full. Jackie Reaper, the legend, was back, and so were all the sponsors and bigwigs who had slipped away under the shadow of the dinosaur.

I kept my cap and sunglasses on, so only MD and Ruth recognised me outright, while a few others recognised me by my girlfriend. She was wearing a Chester FC beanie a stallholder had given her for free. He was probably thinking it wouldn't do his sales any harm if people saw her in it.

"Oh, this is exciting, isn't it?" She was all smiles. "Big buzz around the place."

"Yeah," I said. "The prodigal son returns in the team's darkest hour. It's a great story. And they're hoping to see some good football."

"Will they?"

"Why not?" I said, smiling. "He's doing three-five-two with D-Day on the left and Anka on the right. Raffi's in the middle, Henri's up top with Tony. It's almost the strongest possible team. And no left back, no problem. I swear Evans was sticking with four-four-two to make me look bad."

"I thought you don't like D-Day."

"No one does. Not even his mother. But he's the only real option for a left-sided player in this formation. And Jackie probably thinks, new manager, clean slate. Everyone starts fresh."

"What else? Something's making you smile, and it isn't the formation."

"He's got Pascal and Youngster on the bench. There's finally a pathway. It's happening." I shook my head in quiet amazement. "Did you see the way they were warming up with those little cones, those little shuttle runs? That's what the big boys do. We've got a manager who's a top coach. We've got a manager who gives a shit about the youth team. He came to watch the women! It's . . . it's so weird."

"Weird?"

"You know, like . . . I've been running up the down escalator. Now when I think about my job, it's like . . . easy. There's no friction. There's no one putting the brakes on. Jackie gets it." I exhaled. "We can finally focus on making the numbers go up." I tried to smile, but didn't. The turnaround had come so suddenly. It'd take a lot of getting used to.

"So . . . you aren't going to play rugby tomorrow." Emma had been moderately angry at me for signing up to play what she considered a barbaric sport, partly because I'd rushed to join the local team instead of taking her out for Valentine's Day.

"Babes," I said. "I have to play. I made a big fuss. I went on the radio. I did an interview with Bingo. They've sold two thousand tickets. Hundreds of little kids want to watch me. I have to go. But it's the first and last time. Probably."

"Do you promise?"

"It's a thousand pounds for kicking an egg. I can't *promise*. But I feel good about football again. I feel refreshed. I'm ready to grind. Ah, here they come!"

We had the windows open, despite the chill, and we heard the roar as Jackie Reaper led his team onto the pitch. He waved to all areas of the ground.

"Crackers will love this," said Emma.

"And it's only going to get better," I said. "It's only going to get better."

4

THE NINETY-MINUTE WORK WEEK

Football glossary: The New Manager Bounce. A theoretical upturn in results that takes place when a bright, shiny and new manager replaces a tired, worn, and cracked one. The new manager bounce has been scientifically disproven multiple times but what does science know about anything?

Saturday, February 25.

I met Emma at Bradford Interchange and we drove to Horsfall Stadium, home of Bradford (Park Avenue), my favourite team that includes brackets in their name. I asked for help, and Emma used some brackets of her own in the form of a mumbled disclaimer.

"Absolutely. Of course. (My advice is for informational and entertainment purposes only and I cannot be held liable for damages arising from its use.) What's up?"

"I don't know if I'm doing the right things. I'm not sure I'm using my time the best way. I've got loads to do but none of it's urgent. I think I'd like a second opinion."

"Opinions are like a favourite lipstick: Everyone's got one."

Minute 1.

It was a pretty big match. Jackie's first away game, and against a relegation rival, too. We were four points ahead of them, so a win would take us seven clear—a gap that would become insurmountable as matches ran out. A draw would be okay, depending on what the other teams around us did, while a defeat would put us right back in the shit. Our fantastic away support was as loud as ever. They ate up Jackie's sudden reappearance like manna from heaven.

Emma's work week had been unusually busy, and we hadn't spoken much. She looked tired and vaguely unhappy. Me being me, I leapt straight to the conclusion that she was done with going to tiny stadiums to watch awful football.

"Do you want to go somewhere else?"

"What?"

"There's an alpaca farm nearby. They've got alpacas."

"How do you know?"

"I always look for things to do if you get sick of the match. Alpacas, then al-pack-ya home and you can go clubbing. I know you miss it."

She smiled, and my heart lifted an absurd amount. "I like that I can come to your job. Being bored by *your* job is way better than being bored by mine."

"Tell me what you've been up to."

She told me about her week and her shitty clients and all the mad hoops they made her jump through. When the players came out for the start of the match—BPA in green shirts, white shorts; Chester in their striped blue kit—she decided she'd vented enough. "Right. Tell me what's happening here, then tell me about your week."

"Bradford brackets Park Avenue more brackets are twenty-second. We're nineteenth. This is called a relegation six-pointer."

"Because you get six points if you win."

"No, it's the swing. They go into the match hoping for those three points, so when you beat them, it's like you've taken their three and added three of your own."

"Sports logic is my favourite logic."

"Jackie's been slightly unlucky with the postponements. He's got three away games in a row. Then a home game, then two more away games. Tough run. But the training's so good. As Pep Guardiola says, it's so, so good. *So so good.*"

"*So so good.*"

"I'll tell you about training in a second. First, you need to hear about rugby."

"About what?"

"Rugby."

"What?" So it was going to be like that. She'd gone ape when I told her I was doing rugby. She sent me links to stats that showed how dangerous rugby was, then got even more upset when I pointed out that football was rated as more dangerous *on those same lists*. She found a brutal video of rugby dudes wandering around, dazed, with blood pouring from head wounds, being lifted onto stretchers, and some really, really nasty cheap shots and clotheslines. She thought I was going to break my neck in a scrum, or at least have half my teeth knocked out when a dozen men jumped on my back. I'd tried to assure her it wouldn't happen to me, but it was like reasoning with a brick wall.

"Rugby. It's a sport. I'm one of the world's best players."

"Hmm," she said, peeling herself away from me, taking out her phone, and loading *Hedge of Reason*, the maze-based puzzle game.

"So I scored about a hundred points." It was actually thirty-seven, not that I was counting. "And I got a standing ovation. *Veni, vidi, vici.*"

Not even a hmm this time.

And her entire demeanour confirmed something I was almost sure of: She had instructed all my friends to *not* mention rugby, ask about my match, or show any interest in what I'd done against Hartlepool. The idea, I'm sure, was to dissuade me from playing for Darlington ever again by starving me of the praise and attention I "needed." The texts I got after my heroics were all about Jackie. Oh, and one from Henri, who I knew would have loved to see me scrapping and fighting. But his message simply reminded me that someone was coming to service the gas boiler.

I sighed. "So you remember last week, Jackie played three-five-two." Emma put her phone away and gave me an intoxicating blast of attention. "Chester controlled the match from start to finish. Seventy percent possession. Good substitutions. He went defensive a bit early for my liking, but three–nil, take the points, let's go. Jackie Reaper blue and white army! It's an identical setup today. Only change is that Pascal isn't on the bench. Magnus is there instead."

"Oh, no."

"It's fine. Pascal's a long-term project, not quite ready for the first team, and Magnus is really interesting. Could be a valuable squad player. I'm surprised Youngster is still there, to be honest. Jackie must have liked what he saw in training."

"You were excited to take part in Jackie's training, right? Was it as good as you'd hoped?"

Monday, February 20, 9 a.m.—five days earlier. Jackie's first training session as Chester FC manager.

I drove to Chester to watch, and maybe even join in. Why not? I knew I'd love it. But MD intercepted me. Suggested that I might want to let Jackie get stuck in without my unique brand of distraction. He asked me to be "undramatic" for "a couple of weeks." Annoying, but probably right. MD said he was off to do a conf call for his pharma consultancy but he'd be back for our big first meeting with JR. "The Three Amigos," he said, and he looked genuinely excited about it.

I was happy for MD—he deserved some good news, some good times—but couldn't quite share his excitement. Maybe it'd come. Maybe I just needed to find my place in the new dynamic.

I found the spot farthest away from the training pitch that would still let me see the player profiles, and I sat there, analysing.

It almost goes without saying that the training was stupendous. Maybe they did it better at Man City, maybe for really elite sessions you needed a team of six coaches in super perfect surroundings. But for what one man could do with these pitches—wow. The body language of the players was better from the first minute. It wasn't just the so-called "new manager bounce." It was the drills, too. They were challenging. Often, they were fun; drills would descend into farce and there would be a big laugh. Jackie would explain it again—to Vimsy, too, who had to learn all this stuff, same as the players—and then the drill would restart, a little slower, then would catch up and finally turn into a dizzying whirl of bodies and balls. For unlike Ian Evans's drills, everything was done with a football.

I knew about Jackie's coaching. I knew he'd improve the players. But what I didn't know was just how good he was at man management. He took Pascal and Youngster aside a few times, giving them individual tips. During another break, he put his arm around his Carl Carlile's shoulder. They had a big old chat, and when Carlile returned to the main group, he seemed ten percent faster.

But he had a totally different approach for Henri. At first, Jackie ignored him completely. Then he laughed when Henri failed to control a pass. Finally, he got in Henri's face, calling him shit, calling him a waste of money.

Henri reacted to being ignored with apparent indifference; to being mocked by striding around with his chin in the air; to being attacked by storming through the drills.

Henri gained a point in CA after mere minutes and a second one near the end. Youngster saw similar improvement. Pascal, Raffi, and six others added one point during the session. Green green green! The squad left the pitch in boyish excitement—almost everyone, including Youngster and Pascal, who had become friends. Henri left in rapture. I couldn't remember him ever being so . . . so open. It was mind-blowing. Jackie was a wizard! I didn't need to buy the Morale perk!

Jackie checked his watch and wandered over to the goalkeepers. They'd started a bit late because Jackie wanted to get a proper look at them, too.

Livia appeared next to me. "Morning, Max."

"Good morning."

"Someone saw a homeless guy sitting out here. Wanted to call social services. I said it's probably our director of football." She smiled at me. "Do you still use my Disney?"

"Oh, yeah, sometimes. Sorry, is that rude? Yeah, I should have checked. I'll stop."

She waved about my worry. "It's just when I log in it asks if I want to continue watching *The Mighty Ducks* or *Air Bud*. I thought Jackie had done it as a joke."

"No, it was me. I'm in a cheesy sports movie phase. How's he taking this?"

She looked shifty, which was jarring. I don't think she had much practice at deception. "He's very excited."

I grinned. "He should be. It's huge."

She pulled at her earlobes. "Yeah. Huge. But . . . you're going to help him, right?"

Something was up. This was weird. "Of course I am. That's my job. But listen, he's a natural. Three–nil. Seventy percent possession. Couple of in-game tweaks. It was flawless. He's gonna be fine." She bit her nails and looked away. She dropped her hand with an annoyed look. An old habit she'd worked hard to break. "Look," I said. "He wants to do it his own way. And that's right. But if he's struggling, tell me. We'll cook up some scheme together. Help him without making it obvious."

"All right." She sighed. She was disproportionately worried. "How did your rugby go?"

"Top. I'm an all-time legend already. Statue worthy."

She rolled her eyes. "You didn't break anything?"

"Broke some hearts. Broke some records. Broke rugby TikTok."

"Really?" she said and took out her phone. In the TikTok app she typed "rugby." She gave me a disapproving look.

"Try 'rugby Darlo.'"

"Ah, there you are. First hit." I guessed she was watching the clip of me chasing the high ball and scoring my try. "Is this sped up?"

"No clue. I haven't seen it." She handed me the phone and I replayed the fourteen-second clip. The hits looked worse on camera than they actually felt. I winced as the main one came in, but then I was off, sprinting away to the other side of the pitch in two seconds flat. The video ended with two seconds from a different video—an American church lady going "Whuuut?"

"Yeah, it's sped up," I lied.

She shook her head. "Those impacts looked pretty bad. Let's take a look at you."

I shrugged. I wasn't in pain, but the training session would go on for another quarter of an hour at least. "Fine."

Saturday. Chester versus Bradford, minute 5.

Emma was interested in Livia's strange comments about Jackie, and was pleased that she had wanted to take care of me, but she heard the word *rugby* so had to express massive disapproval somehow. She did it by saying, "Oh, so when *Livia* shows you a TikTok, you're interested."

"If I'm in it, yes." Chester were dominating possession, much as they had done in the previous match. They looked sharp.

"What do you think she's worried about?"

"No clue. He's walking around like he owns the place. Super confident."

"Huh," said Emma.

"What?"

"Sometimes when guys do that you can tell they're trembling inside."

"He's not some rando trying to chat you up at a bar. He's a former pro, great defender, great thinker. He's been preparing for this moment since his injury. He's ready."

Emma's face stiffened into an angry sort of pout. "So what did Livia say? Were you all right?"

It took me a half a second to remember what she was talking about.

Monday, 10:45 a.m.

The first thing I noticed in the medical room was the smell, or lack of it. The diffuser in the corner of the room was off. That was weirdly depressing. Filled me with doubts. I tried to let the feeling slide off me.

Livia asked me to take my top off while she put on gloves. She turned and gasped. It's not good when a medical professional loses control of their reactions. "The fuck?"

"What?" I said.

"The bruising, Max!"

I went to one of the full-length mirrors. The left-hand side of my torso looked like a banana that was an hour away from being home to four thousand tiny flies. "That's the lighting in here. It's not that bad."

"Turn this way," she said, holding her camera up.

"Whoa, no way," I said. "Jackie will kill me when he checks your phone and sees you've got nudie pics of me."

"It's for the insurance. If you've got a smashed spleen, we're not paying for it. Your rugby team is on the hook for this."

"Are you serious?"

"Yes. Stand still. Oh, my days." She took the photo. "And it doesn't hurt? You can lift your arm and everything?"

"I mean, I'm aware that I took a hit. But it's fine."

"Are you coming back tomorrow?"

"I think I'll be around almost every day now."

"I want to keep an eye on this. Let me know right away if anything weird happens."

"Weird like what?"

"Like you drop dead."

"You'll be the first call I make."

Saturday. **Chester versus Bradford, minute 10.**

On the pitch, across the running track that separated the fans from the action, Chester continued to zip the ball around. Raffi was on 7 out of 10. His CA had been steadily improving and was now 27. He'd overtaken Angles, Trick Williams, and Magnus. Under Jackie, he'd kick on even more. Could he finish the season on CA 40? Next season he'd turn into the most dominant central midfielder in the league.

In the stands next to me, Emma placed one finger in the space between her eyebrows. Like almost everyone else, she was way better at controlling her emotions than I was.

"I want to see," she said, meaning the photo of me disguised as an overripe fruit.

"I don't have the photo," I said.

"I want to see it *now*," she said.

I knew this was a bad idea and would bite me on all my asses. "Oh, good pass, Carl!" I yelled, applauding massively. Carl was also on 7 out of 10. Much improved. The Jackie Effect.

"Max," she warned.

"Babes?" I said.

"Max," she warned.

"Bebs?" Now it seemed I'd do more damage if I didn't show her. I experienced the all-too-familiar sensation of my insides turning outside-in. I swiped through my recent photos and showed it to her. Her face crumpled. "Emma," I said, trying to bring her into a hug. "It's fine. It looked bad but I promise it wasn't."

She was refusing to look at me, sort of crying and stuff. Her fears realised. Well, shit.

"Emma, I swear on all the hedgehogs. The bruising is *gone*. I promise. I'll show you." I started to take my hoodie off, then thought about the optics. "Okay I can't do it right now because I promised MD I'd stop doing weird shit for a couple of weeks. I'll show you later. I promise, it's all gone. There's one little yellow patch about here, but I don't know if that's the last bit of bruise or some tea I spilled."

"How can it be gone?"

"Because it wasn't that bad. Honestly. I know you don't like the thought of it, but rugby's safer than football. There was no one within twenty yards of me almost the whole game. Livia checked me again on

Wednesday and said she'd overreacted. Okay? Babes, come here." She allowed me to hug her.

"I don't want you to get hurt."

"I also don't want me to get hurt." I held her for a while, until I sensed an opportunity to change the mood. "Do you want to hear about the podcast that's been slandering me?"

"What?" she said, sitting up, liquid eyes blazing.

"Jackie tore them a new one for me."

Monday, 11 a.m.

I wandered up to Jackie's office, which until a couple of days prior had been home to Ian Evans. It seemed like the pensioner had been in to collect his belongings. The photo of him with that kid was gone and the drawers were empty, but otherwise, it was much as I'd last seen it. The flipchart was there with a 4-4-2 formation displaying the names of fit and unfit players. I noted that Magnus Evergreen's name had slipped off the radar. I hoped Jackie would take me more seriously.

Through the big windows, I checked out the goalies. It looked like Jackie had taken over the session. Tracksuit manager. Getting his hands dirty. Whatever he was doing now, it looked fun.

Fun? I glanced at the chair that Evans had spent so much time in. I did a quick online search for how to do an exorcism but while I had my phone out, went to the podcasts app.

After Saturday's win, Jackie had given a long interview to the unofficial Chester podcast.

There were two podcasts about the club. Boggy produced *The Seals Podcast*, which came out once a month and was fine, if a bit corporate. For the really rabid fans there was *Deva Victrix*, by the fans for the fans. That came out after every game and was based on the Arsenal Fans TV model—hot takes and anger with a generous helping of stupidity. Pure dick bait.

I'd tried to listen a few times and always quit two minutes in, but for this special episode they were much better about knocking their microphones and not talking over each other. That was probably because they were in awe of the new manager.

The start was a load of "oh Jackie you're so great" simpering. Then there was five minutes of "yay we won three-nil" followed by about an hour of "Jackie you're so amazing why are you so amazing?" They read out texts and emails from listeners who described what it meant to them that Jackie was back.

I skipped ahead to the good bit. It was the part where Jackie started saying, "He won't mind me saying" before insulting me.

There were three hosts, and I have chosen to use their real names.

"The other thing that was exciting," said Huey, "was seeing some young players on the bench!"

"Well," said Dewey, "I'd agree if they weren't Max Best signings."

"What do you mean?" said Jackie.

"It's just weird, innit?" said Louie. "An eight-year contract for that little tiny one. He's too short. Eight years for him is the most bizarre thing I've ever heard of, and I've taken ritual peyote in a shaman hut in Blackpool. The other one's his client. Just nonstop weirdness with that guy. You're back now, so we can bin him off, right?"

"Bin Max off?" said Jackie.

"Yes, please," said Dewey.

"I think you might have the wrong end of the stick there," said Jackie. "I'm the one who fought to get him to Chester."

"*You* did?"

"Yeah. He won't mind me saying this, but he's an annoying guy. He's completely normal, good lad, good hang, but put him in front of a football pitch and he turns into a maniac. He won't mind me saying that either. I've seen him do mad things. Twice that I know of, he's taken control of a reserve team and slapped the first eleven."

"What?"

"I know." Jackie laughed. "He's a one-off. At least, I hope he is!" Big laugh. "But seriously, now. When it comes to football, he's the biz. When it came to taking this job, his being here was a weight off my mind. You're worried about the players he's brought in? I'm not. I worked with Ziggy at FC United and saw his growth. I've been watching Raffi progress for a while. And I was actually there when Max discovered Youngster. He was doing cartwheels."

"Youngster?"

"Max. I thought Youngster was some kid who'd walked in off the street, which is basically what he was. Seeing him now, he looks like a proper player already. I need to see him in training, obviously. Have a good look at him to see how he fits in my system. But he was at

Altrincham and they wanted to sign him. If he's good enough for the division above, you'd think he might do all right down here. I don't know Pascal so well, but he's another kid who's dropped down the pyramid to come to Chester because of Max. I don't see how you spin that into a bad thing."

"Well, yeah, that's one perspective, but it's all about the grift, isn't it?"

"What did you just say?"

"What Louie is suggesting is that Best is getting fees on these deals."

There was a pause. I could only imagine Jackie's face going dead, the way it did when I displeased him. But he sounded pretty jolly when he replied to that. "Right, yeah. Max Best, criminal mastermind. Because the way you get lots of money fast is to be a brilliant footballer and not tell anyone. Get a contract where you play for cheap but with a big goal and assist bonus. Score and set up, like, fifteen goals in a month. And just as you start getting offers to play for huge clubs at five figures a week, you take a massive pay *cut* to go and help out a skint team at the bottom of the league. Before you've even got your first wages through, you hear the disabled team can't afford to go to its tournament, so you pay that anonymously, in cash."

"He did that?"

"How do you know if it's anonymous?"

"There were only four people who knew. But back to our criminal mastermind. Half the youth team leave, so while they're at their new club, he pays for a coach to give them some proper sessions so they don't fall behind. Then he takes over and those players come back. But he still pays the coach. So now there's a random team in Cheshire getting professional sessions twice a week. And he does all this to lull us into a false sense of security so he can take a sweet, sweet slice of Youngster's ninety-five-pound-a-week scholarship contract. Mmm. I love the smell of passive income in the morning."

There was a long silence that a normal podcast would have cut.

"Right," said one of the three twats. Don't care which.

"I'd suggest you stop slandering the guy. His girlfriend's a lawyer. Nice girl, but she'll ruin you. How did all this happen? He's a top lad. Why don't you invite him on your show?"

"We did, when he first came to the club. He said he'd do it for six thousand pounds."

Jackie laughed hard at that, then remembered he was trying to have a good relationship with these idiots. "Do you think it's *possible* he was joking?"

"Yeah, at first, but then we started hearing all these rumours."

"You're better than that, Huey. Remember all the fuss about Tony Woodston in the old days? You knew him and you were always defending him. And you were right. Now look at you on the other side of the fence. Max is no angel, but he's better than most. And believe me, you don't pay him to talk about football. You pay him to stop."

Saturday. Chester versus Bradford, minute 15.

Emma listened to me retell the tale, almost expressionless. When I finished, she blinked and whispered, "I'll fuck them up. *'Nice girl, but she'll ruin you.'* You'd better believe it."

"It's okay. I like the way Jackie handled it. It's better like that. They'll stop now."

"Tell me the name of the podcast again."

"It's called *This American Life.*" Emma tutted, but she enjoyed my joke. There was a brief lull in our conversation as Henri made a run to the back post, but the cross was slightly too high—he applauded the intention. He was on 6 out of 10 but giving the kind of all-action performance that would lead to goals.

Emma tried to look innocent. "Tell me the real name. All I'll do is send a threatening letter. Dad and I will do it together. Do you know how much fun it is writing a cease and desist? Choosing the right word is better than twisting a knife."

"I really don't want you to do anything. For now. I think it was Ian Evans who started the whole grifter thing. And he's gone."

"Why did he quit? Do we know?"

"Still no more info. I mean, I have ideas. There's the obvious: His methods stopped working and there's this tough run of games. There's private life stuff: He's sick. His wife's sick. Who knows? For once, the gammons aren't blaming me. It was only a few days earlier that I was chanting for Ian at the Forum. But . . ."

"Go on."

"It was weird, though. At the Forum, someone said I should be the next manager and Ian didn't like that. He sat there all grumpy. I was thinking that maybe he spent a couple of days thinking back through all the things I'd done, wondering if I was trying to get him to quit so I could take over."

"I don't think people think about you as much as you hope."

"Like, the left back thing. I ignore the one he suggested. The other player he recommends is doing great. Fits right in! But I go with my own guy, then with all the transfer deadline day drama, we end up with no fit left backs. And Ian thinks . . . huh. He thinks I'm *publicly* supporting him, but *privately* doing everything I can to undermine him. It's mad, but I could imagine that."

"You overcomplicate everything."

"Maybe. I did tell him how to run the team just after finding out how personally he took the idea he wasn't fully in charge. I might have blown him up by accident." I sighed. If that was true, I wished I'd done it consciously, not by blundering around. "Do you want to hear about the first meeting of The Three Amigos?"

Monday, 11:15 a.m.

Jackie and MD turned up. I pressed pause. "Come in, guys." I wanted to reference the podcast, make a joke about Jackie calling me names. But acknowledging that he'd defended me might have made us both uncomfortable. I decided to pretend it had never happened. I sat in Jackie's chair. Show of dominance. Roar! "Have a seat."

Annoyingly, neither guy seemed to realise I was dominating them, which only added to my vague sense of unease. I realised Jackie had never even been in this room. He probably thought it was my office, not his.

MD looked at his watch. "We've got a lot to discuss, but I've got a hard out in about fifteen. Sorry, guys. But we'll be spending a lot of time with each other over the coming months."

"Max, do you want to start us off?" said Jackie.

Again, I felt weird. Out of place. The only reason for Jackie to ask me to start was to throw me a bone. Good Max! Who's a good Max? "Sure," I said. "Item one. Undisclosed relationships between members of staff."

Jackie shook his head and grinned. "I'm dating Livia. Is that what you wanted to hear?"

"I need a written description of how she asked you out."

"I'll get right on it," he said.

He was on such a high my weird banter was only going to gently bounce off him. I got serious. "Great. The real item one. I want Magnus in full training. I want him on the bench and—at your discretion, of course—used as much as poss. If he isn't working out for you, let's talk about it. But I think he's got something, and I want him given the chance to show it."

Jackie frowned, just a fraction. "Okay."

"What did you make of the kids?"

The smile was back. "Youngster's unrecognisable. We need to teach him the position, but yeah. Max Best, Super Scout. What do you think? Getting minutes by the end of the season?"

"Works for me. I'd like eighty percent DM, twenty percent CM. He's a DM, is what I'm saying. Teach him that. Pascal?"

He squirmed. "Great lad. Fighter. Fast. Everything you said."

"But?"

He spread his hands. "Max. In this division . . ."

I was sick of discussing how he was too short. "Do you think you can give him ten minutes here and there through the rest of the season?"

"A couple of times. When we're safe, all bets are on."

It was frustrating, but I knew things would start slowly for Pascal. It's not like he was CA 50 and bursting to start. "Good enough." We could revisit this topic based on how their CA developed. Now for something more personal. "I'm guessing you don't want me at training." I glanced at MD, who had the sense to look away.

"I'd love you in the team, Max. But you can't play. So . . . you're a distraction. A good distraction, normally. But this is my first manager's job. I don't know that I can let you dick around and keep the rest of the players happy. If you're not there, I can do what I know I can do."

"Okay."

"You don't like it."

"Your sessions are amazing, Jackie. That's like fantasy football to me. I want to do that. I want to learn. But it's fine. I can wait till the summer."

"I'd like to talk about contracts," he said.

"Yeah?"

"When do you plan to start talking to the lads about it?"

He included MD in his question, but I spoke a little louder to show I was, like, the guy to talk to. "Almost everyone who is out of contract is a dick. They can, and I believe this is the technical business term, get stuffed."

Jackie laughed two hearty laughs. "Max, they've got mortgages and stuff. They need to know."

"The idea of banks repossessing their homes makes me tumescent, Jackie."

"Maaax," said MD.

"How about we make a list of players we trust to be left alone with the women's team? Start from there? Yeah? What do you think, MD? How about people who make obscene jokes after I've told them I want obscene jokes to stop don't get fucking invited to stick around? Can we agree on that at least?"

Jackie raised his palms. "Whoa! Whoa . . . Okay, I've missed some stuff."

"This isn't a clean-slate scenario, Jackie. This is a 'me and player X go into a room to negotiate a contract, only one of us leaves' scenario. I am fucking sick of neanderthals. I don't want them here. Shit players, shit people. What's the point?"

"So," said Jackie, carefully. "There's the possibility of having some shit people around if they're good enough."

"Yes. The possibility exists. Would you like a list of players not good enough to have a shit personality?"

I pointed to the flipchart.

Jackie bit back a smile. "That's . . . everyone."

"Yep."

"What about Aff?"

"What about him?"

"He's a great guy."

"He played injured."

"He tried to help the team."

"How much help was he on Saturday, Jackie?"

Jackie rubbed his head. "Yeah, okay. Good point. But you can't punish players for trying to do the right thing."

"The right thing is doing what I tell them to do. If I see a guy running funny, tell him to get checked out, and next thing is he's getting stretchered off and he's out for two months, he doesn't get a new contract."

"Left wingers who can defend aren't ten-a-penny."

"If you're telling me there isn't a single left-footed human being who has the basic common sense to put the oxygen mask on himself first so that he can help the people around him, then yeah, Aff can have a new deal. No problem. If, by some fucking enormous miracle, we can *somehow* find a guy who can kick a ball who can also manage to understand fucking basic principles, then soz, he's out. And by the way, if it comes to it, I'll play left mid next season."

"You?"

"If playing there is what it takes to make people understand that I'm serious when I say things, then yeah. I'll do it."

I was getting worked up, which was the last thing I wanted. But Jackie diffused the situation like a grown-up. "You've thought about this a lot more than I have, Max. Let's get through the next week or so and maybe I'll see what you mean. Okay?"

"Okay."

MD looked at us like a proud father, then said, "Shit. I have to run. Don't talk about football when I'm not here. Ian never let me hear this stuff. I'm in absolute heaven."

Jackie and I smiled at each other as he sped away. We were left alone.

"Are you going to be difficult, Max?"

"No. I'm cutting out the rot. There's a lot of bad apples."

He nodded a few times. "I trust you. Mostly. I don't think we can afford to be too . . . idealistic."

"I don't think we can afford not to be."

He grinned. "Max Best."

I had to grin, too. But then I got serious. "Jackie. You've got three away games in a row. It's not going to be an easy run. I want to get out of your way, if that's what helps you. If you want me on the bench next to you, I'll do that. You just tell me what you need and I'll do it. Everything else can wait a minute. Tell me what you want from me."

He rubbed his hands together like he was washing them. "I need to do this on me own. The training, the tactics, the matches. It's got to be my team out there. I've worked hard to get here. It's my time. Stand on my own two feet. D'ya know what I mean?"

Of course I did. But one of the next matches was against Gloucester, and I'd played against them not that long ago. Torn them a new one, too. It was kind of moronic that Jackie wouldn't ask for tips. But I had to let him do it his way. The first team was his realm.

Saturday. Chester versus Bradford, minute 30.

His realm had its first earthquake, just about then. A rare Bradford attack led to a simple goal being scored. One of those where no one's to blame and you can't work out why it's happened. But the guys continued to play as they had—they weren't letting this one little hiccup derail them.

"I can't tell if you're going to be a good match," said Emma, thinking about how I'd described working with Jackie. "Or if you're going to be like Kendall and Roman Roy."

"Is that from *Succession*? I'm guessing those guys don't get on? No, I think we're going to work. I find rough diamonds, he smooths them out. That's ninety-seven percent of it. We're not going to fall out over some lowlife scum. And even the good players . . . I mean, I can't make him see what I see in Pascal. Pascal has to do that. And I really liked how he handled Henri. He challenged him. If he ignores Pascal for six months, maybe that's what he needs. I'm . . . optimistic."

Just then, a cross came in from the right, and like before, it was slightly too high for Henri to head at goal. But he leapt, a huge effort, and nodded the ball square, back into the danger area. Tony, the second striker, was there for an easy finish. One–all!

We stood and applauded, then fell into gossiping about Henri and Gemma, speculating about what Jackie said to Carl Carlile, and wondering how Youngster would cope if he came onto the pitch.

At halftime we retreated into our hospitality box and made friends with the directors of Bradford. Bradford's a big rugby town, and they had seen clips from my debut. Emma kept trying to bring the subject back to football, but in the end she gave up and let me have my moment in the sun.

The guys were huge fans of Max Best brackets rugby close brackets. One guy raved about my kicking accuracy—ten out of twelve hits!

"Whoa," I said, with a little laugh. "You can't count those other two as misses. The ball was flat. The kicks were *perfect*."

They took this as good-natured banter instead of what it was: factual truth.

There was a lot of talk about Jackie then. How young our setup was—young manager, even younger DoF. How dynamic and exciting. They wanted us to go down, obviously, while they stayed up. But they were big Jackie fans. Who wasn't? They wished him well.

Near the end of the break, one of the guys said he was also on the board at Bradford Bulls, the rugby league team. I think that was the first time Emma heard there were two kinds of rugby. The guy said if I ever wanted to go for a tryout there, I should give him a call. I looked at Emma, remembered how stressed she'd been. "I should stick to safe things like being the most-fouled player in the National League," I said.

Back in our seats, Emma gave me a kiss. "Is there a sport you'd be good at where you wouldn't get hurt? What about cricket?"

I gave her an "Are you crazy?" look. "Cricket's way more dangerous than rugby. Next time we're shopping, let's get a cricket ball in your hand. No, not cricket. Swimming? Nah. Has to involve kicking and a ball. I'll just— Listen, I've been thinking. What are we going to do?"

"About what?"

"My job's in Chester. You're in Newcastle. How are we going to . . .?"

She sighed. "I see. This is what this whole conversation's about. Transfer window's closed. There's no need for you to storm around demanding change, because Jackie's there now and it'll come naturally. You can't train. You can scout but it's not urgent and you don't know what division you'll be in next season. What else? The youth teams are in good shape. You've got nothing to work on, so you want to do your little progression fantasies on our relationship. How'm I doing?"

"Sometimes I like to think about the future."

"Sometimes it's nice to be in a place and enjoy being in that place."

Monday through Thursday.

After the meeting, I trudged to my car. Not sad, exactly, but not happy either. I seemed to be the only person in Chester who wasn't jumping for joy.

Jackie had his job. I had mine: Turning the women's team into a powerhouse. Grinding for XP.

XP balance: 2,777

Debt repaid: 862/3,000

I had a healthy chunk of XP, then. But what did I want to spend it on? What did Jackie need? What did Chester need?

The Scouser seemed to have his own ways of dealing with morale. And he didn't seem to think players playing hurt was a bad thing—just the opposite. So Staff Search shot up my wish list, and I also started to think more about working on myself. Unlocking another formation was extremely attractive, especially because 4-5-1 was next, was only 400 XP, and would be an ideal formation for my women's team in its current composition. I only had one striker!

And if I was being truly selfish, there was the monthly perk. After I'd told Old Nick's imp that I wouldn't be doing football anymore, but before I'd taken control of the match against Puddington, it had dropped into my inbox. It was priced, moronically, at my XP balance at the time PLUS five XP. Nick was THAT desperate to get me back to grinding.

So for 2,458 XP I could buy Fantasy February.

UNIQUE SPECIAL OFFER!

New perk available until the end of February: Fantasy February.

Cost: 2,458 XP (KERRAZZZY VALUE)

Effects: Extends the reach of the Fantasy Football perk beyond one game per season. When you buy this attractively priced perk, the Fantasy Football suite will become available for one match in every competition. Example: If you are the manager of CHESTER FOOTBALL CLUB, the Triple Captain and Bench Boost abilities can be triggered in one league match, one FA Trophy match, one FA Cup match (including qualifiers), one Cheshire Cup match, one friendly, and one match in any other competition for which the team qualifies.

Okay, so I was pretty sure Old Nick had made a mistake here, and that this perk was massively underpriced. It reconfirmed my suspicion that he really, really needed me to grind for his own benefit. Buying the original Fantasy Football perk had been one of my best-ever decisions. Because I'd been bouncing around all sorts of teams and clubs and age groups, I'd been able to use Triple Captain and Bench Boost quite frequently, to great effect. If I bought this, I'd be able to use it even more. Old Nick was lazy, but he wasn't stupid. He'd chosen wisely with this perk; I wanted it.

So grabbing it was a no-brainer, and adding 4-5-1 wouldn't take more than one evening's grinding.

I texted Spectrum and Jill.

Me: Please prepare the women to do 4-5-1 on Friday.

But what next? Morale seemed less important than it had a couple of weeks earlier. Injuries seemed less important. The Contracts perk wouldn't help me get rid of Ian Evans. Woot woot! More attributes, then? Maybe a big push to unlock the complete staff profiles.

I called Inga and asked her to get me tickets to any women's game she could find, and that I'd take tickets for any match of any kind any evening that the men's and women's first teams weren't playing. That sounds a lot more complicated than it was. Put simply, her mission was to get me into as many matches as poss.

Monday night I spent in a five-a-side joint, watching crap players while listening to podcasts I normally liked but suddenly found aggravating. Inga came through, and I found my schedule filling with a smorgasbord of matches. Tuesday was Rochdale versus Stockport County (League Two, men's). Wednesday was Burnley versus Fylde in the Women's National League Northern Premier Division (tier three). Thursday was another women's match, but it was in Cheltenham—four hours one way. I treated myself to a night in instead and powered through my coaching coursework.

Regardless, it was some good grinding, and going to higher-level matches really pushed my debt repayments along. Fylde were not impressive; it was more proof that once we got a few more good players, Chester Women would have nothing to fear.

Going to all these matches meant no evening Playdar, because I couldn't do both. Daytime Playdar mostly brought me to schools, where it was weird for me to wander in and stare at the children, while evening Playdar tended to bring me to teenagers and adults, which was more of what I wanted. I noted the schools that seemed to have good players and emailed them asking if they'd let me watch their Sports Days or let me know when they played matches against other schools or whatever. I wasn't stressed about it—I had years to find those kids.

All in all it felt right to put my needs first. Every power-up helped Chester as much as it helped me. I wouldn't think twice about putting my oxygen mask on first. Because I'm not a fucking moron.

Saturday. Chester versus Bradford, minute 55.

"So you've been studying a new formation," said Emma, after I'd explained this thought process to her. "Studying the competition. And you're working hard on your coaching badges. That's all great. Sharpening the axe, but taking days off, too. It seems perfect. What are you worried about?" She waved at the pitch. "Am I crazy or are we getting a bit overrun here?"

"You're not crazy," I said. Since halftime, Bradford had been on top. "They switched to three-five-two, mostly matching us, but they've dropped one of their CMs to be a DM. Raffi's a bit lost now. It's a bit too busy for him in there. They've got a grip of the centre and our wide players aren't really good enough to hurt them. Like, if we had Aff, I don't think they'd have made that switch. He'd have all that space to attack. But D-Day's nowhere near Aff's level."

"What would you do if you were in charge?"

"Bradford aren't very threatening. I'd push Carl from centre back to DM. See how that went."

"Two-six-two?"

"Basically, yeah. It's not as wild as it sounds. Next I'll be studying four-two-four." The curse's demented pricing model had doubled the cost of the next formation. 4-2-4 would cost 800 XP. "The problem with formations and tactics is that you need players to make them work. I can say four-two-four would work today, but if you don't have two fast wingers, it's empty words." I paused and had a think. "Next season we could do Pascal and me as the wingers. That'd be the fastest attack in the division."

"You're talking about four-two-four a lot. I thought this was the week of four-five-one."

"Yeah, it's not my favourite."

"Tell me about last night."

Friday, 6 p.m. Elton Joans versus Chester Women.

Friday's friendly was away to the Elton Joans in the small town of Elton. I worried Ruth would have upgraded the cheap minivans I'd hired to some kind of super premium battle bus, eating even further into the budget she'd given me, but that proved unfounded. The players were nervous after their big defeat the week before, but excited to try what they'd learned during the week. The banter was a lot different than on a men's bus. There was a lot more singing Beyoncé songs, for a start.

We arrived and Jill and Spectrum took over, giving me the chance to frolic around. I smacked a few free kicks into one net, just to blow off steam, and found the referee and linesmen had come to watch.

"I'd hate to be on the wrong end of *that*," said the ref. She reminded me of the one we'd had in the Beth Head matches—short, young, knew the game, wouldn't take any shit.

"Oh, I don't hit it that hard when there's a goalie," I said. "It wouldn't be fair."

The ref didn't know how to respond until she realised her linos were sniggering. "Right. You're Max Best. I saw that video you made. Loved it."

"Great! My IT guy said barely anyone watched it after the first few days."

"It's going around."

"Top. Listen, we've got a deaf player."

She briefly looked horrified, but not for the reason I initially feared. "I'm not going to carry a flag if that's what you're asking. This match uses IFAB rules." She meant this wasn't disability football.

"I know. I'm just letting you know she can't hear the whistle and if you tell her off, she won't know what you said until we explain it to her at halftime. She's good as gold, though. Won't give you any trouble."

"She'd better not. I'm behind on my yellow card quota."

Now it was my turn to not realise someone was joking. It clicked eventually. I smiled at the ref and gave her a friendly finger wag. You got me!

When the Elton Joans started warming up, I relaxed even further. They were going to play 4-4-2, and their average CA was 5. Ours had climbed to 3.5. It seemed we'd add a point per player per week for a while. We still didn't have a left back, so that was one major flaw. Overall, though, I thought it'd be a close match and that Dani and Pippa would create lots of chances for Bea Pea.

Spectrum came up to me. "Max, can I have a quick word?"

"Yeah, one sec. I just saw Tyson and his dad. Let's talk to them first." Spectrum followed me over to the side of the pitch. "Guys! You're our first away fans."

"Suppose we are!" said Bulldog. He was in a good mood.

I looked at Tyson. "Just saying, I appreciate the support and everything, but you don't have to do extra. You're in. Proper in."

"We want to come," said Tyson. "Well, I do, anyway. You're starting a whole new team. We get to see what you do. How it changes from week to week. That's really interesting."

I stuck my bottom lip out. "Yeah, okay. It's going to be slow going, though. Small steps. Incremental progress."

Tyson's face said: *Duh, that's what I like.* "But Dani will get better faster than the others, right? That's what you think, isn't it?"

I rubbed my chin. "Great question. I did, but now I'm not so sure. I'd say she's improving at the same rate as the others, but where they stop, she'll keep going."

"I think she doesn't really believe in herself."

"Yeah, well," I said. "The ball doesn't know that. How are you doing in the sixteens?"

"It's hard. They're all bigger and faster than me."

"Right. Which is the point. But every day you get a bit bigger and a bit faster, but they don't get any less shit."

"Max!" said Spectrum. He pointed at Tyson. "Don't repeat that."

"Okay," said Tyson, with a laugh.

"Obviously I misspoke," I said. "I meant to say that Tyson will soon be pissing all over them from a great height. Better?"

"Not really," said Spectrum, and he pulled me away. Assertive! As we crossed the pitch again, he sighed. "This is a bad time, I know, but I need to get this out. I would like to stay at the club."

I nodded. Jackie's return had fixed a lot of problems. "I'd want to work under a coach like him, too."

"It's not Jackie," said Spectrum. "Of course he's amazing and I'll learn a lot. No, it was Das Tournament, and especially Beth's article."

"Ah. You want to be the Sorcerer's Apprentice."

He laughed. "No, Max. It's more . . . The things you do *actually* make sense. To you, anyway. And to Beth. I guess she knows you quite well. So I stopped thinking 'What's he up to?' you know, negative, and now it's more like 'What's he up to!?'" He said that last phrase in a cheeky, playful way. "I've still got doubts. But I don't doubt you're trying to do something good for the club and the community. So I want to be part of it. If you'll have me."

I stopped about fifteen yards from the edge of the pitch. "Yeah, let's finish the season." I looked at the guy. He hadn't dealt with the Tyson situation well, but he had showed signs of getting a bit tougher. I wanted to tell him he needed to keep improving without being a dick about it. "Everyone who wants to stay here needs to step up. The players, me, you. I'll try to be better at explaining my long-term plans and how you fit into them. And you can improve in the areas where you're only scoring six out of ten."

I think we both thought my framing was pretty lame, but he appreciated that I'd made an effort. "You're going to tell me what those are, right?"

"I think the scam is that I get you to say it first."

Saturday. Chester versus Bradford, minute 65.

"That's good, isn't it?" said Emma. "I know you complain about him, but you like him. I can tell."

"Yeah, he's great. He just really wants to be a football insider. You know, be one of the blokes. Did you know *bloke* is a bad word?"

"Bloke? Yeah. It's as bad as *lad,* but better than *bro.*"

"Wow. I'm trying to get rid of blokes, and Spectrum is bloke-curious."

"Go bloke, go broke."

"Jackie does that blokey banter stuff, always has a one-word response to everything ready to fire. But he's got emotional intelligence and makes people feel included. I can't believe Spectrum would want to be like Vimsy or Sam Topps instead of him. It's probably going to work out fine. Ah, this is not good." Bradford had slowly pushed the match up the pitch, and the game was now being played almost exclusively in Chester's half. The dugouts looked transparent, but somehow weren't. I couldn't see Jackie, except for the top of his head sometimes. Gerald May, our overpaid centre back, got the ball and kicked it miles down the pitch. Bradford worked it forward again, and the pressure was back. Booting it away with half an hour left to go? Mate. "How have we got a possession-based system and no possession?"

"What about the actual match, though?" said Emma. "I still don't know if you won or lost."

Friday. Elton Joans, first half,

We lined up in our shiny new 4-5-1 formation. I put Dani in the middle so she'd get on the ball more, but I had the option of moving her back to the right mid slot, with Pippa next to her in either scenario.

It's a decent formation, 4-5-1, if a little dour. You have the flat back four, which almost all players are familiar with, plus five across midfield. That gives the defence lots of cover, and there's always someone to pass to. You can get high possession stats and stop your opponent from creating too many chances.

The downside is the lone striker. She has to do a *lot* of work. A lot of running into the channels—the sides of the pitch. A lot of hold up play, which means getting to a forward pass and bullying the defenders long enough for midfielders to get forward and support her. You need to be strong, you need stamina, and you need to be unbothered by the fact that you're not going to score many goals.

You're probably thinking, *Ah! Max Best is a genius. He knew that Bea Pea was perfect for such a role.*

Nope! She was more the Ziggy type, a dynamic, never-give-up fox-in-the-box. Just as delighted by scoring from a scuffed tap-in than from a thirty-yard screamer. I knew she'd be frustrated in the role but that she'd do her best. I tasked Jill with giving her pep talks through the match. Keep her spirits up.

I declined to use Bench Boost or Triple Captain because even with the upgraded Fantasy Football perk, it would only work in one friendly, and all the matches on the horizon were friendlies.

The first ten minutes were pretty sedate. We were far superior in terms of technique and passing, and we let the ball do our running. Elton chased and pressed. I was sure they'd tire towards the end, but their manager saw it wasn't working and put a stop to it. No late-match advantage in fitness, then. We had a fairly cagey first half. I used Free Hit on a corner, but it didn't lead to a shot. We didn't have a lot of players with good heading.

"I'd like a bit more threat from dead balls," I said.

"I'd like my husband to leave the bathroom window open," said Jill.

"You love a technical midfielder, Max," said Spectrum. "You go all googly-eyed when you see a tiny playmaker with a low centre of gravity."

"I do not."

"You do. You're like Arsene Wenger. Remember that kid from Notts?"

I broke into a huge grin. "Oh! That guy. He was like a tiny baby Tielemans."

"See? Maybe you could try looking at some other types of players. Just saying."

"I look at the cavemen. I do. The problem with cavemen, mate, is that they live in caves."

The ref blew for halftime. Dani kept running around for a few more seconds before spotting that the others were walking away.

"Someone could use that against her," I said.

"What?"

"Did you ever see that old clip where a player was through on goal and the Man United goalie didn't try to save it? He just pointed to the linesman, hoping the guy would go "Duh, I'm offside? Okay." But the player didn't buy it, and he scored. Defenders could stop defending and start walking away, trying to trick Dani into stopping, too."

Spectrum laughed. "Only you'd come up with that, Max."

"We'll make sure she keeps playing," said Jill. "She only stops when she sees Bea Pea stop."

"Top," I said, and went to give my halftime speech.

Saturday. Chester versus Bradford, minute 70.

"I think I spaced out when you were talking about old clips," said Emma. "That was nil–nil at halftime?"

"Yeah."

"I don't get it. Why's it so easy when you've got the under-fourteens and so hard with the women?"

I smiled. "It's not *easy* with the boys. But that team has decisive players. The centre backs win headers. Future is a passing machine. Seven can dribble and makes great decisions. Tyson's got the X-factor, Benny has great movement. So far, the women's team are just learning the basics. There's no one who's, like, really tall, or super fast, or who locks down one part of the pitch. Do you know what I mean? You need players to sort of dominate their area so you can plan around that."

"Oh." Emma wasn't impressed.

"It's coming. Dani will be that player. Then she'll start getting double-marked and that'll make it easier for the others. Right? But for now, it's a bit of a slog."

"That's why you're doubting yourself? Because you can't do tactical masterpieces."

"Maybe."

Friday. Elton Joans, second half.

At halftime, I switched to 4-4-2 and put on a CA 1 rando as a second striker. It worked—we scored, then I urged the women to keep attacking. We scored another. Nice, easy 2–0 win on the horizon! The match ratings were hugely in our favour. Pippa was on 7, as was Bea Pea. Dani was on 6, but flitting with a 5. It wasn't quite working for her, but she showed nice flashes of skill.

Things started to go wrong when Elton got a lucky break that led to a shot that our goalie dived towards. The ball deflected off a defender and span to the unprotected side of the goal. Two–one!

But it wasn't an issue. We were still playing much better, and the match ratings barely changed. Then Dani combined with Pippa and was in a lot of space on the right. She squared to Bea Pea, who played a nice return pass into Dani's path. She was through against the keeper! Dani shifted onto her left foot and curled it into the corner. Really, really, nice finish. Dani turned to celebrate and found no one near her.

The ref had blown for offside, so the goalie's attempt to save had been half-hearted and the defenders had given up. Bea Pea gave Dani a big clap—great job! But the ref was moving towards Dani, hand reaching to her pocket. She was going to give a yellow card for kicking the ball away after the whistle had gone! I went mental, and scampered down the touchline.

"No! No! What the fuck?"

The ref heard and looked at me. She glanced at Dani, moved her hand away from her pocket, and simply showed Dani her whistle. Dani looked to her left and saw the lineswoman's flag was up. She realised the ref had been about to book her for something she couldn't help.

I calmed *some* of the way back down, gave the ref a stern nod, and walked back to my spot.

Dani was shot, though. The incident had unnerved her. Her match rating started to plummet. I called her over and showed her what I'd typed on my phone.

Me: I'll sub you off now. Thumbs down if you really, really want to stay on the pitch.

Not even a thumb. She walked off the pitch and threw herself to the ground among our gear, pulling her coat over her head. I made the sub. Tyson ran around to talk to her, to gee her up. His dad didn't know whether to stick to his spot or come round, too. I waved him over and talked him through the disastrous end to the game.

The unlucky goal and the weirdness with Dani affected the team in a truly astonishing way. Their heads went. Elton scored another. I demanded we attack. Did my chant and everything, but I couldn't get through to them. I switched back to 4-5-1, just to check they were still obeying me. They were. They just couldn't get a grip.

We lost 3–2, and I couldn't really understand why.

Saturday. Chester versus Bradford, minute 75.

Emma had gone from mild interest to barely contained fury as I described the incident.

"But you told the ref she was deaf! What's she supposed to do?"

"I know. Nothing actually happened, but it was a close call. Next time I'll point to Dani or give them a picture or something so that there's absolutely zero possible risk of this happening again."

"Can I sue the ref if she books Dani?"

"No."

"Can I write a strongly worded letter?"

"As long as you never send it, yeah."

"Max, it pisses me off. I'm livid."

"I know. I went a bit apeshit myself. When I was complaining to Jill on the way home, she whispered that maybe it had turned out well. Like, she thought I was maybe a bit overly distant—she said mathematical—on the touchline, and sometimes players like to know that their manager really, really cares."

"Huh. I can see that. I think."

"We just weren't there in the last ten minutes, though. That hasn't happened to me before. I've always been able to sort of communicate with my team. It's almost like telepathy," I said, carefully. "I get emotional, I get determined, and so do they. We can summon up some energy to put into our legs."

"You've been overworking recently. You can't have much in the tank."

"That's not it. I was up for it. I was, like, crackling with energy and all that. It just wasn't getting to the players."

"What do you do about it?"

"No clue. Maybe it's just one of those things."

"Max," said Emma, turning to get a proper look at me. "I sort of think . . . Okay, if you ask me, you've had a good week. Not outstanding, maybe a bit weird. But things always seem a bit worse if there's a bad ending. Like that meal we had in Darlo. Great soup, great main, crap dessert. But overall, it was a good meal, right?"

"But that's just it. This morning was totally awesome."

"This morning? What did you do this morning?"

Saturday, 10 a.m.

The stars were finally aligned for our goalkeepers to join me at the local goalkeeping school, something we'd been trying to arrange since my first training session with them.

The JM Academy, motto All You Need Is Glove, was run by a former pro called Jay-Mo. He welcomed us with great enthusiasm but then got back to work. We pottered around while two different age groups got on with drills, supervised by Jay-Mo and an older keeper who was helping out in return for some private lessons.

Handling, positioning, and fitness were being improved on one side of the hall. On the other, working with the ball at your feet, drop kicks, and agility.

Angles, Ben, and Robbo were fascinated and extremely enthusiastic. They all agreed it was much better than anything they'd experienced when they were young. The arrival of the three pro goalies from the local club was a big deal; lots of selfies were taken. I was the fourth most requested selfie, a fact that I barely noticed.

While there, I triggered Playdar, which was a neat trick because it showed me most of the player profiles in the area as well as telling me which kid had the highest PA.

I tried to keep the glee off my face as I went on a goalkeeper signing spree. The most talented was nine years old, an agile little dude with PA 130. I nicknamed him Tadpole. There was an eleven-year-old with PA 61 who already had a nickname: Big Sam.

Then there was a good goalie for the women's team with PA 72. Amazing! The only problem was she was eleven. Another long-term project.

Finally, the most unexpected thing of all, a left back. I'd found so few left backs, and no wonder. They were in goalkeeping classes. Lucas was fifteen and had PA 62. I only needed to persuade him to play outfield . . .

Saturday. Chester versus Bradford, minute 80.

"Wait wait wait," said Emma, using both hands to keep her brain from exploding. "Let me see. You've seen that all your players are getting proper training and are improving. You've worked on your coaching badges. You've had your second game with the women's team and you were unlucky to lose. Some rugby blokes said you were good at rugging. And you found a bunch of players so talented you can't stop *beaming* when you talk about them." She paused, allowing a cute little frown to scrunch up her features. "What's the problem?"

"I don't know," I said. "Time. Not enough time. But so much time! But it's something else. Something . . . Or, it's sort of . . ." My voice trailed away.

Emma saw why—Bradford's constant pressure resulted in an overload on the left. A fast guy with a big fluffy afro got to the byline, pulled the ball back, and a striker had a tap-in. Two–one Bradford.

We sat in silence for the next five minutes. Bradford were happy to sit back now, but Jackie didn't do anything. Finally, he subbed Raffi off and put Magnus on as the left back in a 4-4-2. "Yes!" I said, punching the air.

The momentum gradually swung our way, but just as we were piling on the pressure, the ref blew his whistle. Game over.

The home fans went nuts. They were only one point behind us now. I didn't have the Live Tables or Live Scores perks, but we were unlikely to have actually slipped into the relegation zone. We'd be there, out of danger by the skin of our teeth.

Jackie led the team over to the extremely noisy away fans, acknowledging their superb support. They got a generous round of applause. No one could doubt they'd put a shift in.

I watched for a while, my mind churning. The tactics, the players, the substitutions. What could have been done better? What could have been done sooner?

"Max," said Emma. She took my hand. I looked at her and some of the mental turmoil subsided. "You've got to let it go. That's not your fight. Leave it to Jackie. You had a good week. Have more weeks like this one."

I smiled. I'd planned to go to London to watch Crystal Palace Women, but six days of football was enough for one week. "This one's not over. It could end on a high."

"Oh, could it?" she said, with a very provocative smile. "Why don't you check if the alpaca farm is still open?"

"It's not."

"So what do you think? Quiet night in?"

I looked around the ground. Two hundred away fans. Eleven play-ers, five subs, one manager. Jackie had fought for me. I had to fight for him—by staying out of his way. "Quiet night in. Yeah. Or . . . I just got a big burst of energy. How about we go clubbing?"

"You hate clubbing."

"I like you."

Emma bit her bottom lip. "Let's go home and check out your bruises (and we'll see if there's time for anything else)."

5

MENTALITY

Date: Monday, February 27, 2023
Purpose of Form: UEFA C Licence Session Report
Candidate Name: Max Best
Coach Developer: Michelle Lomas
Participants: Darlington FC Under-Twelves

Session Goals

Create and exploit overloads in and around the penalty box.

Session Plan

Max has prepared a highly detailed lesson plan entitled "The Art of Slapping," which includes contingencies for having too many and too few participants. The session begins with Max handing out colourful tactical maps to every player. Max then demonstrates each skill, sequentially, inviting one participant to replace him until all positions are filled with participants. There is no mention of goals. Max talks in terms of "slaps" and "attempted slaps," meaning successful or unsuccessful forward passes and penalty box entries.

In the base model, four players attack versus four defenders and a goalkeeper. Teams switch from attack to defence with every successful or unsuccessful slap. Individual participants rotate roles with every attack. Goalkeepers act as servers. Participants are required to enter the penalty box through the sides, not the front. The attacking team manoeuvres until they have a two-on-one advantage on one flank, then attempt to create a goalscoring opportunity for teammates who arrive in the six-yard box late.

Communication

Max remains positive throughout, with one exception (described later), communicating clearly and dishing out praise where he feels it's warranted. He ensures the participants stay on task by asking them pertinent questions, such as "Did that slap?" and "Defenders, do you feel slapped?"

Participant Engagement

Through the roof. Max allows the boys time to master the drill before he begins demanding more of them. The specificity of what he asks for is exemplary; it's all based on their personal strengths and weaknesses. He seems to have been coaching the group for years. Note: This was only their second session together.

Positives

Max rides waves of motivation incredibly well. During these "up" periods, his sessions are as focused and serious as any I've ever seen. Max is very comfortable letting energy fade and drift, and he has a unique gift for distraction and outright silliness that serves as a natural break. During one lull, Max gathers the participants around him and begins threatening to sack them. "You call yourselves footballers? You've got one week—just one week to regain your jobs." The group eventually realises Max is performing a monologue from a movie, though I couldn't find a movie where a character orders people to "always be slapping."

With the participants newly relaxed and energised, the drill recommences with one participant showing off. "Oh, wonderful," says Max, as he pushes the participant away and takes his spot. "But have you ever thought about doing this?" Max stands touch-tight to a defender, demands the ball, flicks it up, and somehow contorts himself so that he's facing the defender but with the ball trapped behind him, in the crook of his knee. "Where's the ball, mate?" demands Max. "Where's the ball?" He hops towards the goal. A defender tries to kick the ball loose. "Ow, you dick. My wife will sue you. She's a judge. Oi! Stop that." He laughs and continues hopping towards the goal. More defenders arrive and try to wrestle Max to a halt. One punches the ball out of its slot and Max runs around trying to regain it. The participants form an impromptu rondo that succeeds in keeping the ball away from him. He blows his whistle and awards "five slaps to Slytherin."

When the giddiness subsides, Max turns to the showboater and says, "That's what you look like." The participant acknowledges the criticism. But Max understands the impulse behind the original showboating. "If you want to get a professional contract with my team, take your training seriously. If you want to play in the same team as me, make this pass ten times out of ten and that cross nine times out of ten. Yeah? But if you *really* want to impress me, play your passes to the receiver's strongest foot. Do you even know which that is? Because I do." Max walks around pointing at every participant. "Left, right, right, right, both, right." The showboater is suitably impressed. The drills reach a new level of intensity.

Areas for Improvement

(1) Participants were initially confused about what constituted a slap. When I suggested this to Max, he said, "Yeah, *duh*. They have to work it out, otherwise it's your bog-standard final third entry routine, innit? Come off." I'm not sure I agree, but there was certainly some enthusiastic discussion about which moves counted as slap-worthy. Max listened to all participants and explained why he agreed and if he disagreed, what modifications would make a certain sequence a slap. The participants followed his reasoning with much more ease than I did.

(2) Max does not ask the participants for feedback, as per best practice. When questioned, he says, "Yeah no point that was fucking mint they loved it the little shits."

(3) This is the seventh session in a row where I have observed Max leading only attacking drills. I reminded him that we expect to see some defensive drills also, and he replied, "Nah dog that's not for me dog anyways my DoF says I should stick to teaching kids how to slap." Note: Max is the DoF at his club.

Final Comments

The session meets the competency required at C Licence level. The session demonstrates a high level of technical expertise, reinforced by Max's answers to my questions at the end and the way he gave tips on how I could analyse his sessions better—where to stand, how to know which sides the attacks would develop based on the participant's social hierarchies, and so on. Feedback I sourced from the participants was universally positive.

From the Chester Standard, *Tuesday, February 28*

SEALS BATTLE TO BRAVE POINT AGAINST IN-FORM TIGERS

A dominant opening presaged a nightmare second half for Jackie Reaper's Chester, as they survived wave after wave of Gloucester attacks to bank a valuable point. The first half saw Chester play some gorgeous football, and they deservedly took the lead through a thumping Sam Topps header. However, they couldn't find a way to double their advantage while in the ascendency, and Gloucester's halftime tactical tweaks turned the match on its head. Reaper's substitutions failed to stem the tide, and in some views, invited even more pressure.

The main bright spot for Chester was the return to first-team action of Trick Williams, finally recovered from a troublesome muscular injury. "It's very welcome news," said Reaper. "He brings balance to the defence and allows us to switch formations. Second half wasn't good today, but a point is a point is a point. I hear Bradford lost, so it's really a good night for us."

	TEAM	P	GD	PTS
19	Blyth Spartans	34	-29	39
20	Chester	35	-11	37
21	Bradford	33	-22	35
22	Leamington	33	-15	34
23	Kettering	35	-27	30
24	AFC Telford	35	-38	22

Wednesday, March 1.

When I woke up, I had cursemail. The monthly status update.

Your reputation in England: Unknown

Your world reputation: Unknown

Bit annoying. I *was* known as a player, albeit in a low division. And I was a director of football! I was also the manager of Chester Women, and I didn't appear on the ever-growing list of women's football managers. Like certain media personalities, the curse was struggling with the very concept of women.

I suspected that my version of *Champion Manager* didn't have any women's football, and the curse was slowly bringing itself up to date. It had chosen to have two lists of manager reputations: one for men, one for women. The England Women manager, Sarina Wiegman, topped the second list, of course, but she also appeared in the first even though she'd never managed a men's team. My guess was that her achievements were so huge even a gammon would give her a chance as manager of a men's team.

I also got a special director of football message.

The board are generally satisfied with your performance but are worried about the club's precarious financial position.

I couldn't fix the last part without a time machine, so I ignored it. "Generally satisfied" felt very 3 out of 5. Bit annoying. I texted Emma.

Me: How would you rate my performance as your boyfriend? Generally satisfied / very satisfied / extremely satisfied.

She replied with a bicep emoji. What?

Despite the curse winding me up, I felt great. My big talk with Emma about my inchoate, uncongealed feelings had done wonders for me. I had a long-term plan and very few short-term responsibilities. So it didn't exactly matter what I did or the order in which I did things. As long as I was progressing, I was allowed to feel good about myself.

XP balance: 1,242

Debt repaid: 1,009/3,000

I was torn about what to do on Wednesday evening. Spectrum asked me to let him know if I was going to watch any of the boys' training sessions, which was an unusual request from him. Jill did something weirdly similar for the women's team. All quite curious. I wanted to know what they were up to, but Burnley were playing Fleetwood in the FA Cup, and if I could convince Jackie to come, he'd see the future of football. And I'd pile on enough XP to buy Attributes 4, which I'd got my heart set on. It had been far too long since I'd unlocked any cells, and without being able to see a player's full profile, I was flying through clouds. And I only needed another 325 XP! (I'd decided I'd save my coupon codes for perks that cost at least 4,000 XP, unless there was an emergency.)

In the end, though, despite the prospect of a power-up, I decided to put my staff first.

I started at the under-sixteens. They'd gone from having so little talent that Kian was instantly their best player, to having four guys in the PA 30 range, plus Vivek (PA 66), Tyson (PA 58), and Lucas Friend, the left back I'd found at the goalkeeper school. He was PA 62.

Not going to win any tournaments any time soon, but they'd come a long way in a fairly short time. The session wasn't very intense, and when I mentioned it to Spectrum he grinned and said, "They're saving their legs." He was up to something and I liked it.

Then came a meeting Spectrum had set up after I confirmed I was going. While the players went through their end-of-session cooldown, a good-looking older guy arrived. Last time I'd seen him he'd been wearing a puffy jacket with a fake fur hood that made his hair pop. Now he was in a well-cut suit.

It was Sullivan's dad. I'd released his son from the under-fourteens because he had the skills but not the mentality. He was too cautious and wouldn't make forward passes. He was too cautious because his dad screamed at him every time he made a mistake, but even when I banned the dad from going to matches, we couldn't change Sullivan's style.

Now the dad was asking for a second chance for the kid, just like Tyson had got. But the situations were different. First, Tyson had the potential to become a pro footballer and Sullivan didn't. Second, I saw evidence that I could help with Tyson's problem—his teamwork attribute turned green when we hammered him about it. But I couldn't see an attribute that explained why Sullivan wanted high pass completion stats more than anything else in the world. So it was a pointless endeavour.

I told the dad that his son wasn't going to get another chance. The conversation started out civil, but the dad quickly became angry. He said a lot of things that a healthy member of society would regret. He pointed out, correctly, that his son was more talented than most of the players in the youth system, that Tyson only got a second chance because his dad was a sponsor (you can decide if you think that's fair), and that I was a damned fool and he'd tell everyone about this travesty.

He vowed to get rid of me. I think his exact words were, "You won't make it to the end of the season."

I stayed really calm throughout—I know. I was surprised, too—because in the end it's a dad who wants good things for his kid. I didn't mind letting him vent.

When he finally fucked off, I turned to Spectrum. "Thanks, mate."

He cringed. "I didn't think it'd be like that. I'm really sorry."

"It's fine. That guy is a mess. Holy shit."

"Yeah. Poor Sully. That wasn't why we wanted you to come today, though."

Exciting! But I wondered if I should let the Sullivan kid back in, after all. Try our best to fix his issue, heal one of his wounds. I shook my head. I couldn't run the club like a charity, and I already asked way too much of the coaches. "Who's hardest to coach? Dani or Vivek?"

Spectrum adjusted his glasses. "I don't think like that."

"Come on. I'm just interested. I know I give you weird things to do."

"Er . . . Dani makes me realise how much I rely on talking. I've started using the whiteboard a lot more. Laminated handouts that explain the drills. It's not just Dani who uses them—a lot of the players like to see the pictures. So that's good. But the first time we do something, it's quite slow. Which, again, sometimes is good. Vivek hasn't played much football and sometimes there's big gaps in his knowledge. You can't make assumptions with him. We realised the other day he'd never taken a throw-in in his life. And he's very passive on corners. We're trying to make him realise it's *his* job to head the ball! You have to be patient with him. So the question is, do I find it easier to communicate nonverbally, or to be patient?" He laughed. "I think I'm six out of ten on both."

"If it was easy, some other club would have found them." I went internal for a second, thinking about all these young people and how exciting it was to watch their CAs turn green. "Dani needs to realise she's a sword and Vivek needs to realise he's a shield. They've got enough natural talent I'm not worried about the rest. You're doing great. I'm happy. I'd promise to stop bringing you randos with unique challenges, but, you know. I'm *gonna*."

Spectrum grinned and went off to start the next session.

The under-eighteens was a talent desert, then one thimbleful of water (a guy with a PA of 22), then two lush green oases in Pascal and

Youngster. The stars were in a CA race. When I met Pascal in January, his CA was four points behind James's. Now, thanks to his full-time contract, he was only one behind. James was on 26, Pascal on 25. Being named on the bench for the first team had been a big deal for both, and even James's infrequent training with the first team had done a lot to arrest a slight stagnation in his CA. The rest of the under-eighteens simply weren't good enough to challenge him. Frustrating, but that's what years of neglecting a youth system will do. Ian Evans had quit at just the right time to make sure the club's young talents could keep developing.

I hung around for a bit and joined in a couple of drills. As I was leaving, James invited me to church, and Pascal said he had updated his personal scouting report if I wanted to read it. I said I only had time to do one of the two things and they should discuss which. Then I fled.

Across the King George complex, the women had started to arrive. I saw Dani and did the latest sign I'd learned: *Wassup?* I had a quick chat with Pippa—she was feeling low because it was all much harder than she had imagined. I assured her she was doing great and I had absolutely no doubts about her.

Then I went to see what Jill wanted. She was with a younger, taller version of herself. By younger, I'd guess . . . forty? The daughter maybe?

"Hi, Max. This is Lucy. She was a young player coming into the Chester team when I was near the end of my playing days."

"Ah, another former legend," I said, shaking her hand. "Awesome." I noticed that Lucy was dressed in a very sporty way. "Do you still play?"

"That's the point," said Jill. "Lucy was our left back. And she scored from headers." She left the thought hanging. I was supposed to say something.

"Right," I said, bursting with wisdom.

"I've brought her to fill in this evening," said Jill.

"What?"

"Oh, I mean, if I've overstepped, I'm sorry. Oh, no."

I put my hand up. "Let's all stay frosty. I'm not mad. Not even a sub-atomic amount. Mostly because I have no idea what you're talking about."

"Didn't Spectrum tell you?" Her eyes flicked to a point behind me.

I turned and saw the under-sixteens marching towards us. "Oh! A mini match, is it?" I got excited. That's why they were saving their energy. "Ooh, this is going to be chaos. I love it. Wait!" I said, suddenly bouncing. "It's Tyson versus Dani!"

"Er . . . stay frosty, Max," said Jill. "It's mostly going to be positional work. Everything slowed down."

"*He*," I said bombastically, "was the son of a no-good lowlife who founded an empire. *She* was the daughter of a couple of fucking *weirdos*. Brought together by fate and football, destiny has pitted them against one another. This isn't Old Trafford. *This* is the Amphitheatre of Screams."

"I'd watch that movie," admitted Lucy.

"Are you saying you don't want us to do shape work?" said Jill.

"No, do it," I said, a bit whingey. "There'll be a bit of a match at the end, though, right? Right?"

"Yes, Max," said Jill.

I had to suffer while Jill and Spectrum did a walking-pace "match," which stopped every three seconds so they could point things out to the players. Youngster and Pascal came to join me, so it was much less boring. Pascal asked why I looked frustrated.

"This is good and important, but I want to do the fun bits. Do you know what I mean?" Both kids gave me blank looks. They were the type who enjoyed the defensive parts of the game as much as the attacking ones. Both loved hard work and had a very high boredom threshold. "One good thing is both sides are getting something out of this. I heard that Conte does this with the Spurs first team and a load of under-eighteens. You'd think the young players would be in heaven, training with Harry Kane and all the stars, but they're really just mannequins. It sounds horrible. Like this we can work on two teams at once."

"Jackie told me I'll be on the bench again this weekend," said James.

"That's away at Hereford, is it?" I said.

He looked surprised that I wasn't sure. "Yes. Aren't you going?"

"Ah," I said, complaining. "I have to go to a course day to get my UEFA C licence. I'm doing one on Saturday and one on Sunday. I need to do six days. I missed two at the start that I caught up on, did the next two, and these are the last ones."

"How do you enjoy the course?" said Pascal.

"It's fine. It's not for us, if you know what I mean. It's for civilians. It's like this drill—for Vivek, it's amazing, because he's inexperienced and in his position, mistakes are punished. Every time you do this drill with him, he's going to get more confident. But I'd hate it, and I'd hate being the coach. These course days are like being back in school. Teacher gives you a task and you talk about it with your table and then you get feedback. Except in my case, at the end of the day, the teachers hand me their CV when they think no one's looking."

Pascal looked worried. "Are you being given favourable treatment because of your position?"

"Not really. If I was, they wouldn't schedule the course days on Saturdays when we've got a big game. And I'm pretty open about what I know and what I don't. There are times when I'm the expert in the room, and times when I know as little as the rest of the students. I'm only doing it to get the paper so I can become a proper manager. I don't think I'm a good coach. I'm certainly not a natural. There's one thing I'm quite good at, I think, and it's mentality. Especially with the young players. When I tell them what I want and what I don't want, they listen. I imagine a future where I take four sessions a year with each age group, to really drill into them the kind of football I want them to play, and the kinds of players I want them to become. Day to day training? I don't think it's for me."

"I hope you are there to see my debut," said James. "You made all this happen."

"Listen," I said, putting my hand on his shoulder. "If you make your debut and I'm not there to see it, don't worry. There's just one thing you need to remember. The absolute, most vital, most important thing is . . ." I pretended to get distracted by one of the players being out of position.

"Is what?" said James.

"Huh? What are you talking about? Ah, finally. We're going to get some action!" The coaches had decided they'd done enough shape work, and it was time for a match. I tried to make Spectrum push Tyson to left back so he'd have to defend against Dani, but Spectrum refused. I turned to Pascal. "What's the point running a football club if you can't have some fun? Jesus."

"Mr. Best," said James. "What's the important thing?"

I was going to leave him hanging, because that seemed pretty funny. But I decided to give him a boost. "First thing is, when you step up a level it's a shock. These guys seem so big and fast and they're all trying to murder you. But at some point you'll win a tackle or make an interception and you'll realise, *I got this.*"

"I understand."

"And if I'm not there to see it, that's God's plan. Isn't it? Because he knows if I hear your name being announced to the whole stadium, and I see you there on the touchline ready to go on the pitch, with your big, goofy smile . . . I'll actually pop."

"Pop?"

"I'll burst. With pride."

He looked away, trying to keep his face neutral. He mostly succeeded. Pascal gave him a pat on the back.

The match was strangely well-balanced. The boys were faster and stronger, but the women were a better team and had higher technique on average. They trusted themselves to pass through the boys, to keep the ball moving, to wait for opportunities. But then came a mistake and the ball was fed through to Tyson, who lashed it into the top of the net. Tyson had the killer instinct all right. The thought occurred to me that I might not want his teamwork to go much higher.

A mistake being punished was what had caused the women's heads to go down in recent matches. This time, though, they kept playing. Pass pass pass. They struggled to get the ball forward, but they kept trying. During a break, I crossed the pitch to where Jill was running the women.

"Jill, this is top. They've stepped up a level. Why do you think that is?"

"Have they? It looks the same to me."

"No, the mentality. They're sturdier. Calmer. It's more professional."

She scratched her cheek. "I mean, the only difference is Lucy. She's experienced. Maybe she's a good influence."

Influence! It all clicked into place. I had three good players—Dani, Pippa, and Bea Pea—plus a bunch of okay ones who would do a job. But I didn't have any leaders. Pippa wasn't a natural captain type. When things had gone wrong, she'd been unable to effect change. My sideline rants did nothing; I had no conduit to the pitch. With the under-fourteens I had Captain. With the Beth Heads I had Beth.

The captain was my on-pitch avatar. Some thought nagged at me, but I couldn't bring it to the surface. If I didn't chase it, it would probably come to me.

Lucy was forty-one. She had PA 90, CA 3. At a guess, with regular training and game time, she'd get up to CA 20. Far short of the level I'd hoped us to be, but I needed her.

I demanded Jill's whistle, blew it, and went over to the left back.

"I'd like you to play for Chester."

She laughed. "I'm a bit old, Max. I'd double the average age."

I didn't laugh. "I'd like you to play for Chester. You're my starting left back. This season and probably next."

"Until you find someone better."

"Yes. But then you'll be my left-sided centre back. You'll deffo play every time we do three-five-two. You won't be short on game time."

She didn't know what to say. "I only came because Jill said you don't think women are good in the air. It pissed me off. I wanted to show you up."

"I never said that. You got scammed. Jill knew this would happen."

"But I haven't even won any headers yet!"

"If God wanted us to play football in the sky, he would have put grass up there." The joke didn't help her realise that I was serious about my offer. I stepped away and opened myself up to as many players as possible. I called out, "Match is on hold until Lucy agrees to play for Chester Women."

The nearest few women rushed over to welcome their new teammate. Tyson came over and asked for a selfie—pretended to hold a phone up while they both smiled at his palm. He ran around showing it to everyone in the area. Lucy was overwhelmed by the attention. She needed a minute. I went over to Pippa.

"Are you okay with not being captain?"

"Oh, thank God. Yes, I'm okay with it. Yes!"

"You don't get to boss the girls around, but I do need you to boss the midfield. Good?"

"Good."

I turned to Lucy. She nodded at me. Energy filled me to the point I barely felt my feet touching the grass. I grinned as I strode towards Dani. It was time for her second masterclass. I escorted her to the side of the pitch and took her place at right mid. I pointed to my eyes. *Watch.*

My direct opponent was Lucas, the left back who wanted to play in goal. "Oh, no, no, no!" he said. "This isn't fair. I didn't sign up for this."

"I have a new move," I announced. "It's called *Death by a Thousand Slaps.*" I winked at him and blew the whistle.

I showed Dani a couple of things. One, how to get a bit more space by dropping a bit deeper. If her opponent stayed with her, that only left more space to run onto. If her opponent stuck to the defensive line, Dani would have a few yards of the pitch all to herself. Two, how to combine with Bea Pea by driving forward, playing the ball square, and then having two options for the return pass.

I wanted Dani to be extremely aggressive in the moments after the last pass was played. I didn't know sign language for "please kill everyone," so I mimed swinging a sword. She looked around, uncertain, wondering if everyone else was seeing the same thing she was. *Yes!* I confirmed. Fast, decisive movements. I took a pass and cushioned it in front of me, burst forward, and smashed the ball into the net. I mimed like I was decapitating a few enemies and then I put my sword in the ground and, kneeling, prayed for their souls. Prayer complete, I picked up my imaginary weapon and handed it to Dani. She didn't want to take it, but I made her. *You are my sword*, I tried to mime.

Dani repeated the move. She took a touch, thundered through the gap between defenders, and struck the ball low and to the left. I celebrated like we'd just knocked Newcastle out of the FA Cup.

I got so sucked into these scenarios that the rest of the players faded away. The entire world was me, Dani, and Bea Pea. When I came to my senses, I worried I'd bored everyone, but it seemed the opposite was true. Everyone else was riveted, and when the mini match ended, Tyson raced to Dani and was so excited to talk to her he forgot she couldn't hear.

Jill was joking around with Lucy. I think I heard her say, "Yeah, it's always like this." Having an older head in the team was going to be huge, I could feel it. But I was missing something. That thing on the edge of my memory was still there. A penny waiting to drop.

Penny?

No, not Penny.

"Shit," I said, and scrambled for my phone. I called Joe, the club secretary.

"Max," he said, in a panic, because he knew I'd text unless it was an emergency. "What's happened? What have you done now?"

"Do you still go to Footy Addicts?"

"Yes, sometimes."

"I need Bonnie."

"Bonnie?"

"She's a centre back. She's twenty-four, quite talented. Massive leadership qualities. I need her. Can you use your contacts to try to get her?"

"Get her?" he laughed. "You want Barnesy. He was in the army. If you want to kidnap a woman . . ."

"Great," I said. "You try phoning everyone you know. Meanwhile, he can assemble his strike team. Joe, I need her. Okay? Chester needs her."

Tiny silence. "I'll see what I can do."

He hung up and I started biting my nails. Bonnie had PA 41. I'd met her the day I'd found Kian, but back then, I wanted everyone on my women's team to have PA 100. The way I was thinking now was that PA 41 with high leadership was worth PA 60. Bonnie could be a mainstay for two or three years.

On Thursday I joined a Footy Addicts lunchtime match in Darlington, and in the evening went to Middleton Rangers to grab some XP. It wasn't much, but there weren't any professional matches that I could get to.

At halftime, I used Playdar and whizzed round to a little field where I found a teeny tiny PA 56 midfielder. I got him to take me to his house, where I told his very confused mother who I was and that I wanted to organise a trial for the kid with Darlo.

"What if it doesn't work out?" she said, after loads of back and forth.

"Then you'll have to move to Chester," I replied, before racing back to my car to catch the second half.

XP balance: 1,404

Debt repaid: 1,027/3,000

Also on Thursday, I got my agent fee from Henri. He liked to pay his bills at the start of the month instead of when he got paid on the 15th. He said it was more orderly, more civilised, and if he wasn't going to show this country a better way to live, then who was?

Not for the first time, it felt strange to take money from the guy when he was letting me live in his house for free. He didn't think about it like that, though. The agent fee was payment for a professional service. The rent was an agreement between friends. He was able to separate the two concepts much better than I was.

When was my income going to increase? There was nothing on the horizon. One day in the distant future, James would move to a big club, and my cut of his wages would set me up for life. Between now and then . . . what? A boot sponsorship deal? They were normally only handed out to active players.

I fumed about Old Nick and the weak-minded simpletons at the FA for a while, but then thought of a way to pay Henri back for his generosity: by doing my job.

I emailed a few clubs in League One and League Two to see if they'd be interested in signing Henri next season. The calls started coming in almost immediately.

Chester Women versus Buckley Commoners.

We travelled to North Wales to play against a team from a former mining town called Buckley. It wasn't a glamorous destination, and even Tyson didn't come to watch. Spectrum had a day off, so it was just me and Jill. But with the addition of Lucy, we had ten players with a bit of quality—their average CA was 4.8. Then for the last slot, we had a variety of CA 1 options I could use depending on the formation we went with.

Buckley had five players with PAs ranging from 5 to 20, with CAs almost maxed out, but the other six were PA 1. Their average CA, then, was a smidge over 5. We were the underdogs again, but only slightly.

Before the match, I took Dani and our new captain, Lucy, over to the referee and explained the former couldn't hear the whistle. The ref said, "Yes, yes, fine, I hope the floodlights stay on; they're very unreliable here." She didn't exactly fill me with confidence, but what could I do? (I needn't have worried; the ref was inept but not cruel.)

Buckley were going to play 4-4-2, and I matched them.

The match kicked off. We started passing the ball around, settled into our shape nicely.

"I like the way they involve Robyn," I said. Robyn was our goalie. Only PA 14, but a fun hang. You need a couple of bubbly characters in the dressing room. The dream would be to find a high-PA goalie but to keep Robyn around.

"She's good with her feet. They trust her."

While most of the team stayed solidly in their positions, Dani experimented with hers, the way I'd showed her. She dropped a little and her opponent didn't come. Dani played a few one- and two-touch passes to keep the ball circulating. Her opponent started to creep closer, so Dani went all the way forward into an offside position. I'd explained to her that she wouldn't be called offside as long as the ball wasn't passed to her, but that her being there would mess with the other team's heads. And so it proved. Her opponent didn't know what to do and ended up bickering with the nearest centre back.

While Dani was high up the pitch, we broke through on the left-hand side. Lucy combined with Gracie and played it to Bea Pea. Now Dani was in an *onside* position, and Bea Pea's diagonal pass was perfect.

I'd tried to get Dani to be more assertive in these situations. At heart, she was still the shy girl lost in the middle of a disability football whirlwind. I needed a killer.

Bea Pea's pass is a good one.

Dani is in acres of space.

Her first touch is excellent. She looks up and hits a fierce strike towards the far post . . .

GOOOOAAAALLLL!!!!

A clinical strike!

The keeper had no chance!

That . . . that was exciting. She was merciless! Dani the Destroyer! Football management was easy. Get hot talents, train them up, profit.

I knew then that I was going right to the top of the game. Not long from now, there would be a camera following my every move. I needed to make sure my face looked managerial at all times.

I tried to be the cool, calm, and collected manager. You know, Carlo Ancelotti meeting triumph and disaster just the same. But first I did a little dance. Had a little smile. And *then* it was back to being impassive.

Pippa wins the ball in midfield. She plays it back to Lucy.

Lucy passes square to Mo.

She plays it on to Robinson.

Dani wants it short. She's screaming for the ball!

Robinson starts to play the pass but pauses. She chips it long.

The defender is in no-man's-land! Dani has the freedom of the pitch!

She races forward. The centre backs are storming towards her.

The goalkeeper comes to narrow the angle.

Dani has played it too far wide . . . hasn't she?

She lashes the ball towards the near post.

GOOOOAAAALLLL!!!!

She celebrates with Robinson—they combined so well for that goal.

I am a pebble on top of a mountain. I may stay for another million years, or I may fall. I am indifferent. I concentrate on being the best rock I can be.

Robyn takes the goal kick long.

Butler competes for the header. She can only glance it to the right.

Dani appears out of nowhere and skips past two players!

She puts her foot on the ball, then picks a pass to Bea Pea.

The return pass is crowded out, so Bea Pea turns left.

Lucy has bombed forward!

She touches the ball and shapes to cross.

The fullback throws herself into the way.

But the cross didn't come! A great feint by the Chester captain.

She pushes towards the byline and whips in a cross.

GOOOOAAAALLLL!

Bea Pea stooped to conquer!

Lucy with the assist.

I am a sunflower. I turn to the sun. I bask. I show no emotion.

My halftime speech focuses very heavily on the interconnectedness of all living things. At times I forget I'm a sunflower and lean into rock-based imagery.

My players say that the other team's number 10 is very good and ask for advice.

My advice is: bask in the sun.

My players complain that it's nighttime.

"Just keep doing what you're doing, Jesus Christ," I snap. "I'm trying to work on my persona over here. When we're on TV all the cameras are going to be pointed at me. *'Ooh, what's Max Best going to do now?'* they'll say. I want to look unbothered and calm. That's how Carlo Ancelotti keeps winning everything. Because his players think he's so calm that everything must be part of the plan. All right? Can I get back to practising? Fuck me."

Chester are still well on top in this game.

They win another corner. Gracie is in no hurry to take it.

The corner is played short. Dani whips in a first-time cross.

Lucy rises highest . . .

GOOOOAAAALLLL!!!!

The captain scores!

She'll never have an easier header.

"Four–nil, wow," said Jill. She twinkled. "And a goal from a corner. Like you wanted."

"Might be a good time to thank you," I said.

"What?"

"Lucy. The missing piece. You saw what we needed and you made it happen."

Jill shook her head. "It was luck. I thought about what you said about headers. I know Lucy's been keeping herself fit with her runs and her mountain climbing and all that adventure stuff she does. I didn't realise she'd . . . I don't know."

"Bind the team together."

"Is that what you think it is?"

"Yep."

Jill blazed with pride, just for a second. "One thing about the old days. They toughened you up. She was a weedy little thing when she first walked into our dressing room. Look at her now."

I thought about that. "How do we get, say, Dani or Bea Pea to go on that kind of journey without, you know, bullying them?"

Jill looked down. "Don't know." Her head jerked back up. "Come on, Dani!"

Lucy loses the ball.

Erin is there to cover. Great tackle!

The ball breaks to Gracie. She passes to Pippa.

Pippa sweeps the ball wide to Dani.

Dani combines with Bea Pea—the Buckley defence must be sick of seeing that!

Bea Pea's return pass runs wide.

Dani shoots . . .

But it's a tame effort.

The commentary said it blandly, but I saw and experienced it on a visceral level. A full-body, guttural *nuuugggghhh* that was *not* managerial.

Dani had let the ball run a few more yards to improve the angle of her shot. But then she'd taken her foot off the throttle and, basically, tapped the ball straight at the goalie.

She didn't want to embarrass the other team.

She didn't want to hurt their feelings.

Dani the Destroyer had killed enough for one night.

In *her* opinion.

I used the tactics board to bring her off and told the nearest sub to get ready to go on.

"What?" said Jill.

I didn't want to make the same mistake with Jill as I had with Spectrum, so I told her, as calmly as I could manage (I was actually fuming) what I'd seen. Dani trudged off the pitch and her replacement sprinted on. I took out my phone and typed in the team chat.

Me: We're not dicks. We're not sociopaths. We don't want to hurt, maim, or humiliate our opponents. But if we ever, ever take our foot off the accelerator, we'll get slapped. We cannot feel sorry for other teams. We shouldn't think about other teams, ever, full stop. We have our team targets. Your teammates have their personal targets. We score every chance we get because leagues can be won or lost on goal difference. Because matches are never over until the final whistle blows. Because our fans pay to see goals. Because your teammate gets an assist and with enough assists, they get a big transfer or a scout from their national team comes to watch them. Anyone who stops trying will get subbed off and I'll play with seven if I have to.

I sent that and felt Dani become emotional behind me.

Jill felt the change in the mood and got her phone out. She read the team chat. "Pretty harsh," she said. Her eyes flicked backwards. "What if she quits?"

"I can't live in fear. I have to do what I think is right. What if she does *that* in the World Cup final?"

She read the text again. "They're called truth bombs because they have a habit of exploding."

"That wasn't a bomb. That was the opposite of a bomb. A seed. That's a truth seed. If it grows, we've got a legend. If it doesn't, we never had anything. How does she look?"

"Bright red. I'm guessing less than perfectly happy."

I turned to the next sub. "You're on soon. You ready?"

Then I took Lucy off. She gave Pippa the captain's armband.

"What are you doing?" said Jill. But it wasn't accusatory. It was inquisitive.

"Lucy's old. She's tired."

"She's fitter than you," said Jill, which was probably true.

I congratulated Lucy as she left the pitch and asked her to think about what pose she wanted for her statue. "Giving you the middle finger for subbing me off," she said.

"I think a lot of people would like that," I said.

So then I was just waiting for the moment. The incident that would teach Dani a lesson. And it didn't take long to come. Buckley's number 10, the player with the highest CA on the pitch, started to get on the ball more. Started creating danger. Buckley's first goal caused a ripple of panic to spread around my team. I was attuned to it now. I could feel it. Lucy would have absorbed some or most of it. But Lucy was off the pitch.

I made eye contact with Dani for the first time since the incident. I thought there might be a battle, but she looked away almost instantly.

Four–one up, and I was hoping to lose. What would Beth call this story? *The Architect and the Arsonist*, the twist being both characters were me.

But I felt it in my bones. I didn't often have such strong reactions to incidents on a football pitch. I knew Dani had eased off. I knew it to my core. I had to let my solution play out.

Buckley had another attack that we just about defended, and from the corner they put a header miles above the bar.

Jill looked at her watch. "It's going to be a long fifteen minutes."

And so it was. Buckley scored, attacked relentlessly, but their third came in the last minute. Too late to find another.

We won 4–3, but it didn't feel like a victory. No one celebrated. People tried to put their arms around Dani, but she shrugged them off. She tried to get Jill to open the minivan so she could get on board already. Jill refused and insisted Dani take a shower along with everyone else.

The next act in the drama would probably happen when I wasn't around, so I asked Jill if I could leave her to gather our gear and whatnot, thanked the ref and the other team, then got in my car, ready to zoom away. Jill knocked on my window. I wound it down.

"Can I check this? Dani's by far our best player. You went OTT trying to get her here. Now you're pushing her buttons."

"She'll learn something from this. We were four–nil up and she let them off the hook. We nearly lost. She can blame me, or she can blame herself. Right?"

Jill lifted her eyebrows. "But if she quits . . ."

I shook my head. "I refuse to think like that. If she quits, I'll be gutted. If she stays, I'll wait a few weeks, and then find the next thing to fix." I smiled. "I'm no expert but I think if she doesn't hate me from time to time, I'm not pushing her hard enough. What do you think?"

Jill stood straight. "I think we won't need to toughen her up. If she survives your brand of management, she'll survive anything. But, er . . . if she does quit, will you make another Harry Styles dance video to win her back?"

I laughed. "Sure. If there's a song that fits."

Jill tapped the car twice, then went back towards the pitch.

The final two-day module in my UEFA C licence was called "Helping Players Love and Learn Football through Match Day."

I passed with flying colours.

Who said irony is dead?

6

THE ART OF PHWOAR

UK English glossary: *Phwoar! The sound a British person makes when they find someone sexually attractive. Have you seen Max Best's girlfriend? Phwoar!*

The concluding section of my UEFA C course was delivered by some guy high up the FA gravy train who, presumably, had a free half-hour in between seven-course meals. He was extremely tall and good-looking, and caused a sensation when he walked into our classroom like he owned the place. He was one of those middle managers who read *The Art of War* (getting on for 3,000 years old) and imagine it has modern-day applications. It was around 4 p.m. on Sunday when he showed us his last slide. The last minute of a four-month-long campaign.

"Whatever you do in football," this chump said, "there will always be people who think they know better. Captain Hindsight. Monday Morning Quarterbacks. So I want to leave you all with this quote from Sun Tzu." He clicked his little button and read what came on the screen. "'*One may know how to conquer without being able to do it.*' That's it. That's the takeaway. Everyone's got an opinion, but put those people in the hot seat and all they'll do is warm their arse. Ninety-nine percent of people who've ever seen a game of football will tell you, whatever you're doing, that you're doing it wrong. But they couldn't stand in front of twenty players and tell them what to do. They couldn't stand on that touchline on a match day and make the big calls. I know this is cheesy, and every intake they beg me to stop saying it, but I won't. I really believe this. By being here, by improving your skills, by doing things the way you think they need to be done . . . you're all winners."

All right, yeah. Maybe he wasn't a chump. And maybe I bought *The Art of War* five seconds after the guy finished staring into my soul.

And maybe it was kinda boring actually, so maybe I looked up "best Art of War quotes" and read that instead.

Monday morning's training was superb, of course. I watched from Jackie's office, which was too far from the pitch for the player profiles to show above their heads, but it didn't matter—I could track the first team and the women (though not the youth teams) through my squad screens. I could, to take a random example, see that Dani's CA hadn't increased after the last match, whereas almost everyone else's had. And I could see that she appeared to be in perfect health. No red attributes.

So the text message I'd just got was . . . worrying.

Mr. Smith: Dani can't make training tonight. Her ankle is troubling her.

I sighed. So it was going to be like that. I passed the message along to Jill and Spectrum, adding one of my own.

Me: Please prepare the women to play 4-2-4.

That formation was the next perk I'd buy, possibly even ahead of Attributes 4, though with some good grinding I expected to snatch both before Friday's match. Another formation, another new ability. I felt like my football management powers were starting to get serious. I had enough basic skills to be dangerous, and I was adding to them all the time.

I sighed again. While I was out getting my B Licence, the first team had travelled to Hereford and been slapped 3–1. I tried to get a sense of what had gone wrong, but it was one of those ask-six-people-get-seven-opinions scenarios. Henri, for example, started his explanation by saying, "Henri was not at his magnificent best," and added that his marker was unusually good at denying him space. Pascal blamed Jackie's slow response to the other manager's changes. Youngster, who didn't get on the pitch as I *thought* he'd been promised, said the team followed the plan to the letter and they were merely unlucky.

Despite the setback, Jackie's training was as good as I'd come to expect. My women's team were improving by one CA a week, but *they* were starting from zero. Improvement came on a curve with heavily diminishing returns. Jackie was adding one CA per week to *experienced* players. Players far down their personal curves.

Our best eleven now had an average CA of over 42. Henri had powered ahead to CA 53, just ahead of Sam Topps, the prick, on 52. With Glenn Ryder also hitting 50, we had three players with a half-century. All were guys who loved a scrap, and they loved Jackie's sessions, which were all about winning your duels and then bossing the match with your superior technique and passing.

Of course, there was a big drop-off from my dream team, which included Aff, to one that included D-Day. Aff's recovery from injury was going to be one of the topics of this morning's meeting.

Still, although results had been grim and we were only above the relegation zone by a whisker, the way our CA was rising would soon make us one of the strongest teams in the division. That spine—Ryder, Topps, Henri—was as good as anything in the league, and it was still improving. The risk was that we'd run out of runway. There were only ten games left.

MD arrived a couple of minutes early, followed by Dean and Livia. Jackie and Vimsy came in soon after, smelling of grass. Jackie was surprised to find I wasn't sitting in his chair.

"Hi, everyone," he said, rubbing his palms together. "Big week ahead!" For some reason, his immense positivity made me turn to his girlfriend. She made eye contact with me and looked away. I understood it completely: Jackie was stressed off his tits. Four points from twelve, relegation looming, being the guy who'd get all the blame . . . understandable. It was only later that I realised he'd tricked us into not talking about Saturday's defeat, instead focusing on the future.

"Max," said MD. "I have a hard out. Can we power through?"

"The frequency with which you tell us how hard you are is upsetting," I said. "Where do you want to start?"

He glanced at his watch. "Tell us about your course."

I shook my head. "Yeah, done. Easy. Licence in the post. Head honcho was a big Sun Tzu fan and I'm starting to see why. It's pretty top stuff. People never change, I guess. There were lots of lovely people, people trying to make a difference in their communities. I enjoyed it—no, really—but the actual football content was a bit basic, even for me." I gave them a self-deprecating smile. That was less and less effective, I was finding. Maybe it'd still work on civilians, but the people in this room knew I was a floating megabrain. "I'm going on the B course as soon as. That's *much* beefier. A year from start to finish. Ton of work. Some of the teachers said they'd send me all their materials from when they did it so I can get stuck in. My plan is to have everything ready on day one of the course, hand it all in, then I can focus on the face-to-face sessions and all that."

"Making friends," said MD, with a smile.

"That's what I do. Oh!" I said, only then remembering something incredibly important. "One guy was really interested to hear what we're doing here. The pan-disability team, the women, the way we're building a positive, inclusive culture. He watched my tekkers video and was like 'yeah mate, yeah.' He said it was right up his alley and he asked if we were looking for sponsors."

MD perked up. "He did?"

"Yeah, his dad runs a fast-food chain. They're always looking to partner with sports teams because, you know. Shit food, healthy image." I fished in my pocket for some notes I'd made. "Right. They're talking about a test run of twenty K."

"Twenty thousand pounds?" said MD, ecstatic.

"Yeah," I mumbled. I looked down at my notes. "Just one catch. It has to be Jackie."

"Me?" said the baldest man in the postcode.

"Yes, Jackie," I said, with aggravating patience. "You're the local hero. You're the manager. It can't be me, can it? Everyone in Cheshire thinks I'm a prick. Guess who is loved and respected. You. Now, look. Step one is we film a quick video. I send it off, my new mate shows it to his dad. If he gives the green light, we go from there with, like, proper cameras and a crew and all that guff."

The stress was plain on Jackie's face now. He had a haunted look. He'd only been a manager for ten minutes, but he'd aged ten years. "I'm pretty busy, Max."

"Yeah, you're not too busy to earn us twenty grand with thirty seconds' work," I said, getting angry. I made a big show of calming down. "I've got the text here on some little flashcards. Read it out and we can all get on with our days."

I stood and moved him in front of a blank wall. I handed him his lines on three pieces of card and started filming.

"Charcoal," he started.

"Fuck me," I barked. "Smile or something. What the fuck? Have you never seen an advert? For twenty fucking thousand pounds you can smile, you miserable bastard."

"Come on, Jack," said Livia.

Jackie gave me a blast of evil eye, then composed himself. His best cheeky Liverpudlian face appeared, and he twinkled at the lens.

"Charcoal Chicken is proud to sponsor Chester Football Club and here at Chester Football Club we're proud to be sponsored by Charcoal Chicken."

I waved a thumb at him. Keep going! Next card.

"When you add charcoal to chicken you get a taste explosion; it's dead nice. Chicken burger and chips is only five pounds at Charcoal Chicken."

Another thumbs up. Jackie moved to the third card and read it perfectly until he got to the last word.

"And best of all, it's open seven days a week. Charcoal Chicken—I'll see you . . . there."

The text I'd given him didn't say "there." It said "dere," which is "there" in a Scouse accent. It was just a subtle hint that something accent-related was going on.

Jackie's eyes rolled left to right as he shuffled the cards, reading through the text again and again. He blinked. "Oh, you bastard," he whispered.

I started to back away.

A huge, pained goose honk emerged from MD. Vimsy had been leaning against the window but now he was slumped forward, clutching his stomach like he'd been poisoned. I assumed Livia and Dean were doing something similar but I couldn't take my eyes off Jackie in case he tried to actually murder me. I kept the table between me and him, but he made no attempt to assault me. He had flushed red but was now laughing along with the rest of us. His whole body shook as he wiped a tear away. "You bastard," he said again. "You didn't record that, did you?"

"Course not," I lied.

"What's so funny about the way I say chicken?" he asked, which landed like a nuclear bomb. Another round of laughs, the kind you fear might go on forever. "Come on," he said. "What's funny about it?"

"You do the first *ch* with your mouth extra wide, so that's already funny. But then the *ssshhhggg* sound in the middle doesn't actually exist in English. You Scousers can vibrate your throat, but it's a wet vibration." The phrase *wet vibration* sent MD honking again. "When I try to recreate the sound, I feel like I'm waterboarding myself."

Jackie read the text again. He became about twenty percent more Scouse. "The 'ole time I was thinking, *why 'ave I never 'eard a dis?' Charcoal ch . . . charcoal poultry. I dunno what it is but it sounds amazing. My mouth was watering! Someone should do that as a business. I'm not even joking."

We gave ourselves twenty seconds or so to finish wheezing, and to do those long, luxurious final laughs that are so, so satisfying.

That little bit of one-upsmanship wasn't just to score some banter points. I felt that Jackie needed a good laugh, and the approval in Livia's glance made me think she agreed with me.

"Right," I said, clapping my hands and going back to my seat. "Now that I've won the banter wars, let's talk about injuries. How's Trick?"

"Right as rain," said Dean.

"Aff?"

"Could be back in full training sooner than expected. He wants to rejoin first-team training this week."

"Does he?" I said, some of the warmth I'd generated fading away.

Dean had just enough sense to realise he was entering a minefield. "Yeah. He's been very diligent. Takes care of himself."

"Does he?" I said, even more frostily. From my point of view, Aff had tried to hide a hamstring tweak and played at full intensity instead of resting, putting himself out of the team for two months.

"I'd love him back in the lineup," said Jackie.

I looked up at the ceiling. I didn't want to bring any stress into the room, especially not five seconds after I'd basically given everyone the joke equivalent of a full-body oil massage. "My bro Sun Tzu says, '*He who wishes to fight must first count the cost.*' So let's talk about the cost, and I'll put this in the plainest possible language. If Aff is rushed back from injury and the injury reoccurs, or he tears something else because he can't move freely, then at least three people are going to lose their jobs." I looked at MD when I said the last part. His eyebrows rose just a little, but he didn't gainsay me. I later realised that, as a middle manager, MD had probably been through multiple *Art of War* phases.

"Max," said Dean, but then he stopped. I think he was trying to work out who the other two were. It should have been obvious: Jackie and Aff himself.

Jackie certainly understood me. "So he's scheduled to come back on the eighteenth of March, right?"

"We're at home to Blyth Spartans that day," I said. "Give him twenty minutes at the end. Back in training, carefully monitoring his workload, letting him or I suppose in his case *making* him skip anything that's going to be a risk. He can do his glute bridges and his lunge jumps instead. Tuesday match against Kettering might be a bit too soon. Maybe another twenty if we're desperate? Home to Chorley, second half. That should do it. Last four games of the season he's back to full fitness. The last four games are Southport, Farsley, Scarborough, and Peterborough. With Aff in the team and another month of Jackie's training under our belts, there's nine points. Twelve if we go for Scarborough. Really go at them." I realised I was getting into the territory of messing with the first team, so I shut my gob.

"That's the plan, then," said Jackie.

"Sorry," said Vimsy, "but okay, he can't play tomorrow, fair dos, but it sounds like he could be on the bench this Saturday. Six-pointer against Leamington."

"Vimsy," I said, scrunching my face closed and kneading my eyebrows with my thumbs. I had options, though. I could explode, sure. Or I could try to be funny. One of my new quotes seemed apt: *In all walks of life, diplomacy should be our first option.* "Oh, I get it. Good gag. Good wind-up. Thanks, I needed that. I *was* getting too tense, you're right."

Vimsy considered taking the safe route out but stuck to his guns. "I'm just saying, he's quality. He gives us something extra."

"I know that," I said. "But if he gets injured a-fucking-gain, then I'll have to sack four people." The change of the number from three to four hit home. "This is now a football club that makes good decisions.

We don't make bad decisions to get us out of a mess caused by terrible decisions. There's a quote about this. Hang on." I got my phone out and whizzed through the *Art of War* quotes I'd saved. "'*He will win who knows when to fight and when not to fight.*' That is pretty fucking clear, isn't it? This guy three thousand years ago literally wrote a book called 'Don't Rush Aff Back from Injury.'" I couldn't resist adding one last dig at Physio Dean. "If Aff doesn't feel comfortable in the medical rooms for whatever reason, that's something we can address going forward." He shoots, he scores! Dean was staring at his feet. I can't be sure, maybe it was wishful thinking, but I thought I saw approval on MD's face. "If Aff is bored, he can go and scout Southport. He can study their right back, find weaknesses. Tell us what formation they're playing and what subs they make. Right? He can be useful. Sun Tzu loved a good spy. Aff's boredom can be *managed*."

Big pause. Lots to think about there.

"Anyone have anything else?" said Jackie. It seemed to me that he had shrunk when he'd retaken his seat. It wasn't Jackie. It was the *chair*. Evans made it seem like a throne. Jackie wasn't Evans, but he'd grow into the role. I was sure of it. For now, though, the chair didn't feel like his. The room didn't feel like his. Jackie was too busy to think about such mundane things.

While MD talked about finances and the coming "Boost the Budget" campaign, I texted Livia.

Me: Can you sneak some Jackie stuff in here? A framed shirt? Big photos of him? I assume he's got loads of that. Make him feel that this is his space. Yeah? Just . . . choose photos where he's still got hair. So I don't vandalise them with devil horns and moustaches and the obvious.

I pressed send and surreptitiously looked at Livia. She read it on the screen, then gave me a little nod.

Livia: Great idea! I'm on it. Thanks, Max.

I can't explain it, but the way she added the word *Max* on the end made me nervous. Really, really nervous.

I had lunch with Henri, Raffi, and Pascal. They wanted to go to a new place they'd heard about, but for some reason I was craving chicken, so we went to Nando's.

It was nice. Good group. Pascal's mania for detail and his desire for control; Raffi's cool acceptance that sometimes life be like that; and Henri, floating above, giving us the thirty-thousand-year perspective on whether we should order dessert or not (answer: we should)—it all reinforced something I'd noticed while watching them train: Pascal brought out some fraternal qualities in the older players. Raffi, in particular, didn't like when I teased the little guy.

They asked how the women's team was going. "Making progress," I said. "Jill knows the next team we're playing very well. Northwich Vixens. Apparently the manager is good with tactics. I'm excited. Going to beef up my skills and see if she can deal with it."

"What if she beats you?" said Pascal.

"Then I'll steal her moves," I said, laughing. "What do you think? Thing about Sun Tzu is, he's all about not fighting if you aren't going to win. Which is cool if you're a general. But if you're a football manager, you're going to have defeats. You can't say, 'Ah, Queen's Park Rangers are too strong. I'll skip this battle.' You do your best, and if there's nothing you can learn from it, you aren't trying very hard. You should be able to learn something from every match you watch."

With that in mind, I set off to London to watch Brentford beat Fulham 3–2.

Brentford were considered a model of good management. They used data to find cheap players with potential, and they'd done this so well they had won promotion and were ninth in the Premier League, ahead of Chelsea, and pushing for a place in a pan-European tournament. My plan was to be Brentford on steroids. When I had more time, I needed to set up a fake data science team to explain how good we were at finding new players. AI was the big hype of the year, with impressive tools like DALL-E and ChatGPT making headlines. I could tell people I was using AI to analyse football data. That could be funny when other clubs tried it for themselves.

The drive down took four hours and I had to buy my own ticket, but I gorged on XP: 672 in total. Such a big injection gave me the confidence to buy Attributes 4, knowing I'd have enough to buy 4-2-4 by Friday.

Just as I was about to unlock a new cell, Brentford got a penalty. The home team's star striker, Ivan Toney, scored it. That was his twenty-second successful penno in a row. His technique was amazing. I couldn't quite work out how he did it. He took one slow step towards the ball, made the goalie move the wrong way, and then passed it into the net. (When I got home I watched a video that showed a bunch of his other pens, and what was interesting is that very, very often, the goalie dived the *right* way, but Toney scored regardless. I probably wouldn't change my method, but it was interesting to see a fellow expert at work.)

So. Attributes 4. The curse did its little cell dance and seemed like it would land in the one I knew had to be Influence. The one I wanted most! But I'm pretty sure that was just Nick yanking my chain. The cell bounced forward three more times, coming to a rest in the twelfth empty slot.

A new word appeared in the player profiles: *positioning*. Great. What did that mean?

I sat on the edge of my seat, leaning as close to the pitch as possible. The first thing I noticed was that the defenders generally had higher positioning scores than the strikers. That suggested it was a defensive stat. The starter with the highest positioning was Fulham's American centre back Tim Ream. The lowest was also a Fulham player—their star striker, Mitrovic.

So . . . this was what? How good players were at being in the right defensive position? But they were supposed to stand where I told them, right?

I fired off a text to Spectrum. He probably played *Champion Manager* and *Soccer Supremo*, the big nerd. I'd never discussed it with him, for obvious reasons.

Me: I want a young player to improve his positioning. Who do I tell him to watch from the first team?

He replied almost instantly.

Spectrum: Glenn Ryder.

I supposed I'd find out if that was right the next time I watched them train. I mentally slapped myself in the forehead. Since I'd become DoF, I'd been given access to every first-team player's real-time profiles. I knew their positioning scores already!

Sure enough, Ryder did have the best positioning skill: 13. Trick Williams, the prick, was one of the best, with 12. It was annoying that the ghoul had good qualities. It made it harder to seethe at him. Aff also had 12, which made sense given how good he was defensively. Pascal and Youngster, predictably, had relatively high positioning scores: 9 and 10, respectively.

Carl Carlile's was only 7, which helped to explain his poor performances.

On the women's team, Lucy was the only one with a score higher than 10. Bit worrying.

I drove back to Chester, thinking about positioning almost non-stop for four hours, slept in the stadium, and pottered around the quiet, gloomy streets of Chester all day, house-hunting and staying out of Jackie's way, hoping our position in the league table would improve.

XP balance: 604

Debt repaid: 1,112/3,000

Match 37 of 46: Chester versus Kidderminster Harriers.

Jackie set the team up in his favoured 3-5-2, with an average CA of 41. Kidderminster were sixth in the league, fighting for a playoff place, and had CA 46 with two strong strikers in their 4-4-2. Their away form was much better than their home form—pretty rare—and their goals for was only slightly higher than their goals against.

From that info, I expected a close match decided by one or two key moments: a slip, a moment of magic, maybe a refereeing mistake.

So it was pretty thrilling to watch us play like giants. Sam Topps and James Wise took the midfield by the throat and let Raffi drift around connecting the other parts of the team. D-Day was inspired—9 out of 10—and Henri struck two powerful right-foot shots into the old onion bag. After the first goal, he ran around like a baby goat, hopping and skipping and doing lousy high-fives. The second time, he celebrated without moving. He turned on the spot, checking all eyes were on him as his skill demanded, while slowly raising his arms. Extremely cocky, extremely narcissistic. The crowd fucking loved it.

Two–nil up after half an hour, dominating possession, playing like a top-of-the-league team. Amazing.

Harriers, though, didn't give a shit. They kept doing their thing. Grinding, Ian Evans-esque football. High balls to their beefy boys, looking for knock-downs, hoping for a lucky bounce. One fell their way, and they scored.

"Just one of those things," said Ruth, who was with me and Emma in the director's box. She'd become a lot more interested in football since the day I went to her house and told her I didn't care about her vote.

Just one of those things? Sure. Maybe. But my obsession with the positioning attribute made me wonder. Was Carl just slightly in the wrong place? Had he switched off? I'd need to review the tapes, but it seemed to me like his positioning *was* at fault.

The goal was catastrophic; the rest of the match was played in our half. But like at the beginning of this adventure, the new knowledge was weirdly exciting. Knowledge was power, and I'd never felt more powerful. As a wise man—can't remember who; Neymar maybe—once said, "If you know the enemy and you know yourself, you need not fear the result of a hundred football matches."

For now, I still had to recruit players based on their PA. That was the quickest route, surely, to making some transfer profits. But as we rose through the leagues and I chose players to keep, my defenders would need high positioning. How high? At the expense of what other attributes? I wasn't sure, but I had years to find out.

And in the meantime, if I found some high-positioning youngsters, I'd be on them like devil horns on a vandalised photo of Jackie.

At halftime, Ruth and Emma wanted my full attention. I was at the window, leaning on the glass. Since Kidderminster's goal, our match ratings had declined slowly and steadily. D-Day had two assists to his name, but even he'd fallen from 9 to 8. We'd won some battles, but I knew we'd lose the war. Here I was, in theoretically the most powerful role in the club, and I could do literally nothing to help.

"I've got good news and great news," said Ruth, inviting me to choose. I was still thinking about how reliant the club was on the man in the dugout, so I didn't reply. Must have looked pretty gormless, because she pressed on. "Inga arranged a match against Wrexham, didn't she? And you were going to play it on a boggy field somewhere, weren't you, Max?"

"Yeah. It's just a friendly. Warming up for bigger things to come. End-of-season showpiece with two of the most famous women's teams."

Ruth closed her eyes while her eyebrows shot up. Patient annoyance? "Wrexham are Chester's big rivals, Max. Even you should know that."

"We literally never play them. We haven't been in the same division since the sixties."

"That isn't true, but I take your point. Nevertheless, the rivalry is there. My dad was always very affected by the Wrexham matches. It's still a big deal in this city. So we've moved the match to here." I looked around the box. Ruth snapped. "Not *here*. What's wrong with you tonight? Emma, what's wrong with him?"

"He's playing football matches in his head. He's trying to give you his full attention. Sort of."

"It's off-putting. Max, you'll need to do some publicity. Sell some tickets. Call your journalist friend and get another story. I liked that *Wizard of Oz* one. I want that for my team."

"*My team*," intoned Emma, and my mouth dropped open. I'd never seen her make fun of someone like that, apart from me.

Ruth thought it was hilarious. "Yes, yes, I know. It's Max's team. I'm sorry. I've been getting quite caught up in it. It's a good story, isn't it? The seven–nil was embarrassing, but things have perked up since then."

"Who was the sexy dude who was with you? Phwoar!"

"Oh! The things he pays attention to. None of your business. So that's the good news. The great news is that Emma and I have decided we want to do the agency. There's just the question of the split."

"Fifty–twenty-five–twenty-five," I said, frowning at the tactics board in my head. Chester's formation was changing and morphing, going from 3-5-2 to 4-4-2, 4-4-2 with a split striker, 4-3-3, 4-3-3 with two forwards set very wide, and so on. What was that? Jackie talking out options with Vimsy in one corner of the dressing room? I closed the whole interface—it felt wrong to spy on him like that.

"I was thinking one-third each," said Ruth. "Possibly a little higher for the person who does all the actual work."

"Oh, thank you," said Emma. "Going through contracts with a fine-toothed comb is painstaking work."

"Let me stop you both right there," I said. "It's fifty for me because my skill is extraordinary. It's mad to give up half, but I can't do it on my own. I think you'll both work hard. There are times when Ruth will do more, times when Emma will. If the thought of the other one being on a beach while you're grinding makes you insane, that's okay, that's fair, but then there's no company. If you do this, you'll have to put some time in and deal with some unpleasant people. Learn about image rights and boot deals and stuff you don't care about. But you'll make millions. There will be disgusting amounts of money. I thought about the split at the beginning. I can't remember my exact reasoning, but I felt sure that you two having the same share does away with loads of BS. If one of you wants twenty-six percent just to be top dog, I don't want to be part of it."

"Easy for you to say, Mr. Fifty Percent," said Emma.

"All right, well, it was just an idea," I said, going to sit at our little table. "I wish you all the best in your future endeavours."

"God, he's such a drama queen," said Ruth, following me. "How do you stand it?"

"I'm a glorified paralegal in my dad's company. Max's drama keeps me sane." Emma sat and did a weird gesture. She crossed her arms in front of her at a very oblique angle. I realised what she was doing and did the same.

Ruth looked at us like we were crazy, but then caught on. She copied the gesture, and then we were able to do a simultaneous three-way handshake. Or was it a six-way handshake?

"You don't realise it," I said. "But you just agreed to get filthy rich."

We clinked our glasses. A new sports agency was born!

"We're going to start with Bark," said Ruth. "Learn the ropes. What about Dani?"

"Er . . . Dani's mad at me right now."

"What?"

"It's fine. Don't worry about it. Maybe just hold off on the whole being her agent thing for a bit. Until, you know, she sets foot in Chester again. No," I said, waving my hand in front of Emma's phone. "Please don't text her. Please. The team has to do it."

"Do what?"

"Do the nothing that needs to not be done."

"You're infuriating," said Ruth. "I think I can guess what happened: You pissed her off and she's done a runner."

"Everything is going to be okay," I said, which was stupid, because that was the moment the Chester players emerged from the tunnel and jogged onto the pitch.

Kidderminster's manager changed to 3-5-2 at halftime, and they came out in a blitz. They equalised and dominated for ten minutes. Jackie switched to 4-4-2, subbing Raffi off for Trick again. That would have helped, but Kidderminster's manager immediately changed back to 4-4-2, regaining the upper hand. When Jackie made another sub, the Harriers guy copied him. In fact, Jackie made three substitutions in the match, and the away manager made a change of his own almost instantly each time. It could have been a coincidence, but it struck me as odd.

The second half was all Harriers, and they ended up winning 4–2.

There were a few boos from the home fans. Since Evans quit, the team had played well but taken only four points from a possible fifteen. Jackie, to his credit, went onto the pitch and applauded the supporters. I saw one guy rush forward and make some rude gestures. Jackie pretended not to notice, but I know he saw it.

I was burning with curiosity to know what Vivek's positioning score was, because it could have been anything. Low would explain why he was struggling to learn his role; high, and his mistakes were just inexperience. But I couldn't watch any training on Wednesday; I'd decided the best source of XP that day was in Edinburgh. I drove across the border, thinking about Dani's ongoing fake injury, fretting that I'd pushed her too hard too fast. Watching Hibernian 1, Rangers 4 took my mind off things. Hibs let me in free as a scout, which helped me guess how much XP I was going to get. Despite being the highest league in Scotland, the Scottish Premiership matches only gave 5 XP per minute.

Several of the Scottish cities with big teams were only about three hours from Darlo, though, so it was well worth adding Scotland to my scouting repertoire. And I suspected, based on absolutely zero knowledge or research, that Scottish women's football would be underdeveloped. Maybe in the off-season I'd spend a week up there trawling for hot talents. The only fly in that particular ointment was that I'd told Emma how much I loved the Celtic accents. Would she trust me to be surrounded by lovely Scottish lasses all day every day?

On Thursday I bought myself a ticket to see Man United at home to a Spanish team in the Europa League, the second most prestigious pan-European tournament. Strangely, it was also 4–1, so it didn't really take me on an emotional journey. I mostly focused on the new attribute, and it helped that I knew United's players so well. Their key centre backs had positioning 17 and 15, while the legendary defensive midfielder they'd bought from Real Madrid, Casemiro, had the highest one I'd yet seen: 18. The attribute was starting to seem pretty fundamental—it didn't matter if you were great at heading, for example, if you were always five yards away from where you needed to be.

Positioning, then. My hypothesis was that all players mostly stayed in the zones required by their formations, but within those zones there would always be an optimal defensive spot for a player to be, based on the game state. And a high positioning score meant they'd take up those positions most of the time, and their team would concede fewer chances.

It was also interesting to see how United had developed under the new manager; the answer was very well. Lots of green, lots of CAs on the up. Garnacho, the talented youngster I'd seen soon after I'd gotten the perk that showed me CA and PA, had added something like 40 points of CA through the season!

But while I enjoyed the lessons and the experience points, being there in the stadium was unsettling. This was supposed to be my team, but I felt disconnected from it. I liked the players and the manager, but the owners were grotesque. More than a dozen times during the match, the United fans called for them to get out. The chants were even more powerful after United's goals. The fans were saying that even winning couldn't mask the horror of having bad owners. So far, so good.

And yet when I talked to the people in the seats around me, they said they'd welcome *any* new owners—hedge funds, Qataris, a mining billionaire. To me, it was replacing one horror with something even worse, but I was a voice in the wilderness, it seemed. New owners would put money into the club. Especially the Qataris. That was by far everyone's preferred bid.

I found I didn't really celebrate United's goals.

I took my XP, bought 4-2-4, and left.

XP balance: 938

Debt repaid: 1,238/3,000

Friday, March 10, 2023.

We were away at the Northwich Vixens. The men's team in the town was called Northwich Victoria, one of those grand old clubs you saw sometimes in the FA Cup draw and thought, *Wow, what a top name.* The women's team weren't affiliated with them, but it seemed pretty obvious the name had been chosen with integration in mind. Evidence of long-term planning and a devious mind—exactly what Jill had warned me about. Tonight I'd be up against Tammy Tactics.

The Vixens were a small but formidable outfit. They had a history of breaking goalscoring records in the minor leagues they played in, but had settled in the North West Womens Regional League, tier six of the women's game. That was too rich for our blood, but they had a development team that played at tier eight. I worried they'd throw a few ringers into the mix, just to make sure they won, but then again, they probably weren't taking this as seriously as I was.

We had almost no spectators. Northwich was a bit too far and un-glamorous for a casual drive.

But we had five special visitors.

First, Dani turned up, ready to play. She didn't acknowledge me or make eye contact. Her turning up was . . . perplexing. She couldn't not train and expect to play. Could she? Surely that was obvious, even to a noob?

Second, Livia had volunteered to come be our physio. That made me uneasy; she hadn't *offered* to do it before. She was distracted and hadn't done anything with her hair. Sometimes she'd just be standing there, hair billowing in the light breeze, cheeks flushed slightly red in the evening chill. An absolute masterpiece. I wasn't the only one smitten; plenty of the players on both teams chased after a loose ball only to catch a glimpse of her and stand, dumbfounded, moonstruck, before turning away, cringing at their own weak-mindedness.

Third, MD. He asked if he could hang around with me on the sideline. Asked for a lesson in football management. I was happy to oblige.

Finally, Ruth and her sexy dude. He got a lot of "Phwoar!" attention from the straight women, a lot more than me, which didn't bother me in the slightest. Ruth introduced him as David, pronounced dah-VEED. He spoke crisply with an unfathomable hint of an accent (German?). "Max Best. Splendid to meet you at last. I am an Arsenal fan. For a long time, our greatest goalscorer was Cliff Bastin. Do you know the name?"

"Vaguely. Might have read it in some old annuals."

"He was deaf. I always wondered how a deaf player could be so good. I am fascinated by the story of your Dani. I'm glad to see her here tonight."

"Oh, right. But she won't play."

"What's that?" said Ruth.

"She didn't come to training," I said.

"Oh, dear," said Dahveed.

"Oh, wait," said MD. He'd been glaring at Dahveed, but now he whipped out his phone. "I have some *Art of War* quotes, too. Here's one . . . ah, yes." He cleared his throat. "'*If soldiers are punished before they have grown attached to you, they will not prove submissive; and, unless submissive, they will be practically useless.*'"

"What's that supposed to mean?" said Ruth.

MD winced, almost imperceptibly. "I'm saying it might be a little early in the project for Max to become a disciplinarian."

Before I could really think about that, the referee joined our huddle. She was middle-aged, and had flushed, rosy cheeks. Would have been a good barmaid in medieval times. She looked around the circle. Her mouth started to form the word *phwoar!*, but she was able to transition into something slightly less insane. "What are you? More Hollywood people come to buy a football club?"

"Got it in one," I said, and I went around the group pointing at Livia, Ruth, Dahveed, and MD in turn. "May I please introduce

Kate Beckinsale, Charlize Theron, an older Tom Hardy, and Benedict Cumberbatch's stunt double."

"Oh?" said MD. "And who are you?"

I spread my arms wide. "I'm the biggest star of all."

"Right, that means you're Max Best," said the ref. "I've heard about you. I need your team sheet."

I checked the time. Fifteen minutes before kickoff. If I could get her to wait five minutes, I'd be able to see the other team's lineup.

"Can we wait a couple of minutes? There's a player who should be arriving any second. I'd like to put her in the starting eleven."

No such luck. The ref wanted the form. But she did agree to give me literally one minute to discuss something with my team. I gathered them around, while my unusually attractive companions hovered, interested in the process. They were way too hot—my players didn't know where to look. Sun Tzu never said anything about sexy generals distracting the soldiers.

"Guys, shut the fuck up. Robinson, are you typing this for Dani? Amazing, thanks. But tell her we're talking about her and then stop. Good?" I thought about what I wanted to say. "All right. With the men's team, if some prick doesn't show up to training and has a lame excuse for why, he doesn't get in the first eleven. Simple as that."

Lucy, the captain, spoke. "You mean Dani? I thought she was injured."

"Bullshit. Nope. She wasn't. So why not just name Dani as a sub and have done with it?" I asked rhetorically.

"Because she's our best player," said Mo.

"No," I said sternly. "That's absolutely not it. I want to discuss this openly but if that's what you think, I'll drop her just to prove the point. No one gets special treatment because of how good they are. Ever. You're a team. That's the most important thing to me. Absolutely the most important thing. I thought I'd made that clear."

"You did. I was joking. Sorry," she mumbled.

I took a breath. There were times I flew off the handle out of proportion to what had been said. I tried to get back to where I was. Let my face soften a bit. "Why not name her as a sub? One. She's fifteen. Last week I told her some home truths, and did I like people doing that to me when I was fifteen? Did I fuck. So I have some sympathy with that and you guys probably do an' all. Two. I don't know that I should insist on professional standards when we're not paying you. Three. She comes from Crewe. Her parents drive her all over the country according to what they maybe see as my whims. I don't want to be a total psycho about it if they want to skip a week. You know, if that's what it was. But if it was Dani flaking out and I don't punish her this week and then I punish you next week for the same thing, that's team spirit cancer. You're a good team, the vibe is great, but if I can get you to really fucking *believe* in yourselves the way I do, we can get to the top of this game. I'm dead serious. But honestly, I don't really know what to do here. So, thoughts, please."

Pippa spoke first. "I want to be treated just like the men's team, but if you'd punish a player without knowing the whole story, then no. No, thanks."

Livia was next, to my surprise. I thought she was totally spaced out. "What makes you think she wasn't injured?"

"I can't explain it. But . . . I'll give you a million pounds if she was."

Bea Pea was next. "I don't think it's the first thing. The being mad at you thing. Yeah, she didn't like being told off. But deaf people are very direct. She's used to plain talking. And, er, we're getting used to it, too."

There was a lot of chuckling. "From me, you mean?"

"From Dani."

"Oh." I smiled. I sensed bonds being formed around these women. As long as I didn't mess it up, they'd keep growing closer together. "So she wasn't injured; she wasn't mad at me enough to miss training . . ."

Weirdly, the next person with an opinion was the referee. She'd snuck into the discussion. "She was on her period and didn't want to tell you. It's not a big deal. Can you fill in the form, please?"

I looked at Jill; she shrugged. *Could be that.* I had to laugh. "Right. We've heard the verdict from IFAB. Law six, subsection five: Occam's razor shall apply. Who agrees with our match official for the day?" Most hands went up. I pointed my finger around the semicircle. "This one doesn't bite me on the arse, okay? I'm trying my best here."

While I filled in the form, Lucy double-checked the ref understood about Dani's deafness, and Jill, reading over my shoulder, read the team out. There were no surprises. Basic 4-4-2. I handed in the form, and a couple of minutes later, saw that Tammy Tactics was also doing 4-4-2. Huh. Bit of a disappointment.

The feeling of letdown lasted five minutes. Ruth and her exotic boy popped off to get takeaway coffees from a little kiosk. Livia sat on a tiny stool, hunched over. She was in earshot but didn't participate in the conversation. Jill was in front of us, walking up and down the touchline, yelling football things. I was going through our team, pointing out some strengths and weaknesses to a fascinated MD, when Tammy made her first change. Apparently satisfied that I really was playing 4-4-2 and it wasn't a trick, she started making tweaks.

"Ssh, ssh," I said, grabbing MD while staring at my opponent.

"I wasn't saying anything. *You* were."

"She's up to mischief," I said, beaming.

The Vixens were an interesting team. They had lots of pace up front, and a few players with good PA. But the obsession with having pacey forwards meant loads of players were out of position. The forwards included a left back and a right mid, while the left back was actually a natural centre mid. Tammy might have been a tactical genius—that remained to be seen—but she didn't have my ability to put players in the right positions. As such, it was hard to compare the team's average CAs, but I wasn't too worried if ours was quite a bit lower.

I started pacing around, waiting for the Vixen to finish barking instructions. The tactics screen updated, and I dashed to MD to tell him what was going on.

"She's doing four-four-two diamond," I said. "That's crazy. She doesn't have a CAM. See the girl who's moved into the centre, there? She's a winger. CAM is hard; she doesn't have the skills."

"I don't know, Max," said Jill. "Having her there worries me."

I waved the concern away. "She looks good because she's fast. At this level, speed is like a cheat code. You know Michael Owen? Played for Liverpool as a kid. Scored hundreds of goals every season. He was just too fast for any other kid to stop him! The miracle of Owen was that he kept doing it even against top pros. Until his hamstrings popped."

"So what are you going to do, Max?"

"Huh? Oh, I already did it. Didn't you see? It was subtle, but the girls know what to look for. What do you see, MD?"

He scanned the pitch. "Four-five-one?"

"Yeah. They've given up central midfield, so we're going to dominate it. Keep the ball there. Did you notice Dani automatically moved from the right to the very centre? We train that. So our best players, Dani and Pippa, are there in the centre passing to each other. It's fucking hilarious to me. What do you think?"

MD gave me a thin smile. "But what's the point? We don't look like scoring."

"*Be where the enemy is not.* We're not trying to score right now. Right now's all about frazzling."

"Frazzling?"

"Yeah. Tammy's trying to do something. Her players are trying to do something. We're like, 'Nah, don't like your plan. We'll do ours instead. We'll do hundreds of tiny passes in midfield on your home patch.' It's winding them up. See that one there? She's got literal steam coming out of her ears." I laughed again.

"Who's Tammy?" said Jill.

"Tammy Tactics. Their manager."

"Oh." She didn't like it.

"Jackie calls Max '*Tommy Tactics,*'" said MD. "I think Max is trying to pay a compliment."

"Absolutely. I can't wait to see what she tries next."

"Next" took its time. She was stubborn, this Tammy, but finally conceded her idea hadn't worked. She started yelling at her players. I flashed some hand signals to absolutely no one, just so I could telepathically change formation without it being too weird.

"What's this time?" said MD.

"We're flooding midfield, so she's trying to match us. Five in midfield, look."

"Ah, yes . . ." said MD. "Yes. But now *we* don't have anyone in midfield. You changed it *already.*"

"Yeah, we've gone to four-four-two diamond."

MD looked mutinous. "But Max! When *she* did diamond *your* solution was five in midfield, so how can the solution to five in midfield be *diamond*? It makes no sense!"

I laughed and leaned into him to give him a friendly sideways hug. "Mate. Listen. There's only one player on this pitch who can do CAM. Meanwhile, the Vixens currently have no attacking threat, and they're at home so they aren't going to mindlessly pass the ball around the centre circle like we did. So while they're in this lull, I'm going for their throat. Direct balls to bypass midfield. Pippa's not terrible as the DM. She can ping a decent long pass from there, anyway."

"How long until— Oh, shit."

A feeble Vixen attack was stomped out by sheer weight of numbers, and the ball was played to Pippa.

Pippa has time and space. She looks up and sees Bea Pea coming short.

The pass is accurate. Bea Pea touches it first time to Dani.

Dani bursts past a challenge.

She's fouled!

The ref puts the whistle to her lips.

But Dani gets up and keeps going. She plays a one-two.

Another burst forward!

Dani has a clear sight of goal.

GOOOOAAAALLLL!!!!

She makes no mistake.

Dani ran around, celebrating. I turned to see Dahveed holding Ruth's coffee so that she could applaud. They were both beaming.

"What were you saying, Mike?"

"Er . . . How long until she changes the formation?"

"The manager? She changed it during the goal celebrations."

"*What?*"

"Yeah. She's absolutely brilliant. I love her. Let's see," I said, pretending to be unsure of what the new plan was. "I think it's a plain four-four-two. Maybe I'll go back to that, too. Don't want to show my hand. At halftime she'll have the chance to make big changes. *The whole secret lies in confusing the enemy, so that he cannot fathom our real intent.* Actually, that gives me an idea." I spent thirty seconds running up and down the touchline yelling instructions at players, pointing far and wide. Of course, they ignored any positional changes I requested verbally, but it was quite a performance.

When I was done, Jill took a few steps back and mumbled, "What was that?"

"Yeah, Max," said MD. "What did you change?"

"He didn't change anything," said Livia in a pretty flat voice. It was the first thing she'd said in about half an hour. "He's bluffing. Making her feel stressed trying to work out what he did."

"Fuck me," said MD, as Tammy and her coaching team fell into a panic.

At halftime, I let the ladies hydrate and chat to each other about their opponents and all that. Sometimes players said interesting things in those little moments. No one had spotted what the curse had told me: that one defender had a much lower positioning score than the others. I wanted to test my hypothesis.

"All right," I said, when they'd had enough rest. Everyone paid attention. Normally, someone typed in the team chat so Dani could follow, but I wanted to try using my phone's dictation tool. I held the phone to my mouth and tried to speak clearly. "The lazy dog drank the rain in Spain." I checked what it had typed. It had gone for *drink* instead of *drank*, but the rest was accurate.

Me: Huh. Not bad. Dani please tell me if this is shit. If you're still talking to me. I said that last part sarcastically, by the way. So, second half we'll dick around a bit more, just to annoy that manager and see if we can get that centre back to spontaneously combust. Number 5 is a hothead. Just saying. But at some point we're going to stop reacting and start proacting. Shit, that's a terrible line. Cut that. Delete. Fuck me how do you delete? Yeah, so at some point we'll switch to 4-2-4. Dani wide right as playmaker. Now, their weak spot in the back four is their left-sided centre back. Number 4. That's the one closest to you, Dani. So when you and Bea Pea combine, remember that. That number 4 will be out of position more times than not. Watch her. See what you can do with that info.

Dani: I'm not sure I know what you want.

Me: Like, can you drag her away from the other centre back?

If you can get her all the way over to the left back, there's going to be a massive hole somewhere for Bea Pea or Gracie. Or she will play you onside when you're running on to a Pippa special. Just look for it. Number 4. Out of position. It's not a one-off. That's who she is. Number 5, big temper. Good? Bicep emoji. Heart emoji. Er . . . goal emoji.

The second half went great. Whatever Tammy tried, I reacted instantly and shut it down. After a while, MD seemed to get bored of me explaining my dance moves, so I gave him short updates like "She's trying four-three-three. That's a good formation for her fast players. I'm doing five in midfield to shut the supply routes down." Then I blabbed about life, the universe, and everything until it was time to unleash my new formation.

4-2-4 is basically the same as 4-4-2, but with the two wide midfielders pushed farther forward so that they are very attacking. The wormy, fearful right mid becomes a sharp-toothed wyvern. What sight on a football pitch compares to a winger in full flight?

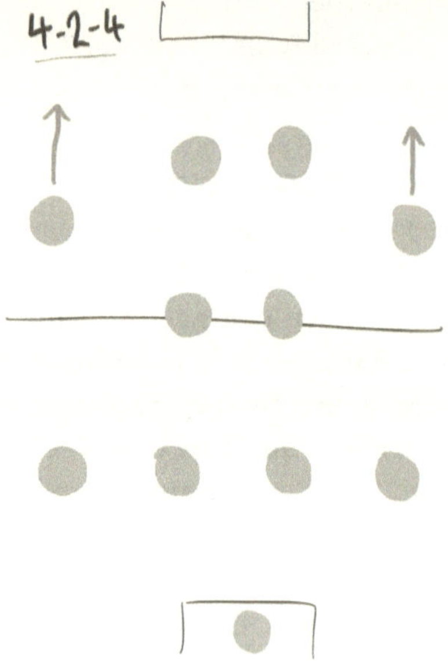

4-2-4 is *all* about the wingers. Like in a battle, the danger comes from the flanks. Imagine Aff on the left and me on the right, getting the ball and firing crosses onto the head of Henri. How many goals would you get from that? That's right. Infinite.

Dani was well-suited to this formation. Gracie on the left, less so. But I instructed almost everyone else to pass right, while making Dani the playmaker. That ensured she'd be first option for a pass most of the time. Then the only questions were: Could Dani win her duel with the left back, and if she did, would she ease up?

What I love about 4-2-4 is how god-damned attacking it is. If you can get the ball to your wingers, it's mayhem. Of course, there are huge gaps in your midfield, so it should be possible for the other team to get a stranglehold in the game and force you to withdraw your wingers . . .

But that's where the frazzling came in. Tammy Tactics couldn't think straight. We played a full six minutes of this flying winger formation before she even realised it wasn't 4-4-2, and when she finally tweaked things, it was too late. Dani had run rampant, torturing her fullback and mercilessly pressuring the CB with poor positional sense. Bea Pea scored the goals, but Dani made them. There was even an incident where the fired-up defender stopped a Bea Pea dribble by pulling her hair.

My players went mental, but it all calmed down very quickly. I loved it. One of those incidents was better for team building than any speech I could give. The Vixens had a young player fresh on the pitch who was covered in tattoos and was keen to put herself around a bit. She yelled something at Dani, who naturally didn't react in the slightest. So this girl, Maddy, gave her a push. Dani was perplexed, but when she realised what had happened, she became furious.

I watched Dani stomp around, fuming, getting herself really worked up. Maddy got the ball and Dani sprinted towards her—I worried my player would do something unbelievably stupid. Fortunately, Maddy passed the ball and jogged away, unaware she'd been in danger. I subbed Dani off, just to be safe, and she spent the next ten minutes complaining about Maddy and her shit technique.

I locked eyes with Jill and we both looked away, trying not to smile too hard.

Our little Dani was trying to be fierce.

The final whistle. Three—nil.

"Ah, well, that was tremendous fun," I said. "Good lark, that. Jill, can you come and help me with some recruitment?"

"What? You're going to poach one of their players?"

"Going to try."

As I walked away, I spotted Ruth and Dahveed walking towards Dani. Laying the groundwork to become her agent.

I went over to Tammy and had a quick chat with her. I was very warm and, in my opinion, gracious. After the pleasantries, I asked if I could talk to one of her players to see if she'd be interested in joining our project.

Tammy wasn't happy, and pointed out that the Vixens were miles ahead of Chester, and we'd only beaten the development team. The actual first team would thrash us. True, but missing the point. I was on the verge of replying when Jill took over. Tammy knew and respected her. Jill pointed out that Chester Women was well-financed and serious, and she said some nice things about me that I don't need to repeat. Things like "I know he looks like a villainous Ken doll, but he's actually really nice." And "I know he talks like an *Apprentice* candidate but he really cares about developing the players."

Tammy relented. "Fine. I suppose I can't stop you anyway. Who is it you're interested in?"

"Maddy Hines," I said.

"You've got to be joking."

"I never joke about Hines," I said, ready to make a quip about beans.

"She only played ten minutes!"

"Right. So you won't miss her."

Maddy was helping to gather the team's gear. She was a sixteen-year-old right mid with PA 80. She'd played ten minutes with a match rating of 5 out of 10 and in a real match would have been at risk of getting sent off. A deeply unimpressive cameo. There was no way anyone in the world would have thought twice about her. I loved the curse sometimes!

I introduced myself and Jill and asked if she'd come over to our side of the pitch for a chat. She was surprised but curious. As we walked, I asked her about her tattoos; she told me all about them. I noticed that Ruth and Dahveed were still talking to Dani, which meant none of our players had gone for their shower. They were all getting as much of an eyeful of whichever one they found hot, while also trying to get noticed by helping with the group chats.

But now there was a new person to gawp at.

"Shut up, everyone." I switched to the dictation tool so Dani could follow. "Everyone, this is Maddy. Very talented right mid. I'd like to invite her to training and all that. What do you think?"

My phone beeped almost instantly.

Dani: Right mid?

Me: Yes. Right mid, Dani.

Dani: That's my slot.

Me: Your slot? Are you afraid of some competition, mate?

Dani: No. She's shit.

Me: In what way?

Dani: Not aggressive enough.

"Maddy, Dani is our right mid. For now. She's saying you're not aggressive enough. What do you think about that?"

Maddy swept her black hair aside. "Aggressive? I didn't see her do anything in the fight."

"Oh, we're not talking about fighting. Dani, show her."

Dani grabbed a football and threw it at me. I caught it. Dani pushed me a few yards back. Maddy and Dani faced off.

Dani pointed at Maddy, really jabbed her finger.

"I think she's saying, 'This is you.'" Dani nodded at me, either because she'd read my lips or because she wanted me to pass her the ball. I kicked it towards her.

Dani took a touch, killed the ball dead. Then she looked around with a gormless expression and put her hand over her eyes. A sailor looking on the horizon! The gesture I'd used to communicate with her in Crewe. Then she kicked the ball a couple of feet away.

"I don't do that," complained Maddy. "What does that even mean?"

"You're too slow," said Bea Pea.

Watch, demanded Dani. She pointed to me. *This is him.* She gestured that she wanted the ball. I passed to her. She touched the ball two yards away from her and sprinted after it. She zoomed past Maddy almost before the new girl knew what was happening. Dani came back and pounded her fist into her palm. *Aggressive!*

"Did you get that?" I said.

"Yeah," said Maddy. She'd found the last few minutes very surreal, but I knew what was happening now. It was her and Dani, me and the ball. A lesson. A chance to learn. Did she want it?

Dani got the ball and fizzed it at Maddy. Maddy took a touch—the passive, safe touch that Dani had spotted while studying her in those ten angry minutes. Dani turned and waved her arms around. She'd been spending too much time with Tyson. "Shit!" said Maddy. "Let me do it again."

Dani hit the ball even harder this time. Maddy was ready, knees slightly bent. She pushed the ball away and chased it. She dashed past Dani.

Dani watched, then gave a short nod. She went back to her phone.

Dani: We need a backup since you keep subbing me off. She'll do.

I summoned Maddy with a reverse nod. She came over. "That's what it's like here. We'll push you. It's not for everyone. We're going to play Wrexham next week, in our stadium. Sold a few hundred tickets already. You could be in that match. Why don't you come to training? Check it out. See if you like it." I smiled. "See if you can hack it."

"I can," she said. Not quite super confident, but good enough.

I thought I had her on football grounds, but sometimes a little sex appeal goes a long way. I introduced her to Livia—*"one of the physios"*—plus Ruth and Dahveed—*"they're on the financial side."* And just in case Maddy was the kind of person whose favourite Beatle was Ringo, I said, "And that's MD." Maddy turned back to Ruth and Dahveed, but I couldn't tell which one she was into. Nor did I give a shit—all that mattered was we had another high-PA prospect. "See you on Monday," I said, and let Jill do the rest.

I tried to keep the smug grin off my face as I walked back to my bag. But 3–0 and a new player? Fuck it. This was smug o'clock. Sun Tzu never won a battle and then brought his enemy's best general to his side. I caught Dani staring at me. She turned red, presumably still mad at me. Pippa tapped her on the shoulder. Showers were unlocked. Dani got up and followed everyone else inside.

"Well," said MD. "That was educational. Er . . . I wouldn't normally do this, but I've invited Livia to chat with us. The Three Amigas." Ruth and her dude had gone. Jill was inside with the players.

"Sure, yeah, of course," I said, not really paying attention. Why *shouldn't* we talk to Livia while we waited for the women to shower? They took fucking hours in there. It was probably the worst part of the job and I was always tempted to drive off and leave them to it. Then I got suspicious. "Oh. You didn't come tonight to talk about women's football." Jackie. He wanted to talk about Jackie.

"No, I did. It was really interesting. It's a bit overwhelming, to be honest, watching you work. It's like watching my nephew play his video games. I can't keep up." He glanced at Livia. "I know this is a hard time for you."

She gulped. "Yeah."

"And you know none of this is personal. We all love Jackie." Livia nodded. "But we're in the relegation zone now. One point behind Bradford, and they've got two games in hand. We're five points behind Blyth, and they've got a game in hand. We're really in the shit."

"It'll be fine," I said. "The team's improving rapidly. Jackie's incredible. Nine games left. Twenty-seven points available. We'll overtake both those teams, no sweat."

"Max, I am sweating. I've been sweating nonstop for months." He pushed his hair back. "Tuesday, while you were surrounded by hot blondes, I was with the directors of Kidderminster. I've known them for years, good bunch. Love a bottle of bubbly, they do. But second half, they confessed they knew they were going to win. Apparently, it's all over the league. How to beat Jackie Reaper's Chester."

"What?" I said. "What?"

"Everyone knows he's good, but he's inexperienced. He's never been in the big chair. He's slow to react. The Kidderminster manager told his board before the game not to worry about the score at halftime, because as the match got towards the end, he'd switch things round and Jackie wouldn't have an answer. I'm sorry, Livia, I'm just saying what I heard. And . . . that's what happened."

"What if he's not slow? What if he's thoughtful? Sun Tzu advises to '*ponder and deliberate before you make a move.*'"

"*You* don't. You see something and react instantly."

I shook my head. The situations weren't comparable. "I noticed that Harriers guy made a sub right after Jackie did. Three times. I thought it was odd."

"Yes!" said MD, animated. "Yes! 'I'll squeeze him on subs,' the manager said. Turns out these old dinosaurs, as you call them, put pressure on the young managers like that. They've got more tricks in their locker, the older guys, more cards to play. The young guys flounder around. Most sink. The ones who swim learn fast. But we don't have time for Jackie to learn the ropes. There's a rope around our neck."

"'*Victorious warriors win first and then go to war.*' We win on the training ground. This win tonight, yeah, I was pretty great, guilty as charged. But we won it before we even got on the bus. We won it by recruiting well and having great coaches." I thought about the first team's green attributes and their rapidly rising CA. "Things are going great. Kidderminster are one of the best teams in the league and we matched them for half an hour. Who's next? Leamington. They're shit. We'll blow them away. We're miles better than them."

"Their manager's an old hand," said MD. "I'm worried we'll have more of the same."

More of the same. Jackie was just as fixated on 3-5-2 as Ian Evans had been on 4-4-2. *Do not repeat the tactics which have gained you one victory, but let your methods be regulated by the infinite variety of circumstances.* I swallowed. Saying out loud that I'd hoped for more tactical flexibility felt . . . wrong. I didn't want to add any more doubts to the mix. We had to be positive. "But what do you want to do?"

MD glanced at Livia. "Tonight I watched you change formations, what, ten times? Instant changes. React, nullify, exploit. You didn't give the other manager an inch. It was almost cruel. It was *The Art of War*. Masterful."

I shrugged. "Jackie can do all that."

"Of course he can. But he isn't. He's struggling, Max."

I looked at Livia. She folded her arms. It was like she was distancing herself from her own treachery. "He's so in his head. He dwells on his mistakes, beats himself up. He feels stupid. I've not seen him like this since the early days of his injury. I'm really worried."

"Look. Listen. Guys. Seriously. Jackie's amazing. Okay? He knows football." I remembered my trial at Chester, and what Nice One had told me. "When you step up a level, you struggle. It's normal. You survive, then you thrive. We've handed him a shit job. He has to build the plane while he's flying it. You've got to expect some turbulence." It was strange that I was the most positive person in the scene. "All right. Let's be practical. What can we do to help him out?"

MD bit his lip. "You could let him use Aff."

"No. Something that would actually help him, mate. Tomorrow's match. The place is called Leamington Spa, right. Is that like a name or is it . . . ?"

"There were spas," confirmed MD. "You used to go and 'take the waters.' Not sure if there still are any. You think a jacuzzi might help?"

I smiled. "It'd help Livia, at least. She's got second-hand stress."

She didn't smile. "I'd rather have three points tomorrow than a back rub." She dipped her head. "I'll check what's in the area. See if I can get him to come with me early. He'll want to be on the team bus, though."

"I'll talk to Vimsy," said MD.

Suggesting a stressed guy went for a massage. That was *truly* a floating megabrain at work. Tommy Tactics to the rescue.

On Saturday morning, Emma came to my place in Darlington and we had brunch together. For ten minutes it was so awesome, so perfect, that I stopped eating and just closed my eyes, trying to hear what utter contentment sounded like.

For some reason I thought of the sound of Old Nick's voice, and the hairs on my neck stood up. One of the quotes from Sun Tzu floated across my mind. *Let your plans be dark and impenetrable as night . . .*

The old demon had been so quiet. He'd stopped me playing football, but what was he up to now? And why had I thought of him just then? Maybe he'd just that second spent a big chunk of the XP I'd collected for him, and I'd somehow felt it. Psychic feedback or something. I tried to shrug it off.

"So. The plan. Head down to Leamington and watch the match. If we lose, we'll check into a spa. Nice oily massage, late dinner. What do you think, bebs?"

She would normally have been on the phone booking the massages and making reservations before I'd stopped speaking. But she barely even blinked. "Max," she said, then hesitated. Quite rare for her.

"'Sup, bebs?"

"My dad was having breakfast this morning. He sits at the kitchen counter on his big iPad. I made a coffee and saw the Man United badge."

"Which is the best badge. Go on."

"He was reading about the takeover deal. Swiping through loads of photos of Arab guys going into the stadium."

"Old Trafford."

"Right. And I sort of stood there, watching him swipe. Didn't seem very interesting to me."

"Me neither, and I'm a United fan. They want to buy the club. It won't happen."

"But then . . ." She took out her phone. She'd saved some of the photos. She showed me the first one. "Here's the guy who wants to buy United. He's the figurehead, anyway. Dad says everyone knows it's the actual country financing him."

"Yeah."

She swiped. "Then it's loads of business boys . . ."

"B-boys."

"Loads of b-boys and more Qatari dudes and all that. Then I nearly dropped my coffee." Another swipe. The next photo was . . . "That guy you had an argument with in Sheffield! The one from the helicopter. He didn't get his way in Sheffield, so he's got involved in the United deal. Why do men always manage to fail *up*?"

I took the phone from her and brought it closer. There he was. Old Nick in amongst the b-boys and the billionaires. Trying to make sure Manchester United was sold to an oil state. In his mind, the ultimate punishment for my disobedience.

Let your plans be dark and impenetrable as night, and when you move, fall like a thunderbolt.

"Max, are you all right?"

"Yeah. I feel like I lost a battle I didn't even know was happening." I went internal for a minute. It was horrible in there. But I came back up and saw this gorgeous woman staring at me. I twinkled. "Forget that. I invited my hot girlfriend to spend the evening in a jacuzzi with me. I hoped for more of a reaction."

"I don't have a swimsuit."

My eyes widened. "Then let's get it booked!"

She smirked. "What if we win?"

"What?"

"You said spa if we lose. What if we win?"

"Oh," I said, realising I'd created a bad incentive. "Huh. Give me a second. Maybe there's a quote about that."

7

WHILE MY SHIT CAR GENTLY WEEPS

Thursday, March 16.

Before lunch, Jackie and I had a quick meeting with MD, whose emotional state was part despair, part anger. He told Jackie the stakes were too high for him to continue ignoring my talents, ordered us to work together, and kicked the door on his way out. One of the photos Livia had hung up wobbled. It was a young Jackie (with hair!) playing one of the two matches he played for Everton in the League Cup.

I rose and adjusted it. "Do you think they put you in the team too early?" I said.

"Nah," he replied. "Moyes let me train with the first team sometimes, so I was champing at the bit by the time Roberto gave me a go. You see that, there?"

I stared into the photo, but I was watching Jackie's reflection. Behind me, he made a face—I couldn't tell what—and pulled himself to his feet. He paused, pretending to be looking out his window, then came over.

"That little circle there, in the background? We're pretty sure that's my dad. That's where he sat, and it looks like him."

"That little smudge?" I laughed. Well, maybe it was. "It's good he was there to see it. The second highest moment of your career."

"What's first?"

I smiled. Gave him a friendly punch on the upper chest. "That's yet to come, mate. Come on. Car's outside. I threw a load of burger wrappers and empty cans in there to make you feel at home."

As fate would have it, Jackie had called me the night before, asking for a big favour. A big, discreet favour. He said he needed a lift somewhere. I said sure. He said I hadn't asked where. I said it didn't matter.

And now MD had ordered us to talk to each other. Work out a way to work together. What better time to bond than during a short, breezy drive?

"Er . . . Max. Your car is leaking." He pointed to a tiny, almost invisible oil stain beneath one of the least important pipes on the entire vehicle.

"Don't tell lies," I said. The truth was, a repair of my tubes would cost seventy-nine pounds. Money I was curiously reluctant to spend. "It's perfectly safe. Get in."

Jackie got in the passenger side and looked around for the rubbish I'd mentioned. As if. My car was shit, and leaked, but it was *clean*.

I eased into my throne and handed him a roast beef butty. "So, Liverpool," I said.

"Liverpool," he said, eyeing the sandwich. He was right to be impressed; it was *artisanal*. The bread was covered in *bits*. "Turn left onto Bumper's."

"Ah, ah!" I said, holding a finger up. "We must observe the formalities!" I made a big show of plugging my phone into the car. "Can you guess what we're going to listen to?"

He shook his head with a grin that said, *So, you're going to be a dick about this.* He looked up at the roof. "Obviously, you're going to blast "This Is the One" way beyond what your sound system can actually handle." When Jackie had taken me to Chester all those months ago, he'd serenaded me with an ear-splitting rendition of "You'll Never Walk Alone," the dirge sung by Liverpool fans. The closest equivalent for Man United would be "This Is the One" by The Stone Roses. That was the song that was played when the teams walked onto the pitch at Old Trafford.

"Sorry, bro. "This Is the One" is a banger. You don't get nice things after what you did to me in your car. I've waited a long time for this moment."

I pressed play, and we set off.

"What the shit is this?" yelled Jackie.

I grinned. "Do you like it?"

"It's torture."

I beamed and slapped the steering wheel in time to the beat.

It was a sort of electro-indie song with an addictive hook and preposterous Auto-Tune effects. It heavily featured a sample taken from a football stadium, and the musician I'd hired had even freestyled a little rap to give it a good bridge between sections.

Best! wickywickywickywakka Best will tear you apart—again.

Best! wickywickyWICKYwakka Best will tear you apart—HAgain!

They call him Best, the maximum of cool,

Risin' to the top, breakin' every offside rule.

A master of the game, no mistakin' his claim,

Best in the business, remember the name!

And back to the chorus. On a global scale, compared to all the music in the world ever, it'd be a 3 out of 10 tune. But to wind Jackie up? Mate, mission accomplished.

We were driving past the university when it ended. Appropriate; I'd given Jackie a lesson in patience and payback.

Jackie rubbed his temples. "I'm speechless."

"Do you want me to teach you the rap?"

"No. Was that you singing?"

"I can't sing. There's an internet guy who makes songs on demand. That absolute *tune* only cost a hundred American dollars. That's under eighty quid. Can you believe it? Maybe he's got an AI to do it in two minutes flat, but I think it's impressive."

"You paid a hundred bucks to annoy me?"

"It'll play at my funeral, too. Double the value. You're going to tell me when to turn, yeah?"

"It's straight for miles. Until the A550." We sat in silence for a while. Well, mostly silence. I might have been mumbling the rap and slapping the steering wheel. Jackie finally stirred and said, "Do you want to know where we're going?"

"I presume it's to the recording studio The Beatles used. To get this pressed. To get this *out there*."

"You're not interested?"

"I'm interested but I think we have other things we should be talking about."

"Yeah," he said, settling back, rubbing his face.

"Let's start with Leamington. How did that go, from your point of view?"

"Not good."

"Okay," I snapped. "We're not doing *that*."

"What?"

"That fucking man-baby self-pity shit. We've got a football club to save, and being a man-baby is *my* job. First half, Leamington mullered us. Two–nil at halftime. What did you say to the lads?"

"Shouted at them. Proper lost my temper."

"You didn't change anything? Tactically?"

"No. The plan was fine."

"As we saw."

"Right. Next twenty-five, we battered them. Bang bang bang, three–two."

I licked my lips. "Then you went defensive."

"I went counterattacking."

"You went defensive." Jackie had reverted to 4-4-2, got men behind the ball, and invited pressure. Leamington had equalised, and there had been an agonising final five minutes. It finished 3–all, but the point didn't help us much in the relegation battle. "Right. The players were scrapping, though? Battling? Because some people are saying they've given up."

"They haven't given up. They were battling."

I nodded. That had been my impression, too. I let out a sigh. A big one. "Then Banbury."

Jackie sighed, too. He rubbed his hands all over his face and head, like his palms were those squeegees in a car wash. "Yeah. Banbury."

"Is it just my imagination or did we set up against them like they were Brazil 1970?"

"That *is* your imagination, yeah."

"Because as you know, Jackie, they're *shit*. It was strange to see us treat their number nine like he was Pelé." Jackie sighed again, was still for a moment, then started squirming around. I needed to have this conversation with him, but I didn't want to nag him so much he shut down. "Do you want to hear my song again?"

"Their number nine is massive and wins every header. You have to react to that."

"Yeah, you should base your whole plan around one gigantic farmer with a huge pumpkin for a head. Heading twenty, speed twenty . . . miles per year."

"He's a danger, that guy. You've got to do *something* about him."

It was actually fun, this, talking about tactics and plans with someone close to my level. At least it would have been fun if Jackie wasn't a broken man. I had the weird feeling that I was meant to put him back together. Who else could do it? I needed to tell him off first. He kept reverting to dinosaur football. "You made Glenn Ryder man-mark him. So our best defender was stuck in one spot the whole match, trying to win headers against a guy who wins every header! It was surreal. Just ignore him! What's he going to do? Win flick-ons? And then what? Charge into the penalty area? It takes him five minutes to turn around. You need Ryder doing his normal job, taking up the right positions, cleaning up the second balls, organising the rest of the defence."

"What would you have done about him?"

"About Jabba the Shit? Nothing. He's nobody. He's shit, his team's shit. Four-two-four, all-out attack, have some of that."

Jackie scoffed. "Four-two-four, away?"

"Yep. What's the worst that could happen?"

"We lose."

"We lost *anyway*, Jackie. We made the *whole match* about some seven-foot genetic throwback. Every team at Chester takes the initiative, poses the questions, every team tries to be the protagonist, every team except one."

"It's not that easy, Max."

"It is, actually. What's the greatest team talk in history? Alex Ferguson. Man United are at home to Tottenham. He goes in the dressing room, and what does he say?" I was sure Jackie would know the story, and I was right.

"'*Lads, it's Tottenham.*'"

"Three words. Done. It says everything. Lads, it's Banbury. While we're playing fantasy football, they'll be kicking it long to the Wicker Man. While we're scoring our sixth goal, he'll start crying coz he ran out of fingers to count on."

No smile from Jackie. Just a mirthless, "Take this exit."

I pulled into the slow lane. "Right. You asked me to leave you alone, and I did. Like all alpha male executive types, I've been reading *The Art of War*. There was one quote that stuck out. I forget the exact wording, but basically, wars always go bad when the sovereign interferes with the generals. Okay, I think I take that point. But you heard MD. He ordered us to work together. So I'm not the sovereign, any more. He is."

"You want me to wear an earpiece while you tell me what to do from the director's box?"

MD had fired all kinds of ideas at us, some more realistic than others. "No. I want to help you in the absolute most minimal way possible. I've been thinking about how to help you without you even knowing it. Mad, underhanded schemes like in movies. But that's not what you need. You don't need me at all. Not in the slightest. What you need is to get out of your own way."

"Oh, is it?"

"Yeah. You're in a doom loop."

"Max."

"No, fuck you, I'm serious. We're doing this. It's not just for you and the club. It's for Livia. She has to put up with your marding around. At first I didn't mind it. A bit of worry makes her look like a sort of pre-Raphaelite Ophelia. But now she looks like a ghost. She wears baseball caps, mate. She never chats. She normally tells little stories about what her weird family is up to. Not anymore. She only talks if you ask her something. It's depressing. So you're going to let me fix you. For her."

"You're going to fix me?"

"Absolutely. Lads, it's therapy. Piece of piss. There's my bag there, can you open it? Get that paper that's wedged into the pen lid."

Jackie rummaged and came up holding the item I'd described. He pulled the pen away and unfolded the piece of paper. He skimmed the page. "No. No way."

"We're doing it or you're fired." I cleared my throat. I didn't have much experience as a therapist. I'd have to learn on the job. "Livia told me this was the sequence they used when you did your rehab for your knees. What's the first step?" He didn't say anything. "Read out the first step or you're fired." Still nothing. "Read the first step or in a month Emma and I will be on a double date with Livia and Henri."

I was busy navigating the maniacs driving around Ellesmere Port, so I couldn't check his expression. His voice was pretty flat. "Accept and acknowledge your feelings."

"Great. Let's do that."

There was a silence that lasted so long I thought this experiment was over. Twice I nearly pressed play on my song to punish him. Finally, he spoke. "My feelings . . . I feel embarrassed."

I waited for more. "Is that it?"

"What else do you want?"

"I want you to be honest."

"That's it, Max. It's enough, isn't it? What do you *want* me to say?"

"Say that your brain is fried. That the walls are closing in. Everyone's looking at you, laughing. They know you're inadequate. Your skin's on fire, heart's pounding, ears are thumping. Clichés make sense: You want the earth to swallow you up. You wonder how it came to this. You thought you were ready. You thought you could do it, but you can't, you're shit, there's nothing there, everything that led you to this moment was a cosmic joke."

I felt Jackie sag. "Is it that obvious?"

"No, you cretin. I was describing myself."

He straightened a fraction. "What?"

I sighed. Talking about feelings was not fun, but we had to get through this so we could get back to formations and training and squad building and all that top stuff. "I've been lucky in a way that you haven't. Remember that day I brought Ziggy to FC United? I managed the reserves for the second half of that training match."

Jackie turned his head towards me. "You said you'd do five-three-two, but that was a lie so you could play with our toys."

"Absolutely. And what did I do? Smashed the first team."

"No, you didn't."

"I did. I realised beating Neil would be bad for Ziggy, so I eased up. What was that, thirty minutes of competing? A tiny syringeful of experience. Now, imagine that was my vaccination."

"Against what?"

"Against the stress of being a football manager. You get your shot, right, and you wait a while. That's how it works. I had weeks to think about my battle with Neil. Months. My first combat against a real manager. And I did fine. Next time was Chester reserves against Ian Evans. And all that stuff I just described to you, that's how I felt for the first twenty minutes. Smasho and Nice One talked me down from the ledge, I kept things simple, I realised there was no mystery to what Evans was doing, I smashed him. That was my booster."

"Huh," said Jackie. The metaphor was working for him.

"But after the booster, you need another break. And then at maybe just the right time, Dave Cutter gets himself sent off in the first ten minutes of a Darlo match. I take over at halftime. I'm not exactly the *manager*, but the lads do what I tell them."

"That was the four–all," said Jackie, brightening for the first time that day. "I heard about it. You went *nuts* in the second half."

"Laser-focused counterattacking," I said. "But it doesn't matter what happened, really, for this conversation. I'm saying, I've had three halves of football management against proper managers, all nicely spaced out, lots of time for me to absorb the lessons. Er . . . please don't tell anyone about the Darlo thing. That's secret."

"It could help your career if people knew."

"Secret." I shook my head at some driver overtaking from the slow lane. Idiot. "I think it was very, very helpful that my first taste of battle went well. Now, take you. You won your first game. The energy was so positive it would have been hard not to. It's like a free hit; doesn't count. The next one counted, and you lost. And it's been a struggle ever since. So you're in the doom loop. There's a match on Saturday, on Tuesday, on Saturday, on Tuesday. Most are away so you're spending half your week on a bus. You don't have time to process the last match. You're stuck. If I'd lost my three halves, yeah, I'd be having loads of low-level anxiety, I think. Doubts. Am I good enough? I might have said, 'Oh, *I need another year. Maybe I'll stick to being an agent.*' But that's not what happened. What happened was: I slapped. I slapped three times and now I've got full immunity."

I focused on my driving for a bit, then nodded. I'd remembered where I was going with that line of reasoning.

"You feel embarrassed? Because why? Because you didn't have the chance to have a quick go in the hot seat six months ago when it would help you now? Because it was a wet winter and all those away matches got shoved to the end of the season? Because MD and the last five managers left you a shit squad full of morons? Feel what you need to feel but I don't think what you're doing is embarrassing. Ninety-five percent of the time you're fucking killing it. What's the next bullet point?"

"Control what you can."

"Right. I read your interviews from the last two matches. Loads of moaning about the referee. What's the point? Focus on coaching and tactics. That's all you can control. I don't want to hear you talking about referees again. Anything to add?"

"I tried to control the Banbury match by marking the dominant striker and you didn't like that."

"Because he's shit. And anyway, it says control what you *can*. Imagine there's a two-metre circle around that guy. Fine, let's say he's got that tiny blob locked down. Control the *rest* of the pitch. We both know you can do that. And when you do that, this trundling siege weapon is a liability, isn't he? Next."

"Have clear aims."

"We're playing Blyth on Saturday. At home. They're shit. We should have a minimum of twenty shots in that game."

"*I'm* supposed to come up with the aims, Max."

"*Your* aims are, like, '*Oh let's all dance around the tallest player. We're a bunch of June bugs. Wheee!*'"

"Jesus wept." He sighed. "Twenty shots. Why twenty?"

"Because I don't want to stress you by asking for the real number, which is twenty-five."

"What about goals?"

"What about them? You can't control how many goals there are. Shots, though. You can get me twenty shots."

"All right. I'll write it down and underline it three times. This is all brilliant, by the way, I'm nearly fully recovered. Next point. Ask for or accept help."

"You've done that one. You asked me for help today. That's why I'm driving you to"—I did a fake vomit noise—"Liverpool."

"And I appreciate it. You've been before, though."

"No, it's my first time in my whole life. I've been putting it off. I half-hoped I could do a whole football career without stepping foot in Merseyside. You know, like Denis Bergkamp never got on a plane."

"All that driving around, all that scouting, and you never went to Merseyside?"

"Nope."

"Well, I suppose I'm honoured." I didn't say anything, so he looked down at the list again. "Use visualisation as a tool."

"On seventy minutes, when you're thinking of making a defensive change, thinking of trying to keep things tight, just imagine Henri and Livia walking hand-in-hand around Paris in the summer. She's wearing big sunglasses; he's got a jaunty scarf."

"Max."

"There's a breeze that brings the smell of onion soup, the distant strains of an accordion. 'My sweet', says the sandalwood-smelling striker. 'He's playing our song.' Livia pauses, smiles. 'Why yes, *mon petit champignon*, I do believe he is.' And they rush towards the music, and they hear . . ."

Best! wickywickywickywakka Best will tear you apart—again.

"Fucking hell, Max," said Jackie, reaching over to press stop on my media player. "I can visualise my own nightmares, thank you very much. Why do you always go straight to the idea of Livia leaving me?"

"Duh! I'm projecTING," I said, in the moronic, sarcastic tone I'd learned as a teenager. I still used it when I wanted to say something serious without taking myself too seriously. "I'm afraid everyone will find out I'm a FRA-UD and I'll lose EV-ery-thing starting with Em-MUH. Oh-KAY? Is that all RIGHT?"

Slight smile. "Okay, Max."

I went right back to my normal voice. "Or you can use visual-isation to, like, create patterns of play like the Max Best Challenge. And the last step, I remember, is cultivate optimism. Optimistic Jackie Reaper in three, two, one . . ."

"Nyeah," he said, optimistically. "I want to be positive. I do. But we're so deep in dog shit. Three points behind Bradford, and they have two more games to play. If they draw both, we're five points behind."

"Holy shit," I laughed. "That's the worst optimism I've ever heard. Try again."

"No, Max. We're in the shit. We have to be serious about it."

"Ah, you're wrong there, Jackie mate. You're in the shit. I'm not."

"What do you mean?"

"After Leamington, there was an emergency meeting. Monday evening. The board, MD, Joe, and I got together to discuss Scenario B planning. The main worry is that relegation means no enthusiasm for the Boost the Budget campaign. So that would mean cuts, and going to tier seven means *savage* cuts. It was all pretty calm. People spoke and people listened. Refreshing. I laid out my vision for life in the seventh tier."

"Go on."

"Everyone who's out of contract leaves. We try to offload Sam Topps, get a fee for Raffi. Pascal can leave if he gets a club. Vimsy goes. Physio Dean goes. We keep the other coaches and Livia. Max Best, player-manager. The team is Magnus and Youngster, plus loads of seventeen-year- olds. I start the season by winning games single-handedly, until the lads get up to speed and I can come on for the last twenty to add a bit of pizzazz to the scorelines."

"Where are you going to find these teenagers?"

"That's just it!" I said, excited. "Have you heard of Exit Trials?"

"Of course."

"I hadn't! Someone told me about it on my coaching course. Players who are getting cut from their clubs get a day to show what they can do. Trials! Hunger Games shit, with a match at the end. Right?"

"It's not always like that, but you get to look at a lot of talented players in one place. I can imagine *you* could get half a team out of those lads. And they'd be keen to come."

"Keen? Where else do they go from being rejects to being first-team regulars? Yeah, look. Relegation would be a disaster. It's not the plan. Not at all. But if it happens, I'll make the most of it. We'll win the league on a literal shoestring. A few months into the season, the Deva will be full. Bunch of kids playing fantasy football! Imagine it. MD was like, 'You think we can cut the budget from fifteen grand a week to three or four and build a title-winning team?' Even Sean and Ollie, the twats, were into it. Maybe they just think I'll fall flat on my face and they can get rid of me sooner, but they really seemed to appreciate that the worst-case scenario had a silver lining. They're going to let me try."

"I'm glad you're trying to help but you're not good at this cultivating optimism business, Max."

I laughed. "I'm just saying, Chester will survive. Come back stronger. I guarantee it." I sucked my lips into weird shapes for a bit. "It's been interesting watching you from a distance. It's been a sort of safe space for me to think about my issues. You know us snowflakes love our safe spaces. I was thinking, I spend so much of my life afraid. Afraid my best player will quit because I annoyed her. Afraid my girlfriend will leave me. Afraid I'll run out of money. Afraid I'll get hurt playing. Afraid I won't be able to help my mum or my friends." I paused. I'd made myself emotional. And I'd been doing *so* well. "We've all got different skills. One of mine has always been exams. Most people are afraid of exams. I was never bothered by them. You either know the answers or you don't, right? When I was moving into secondary school there was a test to see which classes I should go in. I whizzed through the pages, and then there was this question. It was a football league table! You got some scores and some numbers, and you had to work out the rest of the scores and the rest of the table. Like, if team A conceded seven goals and drew two games then that meant they couldn't have lost to team B, so team C must have beaten team D! I loved it. It's one of the most fun things I've ever done. I think I was, like, cackling with delight right there in the exam room. Do you get me?"

Genuine grin. "I can just see it."

"It was the perfect combination of being the right mental challenge for tiny Max and being super motivational. I wasn't worried about the results. I loved the process. You can guess I got an amazing score from that exam. And so what? To work in a call centre? Now, I know you love the football process. I know you're motivated. I know this level is actually easy for you. Fear's got you all twisted up. You're scared of exams. I'd like to introduce you to a little concept I call Fearless Football. Take a big swing. What's the worst that can happen? You see, people say it's always darkest before the dawn, but I say it's darkest just before the heat death of the universe. And that's in, like, loads of billions of years from now. All right? So cheer up, you miserable bastard! You played for Everton! You're the best man manager I've ever seen. You're the best coach I've ever seen. You know, now that I think of it . . . yes, I think you're my favourite employee."

Jackie laughed. We hadn't really discussed the weirdness of our new roles. How could I be above him in the hierarchy if he was the one everyone took orders from and oh by the way, he's also sort of my mentor? "Thanks, boss," he said, which was positive. A bit of his humour coming back.

I slapped the steering wheel. "We get through this, you've got the summer to process it all, we dump some of the trash we inherited. I bring you the best of the best from the exit trials. You whip them into shape. I've never been more optimistic about *anything* than next season, except maybe the one after that. We're putting quality in the pipeline, and when those little gems get to the first team, *you'll* be coaching them. We're going to the moon. Ugh."

"What?"

"Is that Liverpool?"

"Yeah. Nice, innit?"

"I think I need to put on some music. Something upbeat to help me, you know, accept my situation and visualise a time when it will be over."

We pulled into a hospital pay and display. I parked—a study in perpendiculars; I should have won a cash prize—and the situation hit me. "Should I be worried?"

"You shouldn't be more worried than *me*, Maxy boy." He leaned forward and looked at the building. It was a private hospital, but it didn't have the luxury and class that my mental image of private hospitals had. Where were the perfectly ordered French gardens? The fountains? The signage with carefully chosen fonts? "It's me knee," he said. "Hoped I was done with this place for good."

"Your knee hurts?"

"Yeah."

I thought I knew where this was going. "Did it start hurting maybe the morning after we lost to Bradford?"

Jackie leaned forward until his head was resting on the dashboard. He came back up, eventually, with a little indentation in his forehead. "This is me own fault for helping you. No good deed goes unpunished. Come and help me out."

I got out, went to his side, and held his arm as he emerged. "Why aren't you on crutches, mate? Have you been in pain but pretending to be fine for weeks?" The thought angered me. "You fucking dick! We're all relying on you to make good decisions and you're in pain! What the actual *fuck*."

Jackie smiled. Put his palms on me. "I'm not in constant pain, Max. It's not good when I sit in one place for too long. And your car is uncomfortable."

I stepped away, lest I do something the law couldn't forgive. "Apologise to her or you're sacked."

Jackie smiled again and patted the bonnet. "Sorry, luv. I didn't mean it."

"Do you want me to carry you in?"

Jackie's smile vanished. "No."

We glided smoothly, virtually hovering on pristine knees (me) and creaked and cracked and shuffled and slid (him). Reception told us where to go. I asked Jackie if he wanted to be alone with the specialist, and he said, yeah, probably. I asked when he planned to tell Livia, and he said he'd tell her when there was something to tell because otherwise she'd worry and he couldn't do that to her. It sounded like horseshit to me, but he was allowed to fuck up his relationship. My job was to make sure he got us three points on Saturday.

The orthopaedic specialist, Sanj, popped out of his inner sanctum, said he was both happy and unhappy to see Jackie again, which was charming, actually, but that he needed a bit longer with his current patient and he'd be twenty minutes late.

Jackie, being a good person, first thought of me. "Max, I'm sorry."

"How long will your whatever take?" I spoke to the doctor as much as Jackie.

"Oh, half an hour, perhaps? Perhaps a little longer?"

"I'll go explore Liverpool, maybe. I saw some nice bits of concrete over there."

Sanj and Jackie exchanged a glance. Both proud Liverpudlians, not happy being dissed. Jackie pointed to a chair. "You do that, mate. But stick around for the next twenty, eh?"

The doc retreated into his cave. Jackie perched on the armrests between two chairs. Sometimes he pushed himself off and had a little potter. Keep those knee juices flowing.

"What did you say to the lads?" he said.

"When?" I said, though I knew exactly what he was talking about.

"Yesterday morning. Before training."

"How was the session?" I said, though I had a pretty good idea because I'd seen the results on the Chester Squad screen.

"Phenomenal," he said, frowning. "I've got to be honest. After Tuesday's defeat, I was pretty down. Wednesday training starts, my heart isn't really in it. The lads, though. I was looking around, like, what's all dis? It started normal, but then they, like, I don't know."

"Trained like their careers depended on it?"

Jackie gave me a level look. "Yeah." My reply was a smug grin and some little lip pushes. Deeply annoying to look at, I'm sure, but very satisfying when it's happening on your own face. "Max," demanded Jackie. "Tell me. Tell me or you're sacked."

"Ha. Doesn't work that way round. I'm sure you'll hear anyway. And listen, don't fly off the handle."

"Oh, God."

"So you know that email we got from the FA?"

"The new contract conditions?"

"Yeah. There was a big furore about it. The lads were up in arms. They turned up at the training ground at seven a.m. demanding answers, stressed off their tits. Trick Williams wailing and gnashing his teeth about his mortgage. Sam Topps saying he'd just put his kid in childcare and how was he supposed to pay for it. All that, times twenty. MD called me at, like, three minutes past seven to come and deal with the sitch." I studied his face. "You didn't read it, did you?"

"I did, but . . ." *But I've got a million other things to worry about.* Fair enough.

"Yeah, this is the week of Max Best being called to Chester every morning to put out some fire. So the basic point is, from this summer, nonleague contracts are going to stop protecting injured players. In the new system, if you're injured, you get twelve weeks of full pay, and after that, they get ninety-nine pound a week."

"Ninety-nine quid?" spluttered Jackie. "A week?"

"Yeah," I said, delighted. "And the best part is, if there's an injury that'll keep a player out for four months, we can bin them off."

"Bin them off? For getting injured!"

"Yeah," I said, rubbing my hands. "These fucks think they can defy me. Think they've got the power because they've got a *contract*. But now when they get injured, I can chuck them out the door before the X-rays have finished developing!" I laughed, long and hard.

Jackie was getting steamed up by my attitude. "I'm pretty surprised, Best. I expected better from you. What you're telling me is horrible. We're athletes, not cattle. You should understand that." He looked down at his shitty knees. "This could happen to you."

I laughed and pranced around the room. "Don't you get it? I've given you a taste of what I gave them."

Jackie thought that through. "Oh," he said. Calm again, he pitched his chin up. "*Fuck me.* You went full Max on them, didn't you?"

"Oh, mate. I wish you'd seen it. But you'd have stopped me before I got thirty seconds in. I made sure to get rid of everyone. MD, Vimsy, Dean. Kicked them all out. It was just me and the players. I let rip. Said a lot of stuff I've been wanting to say for weeks. I called them worms. I called them brainless morons. I blasted D-Day for his soft penalty. I laid into Aff for getting himself injured. I savaged Trick and Sam for openly mocking me and my attempt to change the culture. I fucking let them have it for, like, three minutes. Three beautiful minutes."

"That's why you're so relaxed today. You've been all, kinda . . . calm. Less manic."

"It was fucking therapeutic. I'd printed out the email, and I laughed in their faces. 'You fucks are fucking fucked,' I told them. 'All these agents sniffing around because they've heard this is Snowflake FC and you want out. Promising to get you moves to proper clubs where you can do your racist, sexist jokes all day. Well good fucking luck, mate.'"

"Wait. Agents sniffing around?"

"Yeah, like vultures. A couple that absolutely hate me. For them, taking one of our players isn't just another new client; it's another poke in the eye for me. Yeah, so, I laughed at the lads. 'You go to some other club, everything's top for a while, you're well rid of that Chester mess, oops, you're injured, fuck you very much here's ninety-nine quid a week.' I really hammered that; it's such a cartoon villain amount of money. I might have focused on Aff more than is justifiable. We should get together with him and have a chat. I do like him."

"Maybe not," said Jackie, calculating. "He was on it in training."

"Keep an eye on him. He's just the highest-profile idiot out of twenty idiots. So I ranted about injuries for a bit, then I turned to culture. I said that all I'd asked was that they treat the club like a normal workplace, stop fucking bullying people, make it a place where anyone of any creed or colour could flourish, and they'd spit in my face. They said they weren't willing to change, that they had the right to bully talented players out of the club, to laugh at disabled kids, to make crude comments about the women, and so on and so on."

"Were they doing all of that?"

"All that and more. The scum. And I told them, in case they missed it, that the people who run this sport just gave them less rights than a checkout girl. That this paper put full power over their careers in *my* hands. And they'd spent the last two months flipping me the middle finger every time they saw me."

"Let me guess, you gave them all the middle finger."

"Some Vs as well. Quite a lot of laughing. From me. Stony, horrified silence from them. And then I put the email away and switched to my low, dream-like voice."

Jackie nodded. "I would have stopped you long before you got to this part. I should have known. This is your MO. The switcheroo."

"I said there was probably only one director of football in the world who'd played professional football in the last year, definitely only one who'd actually had medical treatment at Chester. I said I knew the risks they took when they stepped onto the pitch. Pointed out that I'd tried to make the medical room a nicer place to be, and even *that* was something they'd pushed back on."

"How?"

"Making fun of Dean for buying the diffuser. He has it turned off all the time."

"It's on again."

"Huh. Good. Anyway, that's just a kind of symbol of how no one gives a shit about this except me."

"I'm sorry, Max."

"What for?"

"I should have been pushing with you. You're right about it."

"Shut the fuck up, please, I'm telling a story. So I'm a DoF who gets it, and their manager is a guy whose career was ended by injury. If there are two people in the world less likely to bin a player off for being injured, please let me know who. Kind of left a pause so they could digest that. Would I use this to get rid of a player telling racist jokes? Of course I fucking would. Would I use this against a good guy, a guy who welcomes new players, takes time to do selfies with the fans, a guy who understands what being a community club means? Of course not. I said, 'So you can fuck off to Wild West FC if you want, but you'll regret it. There's one job left in England where people will take care of you, treat you like an actual human being, and you've *got* that job. If you don't want it, thousands will.' Then for some reason I was looking for Youngster, but he was at school. I went Biblical anyway. I held up the printout again, said, 'You feel that in the air, boys? There's a flood coming. And Chester Football Club is the motherfucking ark.' Then I ripped up the paper and walked out. Boom."

Jackie was smiling. Proper, full-mouth smile. No hesitation, no reservation, no dark shadows at the corners.

The doctor's office door swung open. An old woman went first and held open the door while an old geezer swung himself forward on crutches. He looked like he'd been crying, the poor old sod. I hoped my knees were still healthy when I was sixty-four.

"Jackie, do you want to begin?"

"Max?" Jackie said. The smile was gone. "You can come in if you want."

My eyebrows shot up. "No way. I'm in Liverpool. There's so much to see and do!" I said it with a laugh. I think under any other circumstances, Sanj would have flicked me some Vs. "Text me when you're done. I won't go far."

The door closed behind them, and before heading out into the terrifying world of Liverpool, I opened the squad screen again and checked some profiles.

There were a lot of green CA numbers. That was important in the short-term. But the most staggering thing was found on the profiles of Trick Williams, Sam Topps, James Wise, D-Day, and Aff. At various stages of delay since my rant, they'd all done something no professional footballer had done in the time since I'd started seeing player profiles. They'd all added one point in teamwork.

I met Jackie ninety minutes later. "What did you do?" I laughed. "Watch a football match together?"

Jackie was subdued. Sanj had given him crutches. "I'm going to stay here overnight. With me ma and da. Get some scans in the morning." He winced. "Oh, *training.*"

"I'll take care of it," I said, smiling.

"What are you plotting?"

"Maybe we'll give the lads a refresher in four-two-four," I said. Jackie looked away, but nodded once. "And," I suggested, "a bit of four-one-four-one." That was, in my opinion, one of the best formations for our group of players, even if it lacked a certain verve. It was also the next formation I could buy, priced at a meaty 2,000 XP.

"You like your DMs," said Jackie.

"Yup." Seeing his proud, worried little face made me realise football wasn't that important. "Or Vimsy can do it. I'll get Terry or Spectrum to help out. I'll come back up here and drive you around. Yeah?"

"Thanks, Max. But, er . . . I'll have to tell Livia. She'll, you know . . . Unless she, you know . . ."

I put my knuckles to my eyes and spoke in a mock-crying voice. "Oh no, my girlfriend left me because of my psychosomatic pain what I got coz I wouldn't talk to my friend Max waaah." Jackie stuck the tip of his tongue out of the side of his mouth. Trying to enjoy the teasing, since the alternative was attempting to murder me. I dropped the voice. "Are you good for a tiny potter? I want to show you something."

"*You're* going to show *me* something in *Liverpool?*"

"Come on. There's a good Jackie. Try to keep up. Come on! Good boy!"

We walked a couple of minutes and turned onto a busy high street. Pretty normal sights in England: far too many cars, far too much brick, concrete, and asphalt. Really noisy. You could taste the car fumes. If you wanted to design a space where it'd be hard for life to flourish, you could do worse.

I was beaming.

When I got to our destination, I couldn't believe my luck. Two young women approached. Black hair, big fake eyelashes (I guess), a bit too much fake tan, but very cute. Very, very cute. "I'm just going to see if I've still got it," I said.

Jackie rolled his eyes. "I don't want to see you flirt, Max. It's aggravating."

"Hey, gorgeouses," I said as the women neared. They slowed but didn't stop. They were probably alarmed by Jackie's bald head. Perhaps it was an unexploded bomb from World War II? "My friend here's from the area. He tells me Liverpool girls give good headshots." The fractional pause I included in the last word made them stop.

The taller one eyed me with interest. Then it clicked. "You want a photo, yeah?"

"Yes, please," I said, getting my phone ready.

Jackie turned around and saw which landmark we were standing in front of. "Max! I thought you hated The Beatles."

The Beatles were a massive, worldwide sensation. In a few years, they not only changed music, they changed the way people *think* about music. They weren't born into wealth, didn't go to a posh school, didn't learn Latin. In another life, they'd have all worked in call centres. "I love them, mate. They prove that talent can come from anywhere. Even Liverpool." I set my jaw. "Even Manchester. Bunch of random lads, combining their talents, bit of teamwork, made the world a better place. I love it. I just hate the way you never shut up about them." To the women, I added, "He talks about them eight days a week."

"I don't," said Jackie, defending himself to the shorter woman with a cheeky smile. She smiled back at him. That interested me. Jackie was, subconsciously or not, being my wingman.

"Put the crutches away for a second. Jesus Christ. We get one shot at this. I'm not coming back."

While Jackie hobbled away and rested the sticks against a bare patch of wall, I whispered to the tall woman.

Jackie and I got into position. I gave him a sharp glance. "No, I don't want to hold your hand."

He gave me a crazy look in return. Realisation dawned. "Are you doing Beatles puns? Don't do that. Please, anything but that."

We stood with our arms around each other's shoulders in front of the street sign. I smiled. The photographer said, "Three, two, one, say *chicken*."

A few seconds later, we gathered round my phone to admire our work.

The photo was incredible. Jackie and I are both laughing, full blast, happy as clams, having the time of our lives in front of a street sign: Penny Lane.

"I'm going to blow this up, put it on your office wall," I said.

The taller woman—my one—said, "Where do you work?"

"Jackie's the manager of a football club," I said. "Local boy made good."

"Oh, really?" said the shorter one, increasingly interested in her man.

"Yeah, we're just off to sign a player," I said.

"Oh, cool. And what are you doing tonight?"

It was on! "I don't know. Jackie? What are we doing tonight?"

His eyes twinkled, just for a second, but then he remembered who he was. "I have to rest. Might need a bit of surgery soon."

I watched him gather his crutches, then had one last quick eye bang with my Lady Madonna. "Okay. So I guess we're done here. Thanks for your help, ladies. It's a fucking good photo."

"What about you?"

"I have to rest, too. I'm his surgeon." I treated them to my cutest face, ending with a smiling double-blink. Blinkle-and-twinkle. They walked on reluctantly. "Jackie, you dog," I complained. "How could you?"

He exhaled. "Back to the car."

"Nope. This way."

A slightly longer walk took us to a series of fields with a long, low building to the side.

"Sporting Club Merseyside," I said. "Ever heard of them?"

"Don't think so. What is it?"

"Like, a standalone youth academy. Doesn't seem to be attached to a club. I had a chat with some of the coaches. It seems pretty top.

Serious, but fun. They've got more coaching badges here than at Chester! More age groups, too, and knowledge flows down like a waterfall. They've got teenage players working with under-sevens and whatnot. I love it. We could do a lot worse than to replicate this. Hang on, I'm getting a call. It's the coach I hired for Broughton. Hey Jude. Oh, he hung up. Must have butt-dialled. Okay, be nice to this guy. Here comes the son's dad." We walked towards one of the dads who was watching loads of nine-year-olds run around doing skill-focused mini-games. "Mr. Watson, this is Jackie Reaper."

"Oh, this is real, then?"

Jackie smiled as they shook hands. "I don't know what it is, but it's real."

"Hey, this'll be fun," I said. "Mr. Watson, don't say anything. Jackie. Which of these kids is a future star?"

I thought Jackie was about to cry off, but curiosity won out. He decided to play along. He pushed himself a bit closer to the pitch. We watched for a couple of minutes. Finally, he said, "They're all good on the ball. They love passing it around. I see why you were drawn here, Max. It's your kind of football, all right. If I had to guess, right now, I'd say . . . that one."

He pointed to a PA 35 midfielder. Pretty good guess. "Oh, he's mint, all right. But we're looking for a ball-playing DM. Great positioning, lovely technique. Sort of like Rodri at Man City."

Jackie gave me a sceptical look. Scratched his eyebrows. Fell into a blank silence. Then there was this burst of electricity that hit his face. He lit up. "There!"

He was pointing to Steven Watson, a nine-year-old DM, positioning 6 (great for his age, it seemed), technique 6, PA 146.

"Steven," I said. "Named after his dad's favourite director."

The dad laughed. He was a very average English guy. Shirt under a jumper. Probably had some mid-level job. Doted on his son, knew he was special, worried about fucking things up. "Named after Steven Gerrard." The famous Liverpool player. Poor kid.

Three men watched little Stevie W jog around, controlling passes, laying the ball off with crisp, one-touch redirections. A couple of times, an opponent pressured him, and he'd either turn in a semicircle and brush off the challenge or flick the ball away the way I'd taught Dani. But this kid was doing it with his back to his opponent and was flicking it *diagonally* behind him and running onto it—fifty times harder.

"Oh, he's boss on the half-turn," said Jackie. "He's gonna be tall, inne? But he's balanced. He's nimble. His hand-eye coordination must be mad."

I sighed happily. "Mr. Watson. We're obsessed. We're going to spend the next ten years trying to sign Steven before someone else does."

"I looked you up when you were gone. You're not having the best season."

I shrugged. "If it was easy, it wouldn't be fun. It's good, this place. I love it. But players need hard matches to help them grow. And there's two reasons to come to Chester. Two things we've got you won't get anywhere else. Not Liverpool, not Everton."

"Go on."

"One. A director of football who's also the best player in the league. Who knows the names, strengths, weaknesses, of every single player at the club. Right down to the little guys."

"That's you, is it?" said the dad.

"Yep! I also take them on tournaments sometimes. What I'm saying is, I'm involved. Your lad isn't just a name on a list somewhere."

"And what's the other thing?"

"He's right here. Jackie Reaper." I gave Chester FC's manager a little push. "Go on. Tell us about yourself."

Jackie was perfectly comfortable listening to me boast, but didn't have much practice of doing it for himself. He normally communicated his virtues with a well-timed smirk. "Oh," he said. We waited for him to think of some nice things to say about himself. "I'm . . ."

"Youngest," I mumbled.

"I'm the youngest manager in the top seven divisions."

"That's right," I said, helpfully. "I read that."

Jackie rolled his eyes and the dad laughed. "Yeah, look. I played twice for Everton. I had a decent career, then my knees blew out. I've been coaching ever since, and now it's me first manager job." He paused.

"Tell him about your fit girlfriend," I suggested.

More laughs. "No, really," said Jackie. "I know a thing or two about dis game. I know a good setup when I see one, and your son is in good hands here. But what Max is doing with our youth teams, it's incredible. There's nowhere in the world like it. It's the place to be, I promise you that."

"Sounds like . . . something. What is it, exactly?" asked the dad.

Jackie indicated that I should take over, but I shook my head. It had to come from him. "What do you think, Max? The whole truth?"

"I'm game," I said.

Jackie turned away from the dad, slightly, to face me more. It was odd. Some unspoken understanding made us talk to each other, even though we were supposed to be selling the club to this talented player's dad. "Max's first day with the under-fourteens, he doesn't like what he sees. Four boys with bad attitudes, off you pop, we'll play with seven."

"Eight," I said. "We had a sub."

"Eight! Makes a big fuss. He was only supposed to be standing there, looking pretty, but he can't let it slide. Next he's banning parents from coming."

"All of them?"

"No, just the troublemakers. The loudmouths."

"Finally!" said the dad, regarding me with new warmth.

"But it's the football, though. Those same under-fourteens go toe-to-toe with anyone they come up against. They beat Wolves. Can you believe it?"

"I didn't do it on my own. I had a little help from my friends."

"What's the formation?" said the dad. "What's the, you know, philosophy?"

Jackie looked down. Frowned. "Flexible. Customised for every match. But . . . attacking. Entertaining. Sometimes it looks reckless but it's not. Brave, yeah, but not stupid. He'll defend sometimes. Bit of the dark arts, where needed." Jackie groaned. "God. It's a complete football education."

The dad tilted his head. "You sound annoyed."

"Yeah. He's a gobby Manc twat. He's just a kid. He shouldn't be this good."

"Mr. Watson," I said, finally turning to give him my undivided attention. "The women's team are playing Wrexham tomorrow night. It's our first go in the stadium. Big night for us. It's a brand-new team, I can't make any promises about the quality of football you'll see, but you'll get an idea of the kind of football we want to play."

"Or," said Jackie, standing to his full height. "You can come and watch the first team on Saturday. Max is going to be my assistant manager for the day." I nearly broke my neck, I twisted so fast. "Because of my knee," Jackie explained. I liked that. Good excuse for why I'd be there in a way that didn't make it seem like I was looming over him.

The dad nodded a few times. He mostly liked what he'd heard about me, but he really, really liked Jackie. "I think I can do Saturday. Who are you playing?"

I went next to Jackie and put my hand on his back. I stared at him. "It doesn't matter. We're going to go at them. Twenty shots."

Jackie smiled. "Twenty-five."

My blood started pumping so fast I swear I heard it swish. After taking a second to compose myself, I turned to the dad. "Are you a betting man?"

"What? Oh, sometimes. Grand National. Liverpool in the Champions League final. That kind of thing."

"Put twenty quid on Chester to stay up. You'll get decent odds."

He grinned. "Is that a hot tip? I love it."

I thought through the first team's fixtures. "You know what? Put another twenty on Chester to win seven games in a row."

"Seven in a row, Max?" said Jackie. "How are we gonna do *dat*?"

I showed him all my teeth and twinkled. "We can work it out."

8

LET THE DEVIL WEAR BLACK

Friday, March 17. Chester Women versus Wrexham A.F.C. Women.

"Who's there?"

"It's superstar football star Max Best. You're in my toilet."

"Oh." A surprised "oh." She hadn't been expecting that. "One minute!"

I pottered down the corridor a polite distance. Fifty-nine seconds later, Wrexham's manager emerged. She was called Eve and had black hair falling past her shoulders, hazel eyes, and eyebrows that swept up and down at the end, like hockey sticks. All in all, pretty fit. "I'm sorry!" she said, tucking some hair behind one ear.

"Don't be. You're welcome to use it. While you're here, though, can we talk about your team? Your lineup."

"Oh." Surprised again, now with a hint of defensiveness. "Maybe?"

I smiled. "You're not in trouble," I said, pretending to be her teacher.

She laughed at the absurdity of my tone. "Okay, go on. What's on your mind?"

"You've got a really strong lineup, there. Too strong for us. Normally, I'd take my beating and move on, but there's loads of fans who've paid to see this. I'd prefer to give them a bit more of a contest." I scratched my jaw. "I suppose I'm thinking long-term. You thrashing us eight–nil in our first match in the stadium isn't going to do women's football in the area much good."

"Won't help your career much, either," she said, challenging me.

"My career's going great," I said, smugging so hard I nearly tweaked a muscle around my lips. "I can take it. My players can take it. I didn't want this match to be here; it's way too early for that sort of thing. But it's marketing, isn't it? And I get it. Sometimes you need to, like, be realistic. Based on all this," I said, swirling a finger around to indicate the stadium, the spectators, the palpable buzz of anticipation, "a close game would be better. If it's three–all going into the last ten minutes, that's a good night out for everyone no matter the final score."

A tiny smile played around the edges of her lips. "I can't tell what's going on here. I feel like I'm being taken for a ride."

"Can you keep a secret?"

"I can keep *my* secrets. Not sure about *yours*."

"I'm going to be assistant manager for the men's team tomorrow. I don't need this." *This* meant women's football. I sighed. "Did you hear the atmosphere out there? People are excited. Intrigued. I'd love to give them an entertaining match. Do you know what I mean? God knows there hasn't been much of that recently."

Eve had a think about it. "You want me to, what, weaken my team?"

"Yes, please."

"I don't know."

"Show me your team sheet and I'll tell you my proposal."

"I already handed it in."

"To the referee's room, then!" I said, holding out my arm like a gentleman. She was tempted, but with a slight arching of one eyebrow, pushed it back towards my torso and fell into step beside me.

The ref wasn't pleased to see us. She was dressed in the traditional referee garb of black shirt, black shorts, black socks, black heart, and had a rectangular face surrounded by frazzled, tinted blonde hair. It was a quality haircut, actually, but still didn't look good on her. It was something about the way it clashed with the lines around her nose and mouth. Too much time spent scowling. Her assistants were younger and had softer faces. They smiled when Eve said she wanted to maybe possibly change her starting eleven.

The negotiations were quick.

"You're going to do four-three-three," I said, which got another arched eyebrow. How had I worked *that* out? "Do you know you've got someone in your squad who'd be a killer DM? I'll tell you who after the match. You could put out an amazing four-one-three-two."

I twinkle-blinked at her. "Which I wouldn't want to play against, but since we're never going to be in the same competition— Isn't it crazy that Wrexham's men's team play in England, and the women in Wales? It's a messed-up sport sometimes." I mentioned six players. "Those six are different gravy. If you'd be willing to start with three, and replace them with the other three, I think we'd just about be able to stay in the game."

"They aren't like-for-like subs."

"No, but, for example . . ."

I went through various scenarios and options that Eve would have, scribbling formations and branching plan Bs and Cs. I got a bit carried away, such that the assistant referees came over to watch. The head ref didn't like that. She told us to finalise the team sheet and leave.

I grabbed a blank form and filled it in with a starting lineup that would have an average CA of about 17. My strongest team was only 7, but our 4–5–1 formation would let us disrupt midfield and be pretty obdurate. There was still a hint of goal threat with Dani breaking from midfield. She'd kicked on since I'd asked Maddy to join us and was now one of four players on CA 9.

Eve studied the form I'd filled in for her. "Am I going to regret this?"

"If we played ten times, you'd win five. Maybe six. We'd win one. You're giving us a sporting chance. But what you lose in, like, the percentage chance of winning, we all gain in atmosphere and excitement. Anyone who understands sport will think the world of you."

She made a decision and crumpled up the old team sheet. She signed the new one.

"There's one born every minute," said the referee, meaning she thought Eve was a gullible fool.

I frowned. Even if you thought that, it was pretty obnoxious to say it out loud. The timing for what I had to say next was awful, but I tried to keep a cheery look on my face. "On the topic of empathy," I said, which caused one of the assistant refs to cover her mouth and turn away. "We have a deaf player. She can't hear the whistle, but she's good as gold. Won't give you any trouble. I'll point her out to you before kick-off."

"Don't bother," said the ref, doing something on her phone. "Everyone gets treated equal on my pitch. Other sports have rules." She got to her feet and took a step towards me. "Football has *laws*. And I enforce the laws equally and without discrimination."

"Like Judge Dredd," I said, causing a new wave of secret mirth.

The ref didn't flinch. "Exactly like Judge Dredd."

I smiled at her. "Great! I love judges. My wife's one."

Out in the corridor, Eve and I walked a safe distance away, then fell into each other, giggling.

Ruth had laid on a big buffet with free drinks in the Blues Bar. The only thing I really wanted, though, was a chai tea latte, and that wasn't free. I tapped my pockets—I'd left my wallet in the dressing room. I spotted a few lads from the first team.

"Glenn," I said. "Lend us a fiver."

"Neither a borrower nor a lender be," he said, and there was a little pause where I wondered if I should remind him I controlled his contract. But then he laughed. "My niece is doing *Hamlet*. Apparently the guy who said that is an idiot and we're not supposed to think it's good advice." He took out his wallet and pulled out five pounds.

"Sorted," I said, which is sometimes Manc for "thanks."

I closed my eyes while I waited for my drink. Had I done everything I could for the team? For the event? I thought so. My players were sick with anticipation and big-match anxiety; the only cure was kickoff. Kickoff! When the curtain was raised and all eyes turned to the stage. The play, and the play within the play. Me, at the side, conjuring up new twists and turns in the story. I was Shakespeare with a better haircut. It'd be a fine old performance, all right.

I floated around the room, weightless, not a care in the world, laughing and joking with fans and people I knew. It was expected and understood that I'd say a few things and move on to the next group, so it wasn't too draining.

There were a bunch of Chester Knights. *Here* a batch of under-fourteens. *There*, Pascal and the Yalleys plus a few Man City toddlers! Meghan was curiously quiet, staring at James. Lovesick!

The crowd parted and there was Emma, dressed up, backlit by the stadium's hardworking floodlights. Our last date was when we'd spent a steamy, sorry, *romantic* night in a spa hotel. A lot had happened since then, and there was only one way to communicate how seeing her felt.

I didn't hesitate. Decision time: nought point nought nought seconds, rounded down.

I strode towards her, put my hand behind her waist, dipped her, and went full smooch. I brought her back up, slowly, and stared into her eyes. Fireworks! Trumpets! Cymbals!

"Ahem," said someone. I didn't want to tear myself away from Emma, but there was something in the voice that was familiar. I hadn't heard it in ages, though. I turned. Gemma. Emma's best friend and sometime Henri squeeze. "Hi, Max."

"No cheek kisses this time?" I said.

"No." And that was that. She might as well have said, "Henri and I are finished. Like, proper finished."

"Well, it's nice to see you. I love that dress." She was in a patterned thing with buttons down the middle, and a tight denim jacket over the top. If she was here to pick up a replacement footballer, she was off to a good start.

She smiled. "And I love your, er, hoodie. Is it from C and A?"

"Even cheaper."

"Hmm," she said. She reached out to test the fabric. "Something is rotten in the state of Primark," she said.

"Gems," complained Ems.

"But what's the point of having a fit boyfriend if you can't dress him up?" She looked me up and down again and sighed. "It's a good job you're cute, Max. You almost get away with it."

"There's Max!" said a new voice. Ruth, coming at me from the side, with Dahveed in tow. He was wearing an amazing suit that was obscenely tight around his biceps. She was wearing something classy that was obscenely tight in disappointingly few places. She pulled a face. "Oh, and there's Max's hoodie."

Gemma gasped. "See? We all think it!"

Ruth hadn't met Gemma, but they were instant friends. "Big night like this, you'd think he'd make an effort. But no."

"I think you look splendid," said Dahveed gallantly.

I didn't reply. I'd just seen someone I hadn't expected to see. "Wh-hhhhat?" I said, drifting away from the fashion discussion and towards everyone's favourite authoritarian stooge. "Beth. You're here." I leaned closer. She'd done something to her eyebrows, but I couldn't tell what. They seemed . . . nicer.

Beth frowned and leaned away from me until I stopped peering. "Yes, Max, I'm here. The first big match of your women's football project. Could be a good story." She must have heard it was Fashion Week at the Deva, because her outfit had levelled up, too. A plain black top, slightly sparkly, under a black designer jacket. She could do an interview then go to a bar and flirt with men who reminded her of me. She did her best to ruin my entire mood. "Is Dani playing tonight?" I stared at her so murderously she did something she rarely ever did: She backed down. "Topic still off limits. Gotcha. Got any juicy quotes for me?"

"Yeah. Don't buy the *Daily Mail*." Beth's article about me had got some traction and she'd somehow turned that into an actual job at the epicentre of British hate. I'd seen her byline on a couple of articles that I'd been forced to read because of my role as director of football.

"Come on. Let's play nice. Hey, have you seen Ziggy?"

"No."

"He's here. Reminded me of the old days. Do you remember the old days, Max? Me, you, Ziggy, Jackie? We're all moving up in the world."

"One of us is moving down. Getting nice and cosy in the gutter."

"What formation are you going to play?"

"Four-five-one don't buy the *Mail*."

"What do you think of Wrexham's team?"

"Really good don't buy the *Mail*. Look out for their pacey fullbacks don't buy the *Mail*."

"The old gang back together!" This was Ziggy. I hadn't seen him for ages. He handed Beth a beer and had a bottle of water for himself. Quite right, too. He was getting regular game time now, coming on at the ends of matches as FC United pushed for an automatic promotion slot. I wondered what his CA was. Maybe 30? His progress would slow down now that Jackie had left.

I nodded towards Beth. "Watch yourself, Ziggy. Say something she doesn't like, she'll put you on a plane to Rwanda and lock you up."

"What?" he said, laughing. He followed the news even less than me and didn't know what I was talking about. "She's at the *Daily Mail*, Max. Isn't that great? They've got all the best sports writers. Beth's, like, a top reporter now. Gone straight to the top team! It's like being scouted by Man City."

"The ultimate accolade in football," I announced, pompously, "is being scouted by Chester Football Club."

Ziggy's laugh burst through his cheeks and vibrated his lips comically. "Right, Max. If you say so." He turned to Beth. "Are they going to start you on women's football? It's dead big now, innit? I've got to say, I'm looking forward to this tonight. It's a while since I—" He stopped, reacting to my reaction. I'd just seen yet another unexpected face. "Hey, are you all right? You look like . . ." He didn't finish the sentence. Nobody actually said the "you've seen a ghost" line in real life, surely?

"Excuse me," I said, well aware that I probably *had* turned pale enough for him to worry. My heart was suddenly pounding and my feeling of lightness was gone. Old Nick! Like Beth, he was wearing head-to-toe black. He'd drifted between some people—more precisely, they'd moved away to let him pass in a straight line—before going through an exit.

I paced towards the door and stepped through. He wasn't there, of course. Had I imagined it? He'd seemed so real. But someone else was there, someone I was much happier to see.

"Bonnie," I said. The tough defender with high leadership I'd been trying to track down for a while. Joe had finally got hold of her, but she'd flat-out rejected the chance to train with us. "Did you see a good-looking older dude come past?"

"Yeah. He smiled at me."

"One can smile and be a villain," I said.

"You're Cliff Daps," she said.

"Yeah."

"AKA Max Best."

I was quite calm again. Back to normal. Pulse steady. "And you're Bonnie and you don't want to play for my team."

Loads of muscles around her eyebrows twitched, but I couldn't tell what expression they were trying to form. "No."

I took a spot facing her and leaned back against the wall. The music from the Blues Bar gently pulsated through me. She was a mystery, this woman. She loved football; she went to Footy Addicts games. And while she'd said she didn't want to play for Chester, she was here tonight. The first serious game we'd played. Last time I'd followed Old Nick, I'd found James and Kisi. I already knew Bonnie's ability, but being led to her by Ghost Nick was a big hint that she was worth pursuing. Was I supposed to chase her like I'd done with James and Dani? I didn't have time, really, and if she wouldn't open up, I couldn't know what was holding her back.

I tugged on the strings of my hoodie. "I'm supposed to give you a big speech now, but kickoff's soon and they say brevity is the soul of wit. Here's my pitch: You're a great defender. You've got top leadership. The way you manage hotheads in the Footy Addicts games is unreal. The team really needs someone like you, but I'm not going to push it. If you need some time to think about it, take the whole summer. That said, it'll be a tough match tonight. A lot of the women are feeling the pressure. If I had Man City money, I'd pay you five hundred quid to go in there and keep their spirits up. If you want to hang out in the dressing room and get a feel for the vibe, we can do that. You can sit in the dugout, too."

"That wouldn't feel right. Dressing room's for the team."

I mused. Wiggled my nail between two teeth for a while. Bonnie wasn't going to happen. Not tonight, anyway. "All right," I said, pushing myself off the wall and clapping my hands. "But, look. Come inside, get some food and that. I'll introduce you to some cool people. I can't promise they won't talk a lot of shit, but I like them anyway. What do you think?"

The word *no* started in her gut, made its way up through her throat, but didn't come out. She swallowed it back down. "Okay," she said.

I held the door open for her, followed her in a couple of yards, and paused. Who'd be fun for Bonnie to hang out with? Beth and Ziggy? Ems and Gems? Maybe the first-team lads. They'd brought their wives and girlfriends. Would Bonnie like talking to a WAG? I really knew almost nothing about her. There was one safe answer: Beth. She was the ultimate chameleon, and she'd wonder what I was up to and would play along. Yeah, Beth.

"This way," I said, stepping forward. We didn't get far, though, before Ruth slammed into the side of me like a soft, attractive missile. "Max. Oh, Max, I'm sorry."

"What? Are you all right?"

Ruth was looking flustered in a way I'd never seen her before. She was almost always the acme of cool, calm, and collected. She projected the image of being one step ahead. "The league. The people from the FA who will decide what league you're going in. They're here."

I didn't see the problem. "Okay?"

She shook her head with frustration. "They're going to base their decision on tonight."

"No," I said. "We've got three more games, then the PitchWreck Cup." That was a special event I'd planned to cap the season. A double-header against a team from Man City (probably their under-eighteens) and the most famous women's team, the Doncaster Belles. Three matches and a final, and it wouldn't matter if we ruined the pitch, because it would be the very last day of the season. And, because I'm a genius, I was pretty sure I'd be able to use Bench Boost and Triple Captain in one of those games, since it wasn't a basic friendly. It was its own tournament. Loophole! I'd even bought a little trophy for the winner. It was a football with a sort of prince's crown. Top!

"Max. Listen to me. They're here. This is it. Win tonight and we'll go into a good league. Lose and we'll start from the bottom. Do you understand, Max? Max!"

I snapped out of it. A cold sweat broke out all over my back. "Ruth," I said. "We're not ready for this. This isn't the right time."

She took in a slow breath, then pushed it out quickly. "It's my fault, Max. I did this. They're here because we're in the stadium. Because we promoted it. We should have followed your plan. I got too excited." She exhaled again. "I'm sorry."

I'll admit, I seethed for a half a second or so, but genuinely only that long and no more. "Hey, without you, we wouldn't be here. We'll cope either way. But you owe me a Get Out of Jail Free card."

"What do you mean?"

"Next time I piss you off, remember how quickly I forgave you."

"I don't know. You're a lot more annoying than me."

I went internal. What could I do differently? I had named our strongest lineup. I had handed in the team sheet so it wasn't like I could sneak Bonnie onto our bench. I would use Triple Captain, of course, but what about Bench Boost? The players who would come on during the match would be CA 1 randos. Getting a few percent more out of them would do almost nothing to impact the game. Could I change the lineup? The ref was already in a foul mood. Was it worth pushing her more?

I shook my head and hit Bench Boost anyway. There was no point saving it. To me, that was it. That was all I could do. I started to push thoughts of the FA assessors aside; dwelling on it was futile.

"Max," said a distant voice. I'd gone so far away, running through hundreds of calculations, plans, schemes, strategies, and when I blinked myself back into the Blues Bar, I realised I had been completely motionless for no small amount of time.

"Bonnie," I said. I'd forgotten she was there.

"Do you still want me to help? I'll help."

The smile that spread across my lips could not be contained. It was so rambunctious it leapt off my face right onto Bonnie's.

Ruth reached out to take my half-drunk chai latte, and I escorted Chester's best motivator down into the place she was most needed.

Along the way, I asked Bonnie not to mention the thing about this match deciding the team's starting point. "They're under enough pressure as it is. More motivation will tip them over into useless stress."

"Okay."

"So our vibe is relentless positivity. Focusing on their strengths, what they're doing well, all that sort of stuff. Good?"

"Good. But I don't know their strengths."

I grinned. "Ask them."

When we entered the dressing room, the chatter and half-hearted banter stopped. I could feel the worry. The air was heavy with it. Dread. Impending doom.

"All right, shut the fuck up," I said, into the silence. "This is Bonnie. I don't want to make a big deal out of her being here, but she's the fourth most inspirational person I've ever met."

"Who are the other three?"

"Marcus Rashford, Harry Styles, and Captain Sir Tom Moore. Now shush, I'm doing my team talk." I put my foot up on the edge of one of the benches and accessed my dreamy, introspective voice. "Ages ago," I said, but there came a series of loud slaps and thuds. It was the sound of Dani catching up to what I was saying on the group chat, and doing her now-famous clap-stomp-laugh. The rest of the team loved it; it was rare.

I paused a few extra seconds so she could reply.

"Dani says you never met Harry Styles," said Robyn, who was on text duty.

"Tell her that I didn't say anything back to that."

Robyn frowned. "That's very confusing." But her thumbs were going a mile a minute.

I rubbed my forehead in mock exasperation. All this silliness, of course, was intentional. I made eye contact with a sweep of players. "As you know, my favourite movie is *Predator*."

There were a few groans. "Last week you said it was *Back to the Future*. Before that, it was *Casablanca*."

"I *watched Casablanca*," said Erin, one of our centre backs. "I'm obsessed with Ingrid Bergman now, so thanks for that. Your Emma has a real Bergman quality. No wonder you like her."

"I like Emma because she's a goddess and because when I sleep with her I'm not sure if she's going to murder me overnight. Er, Robyn, don't put that last bit in the chat. Write 'I like Emma because she's kind and nice to everyone while working hard to achieve her personal goals through the wider, like, perspective of teamwork and self-sacrifice.'"

"I already wrote the murder thing."

"Her parents read that, you know. Can you filter out the weird stuff I say, please?" I sighed. "Okay. Wrexham are going to play four-three-three. They're good, but they've got some weaknesses. We've got Maddy on the right and Dani on the left, and with no wide midfielders helping Wrexham's fullbacks, I'm expecting a lot of one-on-ones. We'll see who's getting more joy and feed that side, yeah? If we keep pushing, I'm sure we can break something." I grinned, then got serious. "They've got good forwards, though, so we'll have to be on it for ninety minutes. Let the crowd feed you energy—that's what they're there for. Don't expect any relief when they make subs. I've seen their bench. There's no relief. You need to work hard. Talk to each other and all that. The ref is a *Daily Mail* reader, so you know what that means." I spotted Bonnie's confused look. Instead of going on a tedious, humourless rant, I gave her the five-word explanation: "It means she's a dick." I turned back to the players. "Don't talk to her. Control what you can. There's a big crowd, and that can work for us if we make it. Just remember what all this is about. In this world, it's just us."

Lucy roared. "Come on, girls!" and they all clapped and stomped their way out into the corridor, and onto the pitch, for the biggest game of their lives.

Bonnie held herself back so she could talk to me. "That was a pretty strange team talk."

"Though this be madness, there is method in it."

"What?"

"There's method to the madness."

"Oh." She looked around the empty room. "Distract them? Make them laugh? Forget how nervous they are? That sort of thing?"

"That sort of thing," I agreed. "But also, it's fun. They're working hard. Training, morning jogs, yoga, whatever they're doing. Unpaid, so far. Some of them might drop out, some might get, you know, upgraded out. So while they're here, they deserve to enjoy it." I bit my lip. "Not that I need much excuse to clown around."

I went to the door and held it open for her, then locked it behind me.

Kickoff was imminent.

The pitch was green and the stand was a sea of royal blue. We'd sold four hundred tickets, and it would have been double if the men's team hadn't decided to make half the city sick of the sport. We'd also given away a fair number to players, staff, sponsors, schoolkids, and so on. The curse would tell me at halftime, but I guessed there were a thousand spectators. Not bad!

While Jill led the players through a last warm-up, our head hospitality volunteer rushed over to me.

"Tiny problem, Max," she said. "We don't have an announcer and we don't know the teams. If you get the team sheets from the ref, I can read out the names."

"Nah," I said. "I'll do it. Where's the microphone?"

"Over here. But you don't have the sheets!"

I picked the mic up and thought about this pre-match ritual. Normally, stadium announcers read the names, leaving a space for the crowd to react. But today I could do whatever I wanted. And what I wanted was to add a little colour to the match. Virtually no one in the stadium knew anything about these players. I could tell them what to look out for. Some of the play within the play. Some of the Shakespeare bits.

I flicked the mic on. "Ladies and gentlemen, welcome to the Deva stadium. I am Max Best, yes, the guy who completed the periodic table. On behalf of Chester FC, I'd like to thank you all for coming." This got a round of applause for some reason. Crowds are weird. "Introducing your Chester team for the evening! In goal, we've got

Robyn. She's a chatterbox, really good shot stopper. Very good against penalties. Back four is Lucy, Erin, Mo, and Mel. Lucy's the captain. Look for her bombing forward the whole match; she's tireless. Watch out for Mo throwing herself in front of shots. She's absolutely crazy; you won't catch *me* doing that. Our formation today is top secret, but here's a clue: It's four-five-something. Across midfield we've got Dani, Gracie, Pippa, Susan, and Maddy. Watch out for Pippa's through balls and energy. The wide players will be a constant nuisance to Wrexham, and they'll be trying to link up with our striker, Bea Pea."

Bea Pea was the only player to react to my intro. She bowed to the main stand and blew kisses everywhere.

"And I doubt you're really interested in Wrexham," I said. That provoked a chorus of boos and jeers from one pocket of the main stand. I took a few steps back and shielded my eyes. "What's that? Wrexham fans?" A bunch of people in red tops cheered. I smiled. I hadn't expected that. "Wow! Thanks for coming. Wow, top. Okay. Hands up if you were in the documentary." It seemed like they all were. "Lots of celebrities in tonight! All right. Here's the team and what I've noticed." I ran through the Wrexham team, too, pointing out a few of their strengths. The Wrexham fans, maybe fifty strong, applauded my analysis.

"Game on!" I said, and the energy in the stadium increased.

I rubbed my hands together as I strode towards the dugout. This was going to be a load of fun.

The first five minutes were pretty cagey. Wrexham were quite a lot better than us, and they had a lot more experience playing in front of crowds. Still, they were careful. They wanted to see what we were made of before they did anything rash.

My lot were also cautious, but that was the nerves more than anything. Once everyone had a few touches of the ball under their belt, they started to relax and enjoy themselves.

The match hit its stride around the ten-minute mark. Wrexham would get the ball and pass it around before trying some set moves they had worked on. One was a long pass towards their quick forward players—that didn't work too well because we always had a lot of players in defensive positions. Another was for a central player to try to make something happen by dribbling wide. The dribbler was good, but again, we always had plenty of players on both sides of the pitch. Wrexham lacked a player who could "pick the lock," as the phrase goes—play a through ball that would cause panic in the defence. So we weren't comfortable, exactly, but I didn't think we'd get annihilated.

As for us, Dani and Maddy had a lot of joy when dribbling at their fullbacks, but we couldn't get numbers into the attacks. Bea Pea was isolated, and while Pippa could play the through balls that Wrexham couldn't, that's not what we needed in this match.

So it was kind of a fascinating stalemate that I found very enjoyable. There wasn't much for me to do, tactically, so I crouched down and stared at Wrexham's defenders, endlessly looping through their profiles, watching how they turned, looking for weaknesses, looking for some personality defect that could get us a goal.

One unexpected thing was that Dani was finding it hard to settle on the left side of the pitch. She'd been playing and training as a right mid or right winger. Now I was asking her to do exactly the same things, but on the left. She was two-footed. What's the problem? No problem, in my opinion! But she wouldn't use her left foot. She kept coming back towards the crowded middle of the pitch so she could use her right.

I had a long discussion with Jill about it. She hadn't noticed this tendency during training. Nobody had. Which meant either nobody had thought to look—understandable; not sure I'd have spotted it myself—or Dani didn't trust her left in a match.

We were getting into the weeds of how we'd address it, what we'd do short-term, medium-term fixes if the problem recurred, and so on and so forth, when the breakthrough happened.

Dani, again, tried to cut inside onto her right foot, but now her opponent was expecting it and stuck a toe out to poke the ball away. It fell to Gracie, who was enjoying her time playing more centrally. She touched it back to Lucy, who played a quick first-time pass to Pippa. That was one area where we were better than Wrexham. We moved the ball forward faster, based on my mania for what Spectrum called "verticality." Getting the ball forward fast meant it usually came back fast, too, putting more strain on our defence. But as we improved and brought in better players, verticality would pay off with rapid, slick moves that other teams wouldn't be able to defend against.

Dani loses the ball.

It breaks to Gracie. Nice layoff.

Lucy pings it to Pippa. She plays it forward to Bea Pea.

First-time control out to Maddy. She bursts past her man.

She's dashing to the byline.

Is there any support? It looks like she'll have to take a shot from a bad angle.

She passes square.

GOOOOAAAALLLL!!!!

Tucked into the open net by Dani!

Where did she come from?

Dani raced over to Maddy and they hugged and danced around. The crowd loved it. Big cheer, much applause.

But the best moment for me was when the women started walking back towards our half of the pitch. Dani looked over and saw all the people standing, applauding, and it hit her like a ton of bricks. I couldn't really see her face, so I'm only guessing, but I think she was telling herself, "Yes, this is for me, more please."

Bonnie took a few steps from the dugout towards me. "She's fast," she said.

"Surprisingly so, yeah," I said.

"Good late run into the box. Very one-footed, though."

I laughed. "No, she's very, very two-footed. I have no idea why she's playing like that. Dani," I called, then dropped my head as I realised how stupid that was. But Bea Pea heard, and made Dani look at me. I did the latest sign I'd learned. I held my left hand as though hiding my cards in a poker game. Then I put my right hand directly on top, and tapped it against the bottom one three times. Then I turned the top hand into a thumb and jabbed it upwards. *Done good job!*

"Are you learning sign language?" asked Bonnie.

"I'm learning one sign a week. The aim is to become fluent by the year 2250."

"I don't get you," she said.

"Yeah," I said, distantly. I was focused on the match ratings. "Listen. Mo, there. The centre back. She's struggling. She's been really solid for us so far. I'm asking a lot of the defence, asking them to win their duels and keep their shape, and it's hard against the three attackers with runners coming from midfield. Maybe it's just a bad day at the office, maybe it's the occasion. Can you try to help her?"

"How?"

"Watch her. Give her some tips at halftime that might buck her up. I don't know. I'd hate to have to sub her off."

"Because this match determines which league you go in?"

"Er . . ."

"You forgot, didn't you? How could you forget?"

I shook my head. "It doesn't matter right now, does it? It doesn't change what I do. I try to win every game. Playing four-five-one against a better team . . . it's pretty conventional. Even Captain Gammon would be happy with that. It's what a serious team does, yeah? If I'd been planning something mad like a false midfield, maybe the news would have changed that."

"False midfield?"

"Long story."

"I'll watch Mo."

Bonnie wandered off.

A couple of moves later, Wrexham went hard with a fast attack down the middle. The ball popped up and Mo decided to head it back to the goalkeeper. She got it all wrong, and Wrexham very nearly scored the easiest goal of all time. Fortunately, Lucy had sprinted back to cover and cleared the ball out for a corner.

Bonnie scampered towards me. "That was the midfield!"

"What?"

"The midfield let two players run past and didn't track them. Yeah, Mo's header was shit, but that's what happens when CMs don't track back."

I jumped into the tactics screen and made it so that Gracie, Pippa, and Susan, the three central midfielders, couldn't go forward. Maybe that'd make them more likely to do their defensive duties. Were they tiring already? For the hundredth time, I wished I had a fitness monitor. And again, I wished I had freer control over the formation. Dropping someone into the defensive midfielder slot would have solved a lot of problems.

"Four-one-four-one," I said.

"What?" said Bonnie.

"Jill," I said, turning round. My coach was leaning forward, trying and utterly failing to look calm and relaxed. She was far too competitive for that. I smiled. "Jill."

"Yes, Max?"

"We need to start practising four-one-four-one."

"Instead of what?"

"We never drop formations, Jill. We only add to what we know."

"That's unrealistic, Max."

"Nope. I want total tactical flexibility. I'd literally sell my soul for four-one-four-one right now." I said that with a cheeky grin, looking up at the stands to see if Old Nick heard it from wherever he was spying on me.

Behind me, the referee's whistle blew.

"Oh, no," said Jill.

I turned so fast I nearly lost balance (quite unusual in my new body) and I saw the end of the incident. The referee was walking towards Dani. I couldn't see the ball anywhere. The ref reached into her pocket, and the movement of the black sleeve made me remember some old line from a book or poem or something: *She whose sable arms, Black as her purpose, did the night resemble . . .*

On this black night, from her sable pocket, the referee produced a yellow card. Showed it to Dani. Dani looked up at it in disbelief. Then she looked down at her feet.

I shook myself out of some stupor, some spell that had been cast, and checked the match commentary.

Mo plays a loose pass. Erin gets her out of trouble.

But all she can do is kick it long.

Gracie challenges for the header and wins it. Good leap!

The ball breaks forward and Dani rushes onto it.

A very promising break! She has acres to run into!

But she was marginally offside.

And now she has taken a shot!

The referee isn't too happy with her.

Dani is booked for timewasting!

In the first half!

I couldn't believe it. Even the curse couldn't believe it! I stumbled onto the pitch like a wounded man. I felt a genuine ache in my side, a stab wound, perhaps, and gripped myself to stop the bleeding. I checked my hands—they didn't look like mine—but there was no red stain. My scalp was suddenly clammy with sweat, though it felt like blood. I trudged past a Wrexham player, past Pippa, who held her hands out as though she feared I would topple.

But by the time I got to Dani, the initial shock had worn off.

Leaving only sadness.

Dani and I exchanged a look. There was no disappointment in her face. She knew I'd tried my best. But she'd tried to tell me this would happen. My charisma, my manic energy, my relentless positivity and certainty that we could change the world . . . she'd wanted so much to believe.

I held out my hand; she took it.

We walked towards the dugout. I waved my finger around, and just in case anyone didn't get the message, I dragged all the icons off the tactics screen leaving an empty green pitch.

The ref stormed towards me. "What on earth are you doing? You can't come on the pitch. Where's your team off to, eh?"

I stopped walking, and Dani did, too. I turned to see some random woman in black, small, angry, and bitter. Reacting would only give her power. She thought she had some power of her own. But I had a greater one. "Get out of my stadium," I said.

As we got closer to the side of the pitch, more players came to join us. First Bea Pea, bitterly crying. Then Pippa, furious. Then Lucy, who took Dani's hand from mine. "Dressing room?"

"Yes, please."

I watched them go. This team I'd started. This wonderful collection of bone and sinew. What a piece of work it was. Smart, capable, brave, and when they all moved as one, they moved like angels. Never more so than now, as they came together, gathered in a united mass, turning their backs on injustice.

As I followed, people tried to ask me what had happened. What was going on? The hospitality woman blocked my path, shoved the microphone in my hand. I stared at it, blankly, then decided that, yes, these good people deserved to be kept in the loop. Some had come specifically to see Dani. Others would support anyone in a blue-and-white shirt. And even the Wrexham fans would seethe when they learned what had just transpired.

I turned the mic on. "There has been an incident," I said, and for some reason, that's when it all hit me. I felt my lip wobble. I bit it and summoned up a blob of cold fury. "Please give me a short time to . . ." I couldn't finish the thought. I handed the mic to someone and walked away in the wrong direction. Eve caught me and guided me towards the dressing rooms.

I needed a short time to what? To decide what to do next? There was nothing to do next. Chester Women were finished.

In the dressing room, a few women were clustered around Dani, who was hugging Bea Pea. Others were slumped on their parts of the bench, borrowed from the men's team. Pippa was in Henri's spot. Maddy was in Raffi's. It's weird what you think about.

"Max, what do we do?" said Lucy.

For once, I didn't have an answer. "I don't know." I sat down and put my head in my hands. We were all quiet for a minute. I reached for my phone.

Me: Dani, I'm sorry. You knew this would happen. I was arrogant to think I could do it any better than anyone else. I don't know what to say. I'm gutted.

The rest of the players checked their phones, but they all knew it had to be Dani next. Her reply came way quicker than I expected.

Dani: You didn't promise to change the world. You promised it would be a team. A real team, and I'd be in it. And that's what it is. I love it here. It's the best thing I ever did.

Jill: There are hundreds of people out there. What do we do? Is the match abandoned?

**Me: I told the referee to get lost. I hope we can all agree that
we will never play under her ever again.**

This message got multiple hearts and thumbs-ups instantly.

Lucy: What about the linos? One of them could be ref.

**Me: Anyone who trusts them to referee this game differently,
I have some magic beans I would like to sell you. Those three
are a crew. They travel together, do matches together. They're
all tainted.**

"Max," said Susan, startling me with unexpected noise. It was
quite peaceful, doing the text chats. "There are people who want to
come in."

"Who?"

"The hot blonde."

"That weirdly doesn't narrow it down as much as it used to. Go
on, then."

In came Ruth, Emma, MD, and Eve. MD spoke first. "Max, did
that ref book Dani for kicking the ball away? Is that what happened?"

"Yep."

The first three reacted as socially normal, empathetic people would
do. By getting furious. Eve was more puzzled than anything. "But you
told her the player was deaf."

Ruth gave her a savage look that meant *how can you be so naive?* But
she had enough about her to get practical. "We have to finish this match."

"No."

"Do not be a manchild about this, Max. There are many hundreds
of paying customers here. I am one hundred percent behind you on
this issue. You know I love Dani. We all do. We will kick up a stink,
get to the bottom of things, all that jazz. Tomorrow. Tonight we have
to finish this game."

"Why?"

She spluttered. "To fix our position in the league!"

"What?" said Jill, Lucy, and several others.

But Ruth was mid-flow. "To boost women's football. To promote
our team. To delight our fans. And to pay the bloody bills!"

Emma put a hand on Ruth's arm. "Max. If you don't finish the match, the ref has won."

"That," I said, shooting her with a finger gun, "is a very good point. Yeah. Okay. We'll finish the match. But there's no point worrying about the league and all that. There's no team. There can't be a team. Or you do it without me."

"Don't say anything rash," warned MD.

"I'm quite calm, MD. But think about it. If a player was shown a yellow card for being Black, we'd walk off the pitch. For being gay? We'd walk off the pitch. And I wouldn't go back on until the ref was locked up and the FA changed the laws so it could never happen again. That's how I feel about it. No Dani, no me. The rest of you can do what you want, I guess." Suddenly, I was so very, very tired.

"Maybe I can help," said someone who'd been using the newcomers as a shield. She popped out from the side and squeezed towards me. "Er, hi, everyone. I'm Bethany. I work for a big newspaper. On probation, anyway. I wrote the article about Max that some of you liked. Look. What's happened is awful. It's total garbage. But this woman is right—you can't let this referee win. I'll write it up. With your help, we can make this into a big deal. A really big deal. Back page spread, maybe. Four million daily readers and millions more online. People will talk about nothing else for days. Where *we* lead, others follow. *TalkSport*. Podcasts. YouTubers. '*Ref Books Girl for Being Deaf.*' There will be outrage."

"Hold on," I said. I spoke into my phone so Dani wouldn't be left out. "For context, Beth works for the newspaper that *made* the ref into what she is. The *Mail* can't go two days without stirring up hate against someone. Yeah, it's mostly foreigners, doesn't affect me. Right? Wrong. We had an Indonesian nurse at my mum's care home. She quit and went back home to her own country because she read the *Mail* and decided it wasn't safe for her here. My mum was devastated. She was a lovely woman; one of the best. And there's a foreign chap playing for Chester *right now* who was at Reading at the time of the Brexit vote. One of his neighbours pushed the *Mail*'s front page through his door with a handwritten note: 'Time to go.'" I paused. There were a lot of shocked faces. Henri didn't tell that story to a lot of people. "And don't think they're not after *you*, too. Beth's newspaper hates everyone in this room. It hates you for being women, it hates you for being gay, it hates you for being Brown, it hates you for being a single parent. If it doesn't hate you yet, it's working on it."

Emma sighed. "Max, you're being ridiculous. Loads of perfectly fine, perfectly normal people read the *Mail*. This woman is trying to help."

Beth came farther into the room. She—correctly—assumed she'd have to persuade *me* to give her access to Dani for the quotes and photos that would *really* make it a killer story. But she also knew how to press some of my buttons. "I obviously don't agree with anything Max is saying about my employer. My boss is a woman. More than half the staff are women. We don't hate women. I'm not going to say I like every story we run but overall we do a lot of good. No, Max, we do. If we had run a story about how the FA were stopping you from playing football this season, they'd have magically found the right forms ten minutes after the first papers had landed on the streets. No one wants to get on our bad side, not even the government. And check this out." She held up her phone. It was open to a *Mail Online* article.

I read out the headline. "'Tofu Eaters Must Be Shot.'"

She rolled her eyes and took her phone away. "It's a story about a ref who demanded a player remove his hearing aid, and the whole team walked off in protest. Just like you. And just like then, the *Mail* was on the right side of the debate. But this time, it'll be bigger. I hate to say this out loud, but you're not bad-looking, Max. People will click on the thumbnail. And Dani's the perfect girl next door. We will enrage people. Give me some quotes and we can make it so that no referee in the world would ever, ever dare to do this again."

The room stirred. That was very smart of Beth. Too smart.

"So we're going to savage a referee. Drag her over hot coals? Make her life shit? Have it so that even fewer people become referees? You know how I feel about that, Beth! Go through the footage of me playing. You'll find me being a dick. Taking the piss out of other players, winding the crowd up. But there isn't a single second of me yelling at the ref. Post-match interviews? I've got a spotless record. We need referees. Young referees. Otherwise it's just a matter of time before the whole fucking game dies. Yes, I want Dani to be able to play. But play what? No referee, no game."

"There's enough knocking around for the next ten years. Enough for Dani's career. And the fact you're literally the most pro-referee person in the entire sport makes it *an even better story*."

"She's right, Max," said MD.

"It's not your job to make sure there are more referees," said Ruth. "It's your job to do your utmost for Dani."

I stood up. "You're asking me to do something abysmal. Someone hurt me so I should hurt them back? I'm trying to be better than that. What you don't realise is that every time I lash out, I get it back tenfold. Example: I annoyed an agent and he did his level best to ruin our entire season. Going after a referee? No one can think of any possible ways *that* might bite us on the arse? Other refs will hate it. They might band together against us. Have you ever read Shakespeare? What happens when you start looking to hurt people, start looking for revenge?" I paused. "Everyone dies." I looked up at the ceiling. It was grimy. Those awful white square panels. Somehow there's always one in the room that's stained yellow on one diagonal. I checked on Dani and Bea Pea. They seemed all right. A *lot* of people were mad at the ref. *Something* would happen, and that was enough for Bea Pea at least.

"Dani, what do you think?"

Dani: I never understood Shakespeare. Harry Styles lyrics is more my level.

She stamped one foot, laughing at her own joke. Talk about lifting the mood; everyone in the group chat was soon smiling.

I stretched. We'd all been still for too long. "I'll think about it. Let's get this game restarted."

Eve blinked. She'd been watching the conversation with wide eyes, drinking it all in. "Who's going to be the ref?"

"The only person in the world I trust to do it fairly," I said. "Me."

I got my whistle from my kit bag, left Jill in charge, said "Thanks for your patience" into the stadium mic, and strode onto the pitch.

"*You* can't be the ref," said one of the Wrexham players when she saw the whistle.

A few players gathered round. I checked out their faces—they didn't know what had happened otherwise they would have gone back to their dressing room. "I can't be the ref? Why not? My mum said if I believe in myself, I can achieve anything."

"I mean, you can't be the ref if you're managing the other team!"

"I quit. This is my career now. Who's the bastard in the black? It's me. Me or we all go home. Now, listen. I'm not like a normal referee. I don't only give yellow and red cards. If you really piss me off, I'll turn the hot water off in your showers. All right? Best get warmed up again. Break's over."

My lot came back on, looking a bit dazzled by the bright lights. A bit uncertain. Dani didn't reappear, and I felt sick. She'd taken the initial blow well, but a delayed reaction was obviously inevitable. But no. There she was. Coming last. Looking tinier than ever.

I got the match going again, and experienced a brief, crippling headache. I hadn't had one of those for a while, even on nights I'd used new formations for the first time. Fortunately, there wasn't much action at first. While the players readjusted to the fact that 1) the match was back on and 2) there was a new sheriff in town, I was able to take stock of some unique changes. The match overview screen now listed me as the ref. But this wasn't a fresh match with a shortened duration. This was a continuation of the existing match, just like if a ref had injured himself and someone else had taken over. Dani's yellow card was still there, and less importantly, the score was still 1–0.

I realised everyone was looking at me. Something had happened while I was spaced out and I needed to adjudicate it.

I dipped into the match commentary and noted that it was giving me much more detailed information with less colour.

Red 6 passes forward.

Red 8 receives on the half-turn, turning clockwise away from Blue 8.

Red 8 progresses five yards, then cuts between Blue 7 and Blue 10.

Blue 10 clips her heels.

Unintentional, but a foul.

I blew and pointed in the direction Wrexham were attacking. The players got on with the game.

Nice!

I rearranged my vision so that I had the match clock semi-transparent in the top-left corner, the match stats next to it, and the commentary scrolling along the top right.

There was another clash, and the Chester Fouls number increased by one. I blew the whistle and pointed.

"Max! I didn't touch her!" complained Mo.

I strode forward and gave her a stern look. "Excuse me?"

"That was a dive," she said, with much less conviction.

I leaned my head back. "I'm just checking here. You think I don't know what a dive looks like?"

"No, of course not. I mean, yes. I mean . . ."

"Can we play some fucking football now? What do you think?"

"Yes, Max."

"And you," I said, turning to the Wrexham player who'd been fouled. "You don't need to add those roly-polies. Not with me. It's cringe."

She didn't respond. The game continued.

Slowly, it gathered momentum again. The players got into it. The fans started to find their voices again.

My job was incredibly simple: let the curse tell me what had happened, and sometimes explain my decision to the players. A few times I ignored a foul so that the game could flow. A few times I got in a gobby player's face and let her know who was running the game. There was plenty of backchat from the Wrexham players, but Bea Pea was the worst. She was so hotheaded she'd go on rants even when the guy she was ranting at was *me*. Incredible.

The match ratings started to turn in Wrexham's favour, and close to half-time, they equalised. I wondered what Jill would tell them. I wondered if Bonnie would help. What must she be making of all this? The match clock hit 45. Just before I blew the whistle, I tried swapping Dani and Maddy on the tactics board, just to see if I could. No chance. The curse knew full well I wasn't the manager. I couldn't exit the match overview, though, so I couldn't check how much XP I was getting. Probably one per minute, right?

I blew for halftime. There was a bit of applause from the fans and the players jogged off to the dressing rooms.

I couldn't follow them; Jill was the manager for now. I needed to give her space to run the team, and to be seen to remain impartial. The match official's room was full of dog whistles. Where could I go? I was the referee, the man in the middle. So I took the match ball, placed it on the centre circle, and sat on it while the ground staff pottered around poking at the pitch with big forks.

Time to think through my dilemma, then. I could be a total dick and use Beth to attack this referee and make it unimaginable that any ref in the world would ever dare book Dani for kicking the ball away. Maybe if the media storm was big enough, IFAB would write something into the laws of the game to guarantee accessibility. Problem solved, we all get on with our lives. But we do our part in killing the sport. And I ally with an institution so vile that even Old Nick would give it a wide berth. And I set myself up for massive retribution. As per.

I eased myself off the ball, sat on the grass, and held the ball up in front of me.

To be a dick, or not to be a dick. That was the question.

I could suffer some slings and arrows. What's a few more? But Dani deserved better. Was letting a scorpion onto my back the right way to achieve change? Scorpions had a habit of killing their ride.

What could I do on my own, without Beth?

I stared at the ball. Nothing came to mind.

"Alas, poor Max!"

I dropped my hand and switched my focus. "Henri! You're here."

He settled onto the grass in front of me, cross-legged. "I try to attend as many of your events as possible, my friend. Note I say events, not football matches." He laughed at his little joke. "They have a delightful tendency towards the theatrical. This one . . ." He did a chef's kiss. "Formidable. New heights of drama."

"It's not my fault."

"'*There has been an incident.' Mon dieu!* What does it mean, though? The mind propels itself. Tumbles. What on *earth* could have happened to make you look and talk like a spectre? Theories sweep the terraces, growing more outlandish, colliding with others, evolving, forming super-theories. I announce the truth of the matter, but few listen."

"What did you say?"

"I said, '*There* is a man so frugal he refuses to pay a thirty-pound fine.'"

I snorted. "You got me. Wait. Holy shit, if they send us that bill I will go nuclear. Argh! Fuck this world."

"I've been talking to Emma, MD, and the financier."

"Ruth."

"*Précisément.* They say you have a solution. One interview. A few photographs. *Voilà.* The day is saved. So why do you linger in the centre circle like a puddle of sadness?"

"It's not that easy. The solution will have some disproportionately massive cost. And I have a responsibility. To the game. We need referees. You get that, right? I could be a manager for forty years. Year one, I cut the number of people wanting to do the job by five percent? No, thanks."

He pushed his legs out and leaned on his palms. "Do you think I'd be a good referee?"

"More ex-players should do it. That'd raise the standard."

"That was not my question."

Henri as ref? It was hard to imagine. He'd read the game well, but would he give more decisions to the underdog? Would he run the game based on personal narratives he constructed? "Mostly no."

"I agree. But you are very good. I look for bias and find none. As a spectator, I trust you. Did you know there are hundreds of schoolchildren here?"

"Yeah."

"For many, it's their first ever time in a stadium. They've seen a wicked referee, a villain. And along comes a hero. The uncorruptible. The untouchable." He laughed. "Max Best. When he refs, he's a better player than the players. When he plays, he's a better ref than the refs. How many children, here for the first time, will want to be a goalkeeper? Some. A striker? Lots. A referee? No small number, I think. Not with such a role model."

"That's crazy." He was so fanciful sometimes. I discounted most of what he said when he got overly Rococo—he was just enjoying the sound of his own voice. "I don't know what to do, Henri. There's a good outcome that's pretty clear. But the cost? It could be anything. It could be absolutely enormous. I'm . . . indecisive."

Henri gave me a blank look. "That doesn't sound like you. Perhaps you should pretend to descend into madness to buy yourself the time you need to gather the information required to make up your mind."

"What. On earth. Are you talking about?"

But he wasn't listening to me. "I have done it, I think. Yes, I have helped my friend sufficiently. Superb, Henri, superb." He got to his feet. "Will you now stop moping around, perhaps? You are making everybody sad."

"Sure." He reached out a hand and pulled me upright. I hesitated. "There's five minutes to go. I can't go in the dressing rooms, and I'm not going in the ref's room. What do you want me to do?"

"You have a ball. You have a crowd. There is one thing you can do where the only consequence is joy."

I spent a few minutes doing tekkers in front of the main stand. Henri was right—it was pretty fun. Therapeutic. Encouraged by the cheers and gasps of the schoolkids, I did some run-of-the-mill dog walks, flytraps, and washing machines, before unleashing a new move I'd dreamed up but rarely practised. I called it *"I Know Kung Fu"* and it involved keeping the ball aloft with a series of martial arts–style upper kicks.

They were a HUGE hit, so I started jazzing the technique up by switching legs and adding *Street Fighter*–esque sound effects. *Hai! Hai! Hai!*

Finally, with a screamed *Haduuuuken!*, I kicked the ball high, high in the air, set myself, and then made a big show of trapping the ball underfoot and grinding it into the dirt. I pretended it was the head of my enemy and I did a convincing Bruce Lee crushing-my-foe-while-twitching-slightly-with-the-effort face. I was pretty pleased with it. A few people filmed the routine, but I doubted their phones caught the awesome sound effect I added at the end.

The diversion was all too brief. The teams came back out and as the match resumed, so did my torment.

I once read that referees make four decisions a minute, but I was making many more. I was also the linesmen, and many decisions were about not making decisions. Should I stop the game here? Was that handball really? There were the rules laid down by IFAB, and there was practical common sense. I disobeyed the curse a few times in order to foster the kind of match I'd want to play in. I made all kinds of decisions, instantly, smoothly, fearlessly. All kinds of decisions except the big one: What price would I pay to save Dani's career?

As for the match, well, the players had reset themselves at halftime, and the second half started with lots of energy and urgency. Wrexham scored, but then Chester equalised with a long-range Pippa shot. Two–all and the crowd was up for it.

Then came a big moment. From a Wrexham corner, the ball bounced around and Lucy was about to smash it clear. But a cheeky Wrexham scamp planted her foot down in the path of Lucy's swing, and Lucy kicked her.

I blew for a penalty.

The Chester players complained. It was, like, totes unfair.

"Yeah, it's harsh to concede a seventy-five-percent chance of a goal for that accidental kick," I agreed. "But that's smart play. It's a pen. Bea Pea, good news is it works both ways. You're allowed to do that, too."

A weird whispering came from the main stand. Confusion. They couldn't understand why it was a pen, and there were no replays.

In my intro, I'd said that Robyn was good at saving penalties, and here she was standing tall, smashing her hands into the crossbar to try to intimidate the Wrexham striker. The latter, their number 9, stepped up, struck the ball hard, and it crashed into the post. It rebounded straight to the penalty taker. She passed it into the far corner of the net, away from Robyn. Tidy finish under the circumstances.

The Wrexham players ran off, celebrating.

I blew my whistle six or seven times until the Wrexham players realised something was amiss.

I raised my hand and blew again. "Indirect free kick for Chester," I said.

The Wrexham players went nuts. The crowd were deeply confused. I sighed and jogged over to the space between the dugouts. I took the microphone and turned it on. "I gave the penalty for a foul in the penalty area. Clever play from Wrexham's number twelve. The pen isn't a goal because the penalty taker struck the ball *twice*. Think about it. If you were allowed to do that, you could just dribble the ball into the goal. It *looks* like the goal should stand because it comes back off the post. But it's an indirect free kick. She should have let someone *else* shoot."

There were a lot of "oh" faces in the crowd, especially from the kids. A lot of older guys were nodding smugly. Presumably they'd been telling everyone near them the same thing. Overall, the effect of explaining my decision seemed hugely positive, and the Wrexham players accepted it.

I took the microphone with me onto the pitch and used it to explain some of my decisions.

The game went smoothly for a while, with Wrexham getting more and more possession. Jill made some frantic gestures, and the tactics screen told me she'd switched to 4-3-3 in a counterattacking strategy. Sure enough, every failed Wrexham attack led to a fast break with Dani, Maddy, and Bea Pea trying to combine.

After one tackle, a Wrexham player's pace attribute turned red, and I blew my whistle several times and dashed across, summoning the physio. The injury wasn't that bad, which was a relief.

During that break in play, our forwards got together and talked about what moves they might try. It was hard to get nuanced with Dani mid-match, so Bea Pea moved her around and demonstrated a scheme she'd cooked up. I couldn't tell if Dani got it, but I think she enjoyed Bea Pea's energy, anyway.

"Ref, Eve wants a word."

"Aight."

I wandered over to the side. Wrexham's manager pushed her hair back. "Referee."

"Miss."

"We need to sub that player off. Your girls are giving us real problems. Normally, I'd bring one of our—what did you say?—*different gravy* players on, but then we'd have four on the pitch."

"Are you asking my permission?"

"I did sort of promise I'd only have three at any one time."

I looked around, made some calculations. "I like the balance of the match. You're dominating but we might land a lucky punch." I scanned the pitch again. "Ah, fuck it. Go for it. We had a good seventy minutes, yeah? I'm happy with that."

Eve was torn, but she had her own career to think of. She sent on one of her good players, and that really tipped the tide in Wrexham's favour. I noticed Bonnie was right on the touchline, alongside Jill, yelling things. She'd got caught up in it all. *She'd* made a decision.

Ten minutes of strong Wrexham pressure went by before they finally scored to go 3–2 ahead. Our players were on their last legs. We'd have to build more fitness before the first league games next season. Which, presumably, would be in the lowest league the FA would dare place us. The pricks. Would I be there for that match? I kept thinking about all the things that could go wrong if I took up arms against referees. If I got into bed with the *Daily Mail*. Ugh.

In my peripheral vision, I saw Jill shouting some stuff, trying to change the shape, but Bea Pea calling back, "*No! Five more minutes of this!*"

She was a smart cookie, that striker. The three teenage tearaways were still a menace.

I followed the ball around the pitch, but when it went to Dani next, I ran much faster. I didn't want to miss this.

Blue 7 receives the ball in space.

Red 2 moves to challenge.

Blue 7 jinks past. She plays a low diagonal pass towards Blue 9.

Blue 9 prepares to receive, but at the last moment, lets the ball progress through her legs. She sprints forward.

Blue 11 is stationed in the path of the ball. She lays it square to Blue 9.

Another first-time pass sends Blue 11 through on goal.

But Red 1 is quick off her line and gathers cleanly.

Beautiful! So *that's* what they'd been plotting. The old Dwight Yorke and Andy Cole dummy one-two. Degree of difficulty: maximum. Yorke and Cole did it several times in rapid succession to score an all-time classic in a pulsating match against Barcelona.

Where had these teenagers seen it? Yorke and Cole happened before they were born. It was a low percentage move that I wouldn't *really* want my players to try. Certainly not when their highest CA was 9! But what if my players could surprise me with their own inventiveness and creativity? Where could this team go, given the chance?

I really, really wanted to know.

The goalie rolled the ball short and the defenders passed it round. I jogged over to the right, towards the main stand, where the next action was going to be. There was a quick bit of pinball, the ball went off the pitch, and I noticed a kid in the crowd stick her arm out to the left. She was calling the decision for Wrexham! She was all kinds of wrong, but I loved it. Henri was right! I was inspiring kids to be refs. Holy shit.

I had visions of special referee camps hosted by Chester. We'd invite a top ref, some first-team players, loads of schoolkids, and we'd teach them to be referees. Whip up a fun schedule. Have a laugh. Make wearing the black cool.

And what about all the players I had to release from the youth teams? What if being a ref was the best way for them to stay in the game? We'd offer them training at wherever real refs started. We'd support them. Make a fuss over them.

Yeah, man. That was it. We don't hate refs; we create them!

I gave the decision to Wrexham; Bea Pea almost stomped her feet, she was so furious I'd got it wrong. I gave a big Maxy two-thumbs to my assistant in the stands, who was overwhelmed that I was giving her attention, and walked off the pitch. I hopped the advertising boards and went to where Beth, Ruth, and a bunch of others were congregated. One was the match photographer, showing Beth and Ruth something on his camera screen.

"Beth," I said. "Call your boss. Get started. Clean kill. Don't miss. Be nice to Dani; she's going to play for England. Make up whatever quotes you need from me. But don't ask me to look sad in photos."

"Don't worry," she said, eyes shining. The thrill of the hunt. "I've already got the perfect pics."

"Yeah? Weird. Well, don't just stand there. Get busy!"

Decision made, I woke up. Slipped back into my body. Felt whole again. Alive. The buzz from the crowd made me realise I'd interrupted the match yet again. I flicked the mic on. "Soz about that," I said. "Why not pop back tomorrow to watch the first team beat Blyth Spartans? Okay, we're on for a proper last ten minutes now. No more commentary from me. Things are about to get pretty epic around here. The rest is silence."

9

THIS. ISN'T. SPARTA.

Saturday, March 18. Match 40 of 46: Chester versus Blyth Spartans.

I woke up at 8—pretty late for me. Emma squirmed, sensing something had changed in the room. I traced my fingers along her spine, up to her flowing blonde hair. Helen of Troy could have been no more lovely. Helen of Troy, however, may have been more willing to spend the night on a mattress in my windowless office inside a freezing cold football stadium. Emma had dragged me to a hotel. One with, and I quote, a "bed that meets the dictionary definition of a bed."

I had to admit she was right; I needed a proper sleep. Big day ahead. Even the armies of old knew when to rest.

I pushed the covers off but stayed there on my side, staring at the one thin strip of light coming through the heavy curtains.

The unpleasantness of the night before was still there, in my bloodstream, in my soul. But there was no point dwelling on it. There was more good than bad. I'd met Eve, a true sportsman. We'd recruited Bonnie, a fantastic new teammate. We'd lost 4–2 but the team competed hard against an established outfit. Anyway, that was yesterday. Today was all about helping Jackie beat Blyth Spartans.

We went down for breakfast and joined Gemma. She'd decided to stay overnight, too, since Chester FC was a drama sandwich with a shopping trip in the middle. We talked about having a victory dinner in a restaurant called the Sticky Walnut, in a Chester suburb.

"Enjoy your breakfast," I said, in a gruff voice. "For tonight, we dine in Hoole."

Absolutely no reaction. Sometimes I wonder why I bother.

I joined them on a little walk around the old town, pottering around, not even resisting when they made me try on different clothes.

"This looks great on you," said Emma, while Gemma nodded. "You should buy it."

I couldn't tell you what I was wearing. Not a black hoodie is all I know. "I'll dress like a peacock if we stay up. Deal?"

"I'll hold you to that."

What I was doing, apart from killing time until the match, was checking out the atmosphere in the town. It was a big game. A crucial six-pointer, at home. You wouldn't have known it. The town was quiet. Some buskers, some tourists. No sign that the place even had a football club.

Maybe everyone had seen the league table.

	TEAM	P	GD	PTS
19	Blyth Spartans	38	-33	43
20	Bradford	37	-25	41
21	Chester	39	-16	38
22	Leamington	37	-17	37
23	Kettering	39	-32	33
24	AFC Telford	39	-44	25

At the end of the season, the bottom four teams would be relegated and demoted to the seventh tier, where they would probably *not* play FC United. Ziggy's team were on a good run and had settled into second place in their league. How crazy it would be if Ziggy was the only one playing sixth-tier football next season, while James, Raffi, and I played in the seventh. Henri, of course, would move to a club more befitting of his talents.

Telford and Kettering were doomed, leaving four teams competing for the last two slots. Leamington were in big trouble, but had played two games fewer than us. Mathematically, they had a fair shot at staying up, but realistically, they were near the bottom for a reason and their games would come thick and fast. Meanwhile, our run of midweek games was coming to an end, and after this coming Tuesday's visit to Kettering, it was Saturday matches all the way. Jackie would have a whole week to prepare for every match. I was sure that would prove crucial.

Our problem was that even if we beat Blyth today, they would survive if they matched our results for the rest of the season, as would Bradford (Park Avenue).

In a way, I was glad of the clarity.

Everyone at the club knew we needed to win, and to keep winning.

I left the ladies around lunchtime and walked to the stadium. Jackie and Vimsy were taking care of the on-pitch pre-match preparations, and a small army of volunteers were getting the stadium ready and doing the hundreds of little jobs that needed to be done. There wasn't much for me to do, so I took the opportunity to explore some aspects of nonleague football I hadn't had time to dive into before. Namely, I went around the little stalls outside the ground, had chats with the vendors, and tried to get more of a sense of the pre-match experience.

One guy was selling replica kits, scarves, and souvenirs. I had a rummage and found he didn't have any Best 77 merch. Annoying. But he did have a Dani 7 car air freshener. He told me people had started asking if he had any women's team stuff and he was dipping his toes into the water. I bought five air fresheners and an I HEART JR mug.

The food stands seemed to do decent business, the stewards were friendly, and a few volunteers went past along with some fans in wheelchairs. One among the group pointed at me and shouted, "It's Max! It's Max!" so hard it became a bit of an issue. I went over. I'd assumed the guy would be a relative of a Chester Knight or something like that, but it was a total rando. Really strange, but I spent a few minutes posing for selfies and answering questions and the group eventually continued on inside. They were buzzing, despite the fact only one of them knew who I was.

"You're good with *them*, anyway." It was another rando. Forty, balding, one of those faces I didn't trust. Could be the loveliest guy, could be total gammon.

"Them?" I said, with a bit of a challenge.

He failed to maintain eye contact. "I don't know the proper words."

"Me neither, to be honest. I just try to be nice. Normally works out."

There was a group of blokes behind him. Lots of beefy boys. Portly construction worker types. Podgy van drivers. Not my natural constituency, tbh, but they normally made good tea. "I just wanted to say. We've had our doubts about you. Still do. Strange stuff we keep hearing about. Thought you were a soft lad. But what you did last night." He swallowed. Had he already started on the beer? What was

I thinking? He'd probably had more that morning than I drank in a month. "That was right by me."

Another guy came closer. "You can't walk off the pitch, though. You can't kick the referee out! That's no good. That's over the top."

The first guy didn't agree. "Got to make a stand, Dan. Can't let people take liberties."

I put my hands up; I didn't want to re-legislate the whole drama. "Here's the thing. Maybe I overreacted, maybe I did the right thing, maybe both are true. I don't know. I'm an easy-going guy. All the players at this club are nice. All the age groups. All the Chesters. We're all friendly." I set my jaw. "But don't *mess* with us. We'll ruin your day."

"Don't mess with Chesters!" yelled one guy, which was an instant hit. Another potentially inebriated chap started a chant that was taken up by everyone within a hundred yards.

We hate Wrexham and we hate Wrexham
We hate Wrexham and we hate Wrexham
We hate Wrexham and we hate Wrexham
We are the Wrexham
Haters

Football fans, Jesus Christ. I pretended to take a phone call so that I could scarper, but one of the fans thrust a blue magazine in front of me and held out a pen. Asking me to sign it! I leaned my phone flat on my shoulder and took a proper look at the mag.

"Where did you get this?"

"Over there."

I signed it, then went to buy something I'd assumed was extinct: a match day programme.

It was nearly time for the team to be named, so I went inside the stadium. Into the inner sanctums, through the secret spaces, into the holiest of holies—the manager's office next to the dressing room. Jackie was there with Vimsy, the latter sitting back, nice and relaxed, having a cuppa. Jackie was leaning forward, filling the team sheet in very, very carefully. While I waited, I took a proper look at the cover of the programme.

At the top it said *The Cestrian*, followed by the price (two pounds fifty).

The hero image was a photo of Tony Hetherington, the second-best striker at the club (third if you count me, which you should unless you enjoy telling lies). Tony was mid-clap and had no expression on his face. Applauding the fans after a defeat, it looked like. Pretty far in the direction of dull.

Then there was the crest of Blyth Spartans, today's date, and the kickoff time: 3 p.m. At the bottom, the logos of the six main sponsors.

Absolutely nothing *wrong* with any of it. Just a bit uninspiring.

I had the same feeling when Jackie handed me the team sheet. Unchanged team, 3-5-2. The only difference from the recent disasters was that Aff was on the sub's bench. One of my jobs would be to make sure Jackie didn't panic and throw him on too early.

Not that there should be any need; Blyth's average CA was 38. Ours had climbed to 41.9, and if we changed D-Day to Aff it would be 42.9. Slow, steady progress.

I had started to think in terms of bands. The first band—bronze— was players with CA under 40. We had five bronze in the starting eleven. One was Raffi, who had climbed to CA 30. He had nearly reached the point where he wasn't in the team because he *looked* like a good player, but because he actually *was* one. I have to admit I was slightly disappointed with his progression given how many first-team minutes he was getting, but that was probably my natural impatience talking.

The silver band included players from CA 40 to 49. We had three in the lineup: Carl Carlile, James Wise (the on-loan midfielder), and Tony, the striker from the cover of the programme. Carl had only just moved from bronze to silver. He still had a lot of upside, but even if we stayed up, I wanted to see some 7 out of 10 match ratings before I offered him a new contract. What was the point of having decent skills if you didn't show it on the pitch?

Gold was anyone over CA 50. We had three: Glenn (51), Sam Topps (53), and Henri, who'd bumped himself up to 55. I got very excited when I saw that, but 55 was exactly his level when I'd seen him as an unused sub for Darlington all those months ago. Three months of playing and training just to undo the damage caused by his enforced break and his emotional crisis. He seemed much happier these days. Did happy players improve faster?

"Max."

"Yes, Jackie?"

"Happy with that?"

I looked down at the team sheet. "Absolutely. It's our strongest team. I like the formation. You've got options on the bench. Trick lets you go to a flat back four. Youngster if you want a DM. Aff for a late burst. This," I said, holding the team sheet with great reverence, "is one of the greatest documents in this nation's long history."

Jackie sighed. "Is it going to be one of those days?"

"Are you being sarcastic?" asked Vimsy.

"About the team? No. Why, what would you change?"

He hadn't expected the question. "You know me, I'm old-fashioned. I'd play four-four-two. And I'd play Aff from the start." He gestured to show he wasn't complaining. "That's just me. I like the team. It feels solid."

"Yes, well," I said. "Maybe this is a good time to clarify something. I'm going to be in the area, but I'm only helping out. Jackie's the boss. When the whistle blows, Jackie's *my* boss. I'm going to shut my trap so that the players are in no doubt of that. All right? Good? That said," I finished quickly and quietly, "put Aff on too early and I'll go apeshit."

Jackie smiled. "Let's get you started on your assistant duties, then. Take that to the ref."

I felt queasy. "You want me to go into the referee's room? After last night?"

"Quit yer whingeing. Get on with it. There's a deadline on those things."

"I see. It's going to be one of those days." I sighed. "Where's the holy water in case things kick off?"

Jackie tutted. "Piss off and hand in the team sheet. Nutjob."

I knocked on the referee's door. It opened and a guy dressed all in black stood there. Any worries I had about finding some kind of mutated supergammon in there evaporated. He was about twenty-seven and had the friendly, cheerful face of a postman. He reminded me of my mate Longstaff.

"Help you?"

"Got our team sheet," I said. He made no attempt to take it from me. "Chester," I added, stupidly.

"You don't recognise me, Best?"

Oh, shit. Oh shit oh no oh shit. "Er . . . Your car stalled and I gave you a push because I'm actually a good guy?"

He loved that. "No! I reffed you down in Gloucester." I must have looked pretty blank. "You don't remember? How can you not remember? You scored four goals!"

"Oh, right. Right . . ." It was starting to come back to me. "It was snowing. You had to decide if we played or not. Not an easy decision."

"You stood nice and warm in my coat while literally everyone else got stuck in clearing the snow. That didn't sit well, if I'm honest. Made you seem like a bit of a dandy." He shrugged. "Didn't take long to change my mind. Happy to make a mistake *off* the pitch!"

I frowned, hard. "I think I was too stressed to think straight. I really needed that match to go ahead. Can't remember why." I held up the team sheet again. This time, he took it.

"Ah, great. Great! I hate when I have to go looking for them. Let's have a decko, then." He went through the list. "Oh, Sam Topps. He's a handful."

"Not really," I said, without thinking.

"He is. Charges around. Flying tackles. I always keep my eye on him."

I laughed and checked the corridor was empty. "Listen, I've got beef with Sam Topps. I've been waiting for him to do something stupid for weeks so I could take him down a peg or two. Maybe even fine him. Show him who's boss." I checked the corridor again. "But he's smart. Sly. He never actually does anything wrong. Like, ever. He's combative, yeah, but fouls? Dangerous play? Not him. He's very, very controlled. You watch him today. It's his, like, *aura* winning the ball. He's very Sun Tzu. Wins without fighting."

"Huh," said the ref. He glanced down. "Henri Lyons is trouble. You'll admit that."

I squeezed a noise through my teeth and did a couple of head shakes. Before I spoke, I wondered what I was doing. I think I was so relieved that the ref was treating me like a human being that I was overly happy to chat to him. Maybe he was relieved I was treating *him* like a human being. It was probably naive, but I couldn't see any harm in being honest with the guy. "In the Premier League he'd get booked every match. He loves a scrap. There's nothing in it, though. It's like a pillow fight. It's all for show with him. If he starts to piss you off, give him a warning and he'll cut it out."

The ref seemed entranced. I briefly worried he was going to use this against me somehow, but he seemed to be loving the gossip. "I've heard this Raffi Brown was a boxer. Comes from a rough area, that kind of thing."

"He'll be the one calming things down. He's ice cold. Mistimes the odd tackle, same as everyone else, but I've never seen him out of control. Not a malicious bone in his body. Big family man. His daughter's as cute as a button. He's going up up up, that guy. Top player."

"What about Blyth?"

I shrugged. "Never seen 'em. Don't know what to expect, really."

He scanned the team sheet and gave it a little flick. "Very interested to see if you're right, or if you were having me on! Enjoy the match. Pity you aren't playing. I still think about that fourth goal. How on earth did you score from that angle?"

I went into the dressing room and listened as Jackie announced the team—the players already knew it—and reminded them of some things they'd been working on in training. "Fast transitions between lines, yeah? When we go back, we go back. No harm done. But when we go forward, we go hard. When we're fast, no team can live with us. Okay? Henri, Tony, watch your spacing. Like we worked on. When to split, when to go tandem. D-Day, Joe, it's that balance. When to go, when to stay. Keep a clear head. Robbo. That long ball to Henri in the channel, that's our joker, yeah? Don't waste it. Okay, now Aff's been to watch them. What did you see?"

That was surprising. I didn't think anyone ever listened to me. Injured players as scouts? Yes, please!

Aff stirred. He wasn't used to talking in such an environment. "They . . . they fire loads of long balls to their strikers."

"Say the line," insisted Carl Carlile, one of Aff's best mates.

Aff rolled his eyes. "They fire so many long balls it'll blot out the sun."

"Then we'll defend in the shade!" said Carl, rising off the bench, miming that he was thrusting a sword at an enemy. It got a decent response.

I had tried to wedge myself into a corner and not be part of any of it. If I popped down to watch training, the players would always have that doubt: Should they be looking to impress Jackie, or me? But here in the stadium I really wanted them to know Jackie was top dog.

So it was a surprise when Jackie singled me out. "Now, lads. Me specialist says not to stand up too much, so I've asked Max to come and help us out today." All eyes turned to me. "Yeah. I know. Scraping the bottom of the barrel, or what? But seriously. If you know anything about football, you know he sees things everyone else misses. An extra pair of eyes. Two heads are better than one. All that stuff. We're leaving nothing to chance today. Big win and we're back in business. Go get yourselves warm, go through your routines. Hop to it."

Again there was nothing for me to do. I wanted to go up to the director's box and talk to Emma, or Ruth, or MD. Or even go and gatecrash *Seals Live*. None of the above seemed like a good idea, so I hung out with Jackie and Vimsy. Talked shit for a while. They were full of the usual football bravado, but just under the surface, they were terrified. A draw would be a disaster. A defeat? A defeat and Jackie's management career could very well be over.

The Gary Talbot Stand is the main terrace at Chester, named after a club legend. The teams emerge from the very centre, go down two tiny steps, and the players keep going straight onto the pitch. The home team's manager, assistant, coaches, and physios turn right. The away team turn left. There are two fairly large rectangles marked on the grass around the dugouts. These are the so-called "technical areas" where the managers are allowed to patrol. They're certainly much bigger than they seem from match footage, which is filmed from a low-hanging camera on the opposite stand.

Jackie, like most managers, liked to stand as centrally as possible, so that he might better berate the referee and yell obscenities at the other manager. He'd got a little camping stool so that he could sit down when nothing was happening, and he'd placed it with two legs slightly outside of the technical area. He thought, correctly, that it would annoy the Blyth lot. Good gamesmanship, but if I was him, I wouldn't want the match to get too emotional—we were the better team. Compete, win your duels, let your higher quality show. Absolutely no need for drama of any kind. But it was Jackie's gig. I had to leave him to it.

The dugouts at the Deva are slightly unusual in that they're split into two mini shelters. Jackie liked to have the physios over on the far one, and the coaches and subs in the one closest to halfway. So Livia and Dean were in one little hut, and Vimsy, Jackie, and I were theoretically stationed in the bigger one, though in practice we preferred to stand up. The five substitutes did sit down: Ben (the goalie), Magnus (multipurpose defensive cover), Trick Williams (a left back if we wanted to change formation), Youngster (defensive midfield, unlikely to be given a debut unless we were so far ahead that Jackie could truly relax), and Aff (the left midfielder who we were easing back into the team after his painful and totally avoidable hamstring injury).

The worst-case scenario, I mused, would be if one of our strikers got injured. We'd talked about it, and the solution would be to push D-Day up as a second striker. I didn't like it much, but he'd played there for most of the season. Or we could do 4-5-1. Either way, it wasn't totally bonkers not to have a striker on the bench.

The match kicked off, and the first five minutes, as always, were very careful. No one wanted to make a mistake. No one wanted to take any undue risks.

The crowd were in decent voice, considering the general assumption that we were already relegated. Blyth had brought a few fans, but it was a long trip from their coastal town located—impossibly—*north* of Newcastle. They'd been on the road for four hours, at least. Understandable that they didn't travel in huge numbers.

Even more understandable when I saw the way they played. It was so defensive even Ian Evans would have blanched. Their manager, Lee Martin, was on the young side to be a dinosaur type. Middle-aged, very stocky, wearing a grey suit. On seeing him, I imagined a deep, gravelly voice, and as soon as the match kicked off, I didn't have to imagine. The guy never shut up. He played a straight 4-4-2 with enormous, hulking centre backs and, unusually, two enormous, hulking fullbacks. The plan? Keep it tight and score from set pieces.

But today they weren't all that fussed about scoring. A draw against us would suit them just fine. So they were doing lots of tiny fouls. Taking their time on throw-ins and goal kicks. Slowing the game down, making it bitty, stop-start, annoying, aggravating. And from Martin and his cronies, nonstop aggression. Complaints to the referee, shouts at our players, huge verbals aimed at Jackie and Vimsy.

Who, of course, swallowed the bait hook, line, and plonker.

To be fair, Jackie started by focusing on his team. Calling out a few tiny tweaks. Giving individual instructions. Requesting a step to the right from Carl. Asking Raffi to pass left. Warning Glenn about his offside line. Good stuff. Valuable stuff. Which stopped happening because Jackie got involved with Martin, big time.

The more Jackie responded, the more distracted he and Vimsy got, the worse Chester played.

My non-intervention pact didn't survive ten minutes. I rose from the dugout, ambled over to Vimsy, and told him to sit down. He was fuming (not at me) but he obeyed. I think he was experienced enough to know he wasn't helping anyone. Maybe he even liked being told to drop it, since that gave him a face-saving out. I picked up Jackie's camping chair and placed it on the other side of the dugout. Then I walked to his side.

"Jackie, you knob."

"Not now, Max. Kin hell." His face was red. His knuckles were white on his crutches.

"Do you want to go and play with your dinky cars? You're being disruptive."

He ground his teeth, but he made eye contact with me, just for a second, and I think there was the tiniest nod. He understood I was telling him to cool it. "Yeah. Oh, where's my— Max! Why's it over there?"

"I don't want you bickering with nobodies, mate. First you fight with your head. *Then* you fight with your heart. Go over there and sit down. Manage your team. I'll ask one of the physios to give you a shoulder massage to calm you down, yeah?" I waggled my eyebrows suggestively.

He tutted. "You mean Dean, don't you?" He let out an annoyed breath but swung himself away from the Blyth dugout and fell into his chair. He grimaced. His knee was worse than he was letting on.

I turned to Lee Martin and beamed at him. Gave him a Maxy two-thumbs. The temperature on the away bench rose five degrees. They did *not* like me smiling at them. I laughed and mumbled, "Bunch of twats." Footballers are pretty good lipreaders, for a certain subsection of words.

I grinned as I went back to Jackie. From his new position, he could still talk to Vimsy and the subs. I decided that I'd stand between Jackie and the Blyth mob. You know, to help him focus. In fact, the best thing I could do in the first half would be to distract him and Vimsy. Take their minds off the game, to some extent. The big challenge, I knew, would come at halftime, when Lee Martin would unleash some dinosaur power move that would make the inexperienced Jackie cower.

First things first, though. "Livia," I called.

She came jogging with her kit bag. "Everything okay?"

"This prick's knee hurts more than he's letting on. Will you try to keep him still or whatever?"

Jackie gave me a furious look. "I'm fine."

"Is D-Day in position?" I said.

He glared across to the far side of the pitch. "Yes!"

"If you can see that, then you can manage from there. Magnus, will you go and keep Dean company in the other box, please?"

"Yes, Max."

"Physios are social animals," I explained to James. "You're not supposed to leave them alone."

Livia had taken the opportunity to whip out an ice pack that she held against her boyfriend's knee. Tenderly. It was such a sweet moment.

"What are you doing?" demanded Jackie.

"Nothing."

"Stop smiling. It's maddening. Argh." Livia flinched and whipped the ice pack away. "It's not you, Livs. That was the *perfect* moment for Henri to go wide. He was too busy grappling with the defender."

I did my talking-to-a-child voice. "Player was fighting? Was it maybe coz you was losing your tiny mind doing verbals? Jackie? Was it coz you was shouting at the bad man? Maybe the players think they have to shout at the bad man, too? Jackie? Was it? Is it? Maybe? Jackie?"

"OKAY!" he yelled. It burst out of him. Many weeks of frustration summed up in one noise. He squirmed, but he was biting his lip and a bit of the old twinkle was back in his eye. "You're right, Max. Point taken. Will you remind Henri what we talked about?"

"Nope. Shouting is beneath me. A perfectly calm, professional football coach like Vimsy is your man for giving crisp, clear technical instructions." I raised my eyebrows in Vimsy's direction. It was a chal-lenge: *Are you ready to work?*

His answer was to push himself out of the dugout. He took a po-sition on the other side of Jackie. They had a quick chat, then Vimsy stepped forward and barked first at Henri, then at Robbo, who seemed to have forgotten his part of the move, too.

"Good spot, mate," I told him. Vimsy nodded, but then glanced over my shoulder. I took a tiny step to the right to block his view, and did a very clear expression that meant *Are you fucking kidding?* He blinked, exhaled, and concentrated on the pitch.

I stayed where I was, keeping one eye on Jackie and one on the match overview screens. When we stopped getting sucked into Blyth's drama trap, our match ratings started to increase. Things were looking good, mostly. "D-Day is playing shit," I announced.

Jackie frowned and switched his attention to the far side. "Get him up the pitch for five minutes."

Vimsy went to the touchline and barked orders and waved and pointed. It took a while, but D-Day's rating went from 5 to 6. "That's done it," I announced. "Keep him there or move him back into his slot?"

"Back to the slot," Jackie said, and Vimsy made it happen.

"You know," I said, pleased, "this is all very civilised, isn't it? Very professional."

"You're such a hypocrite," said Jackie. "*You* use emotion more than anyone I've ever met."

"Nah," I said. "Not when we're the better team. Fire when you're the underdog. Ice when you're superior." I got very, very smug. "That's why when I play, I play cold. Ben," I said, startling the young goalie. I say young—he was three years older than me. "Which post do they attack from crosses?"

"Not really sure," he admitted.

"Oh," I said. "Sort of thought maybe it was your job to look out for that sort of thing. In case we need you to go on the pitch, like."

"Er . . . yes, Max."

"The answer is the far post, by the way. Youngster, which Blyth midfielder is more likely to go forward for attacks?"

"Their number eight, Mr. Best. He has gone forward two times so far. He is truly one-footed, always cuts onto his right foot. If I am on the pitch, I will be sure to shepherd him onto his weaker left foot."

"What about headers?"

"His runs are very predictable. I believe I can cover him success-fully."

"Ben. Hear that?"

"Yes, Max."

"That's the standard."

Jackie turned and gave Youngster a big smile. "Ice cold."

Youngster beamed. I was surprised his CA didn't pop there and then.

Ice cold. I'd chucked some cold water onto this fiery first half. What if I could do more of that while winding up Blyth even more? "Trick, would you hand me that thing, please?"

"This?" he said, holding up the match programme.

I took it from him. "Exactly. Thanks."

I wandered over to the edge of the technical area closest to Blyth, did a big stretch and a yawn, and started reading.

If you've ever wondered if opposition managers like you reading a match day programme while your team is dominating theirs, turns out, they don't.

I was hitting my stride, mate, let me tell you. I'd found my role in the world. Jackie was the leading man; I was a supporting character. Not seen in every episode, did a lot with very few lines. In this very special episode, Jackie would take care of the football while I took care of the technical areas.

Jackie's problem in the previous games was getting outfoxed by dinosaurs who'd learned a trick or two over their long careers. Those old hands had been winding him up something rotten.

From the VIP boxes, I'd been focused on tactics, formations, sub-stitutions. But now that I was in the mixer, as footballers call the area where the action is, I understood it better.

Jackie was getting sucked into blind rage. Mind games. Losing his focus on the one area where he was miles, miles better than anyone at this level, including me: the pitch.

But now he was free to focus on his players. Free to make the doz-ens of tiny adjustments that uncursed managers had to make to squeeze an extra one percent out of their team.

And in the line of fire, soaking up all the opposition ire, was little old me. Maxy Best.

A premium wind-up merchant. A gobby Manc twat. A guy you really, really want to slap.

Reading the match programme, mid-match, while Lee Martin and his crew were hopping around, hopping mad, was like a red rag to a bull.

"What the fuck?" one of them yelled. "Are you taking the piss?"

I looked up at him, a paragon of innocence. "Sorry, is this your copy?"

"You know what I mean, you prick." He came thundering forward, jabbing his finger at me.

I held the magazine close to him and turned the page. (I don't know how I kept a straight face. His rage was incredibly funny to me.) "Says here we've got a club chaplain. Didn't know that. Don't you think we should be a secular institution?"

He absolutely lost his mind. I'm one hundred percent sure Lee Martin had told his guys to pretend to be all animated and stuff in order to mess with our heads. But if you play with fire, you're gonna get burned, and this guy—a coach, I guess—blew his top. He slapped the programme out of my hands and gave me a push. It took me a few seconds to realise the best thing I could do would be to topple backwards, and the delay in throwing myself to the ground only succeeded in infuriating him even more. From my position on the bare soil of the technical area, I giggled almost uncontrollably.

James dashed forward to help me up, but I spotted Trick and Aff holding back Vimsy. I sighed. Gamesmanship was much easier with the kids and the women. These idiot men, beating their chests, were ruining my schemes. "James, cool Vimsy."

The kid obeyed instantly, leaving me there on the ground. Yes! Someone with a brain. I couldn't see what he did next because the referee had come over. From my position curled up like a shrimp, all I could see were his black socks. He bent and offered me a hand.

He lifted me to my feet. "Best! What on earth is going on over here?"

"Well, sir," I started, like he was my headmaster. Again, straight face, give me my BAFTA. "I was reading the match programme, minding my own business, and this chap assaulted me."

The assistant referee, also known as linesman, also known as lino, was in the area. "That's right! That's what happened! I couldn't believe my eyes. Look, there's the programme."

We all turned to see where the mistreated publication was splayed on the ground.

"You, off," said the ref. The coach, after a long delay, made his way up the tunnel and into the away team's dressing room. Bye, bye! Blyth protested way too much—what was the benefit of winding up a referee? It would only come out in some harsh decision late in the game. God hates an idiot, as I think it says in the Bible. And if it doesn't, it should.

I went over to Livia and pretended every part of my body hurt. She got it; she made a big fuss, did a concussion check on me, and pretended to talk into collar microphones the club didn't even own. Perfect!

Once the scene had settled down and the match got back underway—yes, a match was happening—I put Livia back on knee duty, collected the programme, winked at the only guy in the Blyth dugout who was looking at me, and went over to Vimsy.

"Mate. Go keep Dean company."

I was banishing him. He pulled all sorts of faces. "You're not serious."

"We don't need uncontrolled anger right now, thanks. You can sit over there, or you can go up in the stands." I looked at the bench. "Aff, you don't mind if someone punches me in the face, do you?"

"Not much, no." Last time we'd spoken, I'd gone into a long rant about him playing injured, which he'd had to suck up.

"Perfect. Come and shout what Jackie tells you to shout."

Trick spoke up. "I don't mind if you get punched in the face, either."

"Yeah," I said. "If Aff can't keep it in his pants, you're next up. Please God, there's one person here who wants us to win today."

Vimsy hovered around for a bit, but Jackie gave him some sort of signal and then he wandered off, kicking a water bottle as he went.

Our match ratings fluctuated with a downwards tendency. Too much drama on the sidelines!

I stood in front of Jackie and held my hands out. I lifted him up. "What?" he said.

"Calm them down."

Jackie stood on the touchline for a while, looking serene. He gave someone a thumbs-up. He pushed his palms downwards at the defence. He patted Joe Anka on the back as the right midfielder prepared to take a throw-in.

The match ratings climbed back up; I helped him sit back down.

I shook my head. "Fuck me, you lot are hard work."

Aff's eyebrows shot up. "You're not so easy, yourself."

"Wrong," I said. "Youngster, tell Aff he's wrong."

"Diarmuid," he said, because he wasn't all that keen on nicknames, "Mr. Best is attempting to keep us focused on the task while distracting the opposition from theirs. Napoleon said, 'Never interrupt an enemy when he is making a mistake.' Mr. Vimsy, much as I respect him, did just that."

I slapped the match programme against my thigh. "I love this kid." I smiled. "Let's all calm down for a while. We'll win this match if we stop being fucking moronic. All right?"

I'd only been pretending to read the programme before, but now I had a proper look. Page two was a big advert. Page three was a list of all the main Chester employees. My name was there, above Jackie's. The board were listed, and I learned Sumo's real name. There were loads of people I'd never met. Something to fix in the months ahead! Page four was another ad, and then came the most important text: Jackie's manager notes.

Manager notes were a tradition as old as time. Managers wrote what they thought about the season so far, about their last result, about the coming fixture. In the days before social media and wall-to-wall coverage, it was one of the only ways a fan would ever hear anything from their club's main man.

I had a vague memory of reading a manager's note from Sir Alex Ferguson when I was a kid, and being, like, super amazed at how close it brought me to him. Was Jackie on Instagram, posting pictures of his breakfast every morning? Probably. This section of the programme didn't hit as hard as it used to. How could it? But for ten seconds, I was rapt. I was reading the actual thoughts of Chester's manager! What could be more thrilling in the whole world?

Good afternoon everybody and welcome to the Deva Stadium
for our National League North tie against Blyth Spartans.

Wow! That's . . . generic.

Since I took the manager's position, we have felt that we are moving in the right direction but results on the pitch have not reflected this.

Mate.

We have had the lion's share of possession in our last six games, and we have fought back from behind to salvage a draw against tricky opposition in Leamington.

I'm also convinced that the least we would have got in the game against Banbury is a point, if we had been able to stick to our plan.

A pained moan escaped from my lips. Everyone turned to look at me.

"Jackie, soz, but your manager notes are really boring."

"Can you concentrate on the match, please?"

"No. We're on course. Everything's fine. This 'In the Dugout' bit. Did you write this yourself?"

He replied through gritted teeth. "Yes."

"It reads like someone was holding a gun to your head and you'd been told not to say anything interesting or else."

"Haha." He unclenched his jaw. Glanced at the pitch. Nothing was amiss. We had some kind of chemistry, the two of us. If I was virtually ignoring the match, there was probably a reason. He went with it. "I was never that good in school. Not that interested in English. I'm just happy if there are no spelling mistakes."

"Hmm," I said. I quickly scanned the pitch. We had started the match with 65% possession, and now it was up to 70. Our constant probing was taking its toll on Blyth's defence. Raffi was having an 8 out of 10 match, spraying the ball left and right. The Blyth defenders would cope well, then at some point in the second half, fall off a cliff. Put a fresh, raring-to-go Aff on for the last twenty minutes and it would be carnage. Jackie and I made eye contact, then both instantly looked away. He *knew.* I saw him relax. He looked back at me, encouraging me to keep distracting him. Save him from himself.

Livia wasn't quite on the same wavelength. From her point of view, I was having a go at Jackie at a time of great stress for him. "I suppose you think you could do better?" she spat. Fierce. Mother tiger. Jackie squeezed her hand, communicating, and she turned to check if she'd got the right message. I felt a pang of jealousy, which was preposterous.

I stole another quick look at the pitch. Raffi was on the ball again, superb balance, threatening a pass to the right. Blyth's entire defence shuffled across, as they'd been trained. But Raffi turned like a ballet dancer and fired it out to the left. Blyth collectively did that head dip that tired marathon runners do. Eleven players wasting calories based on a simple feint.

Everyone was waiting for me to talk, but my smile was in the way. I tapped the photo of Jackie that accompanied his manager's notes. "Writing's not that hard. You sketch out what you want to say, then try and find a theme."

"A theme?"

"Yeah, like if the chapter's about indecision, or fear of what dreams may come, you do *Hamlet*. If it's about, I don't know, a trip to Liverpool, there's obvious connective tissue. Now, let's all think really hard about this. We're playing Blyth Spartans. Come on, now. What've you got? Spartans? Hmm? Anything? Trick? Aff? Ben?"

Jackie was grinning. "You said you'd write it and *then* come up with the theme."

I shrugged. "You can work either way. I'm thinking, front cover, 'THIS IS CHESTER.' Who's got the best abs at the club?"

Livia didn't hesitate. "Raffi."

Jackie's reaction to that instant answer amused me, but I was on a roll. "Picture of Raffi with his abs falling out. We Photoshop some golden armour on him. Golden hat thing. *THIS IS CHESTER* in that blood font. Roar! Your notes are all about warriors and battles and glory."

"Very violent imagery," complained James, like the Bible wasn't nonstop massacres.

"Mate," I said. "They aren't the Blyth Guide Dogs, are they? Give me a break." I paused to watch as Henri competed for a header. He didn't win it, but raced off after the ball and won a foul. The ref gave the free kick *against* us. I couldn't help but blame Vimsy, unfair though that impulse almost certainly was.

I think Jackie sensed a change in my posture or whatever, because suddenly *he* was keen to distract *me*. "So I write a war-themed piece. You know, I agree with James. We have enough crowd trouble here. I don't want to put ideas in the heads of those hooligans."

"Good. Fine." I had a tiny think, then gasped. Big eyes pointing at everyone around. "Got it! What year were the Spartans?"

"Lots of years, I think," said James.

I gesticulated. "What year was the movie?"

"2005, or thereabouts."

"Oh my shitting God are you trying to wind *me* up, James? What year was the *battle*? Thermopylae?"

Nobody knew. "Someone look it up. Christ."

I took a few steps to the touchline and looked around. Jackie used the opportunity to send Aff out with some microtweaks. One involved D-Day dropping into a fractionally more defensive posture. Another resulted in Sam Topps having a back arrow on the match tactics screen. Not quite a defensive midfielder, but interesting that Jackie's mind was leaning that way.

I checked the stats and match ratings. We hadn't had many shots, but things were still going to plan. Blyth were frazzled, their bench was a mess, and now *their* manager was the one trying to calm everyone down. He had his head screwed on, that guy. Good opponent. I decided not to provoke him more . . . in the first half. He could easily sort everything out at halftime. Which made the second half fair game. I already had a few ideas of things I could do.

"The Battle of Thermopylae was 480 BC," said Livia, who might have been the only person in our dugout with a phone on her.

"Great!" I said, showing the cover of the programme to everyone. I was asking them to imagine the match programme that I was visualising. "Now, get this. Raffi's on the front cover. His face, but especially his torso. THIS IS CHESTER, abs, golden armour. Amazing." I turned a few pages. "In the manager notes section, Jackie's photo looks really aggressive and scary." I tapped his photo. "Which saves a bit of money because we can use this same one."

Jackie laughed hard enough it gave permission to everyone else to join in. Even the loyal Livia bit her lip.

I continued. "It says, Saturday, the eighteenth of March, 480 BC. Three p.m."

"Oh!" said James, causing me to twist my neck towards the pitch. "No, Mr. Best. Nothing is wrong. It is your idea. So wonderful! How are you so fecund?"

"Watch your mouth," I warned. "Yeah. 480 BC. We write the whole thing like it's, you know, the olden days. We've walked for six days back from Leamington, very excited about today's match."

"Marched!" said James.

"Yes, mate!" I agreed, rushing to the dugout to mash his head. "Marched! That's what I'm talking about. Do you get me? Once you sink into the vibe, it's easy. It writes itself. We're playing football in those times. What have they got? Oracles and stuff? *The oracles make Blyth favourites to win, but if we keep it tight first ten, we've got a chance, especially with the home crowd cheering us on.*"

"In the Deva amphitheatre," said Trick.

"Mate!" I yelled, demanding he raise his hand for a high five. "Come on!" I walked around in a big, fast circle. "Jackie! Jackie, mate. What do you think?"

He smiled. "I think I'd like Henri to drop five yards deeper until halftime."

I gave him a Maxy two-thumbs while Aff did the necessary.

Our technical area? Our little patch of Chester? Smiles all round.

At halftime, we fell into the dressing room. I suggested (via body language and a tiny push) that Vimsy should maybe stick to the back of the room, away from Jackie and the tactics board. The naughty corner. I tucked myself into a crevice again, but this time I was in front of the players. Visible. Checking the scores from other games on my phone.

Jackie looked young and fresh. Light in his eyes. Fierce. Daddy tiger protecting his young.

"Lads!" he cried. "Top half. I'm made up. That was a boss performance. No one could ask for more. Second half, they'll tire. They can't keep up with us for ninety minutes. No fucking chance. All they've got is snide shit. Slowing the game down. Taking time off the clock. This half, every time they slow it down, we speed it up. Glenn, Sam, Henri: You set the pace. Yeah? We're calm. We're in control. This is our patch. They've got no business being on the same turf as us. We're toying with them. We lift it, step by step. I don't care if it's nil–nil with ten to go. We don't panic. I don't care if they scrag a goal. Last ten minutes we're going ballistic out there. They'll be on their last legs. It'll be like punching through paper. Er . . . Max, what is it?"

I'd shot to my feet and taken a step forward before I even knew what I was doing. "They're switching to three-five-two," I said, which kinda sorta verged on moronic, but what could I do? We had to win. I had enough sense to look at my phone, as though I'd got a tip.

"You sure?"

"Million percent."

Jackie narrowed his eyes, turned, and adjusted the red magnets on his board. He rolled his neck. Stared. He turned to me with the Scousest grin of all time. "Am I crazy, or are we going to dick them anyway?"

There were a lot of laughs from the lads.

I grinned, too. "Yeah, we play our formation better than they do. But . . ."

"But what?"

"Nothing."

"Come on, lad. Out with it."

I stuck my tongue out the side of my mouth and looked around the room. I wasn't universally popular, but they all knew something about me. Mostly, they knew I was a total prick. "Just . . . there's winning, and there's *winning*."

Jackie laughed. "Come on! Tell me."

I got serious. "These manager fucks have been taking liberties. Using every trick in the book to put you on the back foot. It winds me up." I looked around the dressing room, right into the eyes of Henri, Sam, Trick, and the rest. "You're the power in these waters, Jackie. You're switched on and training is fucking mint. Am I right, guys?"

"Yeah!"

"Fucking Premier League–quality training, fluid tactics, it's amazing. I want to be part of it. I love everything you're doing. So I don't just want you to win today. I want you to fucking smash the whole idea that these four-four-two fuckwits can get one over on you." My chin fell to my throat, lest I get too emotional. I got a grip, looked round at the players. "Lads, you guys focus on the match. Focus on the ball, your mates, your jobs. Leave the shithousery to me. Whatever's going on around me, ignore it. I've got these idiots on toast, believe me. But

Jackie." I looked down at the grimy dressing room floor, then up at him. Pleading. "Let's do to them what they've been doing to you. Let's take the piss."

Jackie didn't blink for approximately three hours. "What are you thinking?"

"They've gone three-five-two, so let's go four-four-two. Every time they change, we change instantly. We don't *have* to—we'll fucking win anyway. This is about sending a *message*." I glanced around. Not everyone knew what I was talking about, which was unbelievable to me. The message was crying out from every cell in my body, every seat in the stadium. The message was nonsensical, ungrammatical, but powerful. Someone had planted it in my brain and it had taken hold of me. I gripped Jackie's shoulder; maybe it would take hold of him, too. I felt my mouth twisting into a snarl. "Don't mess with Chesters."

Jackie felt it. He got the same half-snarl. The same madness in his look. "You want some four-four-two, Max? You want some back-to-basics football? Sure. Let's *shove it up their arse!*"

That was all I needed to hear. Everything was going to be all right. Don't ask me where my next line came from. It just burst out of me. There was no thought behind it. No strategy. No game. Just *waah!* Football stuff.

"Jackie Reaper's blue-and-white army!" I yelled.

Instantly, the whole dressing room was up. On their feet. Bouncing. Screaming. I've only ever seen it from teams *after* they've won a cup. *We* did it at halftime. Nil–nil in a relegation six-pointer.

"Jackie Reaper's blue-and-white army!"

"Jackie Reaper's blue-and-white army!"

Trick replaced Raffi. At the same time, a hulking Blyth-boy was replaced by a mediocre midfielder. Bad move. The CA gap widened.

The first ten minutes of the half were a blitzkrieg. D-Day was inspired, causing havoc down the left. In the centre, Sam picked up Raffi's role and passed them to death. But it was Joe Anka on the right who stepped up with a gorgeous cross for Henri to head home. Your defenders can be as tall as you want, but if the cross is right, Henri's going to put it away. He wheeled away in a frenzy of delight, whipping up the fans.

We kept piling on the pressure. Chance after chance. It was pulsating stuff.

The crowd sensed something was afoot. They were adding two decibels per minute. I ran and jumped and perched on an advertising board. I screamed at the stands. Waved my arms around. Demanded more. More noise, more passion, more energy.

The response was incredible. It filled up my senses.

Belief. Wall-to-wall belief.

A chant emerged. Unscripted, unimaginable, undeniable.

We. Are. Staying up!
Said we are staying up!
We. Are. Staying up!
Said we are staying up!

I imagined Crackers there, in the main stand, suddenly having his earpiece blown off. I imagined a young boy in the stadium for the first time, scared but excited, watching his dad lose his shit. MD and Ruth, up in their fancy box, turning feral, ignoring the sponsors and screaming obscenities at the pitch.

I fucking loved it.

I'd almost forgotten about Lee Martin. In the words of one podcast I used to keep up with, other teams can do tactics, too. Martin's idea was to drop a midfielder into the DM slot: 3-1-4-2.

I went over to Jackie, who was deeply frustrated that he was chairbound, with multiple people pushing him down every time he tried to get up. I told him what was happening. He turned and looked at his bench. A beatific smile appeared. "Youngster?"

All I could do was smile.

"You do it," ordered Jackie.

"You sure?" Giving a debut to a top talent was a point of pride for most managers. Letting me be seen in the photos was incredibly generous of him.

"I'm sure!" he yelled at me.

I stood to my full height, magnificent AF, and summoned James. I put my hands on his shoulders. "It's happening," I told him.

His eyes shone, his teeth sparkled. "Any advice?" he said.

"No," I said. "This lot are fucking dogshit, mate."

He thought about what I'd said, then closed his eyes ever so slowly. "Mr. Best," he said, as his expression softened. "You have such a way with words."

I kept hold of him, one way or another, until the substitution could be made. Tony, the striker, came off. James ran on. The moment he slipped out from my grasp must be the way parents feel when their kids leave home. Fucking abysmal, mate. Not a fan.

We were playing 4-1-4-1. The key position was held by Youngster, seventeen years old, who'd made me jump through hoops to get him to this point. He would protect our defence in our most important game of the season. As he scampered away, the only thing I wanted in this whole world was to burst into tears.

But I kept it together. One thought, and one thought alone, stopped me from expressing how I truly felt.

I wasn't finished with Lee Martin and his Band of Botherers.

The formations were massively in our favour. We were 1–0 up, and we'd reduced the match to something resembling an armistice. Minutes passed with neither team looking like they had a shot. The newfound calmness suited us right down to the ground.

Blyth had come hoping to drop some emotion bombs. Hoping to mess up Jackie. But the closest target to their lines was *me*.

I wandered over and, leaving the very tip of my heel inside the white paint (so that I was technically in the area), stood in the no-man's land between the technical areas. Waited for my chance.

My first intervention was easy. Two players competed for the ball and it bounced towards our bigger shelter. I jogged to get it, flicked it up, and started doing kick-ups. A Blyth player came to get the ball so he could take the throw-in. I politely handed the ball to him so he could set up an attack. Er . . . wait. That doesn't sound right. Let me try that again.

A Blyth player came towards me to get the ball so he could take the throw-in. I increased the speed and complexity of the tekkers I was doing until my feet were a blur. The guy actually put his hands on his hips and sighed. I smiled. *Okay, here's the ball, mate.* I balanced it on the tips of my toes and raised it slowly towards his torso so all he needed to do was clasp his hands around it and get on with the match. Of course, as soon as his hands moved towards the ball, I flicked it away from him and continued doing tekkers with my back to him. That wound the Blyth bench up something rotten. The referee came over to plead with me to cut it out. I held three fingers up and swore to behave.

That was awesome, but the effects started to die down, so I looked around for more potential dickery. Ideally, something a lot more incendiary.

There was a ball boy behind the advertising hoardings. I signalled that he should send me a ball. He obliged, and it landed just to my right. Ignoring the ball for a moment, I leaned forward. The ball boy seemed familiar. It was Kian! The under-sixteens player I'd found at Footy Addicts. I liked it when people got involved. I gave him a little thumbs-up and returned to my task. But when I bent to pick up the ball, I accidentally kicked it forward a couple of feet.

Weird.

I tried again.

Frowning, I bent down, slowly sent two hands towards the ball, and— Oops! The ball nudged forward off my toes. I scratched my head, then tried again. I couldn't believe it! My stupid foot kicked the ball away before my hands could reach down! I kept trying, and kept getting six inches closer to the away team's dugout.

Now, what happened next is completely inexplicable to me.

One of the Blyth substitutes ran towards me and threw an actual fucking punch!

I dodged it, falling onto my back in the process. Half the main stand rose, appalled, outraged, demanding vengeance. The noise was cacophonous.

I turned and saw our subs bench had the appropriate response: mock outrage. Performative pointing, but not moving more than a metre from their seats. They'd read the sitch perfectly. I relaxed.

The linesman waved his flag so hard the referee whistled and sprinted over to find out what had happened. He listened to his assistant, then showed a red card to the guy who'd attacked me. Big trouble with the FA for that little prick! I put my hands behind my head, rather as though I was on the beach, and began juggling the ball I'd been trying to catch. I bounced it from foot to foot. Great little display of tekkers. It was all very jaunty until yet another substitute ran over to me and leathered me in the ribs.

Now there was true pandemonium. Aff, Trick, Tony, Ben, and Raffi were first on the scene, then the nearest guys from the pitch—D-Day, Sam, Gerald May—arrived to join the scrap. Livia and Dean were by my side soon enough, but they couldn't stop me laughing long enough to check if I'd sustained any real damage.

Livia leaned close to my ear. "You're flipping crazy." When I looked at her next, her eyes were all-white. Shining. Well worth a bruise. And if one rib was broken, so what? The gods had given me plenty of spares.

I turned and caught the exact moment the ref sent Lee Martin off, probably for failing to control his bench. Blyth would play the rest of the match with no manager, and, the curse assured me, with two of their unused subs sent off. To all intents and purposes, it was game over.

I looked at Livia. "How's Jackie look?"

She glanced up. The tiniest fraction of a glimpse, but she had seen enough. "He's happy," she said, and her eyes filled with liquid.

"Yeah?"

"Yeah."

My face hardened. "Well, tell him it's not a picnic. He's here to work. Tell him to get Aff on. Go for the jugular."

My reward was a savage smile. "Yes, Max."

10

IN AND OUT

The last twenty minutes went by in a blur of action and shots, entirely aimed at Blyth's goal. We won 2–0. Could have been 6.

The players tried to carry Jackie aloft, stool and all, but he persuaded them to get fucked. They settled for jogging to the dressing room so they could celebrate sooner. No beer for them—they had an away game in three days.

But I was thirsty, so I invited the referee and his crew for a pint in the Blues Bar. He said they'd love to, but he tended to want to get out of the stadium safely and drink when he got home. I promised I'd look after them, and they joined me for a couple of pints. They were a decent hang, if a bit condescending when I sketched out a loose vision of a referee's academy, but were deliriously happy when Emma and Gemma turned up. Gemma was quite flirty with all three of them, which I found absolutely surreal. Once the match officials had left— got a few stewards to discreetly escort them through the spooky dark alley to their car—I asked Gemma what she was plotting. She denied that she was even flirting with them, and Emma backed her up.

Very odd.

MD came in just as a chant went up. It was based around the famous tune from *The Great Escape*. It's very jaunty and the football version is ninety-nine percent based around the sound *duh* so everyone can remember the lyrics. It's lots of fun, and at the end of the stanza there's a space for a two-syllable word.

Duh de,
De der de duh de,
Duh duh duhh derr de-de d-de-de

There's a bit more, and at the end, everyone yells:)
Ches-ter!

MD danced across the room towards us, but when he got close, he took ten steps back so he could continue to enjoy himself. The chant died down and generic upbeat pop music came through the sound system behind the happy murmurs from the fifty or so patrons.

MD put his hands on our high table and closed his eyes, savouring the atmosphere. He showed us his teeth. "I knew it. I fucking knew it! You and Jackie. The dream team. That was really something, Max. I feel . . . I feel . . ."

"Like dancing?" said Gemma.

Panic filled MD's eyes—she was really out of his league—but then he was smiling again. "May I have the honour?" he said, holding his hand out.

"You may," she said.

They started dancing (her) and shuffling side-to-side with a gormless expression (him).

"Okay what the shit is going on?" I said.

Emma's poker face was rock solid sometimes. "I don't know what you mean. Good win today. Do you really have to throw yourself to the ground every five minutes? I thought I was dating a big strong rugby guy."

"I'm strong but sensitive," I said, rubbing my side. It'd be sore for a day or so. No biggie.

Emma looked around. She knew the room was supposed to be packed. Bursting at the seams with happy fans. The mood was good, but it was only a quarter full. "Is it all right now? Are we all right?"

"We will be," I said. "Bradford got a point against Darlo today. That's not ideal. But MD's right. Jackie and I are a good team. We complement each other. Kettering are going to get slapped."

On Sunday morning, I had another lie-in. Emma went out to get some fresh breakfast and came back with food and a paper: *The Mail on Sunday.*

On the back page, in a blue box: *"I saw yellow . . . for being DEAF."* *Teen star's heartbreaking story, pages 94–95.*

I exhaled. Beth worked *fast*. "Did you look already?"

"No," said Emma. "I was scared."

We placed the paper on Henri's kitchen counter, back page facing up, then peeled over the pages in reverse order, like a Japanese couple might. "Oh, fuck," I said.

The first thing that popped out was an *enormous* photo of me and Dani. It must have been taken as we left the pitch after her yellow card. It was almost black and white, with darkness behind us and mist around. There's an out-of-focus Wrexham player to the side, and what must have been the referee, also blurred, just in the edge of the shot.

I'm striding towards the camera with the same kind of gritty, determined energy as an action movie star who is walking away from a large explosion.

Dani is holding my hand, looking up at me. She does *not* look like someone whose world is falling apart.

I felt the cold chill of unforeseen consequences. "Is this what it looks like?"

Emma had started reading the article. She was in lawyer mode, and lawyers don't answer questions unless you pay them. "The photo? What does it look like to *you*?"

"Looks a bit like . . . she's not into Harry Styles anymore."

"She'll always be into Harry Styles."

"Emma, come on, this is bad."

"Why's it bad?"

"She's got, like, a crush on me or whatevs."

"So?"

"No! That's no good. I can't have that." I wanted a football relationship with Dani. Possibly, once I'd sold her for a record fee to, I don't know, Barcelona, possibly *then* we could be friends. And nothing else. Obviously. One good thing: Emma wasn't bothered by it in the slightest. "How did this even happen?"

Emma laughed. A proper, full-body laugh. Finally, she sighed. "Let's review. You pluck her from obscurity, tell her she's special, film a dance video to woo her—still waiting for mine, by the way— sometimes weeks go by and she doesn't even see you; sometimes you go *whoo* and you *drown* her in attention. Oh, and you're hot and talented and you'd *burn* your career to keep your promises. *How did this happen?* Babes, don't be a moron."

I scrunched my eyes closed and rubbed my eyebrows. "How do I undo it? How do I stop her from thinking about me like that?"

"That's easy. Every time a rival manager walks up to you, fall to the ground and curl into a ball like a hedgehog."

"Emma! I'm serious."

She shook her head. "She's got a crush on you. It'll pass." She looked from the paper to me. "There's another thing you can do to look unattractive: turn every little thing into a crisis." She saw I was struggling and rubbed my arm. Her voice softened. "If it's not your players, it'll be your staff, and if it's not the staff, it'll be the fans. You might want to get used to it. Now shush." Emma skimmed the article, nodded, then went through it again, tracking the lines with her finger. It was all very serious. Big law school energy. "All right. I've read it. It's fine. She's clever, that reporter friend of yours. There's nothing, like, explosive here. Nothing untrue, although your quotes are a little too perfect. It's the plain, simple story of what happened, plus a bit of an interview with Dani. But it's constructed in a way that makes your blood boil. *You* come out looking great, as does the club, and they are very, very sympathetic to Dani. I think this will do the trick, and there's no reason other referees will feel attacked. They've got quotes from two other refs who did matches with Dani. They're made to look like heroes."

I read it through and had to agree with her. It was masterful. They'd even got hold of a photo of the referee leaving an ugly building, glancing at the camera with a guilty look on her face, and juxtaposed that with one of a beaming Dani holding the trophy and medal she'd won in Crewe. On the left, a miserable husk. On the right, the promise and hope of youth.

I sighed and got my phone out. I texted Beth.

Me: Acceptable. Now leave her alone.

My phone spent the rest of the day blowing up. Beth's only reply to my text was the word *TalkSport*. I flew around the kitchen wondering why Henri didn't have a radio. Who didn't have a radio? "Quick! To the car!"

Emma sighed and went over to an oversized rectangular clock. That, apparently, was a digital radio and had all the channels.

They'd already started talking about the story, and half the callers were blowhards banging on about how everyone wanted their own rules and why should the refs have to treat everyone differently and they had their own sports, didn't they?

It was bad for my blood pressure, so I turned it off. Emma tried to reassure me that the producers were actively selecting idiot callers to generate engagement. She was probably right, but I stewed for a while anyway.

But more texts came. The overall reaction was hugely positive. Ziggy asked if I would consider adopting him. Youngster said it was the first time the *Mail* had ever been allowed in his church. Kisi left a three-minute, weepy voicemail where I only understood one word in ten.

MD and Ruth had a much more gammony, reactionary circle of friends than me, and they reported back that people were stewing at the ref. Spectrum told me that "Don't Mess with Chesters" was trending in Cheshire and there'd been an upsurge in people watching my tekkers video.

The funniest thing was that Raffi and Henri swapped personalities for the day. Raffi was normally the one sending brief, emoji-heavy texts, while Henri would sometimes drop me a few paragraphs of his thoughts on a variety of topics, including, memorably, an outline for a book he wanted to write about stealing the secret of silk production from the Chinese.

After he read the article, though, I got this from him. Two words, five emojis:

Henri: Yesterday: *heart heart.* **Today:** *heart heart heart.*

That was followed by one from Raffi. An enormous message that must have taken him twenty minutes to type out. It was very warm, very personal. The most common word was *fatherhood.* It was all about his relationship to his daughter and how she'd changed him. How she'd saved him, how she was the light in his darkness. He said he already knew I'd be a good father, but seeing that pic had reduced him to bits. He wanted to be as strong, as gentle, as selfless as the man in the photo.

It made me uncomfortable. Made me feel like a fraud. I wasn't a father figure. For a start, there was no way I would have kids until I knew there was nothing wrong with my brain that I might pass down. And when it came to football, I thought of myself as a peer. First among equals, maybe, but still just one of the team. Kids? I was just a kid myself. I could run a football club. That was easy. Being a father? Terrifying.

I knew joining forces with Beth would have consequences, but I'd been thinking along the lines of angry referees. Punitive football administrators. Something tangible I could rage against. I hadn't expected it all to get so personal. So emotional.

I really needed a football match. An excuse to stop thinking about my inner life, please.

For once, the universe delivered.

Big time.

Monday, March 20.

I woke up pretty late again, and found I had five messages and two missed calls from MD. The first one said:

MD: Come to Chester asap. Call me on the way. Urgent. (No one has died.)

The latest one said:

MD: Very much hope you're not replying b.c. you're on your way. I've got a conf call I can't postpone. Watch training. I'll be there at half ten, maybe earlier, explain everything. (No one has died.)

So obviously my mind was racing all the way from Darlo to the training ground. What could be so distressing? Something with Dani. The first proper consequences coming in. I felt sick.

When I got there, my hair was a sweaty mess. I'd lost weight and my eyelids were yellow. In olden times they'd have covered me in leeches or drilled a hole in my skull. When MD jogged out of the credit card building, I couldn't get up. I couldn't move.

MD sat next to me and stared straight ahead. The first thing he said was, "No one has died. Don't worry. But . . ."

We had an evening game the following day, so the morning's training was fairly easy-going. Vimsy led the guys through their paces. Got their juices flowing. Did a bit of shape work. Bit of set piece stuff. Finished with some noncontact duels. The guys enjoyed it. Training's twice as fun after a win.

He blew his whistle to end the sesh, then I blew mine, with MD's words still ringing in my ears. I waved that everyone should come in, and a circle formed around me. Everyone from the first-team squad was there, except Angles, the goalkeeping coach, who was out with flu.

"All right, lads, shut the fuck up." I waited until they settled down, which didn't take long. They sensed something was off. I heard a car start. Probably MD rushing off to his next meeting. "You know Jackie's knee's been giving him gyp."

"Chip?" said Pascal.

"Gyp," said Henri. "Derived from the idiomatic phrase 'to gee up,' meaning to strike a horse to make it go faster. The pain in his knee is akin to being whipped to go faster. One cannot relax."

I shook my head. There were times the foreign guys knew English more better than what I did. "His knee's ouchy, Pascal." I checked the time. "Yeah, pretty much now-ish, he's getting that bad boy opened up. The specialist is going to take his knee apart like a Swiss watch, lay out all the pieces, give them a bit of spit and polish, stick them all back in."

"Max," said Tony. "When did you get your medical licence?" Lots of laughs.

"You know me, mate. Max Best, double oh-seven-seven, licence to drill holes in knees. Anyway, that's why he's not here right now. Getting himself sorted out. He didn't want to make a big deal of it before the Blyth game. Didn't want to distract us all."

Also, Jackie was waiting to see the result. If we'd lost, he would have quit. That's what MD thought, anyway.

I pushed my own knee forward and looked down at it. "He's going to be all right. He'll be in and out. They're just seeing what's up. If there's something wrong, they'll fix it, but, you know, there's probably just a little pair of scissors in there from the first op. No big deal. And no point speculating. All we know for sure is that, tomorrow night, he's not getting on a bus for three hours down to Kettering."

That caused a stir. At first, everyone was thinking of Jackie. Worrying for him. Now their thoughts got more selfish. Sam was the first to realise what the news meant. He tilted his head as he appraised me. Next to understand was D-Day. He had the look of a man who'd been caught photocopying his arse on the company machine.

I spelled it out for the dim ones. "MD has asked me to run the touchline tomorrow." Run the touchline was a euphemism for be the manager. I let everyone deal with that in their own time. After about ten seconds, I looked around from left to right. Ben, Carl, Aff, Glenn, and a few more of the good ones. Three more I could trust: my clients. And the ten guys I wanted to replace in the summer. "I know some of us have beef. Which is why I'm trying to turn this into a vegan club." Pause. "Absolutely nothing. Tough crowd. Okay, free talk now. Is there anyone who has a problem with me doing the match tomorrow?" No response. I sighed. "Look, you've got to say it now. It can't, fucking, *bubble up* tomorrow at halftime. Do you know what I mean? Speak now. Voice your doubts. I won't hold it against you. Let's clear the air." Nothing. Bunch of surly kids. Worse than teenagers. Like any teacher, I picked someone out. But instead of picking a yes-man who'd tell me what I wanted to hear, I went to the other extreme. To one of the baddies. "Sam."

Hint of a smile in his eyes. He was about to make a joke. "Am I in your team?"

"I haven't decided on a formation or a lineup," I said. There was no point pretending he wasn't the best midfielder at the club, though. "But yes."

"That's all right, then." Some chuckles. Footballers could get very egocentric. Very protective of their status.

"It's not all right, Sam. I need to know if you're happy with me being the guy."

"Happy? Not *happy*. But I'd say you know what you're doing." He looked to his left. "Took the piss out of Ian Evans, all right. Didn't you?"

He was talking about my trial. "I prefer to think that I . . . suggested some alternate ways of approaching the task." Sam's attitude was helpful. He trusted me enough to take charge of one match. And from a contract point of view, being put in the team by the director of football was even better than being picked by the manager. Unless I tried to play with ten strikers or some mad shit, he'd give me a chance. I looked at a spot of grass for a bit, trying to make sure I covered all the essential points. "Vimsy's going to do training again in the morning. Usual stuff. Just a glorified warm-up, isn't it? I'd ask you to be very slightly more switched on than normal. No need to go nuts. But maybe he forgets a step and instead of nudging each other, grinning, you remind him. Do you know what I mean? Having no manager leaves a big hole. We all need to chip in. I'm going to ask Jill from the women's team to come with us. If she can't, Spectrum. They're quality. They're also the kinds of people you guys might have joked about, you know, in a past life. But obviously if they're giving up their evenings to come and help out, you're going to be *extremely* welcoming to them. Charming, even. Any questions about that?"

There weren't. I'd made my point.

Henri spoke. "What will be your tactical plan?"

"I've just heard the news myself. I need to think about it. I know I won't need a defensive midfielder, so Youngster, you've got the night off. Catch up with your homework."

"I have done all of my schoolwork, Mr. Best."

"Of course you have," I said, and there were some laughs. "Rest up, though. Jackie might need you again on Saturday. Good?"

He looked pretty disappointed, but I only had one formation that used a DM and I definitely wouldn't use it with this squad. "Yes, Mr. Best."

"Pascal, are you fit?"

His eyes lit up. "Yes, Max! I mean, Mr. Best."

"I can imagine wanting a lot of attacking options on the bench. Don't go exploring any abandoned houses tonight."

Ben, maybe hoping I'd put him in the first team ahead of our normal goalie if he got himself noticed, had a cheeky look on his face. "Are you going to get the Kettering manager sent off an' all?" Many laughs.

I looked around the circle. "Maybe we should get this straight. I'm not excited about tomorrow. You know I like a bit of drama. Any excuse to tell a story. But I've played Kettering this season. We were down to nine and our manager got sent off. Blew his lid." I looked at Vimsy. I wasn't sure if he was still upset with me from sidelining him on Saturday. Probably. He was a grown man, though. I could rely on him, at least until kickoff. "We still scored four goals in the second half. I want to be respectful-*ish*. Kettering are good pros. They try. If we're stupid, they'll punish us. If we don't graft, they'll beat us." I thrust out my bottom lip. "But the gulf in quality, lads. They don't have a single player who'd get in this team. Not one. As long as you match them for sprints and energy, I'm going to be bored off my tits while you pepper their net with shots. There's no story. Nothing for me to do. It's going to be a clinical performance. Surgical. Twenty-five shots, seventy percent possession." I sighed. "Routine win."

There was a confused silence. Finally, Henri threw his arms around Glenn Ryder and Raffi. "Poor Max. So young, so talented, and his first management job is with us! No wonder he is unhappy."

I smiled back at him. "Here's what's going to happen. We're going to pop down to Kettering tomorrow night, take care of *bizniz*. Wednesday morning I'm going to go and see Jackie in the hospital or wherever he is. I'm going to bring him a bunch of grapes, some clean undies, and three freshly minted points, all nice and wrapped up, signed by you lot. Yeah? Everyone happy with that?"

"Yes, Max."

I shook my head. "Business as usual, then. One last thing. I'd *strongly* prefer if this news didn't get out, and I bet Jackie would as well. Don't tell your wives, your girlfriends, your kids. You know I was in the papers over the weekend. News gets out I'm doing this, it's going to be a circus, and Jackie will get sucked in when he should be resting. No circus, please. In and out. The match reports are all about *you*. *Your* goals, *your* assists. Yeah? We go, we win, everyone in the stadium assumes Jackie's on the bench where they can't see him." Tiny smile. Tiny frown. "Hey! That's an idea. Why don't we do that? Aff. Have you still got your crutches?"

"Yes, Max."

Leaning some crutches against the dugout to make it seem like Jackie was in there? Pretty simple. But I hadn't got to where I was by doing simple things.

"Max," warned Henri. "Don't say what you're about to say."

I couldn't help it. Huge grin. "Has anyone got a bald mate, about Jackie's height?"

So, I was going to manage a professional football match.

What?

Seriously, though. What?

A massive game, too. Chester needed to win. Really, really needed to win.

Technically, it was a relegation six-pointer. If they beat us, Kettering would have hopes of a late burst of points that would see them survive.

And it was away. Statistics said that home teams won fifty percent of all matches, while away teams won only a quarter. The rest end in draws.

Okay, then!

I had a day and a half to prepare.

I'd spoken to the players. Vimsy would take care of the basic admin stuff, like getting the players on the team bus and setting off at the right time. Jill or Spectrum would join him and help out. The kit man would bring the kits. Physio Dean would bring his stock of medical supplies, magic sponges, and sprays. MD would travel down, too, like he usually did, but I'd asked him not to spread the news. I had the sense that we could sneak down south, grab a nice, quiet win, and go home. We didn't need drama. We didn't need energy.

MD didn't need much persuading. We'd do it on the quiet. Less embarrassing for him if I lost 7–0 again.

I should have had millions of extra tasks. But I didn't. My only real responsibilities were getting to Kettering on time, filling in the team sheet, and giving a pre-match team talk.

For now, though, I had the evening free. I could go watch a match. Maybe even get enough XP to hit the 2,000 I needed to unlock 4-1-4-1. James would forgive me for changing my mind about his night off!

But I was astonished to see that there were no fixtures. No fixtures from any league! Not even Scotland. It made me crazy. I checked every website on Earth. But no, it seemed to be the case that the closest professional football match was in Norway!

I didn't fight it. I'd go home, watch some videos of Kettering, and think about my options.

I went into Henri's office and raided his vast stationery collection. I wanted post-it notes, pens, and inspiration.

Kettering normally played 4-4-2, but the manager had proven unusually flexible. I needed to plan for his default option while considering what I'd do if I were him.

I knew five formations. I had the bog-standard 4-4-2 and its simplest variant, 4-4-2 diamond. The latter needed a central attacking midfielder. I could play that role, at this level anyway. Pascal would be able to do it one day. But there was no way I was going to use it in Kettering. The default 4-4-2 was strangely compelling. The two teams would match up man-for-man, but I'd have better players in every position. End of discussion, surely?

A more daring option was 4-3-3. I had three good central midfielders, and this formation would suit them. It didn't use wide midfielders, which was fine because ours were dicks or had just come back from injury. I only had three proper strikers in my squad, and one hadn't played for a while. The idea of having three strikers on the pitch for, say, twenty minutes, made me feel all special inside. I knew that as we got more attacking, it would scare Kettering into becoming more defensive.

Huh. I could start with 4-4-2, let that play out, then sub off the right mid and put on a third striker. Kettering would throw on another defender. *Then* I'd make two more subs and go to 3-5-2.

I slapped myself in the face. I didn't *have* 3-5-2! The formation the team had been using the most and I didn't have it. Jesus, Max!

I spent a couple of minutes beating myself up about the fact, but I knew it was unfair. How could I know I'd be thrust into the spotlight like this?

Why had I been thinking I had 3-5-2? Because I did, sort of. Every time I'd used that formation, Spectrum had set it up for me. That wasn't an option for the Kettering match.

I had two more formations.

For a more defensive, obdurate choice I had the 4-5-1 I'd been using with the women's team. That would be the closest to the system that Jackie had been using. It *could* work with the men's team, but I had a lot more faith in Dani than D-Day. He was a very flighty guy. If he played well, we'd win. If he didn't, where were the chances going to come from?

Finally, I had 4-2-4. Very, very attacking. An option, perhaps, for the last ten minutes. Aff as the left winger. Pascal on the right?

I took a break and went for a walk. I was overthinking this. Kettering were shit. Four-four-two, keep it tight first ten.

I smiled and went to a caff for some builder's tea and something covered in cheese.

Newly refreshed, I had a breakthrough. Normally, the formation was the starting point for the rest of the decisions.

But I'd be using Triple Captain and Bench Boost. And that meant the players I brought on would overperform.

Now, professional players didn't like being subbed off in the first half. It was −100 relationship points to do that to a guy who wasn't injured. I'd do it if it would be the difference between life and death, but I had to plan for Bench Boost to kick in from the second half.

Okay, so which three players did I want to bring on with a performance boost?

Obviously my gold guys: Glenn, Sam Topps, and Henri.

But that was not going to happen. Glenn needed to play the whole match. Sam, too. Henri . . . Henri was an option. He'd fucking hate it, but if he came on with the boost and scored a goal or two that could be decisive in getting the three points. It made a lot of sense to use Bench Boost with attacking players.

I pencilled Henri in alongside Aff. Aff would only play twenty to twenty-five minutes, but he was so good. He'd wrecked Blyth in the last match. The third guy, assuming there were no injuries, and everything went according to plan . . . Pascal?

I felt like I was getting somewhere. At the end of the match, I'd be relying on Aff, Pascal, and Henri. Which suggested the last twenty minutes, at least, would be 4-2-4. All-out attack. Flying wingers.

I took a clean sheet of paper and wrote out two main options for how we'd start and finish the match.

Option 1: Surprise, Motherfunner!

I could start the match with 4-4-2 and at halftime push the wide midfielders forward, making a 4-2-4. This would have the benefit of initially making me seem like a normal, cautious manager. The Kettering guy would not expect the second-half surge, and even with Pascal coming on, we'd start the match with CA 40 and end it with CA 42.

Option 2: In and Out

The second choice was to start with 4-4-2, switching to a very central 4-3-3 and ending with 4-2-4, where we'd attack down the sides. That could even be done without using any subs if I picked D-Day to start as the third striker (he'd slip onto the wing after the change), and picked the lesser-spotted Chad Flintoff as the third starting midfielder (he could later move out wide). Flintoff was only CA 32, but he'd be fine for a half. Against Kettering.

This idea had the advantage of being quite flashy. Big, noticeable changes in style that would get the Kettering manager thinking.

The price for easy formation changes was a slightly reduced average CA. We'd start with 39.7, but that would rise to 42 by the end.

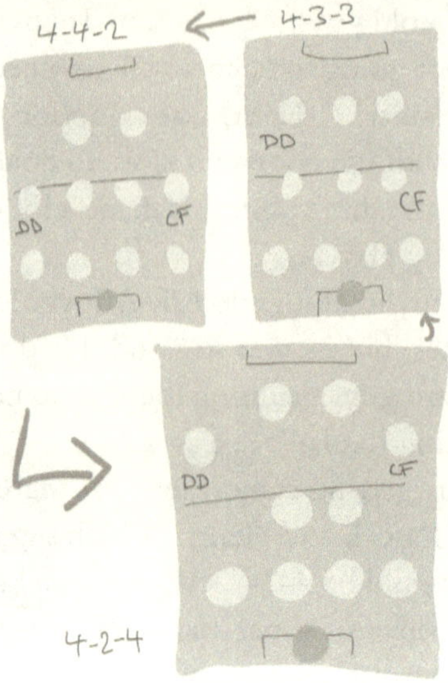

I scrunched up some notes and paced around. Something was off. This was all useful analysis. Thinking through all these options was necessary. Useful. Professional. But I felt I was missing the point. I'd gone from the tactical to the strategic. That was right, surely?

I took a cup of tea out to the crab apple tree and told him my plans. My voice was pretty flat. I was still being very mathematical. Why did that feel wrong?

It wasn't a struggle to work out why. I had to make an even more basic decision than the formation or which players to Bench Boost. There was a more fundamental question: Did I want to manage like Jackie? Imitate his style, since that's what the players were used to?

Or should I go full Max?

I'd had success doing things my way. But it was one thing with teenage boys and a brand-new women's team.

This was the men's team, and if I messed it up and we lost, most of the players and plenty of the backroom staff would lose their jobs.

This was serious.

Tuesday, March 21. Match 41 of 46: Kettering Town versus Chester.

I drove to Kettering early—three hours early, just in case—and when our team bus arrived I waved at the driver to let me on.

"Guys, stay there a minute," I said, and a busload of confused players settled back into their seats. I looked around. "Pascal, need you over here." I handed him some cash. "No one knows what you look like. I need you to buy something for me then go wait by the main entrance. Jill, will you go with him? Take that Chester coat off for a minute."

"Max," she said. "What are you up to?"

"Nothing," I said, rubbing my hands together like I often did when I had absolutely zero schemes up my sleeve.

A few minutes later, Pascal met us at the door to the stadium with a plastic bag. "All right, lads," I called out, circling my finger to show they could start rolling. "Remember what we said. In and out."

I filled out the team sheet, handed it in, and went for a potter. Kettering's stadium, Latimer Park, was very small. A couple of covered stands, lots of low hut-like structures. Nothing matched, nothing made sense. One section had bright red seats, but over there was another new-ish stand that was bright blue. To the side there was a big hill. It all reminded me of my childhood playing footy anywhere and everywhere.

The absolute best part of the stadium was a cute little pie shop that was by the pitch. It was on the wrong side to the dugouts, otherwise I would have added pie-eating to my repertoire of mind games.

With an hour to go before kickoff, it was time to tell the team my plans. I went to the dressing room and all chat ceased. Vimsy turned the pre-match hype music off and there was silence.

"All right, shut the fuck up," I said. I went to our tactics board and moved the red magnets into a familiar shape. "Kettering play four-four-two. Today's no exception. They're not an impressive team, but they're decent at home." Watching them in the warm-up made me recalibrate my expectations. When I'd played against them, their average CA was about 30. Today it was 35. Some of the improvement was from training, but they had three guys in the starting lineup who hadn't been around last time. January signings or guys back from injury. Whatever. "They've got one of those long-throw guys." Some players were able to throw the ball into the penalty box from anywhere in the top third of the pitch. It often caused havoc. "Jackie, how am I doing so far?"

Everyone looked at our new manager. He stared blankly at me. Gerald May slapped him on the arm. "That's you, you dozy twat!"

"Jackie" blinked. "Oh, right, yeah."

Much laughter.

I shook my head and got back to business. "Yeah, so. I want a solid start, build a base, and we'll start increasing the pressure through the half. Second half, we turn on the afterburners. The strategy is: Last twenty minutes, we're attacking nonstop. Good?"

"Yeah, lads, keep it tight first half," said our Jackie impersonator, punching his palm. The squad laughed again. I later learned that at least three players had mates who could pass as Jackie from a distance, and there had been bitter disputes as to who should get the gig. We told the referee he was a trainee physio because one of our medical staff was in hospital, but to everyone else we pretended he was actually Jackie.

"Lineups," I said, moving the blue magnets into position. "We'll start with four-four-two and match them up. Almost the first thing Jackie ever told me was that for pros, the most important thing is winning duels. So the formation is to make sure you don't get complacent. Make sure you start serious. If you're not up for this, some joker's gonna steal your pocket money in minute one. You need to come out of the traps *running*. Start winning duels, start pushing them back. The starting eleven will be able to switch to four-three-three if I want to get funky."

The players looked around at each other as they tried to calculate who would work in a narrow formation.

I put them out of their misery. "Robbo in goal, back four is Magnus, Glenn, May, Carl." Trick's face fell. It was a toss-up between him and Magnus for the left back slot. They had almost identical CA, but I think the single data point that tipped the decision in Magnus's favour was that Trick was a grotesque, subhuman wanker. "Midfield: Wisey, Sam, Chad. D-Day on the left when we're four, pushing on when we're three. You all get that, right?" I moved two of the magnets in and out to show how easy it would be to transition between the formations with those players.

Everyone got it, though Raffi was disappointed not to start. "And up front, last two lads, Tony and Len."

That changed the mood. For the first time there was doubt in the room, and I wondered if I'd got a bit *too* smart.

Lots of eyes turned to Henri. The guys either side of him stopped breathing.

Vimsy came a bit closer, mumbled, "Max, can we talk?"

"I've handed the team sheet in." I slapped the tactics board. "In and out, no drama. Subs: Ben. Trick. Aff. Henri. Pascal. Right. Get on with it." Henri didn't move. He seemed a bit stunned. At least he was on the bench, though. I was leaving Raffi out completely. He was staring at his boots; he wouldn't need them today except to jog around before and after the match. I went to him and tapped his shoulder. "Mate," I said.

He followed me out to the corridor. We found a quiet spot.

"It's only five subs," I said. "I need Trick in case there's an injury. It's the only position I can't work around."

"I'm aight, Max. You got to make decisions. That's football. I'm aight."

"Yeah," I said with a sigh. "It's not fun, leaving you out." We stood there for ten, fifteen seconds. "Listen. I wanted to thank you in person for the message you sent. I didn't know what to say. Thought it'd come to me when I saw you. But . . . still blank. I just . . . Just thanks. How . . . how are you all doing?"

"It's been hard, moving. And the stress. You know. Like, do we have to move back? Is it already over? Relegation and that."

I smiled at him. "Let *me* worry about that."

"You don't look worried."

"Yeah," I said. "That's exactly my point."

Minute 1.

The dugouts were on the base of the hill. Some fans were gathered around the sides, but they were real hardcore nutjobs. Most sought solace from the bouts of drizzle under the various mishmashed shelters on the other side. It wouldn't be a match where the crowd played a big part.

"Jackie" led us across the pitch, then flopped down into the dug-out. Vimsy rolled his eyes at me—he wasn't a fan of the joke. It was working, though. The fifty away fans who'd come down from Chester serenaded him. News of Jackie's operation and my big debut hadn't leaked.

The subs settled down into their slots. Henri's face was completely blank. I guessed he was going to pretend I didn't exist for, maybe, three weeks. That would be my punishment. Pascal was excited. The fact I'd put him on the team sheet instead of Raffi was a massive hint that I intended to actually, really use him. His professional debut! Raffi was next to him, being all paternal and that. I fucking loved Raffi.

"Vimsy," I said.

"Sup?"

"Jackie's all right, is he? I couldn't get much of a straight answer out of anyone."

"Me neither," he said. "I heard the op went well. No drama. Surgeon was in and out."

I scratched my head. "Something's up, though. Don't you think?"

"I'm not paid to think," he said. "It's like you said: It's private. Keep it all between us. I thought one of the lads would blab, but seems like they didn't. Far as the world's concerned, this idiot is actually Jackie. And if Jackie doesn't want to go into the grisly details of what they found when they cut him open, I'm fine with that."

"Yeah," I said, glancing at the Kettering dugout. "So . . . you're going to stay calm, right?"

The referee blew his whistle. And just like that, I was a professional football manager!

Almost immediately, the Kettering coaches and subs were racing forward, demanding a free kick. It was going to be one of those nights. Vimsy closed his mouth tight, and I watched his chest contract. "I'll try," he said.

"No, you'll do it. Or you'll wait on the bus."

"Right." He sighed. Tried to steel himself. "Right."

I waved Jill over. "You two stand down there and watch the match. Go as far away from the home dugout as you can. Tell me anything that you think's going wrong. Anything that could be better. Leave *these* pricks to me. Is that all clear?"

"Yes, Max."

One last quick look at the bench—Henri was somehow watching the match without ever pointing his eyes in my direction—and then it was down to the serious, serious business of looking serious.

Minute 2.

Glenn Ryder, our captain, our *Triple* Captain, yelled, jumped for a header and won it. It might have been my imagination, but I thought I saw a look of absolute astonishment ripple across Magnus Evergreen's face.

Minute 3.

Kettering moved the ball down the right. Magnus tracked his opponent, who was a fast guy with no end product. Magnus waited, waited, then threw himself at the ball. Good tackle! It started to roll out for a throw-in, and I groaned. Kettering had that long-throw expert.

But Magnus clambered to his feet, sprinted after it, and kept it in play. He passed it safely to Sam Topps, and a burst of applause came from all round the pitch.

My heart started pounding. *It's happening.*

Minute 5.

D-Day collected a pass on the left. He pushed the ball to the side and strolled towards the right back. He dropped his shoulder, the defender moved, and D-Day smugly turned back around and kept the ball moving through our midfield.

It was a whole load of nothing, but I'd been watching D-Day closely ever since his pathetic missed penalty. The one that had made me lose my rag with him. He had a bit of the Henri about him. He wanted to be a showman. The centre of attention. I'd given him a key role in the team because he was tactically flexible, but here was a nice side effect. He was up for it. He was in the mood.

Minute 8.

Chad Flintoff on the right was a limited player. CA 32 and no particular strengths. But being put back in the team had lit a fire under his arse. He'd been given one game to show Jackie what he could do. One game to prove the gaffer wrong, prove that he should start every week. He very quickly got up to 7 out of 10 in the ratings and stayed there for a while.

Now, he collected a ball and fired it long towards Len. Len was another out-of-favour player delighted to be back in the starting eleven. He was CA 36, and like Chad, the wrong side of thirty years old. He had a chance to show teams what he could do. A chance to get himself a contract for next season, ideally somewhere he'd get more minutes than at Chester.

He was good in the air, and won the header. His flick-on went to Tony, who took a first-time shot that went straight into the goalie's torso.

Minute 14.

We were competing. My main worry with this match had been that the players would think all they needed to do was turn up. It's what had happened with Darlington when we saw we were playing a team at the bottom of the league. This Chester team, though, were fighting for their lives. Playing for their futures. And were inspired by Glenn Ryder.

Sam Topps won a crunching tackle. The ball spun to James Wise. He fizzed it left to D-Day. He feinted right, burst left, and whipped in a cross that Len headed over.

Minute 18.

We'd started to dominate. Possession was going up. Shots For was going up. Shots Against stayed on zero.

Most players were on 7s and 8s. I asked Vimsy and Jill to keep an eye on two guys with 6. They fell into a discussion and would sometimes yell things.

The Kettering manager was growing frustrated. His on-pitch tactics weren't working, so he tried to provoke us. Tried to goad us. I put on my best poker face, and while I walked over to the guy, I switched to 4-3-3.

"Sorry, what?" I said.

He came close enough to start jabbing his finger at me. "Yous lot are fucking cheats. Yous a bunch of pricks. That was an elbow, that! Fucking red card. You're lucky the referee didn't see it."

"An elbow?" I said, looking down at the grass between us while reading the match commentary. The switch in formation was working well. "That's very serious," I mused. "Would you like to enter into arbitration?"

"You what?"

"Pascal, come here a second." The tiny German jogged across, a study in polite interest. "Mate," I said. "What's the name of that thing that handles disputes in sport? Man City are always trying to scam their way out of trouble with them."

"Oh, CAS."

"CAS? What's that stand for?"

"It's the Court of Arbitration for Sport."

"This guy here," I said, pointing to the manager, who was now flanked by a couple of enormous helpers, "if he wants to, like, start the process, what does he do?"

"I should imagine there is a form to be filled in," said Pascal.

I nodded and looked at the manager. "Have you *got* a printer?"

One of the beefy dudes took an aggressive step towards me. From the corner of my eye, I saw Raffi stand up. He'd let the guy punch *me*, but he'd go mental if anyone did anything to Pascal. I thought I saw Henri lean forward, too. Not quite as detached as he wanted to be. That made me grin, which of course made the guy even angrier.

"You're fucking dead, mate!"

His colleagues gripped him and pulled him away. "Pascal, get the bag."

He ran off and came back. I took out the thing I'd asked him to buy, gave Pascal the empty bag, and shooed him away. Things were about to get very, very messy.

While Sam Topps put his foot on the ball, looking for a forward pass, I draped a red-and-white scarf around me.

I'm ninety-eight percent sure Vimsy was the first to realise what I was doing, because there was a loud "Oh, fuck me," from my left.

Just as D-Day dropped into the CAM slot to collect Sam's pass on the half-turn, just as he got booted up the arse and the ref blew his whistle, I heard the angriest Kettering guy yell, "Oh, no fucking way!" And seconds later I was surrounded by guys who were grappling me, pulling at me, scratching, clawing like wild beasts.

The ref blew and blew and sprinted across.

"What the fuck?" he said.

I knelt, checking myself for wounds. "They attacked me."

He turned to the home team's experienced backroom staff. "Why?"

"He was wearing a Kettering scarf!" yelled the guy who'd started it. He was holding the scarf now. Caught red-and-white-handed.

"It's not a Kettering scarf," I said. "I'm a Man United fan. It's a United scarf."

"It says fucking Kettering on it!" screamed the main hoodlum, causing my entire subs bench to burst out laughing. It got a few chuckles from Vimsy. And even Henri was not unaffected.

I pulled a sad face. "Ref, that guy was really mean to me." More fits of laughter from my subs. Physio Dean was waiting to come and dab me with iodine or whatever, but even he was in fits.

The ref didn't like my antics, but he didn't have much choice about what came next. He gave the bully dude a stern look. "I think you'd better go up to the stands." Another sending off! The prick stormed off, stealing my scarf in the process. Next, the ref got close to the manager, but I heard what he said. "Control yourself and control your bench." I was still kneeling as though *everything* hurt. "Max, how about you don't put on any more Kettering clobber for the rest of the game?"

I jumped to my feet. "Just to check: I'm allowed to wear a Kettering scarf in Kettering *after* the game?" The ref sighed and jogged back to the pitch, where D-Day was ready to take the free kick. I pottered to the edge of the home team's technical area and spoke to the manager. "How about you go over to your little hovel and sit down? Lose with dignity. Good lad."

I watched as D-Day struck the shot just wide—so close! Then I fell to my knee again, feeling my jaw, all kinds of wobbly. Dean gave me some treatment, right there, slightly inside the home team's area.

And there was fuck all they could do about it.

I allowed Dean to take me back to base.

The Kettering lot spent the next five minutes raging. Seething. Kicking things.

While I whistled "The Great Escape."

Minute 24.

Someone in red finally calmed down enough to realise that we'd switched from our starting formation. They dashed up and down the touchline for a second. I almost laughed as I saw the Kettering manager look at his bench. Was he really thinking of making a substitution so early? That would have been incredible. But he came up with another solution. He tried to match our formation with a real hodgepodge of square pegs in round holes.

The second he was finished, I switched back to 4-4-2.

Minute 27.

Kettering turned one of their ugly long-throws into a corner.

"Pascal!" I yelled. He ran to my side. "Outswinging corner. If it gets through everyone, where's the ball going?"

He gestured to an area. "So you start *there*," I said. "If you get it, zoom." I chopped my hand along the length of the pitch. "If someone else will get there first, zoom," I repeated the motion.

"I understand."

Minute 30.

Chester possession: 65%

Shots for: 6

Shots against: 0

Selected match ratings:

Robbo 6 (nothing to do)

Glenn Ryder 8 (utterly dominant)

Sam Topps 8 (loving life)

Chad Flintoff 7 (trending downwards; not match fit)

D-Day 8 (flashes of quality)

Len Kearns 6 (old and not match sharp)

The match had settled down. We were cruising, really, but although we were getting shots, I wasn't totally confident we'd get a goal this half. I switched to 4-3-3 to freshen things up, but this time the Kettering guy was able to change things round a bit quicker. I sensed the guy was counting on halftime, when he'd try to T-Rex power slam me.

I checked his subs again and grew even more convinced that they had come today expecting us to play 3-5-2. The plan had been to switch to 3-5-2 at halftime. After all, it had worked for a lot of other teams recently.

Would they still do it? The guy saw me looking, and his lips twisted into a snarl. Yeah, they'd do it. He'd persuade himself it was the right thing to do.

Minute 33.

Another free kick for Chester. It'll be taken from the right.

Swung in by Flintoff.

Headed away. It bounces loose.

A Kettering player is first to the ball. He hacks it clear.

Anywhere will do!

The defence pushes up.

"Pascal!" I called, spinning. "Did you see that?"
"Yes, Max."
"Good."

Minute 37.
"Vimsy."
"Yes, mate?"
"Let Len know he's got eight minutes left. Big effort, yeah?"
"Right."

Minute 42.

Topps picks up the ball and drives forward.

No one is coming to pressure him.

Is he going to have a crack? He is, you know!

He cocks his leg, and blasts the ball . . .

. . . High, wide, and not very handsome.

Minute 45.

The referee blows for halftime.

Kettering will be glad of the break. Chester have been well on top.

In the dressing room, there was a buzz of chat. The first eleven discussed certain opponents. Moves they were making. Glenn wanted Carl to come closer to him. Flintoff wanted Carl closer to *him*. Sam and Wisey plotted with D-Day.

When the first flush of debriefing was over, the subs got involved, with Trick telling the cavemen how I'd been winding up the Kettering lot. He told the story at least twice, because twice he yelled, "It's fucking got Kettering on it!" Lots of laughs.

I stood at the front, relaxing against the wall, scrolling through cat photos. I was waiting for the other manager to make his move, and sure enough, five minutes into the fifteen-minute break, his tactics screen changed to 3-5-2. I adjusted the red magnets.

I put my phone away, held my arms out, and conducted myself— Beethoven's Fifth—as I sang in a deep voice, "Shut the fuck uppppp."

Didn't need to do more. I had everyone's attention. Could have heard a pin drop out of the real Jackie's knee. I went straight into my dreamy, golden-future voice.

"Seventy percent possession. Eight shots for. None against." I spread my arms. "How does it feel? Feels good, I bet?"

Quite a few nods. It did feel good, but there was still doubt. Uncertainty. Mostly centred around one giant pocket of unused talent. I jabbed a thumb behind me.

"Kettering will play three-five-two in the second half. They've got some whole *drama* planned." I broke character to do a child's voice while sticking my bottom lip out. "To mess with our lickle heads." Right back into dream voice. I made sure the blue magnets were lined up properly. "We're doing four-four-two again. You might be thinking, oh, but Max, what about the dinosaur? How do we stop him? What's the counter to his counter?" I rolled my head around my neck. There was some legit stress there. Not from the football, but from lack of confidence in my man management skills. This could go very, very wrong. "I've got a one-word answer to every question you might have. A one-word rebuttal to anything Tyrannosaurus *Wrecked* out there wants to fish out of his big bag of Stone Age tools. Pascal, put your hand down; no fact-checking when I'm on one."

I scanned the room, this tiny, squashed space that wasn't big enough for every player to sit at once. I looked into every pair of eyes except one.

"One word. You ask: What is the word? What's the word, Max?" I stood to my full height. "The word is: Henri."

There it was. The electricity. I hoped it'd come when I summoned it. It crackled around me, spread from body to body, down through our bones, through the benches, into the floor, into the very air we were breathing.

He couldn't resist. Henri stepped forward. He was wearing a long Chester coat, his shorts and socks unblemished, his hair pristine. But there was no fire in his eyes. "You want me to play?"

I locked onto him. The electricity made me grasp his coat with both hands. I ranted from kissing distance. "No, mate. I don't want you to play. I *need* you to play. I need you to get in that penalty box and save our season. I need you to save Jackie Reaper's career. I need you to save *my* career. If we go down, we're fucked. Everyone in this room is fucked. The Chester Knights are fucked. No more Johnny Winger. No more Wilson. I need you. We all need you."

I released him, hyper now, and pushed the left and right midfielder magnets far up the tactics board.

"We're doing four-four-two again. As the half goes on, we'll turn it into four-two-four. Last twenty minutes, we'll have Aff and Pascal on the wings. They're too fast for this lot. Too smart. It'll be nonstop pressure. Balls in the box, bedlam, mayhem. Chance after chance. Every minute Kettering get weaker. *We* get stronger. Pressure, pressure, more pressure." Back to Henri. "Len's opened the door. Now you smash it down."

"Say you need me one more time."

"I need you one more time."

"Not funny," he said, with peak haughtiness. But he turned and, somehow, seemingly without unzipping it, his coat slipped from his shoulders. He exhaled, and the sponsor logo on his chest rose and fell. "Very well. I will save the club." He turned back towards me. "You lied to me, Max."

"Oh?"

"You said there was no story to tell."

"No, mate. I said *I* had no story to tell. You," I twirled my finger around to include the entire dressing room. "You're writing this one."

Minute 46.

Henri replaced Len, and Pascal replaced Chad. The fear factor we got when the Kettering defence saw Henri was offset by their amusement at seeing Pascal.

As soon as the match restarted I could see that Henri was up for it. Whether he was feeding off the drama of being dropped or my little pep talk, or if it was just the effects of Bench Boost, I couldn't tell you. But he looked light on his feet, fast, powerful. He forewent his usual scraps so that he could concentrate on his movement. He darted around, opening up gaps, making defenders get in each other's way. Once, he made space by standing utterly still.

It was wonderful.

Minute 49.

Chester combine well in the centre of the pitch.

It's fed out to D-Day. He beats his marker and fires in a low cross.

Henri pounces. Flicks it up . . .

GOOOOAAAALLLL!!!!

Into the roof of the net!

The keeper had no chance!

Henri ran over to where our traveling fans were and put his hand to his ear. Then he sprinted across the pitch towards me, gesticulating madly. I didn't see. I was checking my nails. *You think one goal's gonna impress me? Work harder, mate.*

Aff and Raffi fell into each other, bouncing around. Vimsy went tonto. The Kettering manager— Ah, who cares? It was my show now.

Minute 53.

Kettering got a corner. Pascal jogged back into the penalty box to help his mates.

"What the fuck?" I screamed at him.

He shook his head, as though he'd been sleepwalking—which he kind of had; the intensity of the match was frazzling him—and pushed twenty yards forward into the space we'd talked about. It was over on the far corner of the pitch, about halfway inside our half. If the ball went too long, which it often did, Pascal would get it in loads of space and have a counterattack against two slow players.

The corner was fired in—not a bad delivery, to be fair—but Gerald May got his head in the way and flicked it out of danger.

Towards Pascal!

He took a half-step towards the ball, hesitated—had he frozen?—then sprinted away, leaving the ball where it was. I very nearly spontaneously combusted with frustration, but then the patterns and movements clicked for me. Sam Topps chased the ball out, lined up Pascal's run, and played a long pass over the halfway line.

The defender seemed the favourite to get there, but Pascal was lightning. He touched the ball first, and the defender realised he was in big trouble and had a split-second decision to make. He could let Pascal go, and the kid would have a one-on-one chance with the goalie. High chance of going 2–0 down. Or he could take him out. Foul him, get a red card, but only be 1–0 down.

He chose violence.

He rugby tackled Pascal, and for once I wasn't mad when my players and staff lost their minds. It was a really ugly piece of play and Pascal could have been hurt.

The ref tried to defuse the situation by whipping out a card nice and early so we could all see the guy was being punished. But that made it worse.

"Yellow?" screamed Raffi.

"That's a red card, mate!" screamed Vimsy.

"You're not fit to referee!" screamed "Jackie" and got himself a red card. The guy hobbled all the way across the pitch, taking breaks, struggling with his crutches. It was such an annoying performance that a Kettering player ran over to remonstrate with him. Shouted something along the lines of "Would you mind awfully hurrying up off the pitch, old chap?" To which "Jackie" thrust his crutches out to the side, waving them in the physical manifestation of the sentiment *come and have a go if you think you're hard enough*. When challenged, he then picked the crutches up and sprinted off the pitch.

Which increased the tension in the Kettering technical area *a lot*.

Anyway, apart from a scene we'd probably spend the entire summer laughing about, one good thing came out of the incident. Kettering were no longer underestimating Pascal. His speed was absolutely terrifying.

Minute 57.

For the hundredth time in the match, Sam won his duel. Wisey passed the ball to Pascal, who one-touched it back and raced down the line, dragging a defender with him. Wisey turned inside, back to Sam. Out to D-Day. Back to Magnus. Across the defensive line, all the way to Carl. He passed to Pascal and now Carl was the one bursting forward. Pascal threatened to chip the ball down the line, causing three Kettering players to dart towards the danger zone.

Pascal instead played a medium-length ball to Sam, who touched it to D-Day, who was in loads of space thanks to Carl's selfless run.

D-Day touched the ball forward so he could really get some power behind it. He slashed it with extreme prejudice into the area between the defenders and the goalkeeper. Henri darted forward, hurled himself at the ball, and deflected it up into the— No! The goalie somehow threw out a hand and pushed the ball away. A defender was first to the scene and tried to clear it, but Pascal had anticipated where the ball would go. He played it square to Wisey, who chipped the ball back into the mixer. Tony won his header, Henri volleyed. What a great— No! The goalie threw himself to the far corner and somehow got a part of his body behind the shot.

The ball deflected back into the melee of players, and there were hacks, lunges, hopeful swings, brave blocks, and finally Henri was there again. Where most players would have hit the ball as hard as possible and hoped for the best, he had the coolness, the imagination, the arrogance to do a little chip. A little bunker shot. The ball moved in slow motion above the head of a defender who was on the ground, probably shouting "nooo" at 0.25 speed like in a movie, over the waist-high foot of a defender who'd thrown himself towards where he thought Henri's shot would go, over the shoulder of yet another Kettering guy, who tried preposterously but admirably to block the shot with his nose.

But then finally, gloriously, the ball was past everyone. Sailing towards the welcoming embrace of the net.

GOOOAAAA— Wait, what? No! *No!* The goalie's hand—*just* his hand! What?—appeared out of nowhere. The ball thunked into his glove. I saw it wobble and shake, no strength to the save, and deflected, diverted, just enough to . . .

To . . .

To land on top of the crossbar, from where it rolled onto the top of the net.

Corner kick.

D-Day fired it in. A defender cleared it, but as we'd talked about, Pascal was in the right spot to collect, and he sent it back towards the penalty spot. Henri rose, headed, just wide.

Pressure. Pressure. More pressure.

Minute 60.

But the more we attacked without scoring, the more something strange happened.

For the first time, it began to get to me, the enormity of it all.

A win would be such a huge moment in our season. It would propel us towards safety. Maybe even out of the relegation zone completely!

But what if Kettering somehow got lucky and equalised?

A little bit of sweat broke out on my spine.

I checked the match ratings. Henri was on 9.

But Kettering's goalie was on 10.

A gust of wind went past. Didn't touch me at all. But I shivered.

Chester possession: 71%

Shots for: 17

Shots against: 0

Minute 63.

Sam laid the ball off for Wisey. He took a crack, and it flew towards the bottom left.

Annnd the goalie saved it.

Holy shit.

There's a thing that sometimes happens in sport. It mostly happens when you watch on TV. The commentator tells you a story about how one team are doing a lot of fouls, or are wasting time, or whatever, and you notice it and it gets to you. You watch from the point of view of fouls, or timewasting. But on the pitch the players are doing their jobs, unaware of the statistically insignificant change in the number of fouls from a usual match. They're often surprised when asked about a certain aspect of the match that everyone else got worked up about.

But here the story was plain for everyone to see, in the stands and on the pitch.

The goalie was having a worldie.

Ten out of ten. Saving almost everything. Playing out of his skin.

I started to pace the touchline. The guy was CA 35. He was bang average. Why was he doing this to me?

The ball was played to the left back, who thumped it up the pitch. Gerald May missed his header, and the ball bounced up. Glenn Ryder was bursting a gut to cover, so the Kettering striker lashed the ball vaguely at the net. It went miles over the bar, but it was a warning: If we didn't score a second, Kettering would make us pay.

Chester possession: 71%

Shots for: 18

Shots against: 1

Minute 68.

D-Day came off. I gave him a big high five and he slumped onto the bench. He'd worked his socks off. Aff sprinted on.

I switched to 4-2-4.

We had three players who were bench boosted. Three of our four attackers. If we could keep the pressure on, surely we'd get the second goal that would, conceivably, save our season.

The minutes flew past. Time mashed into itself. I saw fragments of moves from future minutes while replaying past ones.

Minute 68.

Aff gets to the byline, sends a cross to the back post. Henri's there! He leaps!

Minute 69.

Pascal scampers to the ball, gets there first, he feints to shoot, but goes for a neat one-two with Tony.

Minute 70.

The ball hits the side netting! He should have scored!

Minute 71.

Ryder wins a towering header and Chester are back in possession.

Minute 70.

Magnus intercepts and fires a long diagonal for Pascal to chase.

Minute 69.

He shoots! Oh, what a fantastic block!

Minute 68.

His header is just too high.

Minute seventy-something.

I'm tearing my hair out. I can't believe this. Once per minute, something happens to make me fall to my knees in despair.

Minute seventy-something plus one.

There's no one on the bench anymore. This is all-hands-on-deck. We're all holding each other. I'm in the middle of the line, but it's not a can-can. It's a can't-can't.

Minute seventy-more.

From the edge of the penalty area, Tony shoots—it seems to be spinning into the bottom-right-hand corner, but it doesn't! It goes wide.

Our wall collapses.

Minute 80.

The narrative sucked me in. I'd gone full Jackie. We all had.

I snapped out of it.

Time to lead. Time to be professional. One by one, I took the players and staff back to the dugout, and I made them sit. They whined. They complained. I was hard, but firm.

The hardest was Jill. She didn't want to calm down. "Vimsy, help me out, here," I said.

He grabbed her wrist and eased her away. They were all safely tucked in now. Nighty, night, children! I swished my finger across the line and commanded, "Stay!"

There was a shared emotional release, a knowing chuckle, that spread across the bench. They knew they'd been tricked. Tricked into thinking there might be some drama here. I'd calmed them. They'd sleep soon. I stood on the touchline, hands behind my back, utterly serene.

The Kettering manager was screaming. It washed over me. We were cruising. Routine victory. Look at my face. Look how calm I am.

Injury time.

The strain of pretending to be calm wiped me out. I was a husk. But the smell of pies wafted across the pitch and I realised I had nothing to worry about. I found serenity in the smell of beef and gravy.

We'd spent the entire half peppering shots at goal, and we'd got that precious goal. We were winning. We were dominating. The clock would hit 90. Any second now. Three points and a pie. No drama.

As soon as I relaxed, the match turned on a sixpence. Suddenly, Kettering were all over us. Attacking, attacking, attacking. Vimsy was next to me. Pleading. Begging me to go defensive. No. We were better. We were attacking. Four-two-four until the end.

We are Chester.

Kettering's right midfielder fizzed a cross across the face of goal. A touch from anyone would have spelled disaster! I stopped breathing. But it rolled safely, all the way across to Carl Carlile. He paused—we had four players in attack but there were only two defenders. How did that happen? He passed to Pascal, who laid it off to Henri. The German put his head down and sprinted with all his might. Henri passed left-footed for Pascal to run onto. His speed was awesome. He burst clear. Aff was haring away—I worried for his hamstring—and Pascal waited, waited, then took out the last defender with a perfectly timed, perfectly weighted pass, and I was dancing. I was hopping up and down like the happiest ever bunny. This was it!

Aff let the ball come across his body, onto his sweet left foot, and he struck it true and hard. I jumped all the way to my knees, like a jockey.

And then I fell to the grass, head in hands. He'd only gone and saved it again! I couldn't believe my eyes. I just couldn't. For the first time, I was aware of the noise from the fans. It was pandemonium. The supernatural goalie got up, dove onto the ball just as Aff was sliding in. The goalie picked himself up, breathed, booted the ball high downfield. Someone won a header, someone lost a header, the ball was on the right, the fast winger pushed past a very tired Magnus, who for once hit a lovely cross—I could do no better—and a Kettering striker leapt like a salmon, bonk, right on the forehead, lovely angles, a gorgeous goal, really; you had to credit them for not giving up, fighting to the end, and there was an absolutely deafening *KLANG* and instead of celebrating the players ran around some more, and then the final whistle went and I was on the ground in bits. I pulled myself up to my knees and looked around. Vimsy was like me, head in hands. Len was on his back, hands over his face, almost like he was crying. D-Day and Dean were on their haunches.

But Jill?

She was running around like a crazy person. Waving her arms around, face contorted. She was yelling, running in random directions. And then she leapt onto Aff, and she punched the air. And I realised—they were celebrating.

What?

I clambered to my feet, but it was exhausting up there, so I hunched over, hands on thighs. And I read.

Great play from Samways. He leaves Magnus for dead.

Can he deliver a good cross?

Oh, he can! It's pinpoint! Curving round Ryder all the way onto Montague's head!

He redirects it towards goal.

Robbo leaps but can't get anywhere near it.

But it hits the crossbar!

The ball is hacked clear. Relief for Chester.

The crossbar is still shaking!

And then, still filled with disbelief, I went to the match overview screen.

KETTERING TOWN	0	CHESTER FC	1
Full Time			
		Lyons	49

Full time! It was really over.

Next thing I knew, I was in the dressing room, standing in front of the lads. Vimsy was on the end of the bench, gazing up at me just like Dani had in the photo. Raffi was listening to Pascal, who was unloading his own private commentary feed into the ether, drunk on dreams. Henri, head back, eyes closed, blissed out. Sam, Trick, Chad, D-Day, huddled together, buzzing, laughing. Aff lying on the one massage table, getting a rub from Dean, who was trying to keep a straight face, but kept laughing.

Victory music was pumping. I switched it off.

"All right. Up the fuck shut," I said. Heads turned. Some lads sat down. Some formed a mini wall, arms round each other, where it was standing room only. "What did I say? Clinical. Surgical. Routine." I shrugged. "In and out, never in doubt."

I lifted a new pad of flipchart paper and attached it to our tactics board. I flipped it open to a clean page and wrote on the bottom left: *24.*

Just above it, I wrote *23.* And above that, *22.*

The players got it. I was writing the bottom of the league table.

21, 20.

Before the match, we'd been in the twenty-first spot. The first of the relegation places.

Next to the number *21,* I wrote *Bradford.*

There was a buzz from the room.

I moved my marker pen a little higher. As I prepared to write *Chester* next to position twenty, a cheer went up. I didn't write anything. Instead, I fixed the players with a quizzical frown.

Then I wrote another number. *19.*

And *there* I wrote *Chester.*

And that's when the party really started.

"We! Are! Staying up! Said we are staying up!"

11

LET IT HAPPEN

Wednesday, March 22.

After a run of mornings when I wanted to stay in bed, I *leapt* out. Quick shower, hoodie, the short drive to the Eastbourne Sports Complex. I burst past the night dude at reception, up the stairs, and into the office used by Darlington FC's manager.

David Cutter was inside, packing things into cardboard boxes.

He'd been fired as I drove home from Kettering. Somewhat took the gloss off my first official win.

Darlington FC announce the departure of manager David Cutter. Darlington will be hoping a new manager can lead them into the playoffs.

"Max!" said Cutter, breaking into a smile. He was worn. Haggard. Looked like shit. "Have you come to apply for the job? You're supposed to wait till I leave. Or do you want a reference?" He laughed.

I didn't know what to say. I looked around. Saw shapes on the walls where photos and paintings had hung until a few minutes ago. "Stop packing," I demanded, racing over to take a photo out of his hands. "This is mental. They can't sack you." I paced away. "I'll talk to someone. Who do I talk to?"

Cutter forced his lips together and returned to his task. Into the box went his Italia '90 mug. His Michael Laudrup shirt. And a long scarf I'd never seen before. Black and white, with a black-and-white crest circled with red. The crest depicted a bridge with two birds flying over it, but it was packed away before I could read the text.

"Will you stop?" I said. "You can't let this happen."

He smiled and took a break. Rested his hand on the corner of a box. "The board wanted to make a change. Maybe with a new gaffer they can still make the playoffs." His mood darkened. "Too many draws. Too many sloppy mistakes. Too many decisions going against us. Terrible referees at this level. Terrible. No, Max. My time's up." He held his hand out, and I was forced to give up the photo. He took a good, long look at it. It showed him holding a slender, angular trophy with black-and-white ribbons tied to its handles. Ticker tape swirled around him. "Maidenhead," he explained. "Great bunch of lads. Left there to come here." He fell into a memory, then slowly emerged. "It's funny what you said. *Don't let it happen.* That's a childish way of thinking, isn't it? None of us have any way to stop it. Events." He put the photo into the box, then leaned against his desk and considered me. "You're a weird one. Most players, they try to make things happen. When you were having a good day, it was like you didn't need to make it happen. You *let* it happen. And the rest of the time, you were holding back." He did a curious little smile. "That's what it looked like, anyway."

He placed another box on his desk and started loading things into it.

I thought about the first time I'd been in this room. I'd come to negotiate a loan move for Henri, and ended up becoming a player. Cutter had let me take shots at the goalies, let me do a couple of drills, indulged me when I asked for them to be made harder. His reward was eleven goals in eight games. But there's no doubt who got the better end of the relationship.

"I feel like I owe you something," I said.

"You don't."

"You gave me my start."

"You'd have got it one way or another. Take that face off you and don't worry so much. I've still got some reputation in this game. I'll take a wee break, get a new job in the summer. Bit lower down the pyramid, maybe. Another Maidenhead. Build a squad, get them promoted. That's what I love. That's what I'm good at. That's the problem, though, see. Expectations rise. The club hits its level, and so do I. But the fans always want more. They're never satisfied. You win two–one, they say, 'Why not three–one?' 'Why no clean sheet?' The pressure grows and grows. You can't see it from the outside. It's brutal. Can't breathe. It's a shit business sometimes. If I didn't love it, I'd hate it." He remembered I was there. "Stop moping. You can help me carry these to my car. I want to be out of here before the players start arriving. Don't do goodbyes. Stopped being sentimental a long time ago."

That was a lie. He was a pretty sentimental person. He'd let me skip training when he thought it was because my mum was in a bad way. He seemed to be more zen than me, though. Sacking the guy who built the squad because the squad hit a bad patch was unfair even by football standards. I scratched my jaw. "You're taking it well."

"What? Oh, no. This part's fine. Busy today. It'll be the morning. Wake up, nothing to do. No structure to the day, to the week. Tomorrow will be bad. Friday worse. Saturday?" He pursed his lips. *Oof.* No football for a football man on the day of football.

"Come and watch Chester. VIP box. Champagne. Things on sticks. You met my Emma. She'll make a fuss over you."

His eyes darted left and right. Calculating how to let me down gently. "Maybe." He handed me a box. "Let's take these ones down. Then you can get on with your day. Sure you've got lots to do."

After being dismissed by Cutter, I crossed the country. Two and a half hours to Liverpool. Plenty of time to reflect. Professional sport is a cruel game. Snakes and ladders but it's mostly snakes and some of the ladders are made of snakes.

Cutter didn't deserve the sack. He'd turned Darlo into a top-three team. Sure, recent results had been poor, but he should have been given the chance to turn it round. Who would they hire who could transform results so quickly? Even Jackie needed time to get his ideas across. I checked the curse news feed, half expecting to see Ian Evans's name turn up. Imagine that. Imagine if he actually got them into the playoffs, and then promoted!

Was Cutter a better manager than Evans? I thought so. A cynical voice popped up. The cold, hard part of me that didn't look back on my time in Darlo with unremitting fondness. When he'd seen how good I was, Cutter should have gone out of his way to keep me. He should have built the team around me. Instead, he was petty, didn't adapt his methods, and was even willing to let me leave for free so long as he got a bung.

So, no. His sacking wasn't black and white.

Cutter's black-and-white scarf made me think of my antics on the touchline of Kettering, and that gave me my first smile of the day. At the final whistle, I'd got a few cursemails. One told me that I would now be able to see my Manager Points. I found the relevant section, and on the very last page, page 742 out of 742, was my name. I'd earned 42 Manager Points. So you got manager points by getting results in matches.

Top of page one was Pep Guardiola on 214,000 points, followed by the Man United manager. It wasn't only based on league matches, then; otherwise Arsenal's manager would have been first or second. United were fourth in the league, got quite far in the Europa League, had won the league cup, and were headed to another cup final. Ian Evans had accumulated 630.

Of course, there was no explanation of what Manager Points were *for*.

Another mail told me about a few achievements I'd unlocked. The most interesting one was Movin' On Up 3, for which I got three XP. That achievement was awarded when I managed at a new high level. I got the first one when I took charge of FC United's reserves. The second when I controlled Chester reserves in my trial. And the third for managing Chester's first team. Another achievement was called Hou(dini) Are Ya? One XP for bringing a team out of the relegation zone. I also got Free Spirit 4, for my continued use of playmakers.

And since I'd been managing a tier-six team, I'd earned 4 XP per minute! Around 360, which took me, including the handful I got for achievements, past 2,000 XP. Just very slightly over the amount I needed to buy the next formation. Ooh, baby. Now I have a defensive midfielder. Ho ho ho.

Jackie lay on his hospital bed with one leg mummified. Livia was beside him, looking pretty relaxed and pretty damned pretty. Her hair was back in a ponytail. MD had been there for a while. If he was annoyed that I'd postponed my arrival so I could go and see Cutter, he never mentioned it.

"Maxy three-points," said Jackie, by way of welcome.

"Jackie, er . . . three ops?"

"I wish," he said, with a grimace. "That's number five, I think. Had an ankle. Dislocated wrist." He looked himself up and down, trying to remember what else he had wrong with him.

"Don't forget your total charisma bypass," I said.

He grinned. He was in such a good mood I could have said almost anything. "Sure, Max."

"Did they find anything?" I said, because I felt I had to feign interest.

I think I pulled a face that showed I didn't want to hear any grisly details, because he skipped to the end. "Yeah, it's all good. Good as new. Rest it up and I'll be out and about in no time." He reached out and squeezed Livia's hand. She leaned closer to him. Sweet. "We listened to *Seals Live*. Have you heard it yet? No? Boggy did his best but there were stretches where all he could do was squeak."

"The last five minutes was only audible to bats," said Livia. "It was exciting, though."

MD grinned. "The Kettering directors were fuming. They were telling me I was about to witness match one of The Great Escape but we played them off the park from start to finish. Most took their thumping with good grace, but there's one guy, very unpleasant chap, who was quite aggressive." MD sighed, smile gone. "He was threatening to send a formal report to the FA for the whole fake Jackie business."

A wet laugh escaped through the sides of my throat.

"Max, it's not funny. It was disrespectful."

I wasn't in the mood for the football world's sanctimonious claptrap, and doubted I ever would be. Fake Jackie was funny. End of. "No, it was fucking hee-larious. I woke up twice, last night, just *laughing*."

MD shook his head. "I need to formally instruct you not to do it again."

"Okay, bro," I said. I held two fingers up and said, "I pwomise." I chuckled. It wasn't likely to come up again, anyway. I looked up at the ceiling—cheap square tiles, one with a yellow corner. Why did I sometimes swear on two fingers, and sometimes on three? It made no sense. I became aware that no one was talking. Back down at face level, the mood had changed. "What?"

MD sighed. "The specialist would like Jackie to stay another night, and then rest at home for as long as possible. We've looked at the schedule. If you take charge of the next two matches, Jackie will get two whole weeks off."

I scratched my head. "You want me to manage the next two matches?" I closed my eyes while I made a bunch of calculations. "Chorley this Saturday. Southport the Saturday after."

I found myself rubbing my forehead with both hands. MD misunderstood the impulse behind it. "Two *home* matches," he said, as though I was a fucking idiot.

"MD, mate. I *played* Southport in December. Unless they signed the Moroccan national team defence in January, we'll smash them. Chorley I don't know, but looking at the league table I'd say they're about as good as us."

"They're tenth, Max."

"Exactly. Just let me think this through." I strung out data points. "Vimsy's doing first-team training now. Thursday, Friday. Match on Saturday. Rest Sunday. Next week, five full days to work on the team. Another five the week after. Just as the shit hits the fan, I get twelve days of Vimsy." I shook my head and pointed at Jackie. "Guys, I need to talk to my subordinate for a while. Could you excuse us?"

I really thought they'd leave, but they had no intention of budging.

Jackie, I think, had an inkling of where I was going, but he didn't seem to mind having an audience. "Go on, Max. Let me have it."

Livia's eyes flashed. Back into protective mode. I thought about putting my foot down, but since Jackie couldn't do that, it seemed cruel. If she ended up hating me, so be it. I had a job to do. "Fine. You might have noticed that I've been pretty chill about the whole relegation thing. That's because I *see* the improvement in the team. It is *startling*. Chorley will be hard, but we've got home advantage. We'll beat Southport unless there's a disaster. Then it's Farsley—should beat them. Scarborough—tough game. Finally, Peterborough Sports. They're about our level, too. So five games left. I reckon we're a shoo-in for two wins, so that's six points. Maybe draws in two of the other three games. That's two points. Finish the season on fifty-two points, very unlikely to go down with that. Am I right, MD?"

"I'll check but I'm pretty sure no team has ever gone down with fifty-two points from a forty-six-match season."

"Great. But we lose one of the easy matches, we're screwed. So why am I so confident? Because we don't play Peterborough tomorrow. We play them in *four and a half weeks*. Last game of the season. They'll finish twelfth or thirteenth or whatever. Those players will have checked out. They'll be on the beach. But we'll have been getting better and better. More intense. More focused. We'll be flying around scoring goals left and right, and Peterborough will just let it happen. Why would they give a shit? And even if they're mega up for it, we'll be so lit we'll brush them aside." I paused. There was another patient in the room who had turned to enjoy my rant. Or possibly to complain about it. "Am I being too loud?"

"No, you're all right, lad. It's dead interesting. Better than Netflix, dis."

"Look, Jackie. I'll do Chorley. And I'll do Farsley. But you need to take training on Monday. I'll round up every coach I know. Vimsy, Terry, Jill, Spectrum, Jude. We'll wheel you out on this bed. We'll build you a golden throne. Whatever it takes. You lie there watching the drills, you look serene, thumbs up for *good job*, thumbs down for *dogshit drop and give me twenty*. But you need to be there."

He tried to squirm but his leg was pretty fixed in place. "Max, I've seen you coach. I've heard about you from Terry and Spectrum and even Vimsy. They all say you're class. You've got your badge. You can do it for a few days."

"No. You'll do it. The whole city is counting on you."

"I can't. Max, you've got to listen. You can do it."

I was getting a bit steamed up. "I fucking can't, you twat. And it's not just the coaching. It's the man management. I risked months of friendship with Henri. I dropped him, I did a whole drama, just to get him hyped to Jackie levels. The same effect you get with a furrowed brow. But okay, this game coming up, I'll be all like, 'Ooh, Jackie's taken a turn for the worse. He might not pull through. We have to do it for Jackie.' All that shit. The lads will play their hearts out, course they will. Week after, we'll slap, no need for tricks. Four points. Six, maybe. But it's not enough. The coaching, mate. The improvement in the players. We need it. I'm not joking. I'll dangle you from four cranes like you're in a baby bouncer. But you're *going* to be there with a whistle in your mouth."

"Like a baby with his dummy," said the other patient, and I rewarded him with a full-beam smile. It's good to have allies.

"Max. You're the one who tells players to stand up for themselves when they're injured."

"Yeah, and I'm telling you to stand up for yourself. Next to pitch one on Monday morning."

"It's not just that, Max." He licked his lips. "It's the other thing."

He was trying to communicate nonverbally, but I wasn't quite on his wavelength. Also, he was the one who insisted everyone else stay in the area. We wouldn't have communication problems if we were alone.

Jesus, why does no one ever skip to the part where they do it my way? It's much easier. "What?"

"My vaccination."

"Your *what*?" said Livia, who hadn't heard anything about vaccinations. It made no sense to talk about that with regards to a knee injury.

"Oh," I said. On our trip to Liverpool I'd used a vaccine simile. Jackie was saying he wanted to use the opportunity afforded by his injury to mentally get to grips with his new position. I had to agree that was smart. I approved completely, except it made us seventy percent more likely to be relegated. I rubbed my temples. This had to be private. "Mike. Livia. I need you to go."

Much reluctance. But with Jackie helping to push, they went.

As soon as Livia left the room, Jackie's entire demeanour changed. He sank into the bed. His eyes closed halfway and the edges of his mouth turned downwards.

"Jackie," I said, leaning forward so the other patient couldn't hear. "I'm not asking you to do something you're struggling with. I'm asking you to *coach*. You're top tier at that. I'll run the touchline for as many games as you want, I don't give a shit. I'm telling you, now, as a handsome maverick genius, that your coaching *guarantees* survival for this club. Give me two hard weeks, you can take two months off. I'll take care of everything in the summer. But we need this. One big push. From you. You're our superpower."

He rolled his eyes. "I'm not Superman. A few days doesn't make that much difference."

I grabbed his wrist. "It does, Jackie. I wouldn't make a fuss otherwise. Come on, you know me. I want to manage a football club. If I thought I was the best person to do it, I'd do it. I'd dropkick you out of here so hard you'd need another five operations. But mate." I smiled at how absurd it was that I had to beg him to realise how fucking mint he was. "Jackie." I shook my head. "It's Wednesday. You've got till Sunday to chill. Monday, I need an hour. One hour! We'll get hundreds of little drone coaches to put out the cones. You'll tell Vimsy and Spectrum what you want and they'll get on with it. All you need to do is say 'go.' And maybe punch Henri in the balls." I trailed off. "You just need to be there."

I trailed off because something weird had happened while I was talking. Jackie covered his eyes with his arms. He was crying.

I gave him some space.

Finally, he took his arms away.

"Max," he whispered. I tried not to look at the tracks of his tears. Mirror neurons, you know?

"Yeah?" I whispered back from a short distance.

He looked at his entombed leg. "It still hurts. I don't think they fixed it. It wrecks. I think this is my life now."

I swallowed. "Mate. Don't." My eyes were instantly damp. I had to stop myself blinking else I'd drown him. I eased away so he wouldn't be in my splash zone. I inhaled, shakily. "Listen. You're off your tits on meds. Of course it hurts. They cut you open, you daft lad. What's it *supposed* to feel like? I cut myself shaving, I blub like a toddler with a scuffed knee. You're not a wimp like me. You're a soldier. A few days you'll be all good. Like you said."

"I'm going to be in *pain* . . . for the rest of my life."

"You're not. Don't be a dick."

"I am. Max," he whimpered. He was like a dog at the vet. I started blubbing. He grabbed my chest, took a feeble hold of my toggles. "Don't tell Livia. I can keep it together for a while. Ease out of coaching. I'll get a desk job." He cry-laughed. "Write match reports! You'd like that, wouldn't you?"

"Shut the fuck up."

"Get a desk job," he said. "Work from home. An hour on the computer. Five minutes stretching. Leg up ten minutes. Ice on hand. Build up the muscle. Back on the PC. Take it easy. Be smart about it. I can do it. I love football, Max, you know I do. But I love her more. I need to give it up. I'll give it all up for her."

"What the fuck are you saying? You sound demented."

"I'm saying it's all on you now. I was . . . I was beating myself up when I came out of the operating room. My knee was on fire. Hurt worse than ever. Christ knows what he did in there, the bastard." He paused. "I don't mean that. He's a great man. He's not to blame for my shitty knees. I was all gutted, thinking, *I'm letting the lads down. They need me bad. Me and Max, we can save this club.* You were the missing link. Missing piece. Fucking psycho lightning rod to attract all the drama, let me get on with the job. But last night, Max. Listening to the radio. You know what it sounded like?" He went full blub, triggering the same in me.

"What?"

"Sounded like watching the Beth Heads." That sent him off the edge. I got to my feet and went to sit where Livia had been. She had all the tissues and stuff. We wiped our eyes for a bit. Jackie went, "Aaah." Cathartic release. "Match day? You're the real deal. The complete package. You're a gobby Manc twat and I love it. You don't need me there. Okay, you need a proper coach. Course you do. I'll get on my contacts. Might be hard to sell someone on the project. No promises. But I swear, Max, same as when I saw you play. You *can* coach. You take training tomorrow and Friday. Tell me if I'm wrong."

"I can't improve players like you."

"Okay. Fine. Let's say that's true. What you did to those kids. What was it called? Das Tournament?" He laughed messily. "That was a wild read. Beth's really something. But you can do that with the first team. Why not? Men need honesty. Direction. Someone who gives a shit about them. They'll go into battle for you, Max. I know they will." His face crumpled as it turned away from me. "Because I would."

I'd stopped wiping my cheeks; there was no point trying to stem this tide. "So if you're not coming back what was all that shit about me taking the next two games?"

He inhaled, accidentally ingesting at least three kinds of body fluids. I gave him more tissues. "Gives me time to work out my next steps. How to leave the scene with a bit of dignity. Know what I mean?"

I can't explain the next part. I found myself leaning closer to him, really peering into his face. There was a cartoonish quality to his expressions. Unexpectedly powerful tremors in certain muscles. Maybe he was born with it, or maybe it was AniMaybelline.

"What?" he said, shocked out of his weepiness by my scrutiny.

"You're catastrophising," I said, dispassionately interested.

"Not," he said.

I stood violently, sending the chair flying, laughed, and slapped my hands together. "Oh! You really had me going." I picked Livia's chair up and put it back in place. I went to the other patient and gave his hand a little squeeze. "Soz, mate. I know you need your rest. It's just my shitty employee over there is winding me up."

"I'm not winding you up," said Jackie, annoyed.

"You're all right, lad," said the second patient. He was having a great time.

I went back to Livia's chair and my soft-spoken voice. "You're off your tits on meds. Your knee hurts because you've just had a *knee operation*. You dick. Fucking getting me emotional over nothing. You know I'm allergic to emotion. So you just relax and keep your mouth shut for two weeks. If you do have a mate who can come and coach for a week, I'll bite his hand off. Seriously, get on that. You know I don't have any contacts. Some guy from Everton, yeah? I'm not joking when I say next week is the most important five training sessions in the club's history. I've changed my mind, though. I don't want to see you there. You're banned. Jesus," I said, with a chuckle. "You had me going. All right, so . . . Rest. Recover. I'm prescribing you ninety minutes of excitement a week. That's to be spent listening to your team that *you* trained go absolutely *mental* on some chumps. All right? Actually, ninety minutes isn't enough. You've got Livia. Let's make it ninety-three minutes of excitement a week? Good? Deal?"

"Deal, Max."

I decided to hang around Chester to watch the youth teams and women train in the evening. While I waited, I had a big old think. It was obvious I'd spend my XP buying the next formation. 4-1-4-1. Finally, a serious formation with a defensive midfielder! I was going to build my hopes and dreams around Youngster. He wasn't quite up to scratch in terms of CA, but he was top quality from head to toe. Every neuron, every synapse told me I could trust him. Told me I could put my faith in him.

So I would be in charge for two matches. I was sure Jackie's pain would diminish enough by the start of the Farsley match that he'd want to sit in the dugout. Who managed which matches when didn't matter a whole lot because I'd already used Bench Boost and Triple Captain.

But I'd have to lead the training sessions, too.

I could do some basic passing and technique drills. I could do my famous Art of Slapping drill. I could copy-paste from fifty drills I'd seen and notated during my time as a footballer. Yeah, I could take training. That wasn't the problem. The problem was no player had ever had an attribute turn green when I was leading a session. No one's CA had ever improved.

One option was to double down on a good resource that we did have available—Vimsy. He could do shuffle-and-slide drills as well as anyone. It'd help with Carl Carlile's shitty positioning, anyway. Another was Spectrum, but using him in the mornings would mean gaps in the evenings. Slower growth for the youth teams. Not ideal, but I think even the kids would understand we had to prioritise the first team in such a dire situation.

I didn't know what to do. Every option was suboptimal. I needed to make something happen, and fast. But if I bought the Staff Search perk, I wouldn't be able to afford 4-1-4-1. No, the curse wasn't going to help me find a genius coach who could start work immediately.

After activating Playdar (a bust) I spent dinner alone in a busy restaurant, then went to my office slash bedroom and texted Emma. Among other things, I told her what Cutter had said about how when I was on song, I didn't try to make things happen.

She sent me a link to a song I'd never heard of by an artist I'd never heard of.

I listened to it, hated it, listened again, hated it more. By 2 a.m. I was jogging around the edge of the pitch, listening to it on a loop in the pitch darkness.

Thursday, March 23.

As everyone arrived for training, I redirected them into the big meeting room. Soon enough, everyone was there. All the first-team squad, plus Vimsy, Jill, Spectrum, and Jude, the guy I was still paying to coach Broughton under-fourteens. Getting involved with Chester's first team was a massive opportunity for him; he looked nervous. And he wasn't the only one. Any break from the routine made players anxious.

I rapped the long, central table a few times and looked around. On the left, a little pocket of allies: Henri, Raffi, Youngster, Pascal. On the right, some baddies: Sam, Trick, D-Day. They all fell silent.

I closed my eyes for a couple of seconds. Trying to get into the right headspace. Find the right tone. The problem was, no right tone existed. I would be mocked relentlessly for this until the day I died. But I didn't know any other way to do it. I had to be fearless. Embarrassment is the cost of entry.

"All right. I went to see Jackie yesterday. Handed over the three points you won for him, as promised. He was made up. His specialist told me he's confident the op went well." He also told me phantom pain was common after such procedures. Turning the emotion dial all the way to eleven was pretty common. "He doesn't want Jackie moving around for a couple of weeks."

That got a buzz. Couple of weeks! I tapped the table.

"I'm going to run the touchline on Saturday against Chorley, and next week against Southport. The aim is to have Jackie back by Farsley. All right? What that means is that I'm in charge for a while." I looked around. "The main topic this morning is training and what we're going to be working on. But I also think it's a decent time to do some admin stuff. Most of you are waiting to hear about extending your contract. We can't have that conversation until we know which division we'll be playing in next season. And I don't think anyone from the club has ever given you a performance review."

Oops! Corporate buzzwords didn't sit well with footballers. Except with Pascal—he was leaning forward. *Review me! Review me!*

"As a group, I'm satisfied with your professionalism. I don't hear about people being late or rude to the drivers or any of that shit. You know how I feel about self-reporting injuries, but I've got no complaints about your effort on the training pitch or on match days. Your heads don't go down, you don't give up. I don't think as a group you do enough to help young players come through, and you're not as community-minded as I'd like. But you're not a negative, either. Next season, we'll work on being better at community things."

I scratched an itch on the back of my head.

"Goalies. Good lads. Ben, I'd like to give you some game time by the end of the season. You need a match. I know that. If we're safe by Peterborough, you'll play that one. Robbo, you keep doing what you're doing.

"Defence. Glenn, what can I say? Proper rock back there. Leadership. You bring the best out of everyone. Gerald, you're a good fit with Glenn. Carl, you've been playing better recently. Keep that up—we need it. Trick and Magnus. I'm planning to use one of you against Chorley and the other against Southport. Trick, you give us more going forward so I might need you to help break Chorley down.

"Midfield. Raffi, great progress this season. Sam and Wisey, you two are dynamite in the middle. I think you've won the midfield battle in every match since Wisey came. Can't ask for more than that. All those tracking runs you make? Those times you chose to stay on your feet instead of recklessly tackling? When you sprint to cover a fullback? I see it all. It's dynamite.

"Wide players. Good mix of attacking threat and defensive solidity. You guys graft, that's for sure. And I love that I can call Chad up, throw him in the team, and get a performance. Doug, Joe, Len, that goes for you, too, and that's what I call professional. I'm not sure I'd be as diligent if I were in your shoes.

"Henri, Tony. Always a goal threat. Always leave the centre backs knowing they've been in a game. Henri, you've been tearing it up in training recently.

"Actually, you all have. Yeah, Jackie's a genius, yeah the drills are top. But you've still got to put the work in. You've still got to want to learn. You're all at a certain level." I held my left hand up. "And some of you have room for improvement." I lifted my hand. "If you've got some growth in you as a player, Jackie'll squeeze it out of you. If you've been showing you've got more gears, showing we can get more out of you, you don't need to worry about a new contract. Because, subject to certain behavioural standards," I said, eyeing the group of dicks to my right, "what we want here are good players who can get better. Sam. You've got another year on your deal. A few more months under Jackie and you'll be the best midfielder in this division. Until Raffi catches you up, anyway."

That had gone . . . okay. I felt it was important that someone in the club say something along those lines. If the team were relegated, it wasn't because the players hadn't tried. It was because the managers hadn't used them right. I couldn't say *that,* especially in front of Vimsy, but I could say the positive part.

"Right. Let's talk about training. Unless we get a Premier League coach on loan for a week, you're stuck with me. I can't do what Jackie does. I only know how to do things one way. My way. So we're doing that. It might get weird. I don't expect all of you to understand what the fuck I'm talking about, but I do expect you to try.

"You'll notice all the coaches. The new guy is called Jude—Hey, Jude!—and you know Jill and Spectrum. Include me and I'm replacing Jackie with *four* coaches." I chuckled to myself; it still wouldn't be enough. "Half the sessions will be small groups. Skill work. Technique. We'll keep you sharp. These guys have good ideas. It'll be fun.

"And the other half," I said, sticking my tongue out the side of my mouth, "will be special sessions. Designed by me."

I put my hands behind my back and looked up. There was a lot to say here, and I hadn't found a single idea that would combine everything.

"There are a lot of things I want to communicate to you. I haven't found, like, an image or phrase that combines everything into one little package. But I have found a song that does."

Joe Anka, MR, CA 36, was the squad's biggest music buff. "What song?"

I smiled at him. He'd have to wait. No spoilers. "I'll just say it isn't 'Friday' by Rebecca Black. And it isn't 'We Didn't Start the Fire.' Now shush.

"Against Kettering, I changed the formation a bunch of times. Four-four-two for a solid start. Four-three-three to play through the centre, give them something to think about. Four-two-four to attack down the wings. I'm sure we can all agree I was very clever and very sexy. But that way of constructing a team comes at a cost: having to pick players who can flex like that. And we could get even more funky. Switch to four-five-one and let them smash against our lines. Etcetera. But there's a cost to that, too. Big shape changes normally cost a sub. We were lucky against Kettering, that we could stick to the plan from start to finish. It isn't always like that. So that's one thing. How do we get to change our vibe, change our focus, change our style, without being locked in to picking certain players, and without costing subs?"

I let that hang in the air. Everyone was interested now. It was kind of abstract, but it seemed like it was leading to a concrete payoff. They had to wait, though, for my answer.

"I don't know about France and Germany, but it seems to me that most English boys grow up in a football culture where they're asked to *make things happen*. Big tackle to get the crowd going. Clever pass to set up an attacker. Try a long shot to test the keeper. You're losing? Make something happen. Your career isn't going well and you've got ten minutes to get yourself noticed? Make something happen.

"Watch Man City. How many games do you watch when you think *someone needs to make something happen here*? Almost none. They've already won most matches before they get on the pitch. They win by buying great players. By training them to work in a system that's impossible to stop. What they do looks effortless because all the *effort* already happened.

"What I'm saying is that when *we've* trained and *we've* got a plan and *we're* fit and *we're* ready, we don't need to *make* things happen. We just need to *let* it happen.

"Example. Don't get involved in melees. Don't let the other manager wind you up. You miss a pass? Who gives a shit? Get the next one. The only thing stopping it from happening is you.

"All right. Another thing I want to tell you is the power of storytelling. When I go on the pitch, I'm always thinking, what's the story here? There's loads of story types. Team gets beaten up in the first half, learns kung fu at halftime, kicks arse. There's your player who scores an own goal from the first corner and an equaliser from the last corner. There's fucking super-goalies where the more you shoot, the better they play!

"And the last thing for now. I've got a great idea for a play. It's about a French spy who goes to China to steal the secret of how they make silk. It's set in the year 4000. I know most of you didn't care much for English Literature in school. But I know you all listen to music. And a lot of music is about storytelling. It's about taking you on a journey. So instead of teaching through dramatic readings of *Silkbot 4000* (first draft), I'm going to teach you how to play football with an eight-minute song."

"What's the song?" called Joe Anka. It was maddening to him that I wouldn't name it. I put him out of his misery.

"It's called 'Let It Happen.'" He'd never heard of it. No one had.

We went out into the centre circle. I had brought out the portable speakers we used to get hyped before matches. I got everyone to sit around in a semicircle.

"Music should be enjoyed," I said. "So first time, I'm just going to play it. If you hate it, great, so did I. This song is a journey. It's an adventure. Close your eyes. See where it takes you. All right. Everyone ready? Eyes closed."

If you guessed that I pressed play on "Best Will Tear You Apart," good job.

"Yeah, okay, okay. That was a joke. I'm allowed to make jokes. Okay, serious now. 'Let It Happen' in three, two, one."

I played the song in its entirety.

Wikipedia calls it psychedelic pop-rock. One review I read praised its ability to "physically command." And that tracked—even the players who didn't like it bopped their head, tapped their feet, wanted to get moving. It's a song that *demands* a physical reaction.

After seven minutes, forty-seven seconds, it ended, and I gave people space to process it.

"Out of interest, thumbs up for good song, thumbs down for barmy craziness. One person, one thumb. Come on." The players voted. "Huh. Pretty much fifty–fifty. I thought more people would like it. It reached number twenty-nine in the charts in Belgium."

"Max, that was epic," said Joe. "I didn't know you had such good taste."

"I don't. Emma listens to that stuff."

His eyebrows shot up. She'd just become his dream woman on two scales. I waved at Spectrum, and he brought the flipchart closer. "Thanks, bro. Before we listen again, here's how we're going to play against Chorley. Four-one-four-one. Youngster is our DM. D-Day on the left for the first half. Trick left back. Joe right mid." I sketched the formation on the blank paper.

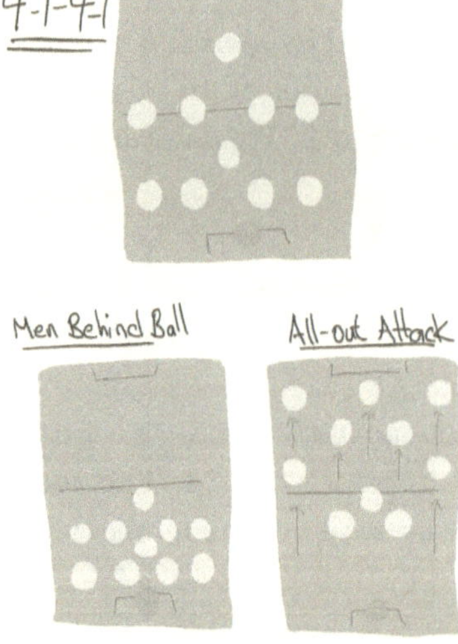

"From here, we can do all sorts of things. We can attack with numbers, with confidence. Even if both CMs bomb forward and we get caught out, Youngster will snuff out a lot of breaks. Get past him, there's Glenn. Get past him, there's a goalie. So it's solid. And we can shuffle and slide and all that shit—if we want. But I see it as unlocking our attacking potential. Yeah, there's only one striker, but we're going to play up the sides like Man City. Fullbacks? Lots of forward runs. Combination play. Sam supporting the left triangle. Wisey the right. Pass it around, break into the sides of the penalty box, defence is all over the place, striker, goal. Piece of piss."

I dropped the marker into the holder.

"We're going to listen to the song again. I want you to think about which instrument, which sound, represents which player on the pitch. Notice as they come in and go out. That's because we're attacking. Or we're defending. But we're not defending because we're being forced back. We're doing it for a breather. We're doing it to take some sting out of the game. We're doing it to draw the other team forward to give us more space to hit in their half. Right? It's all on our terms. We're the musicians. Specifically, Youngster is."

"Me?" he said, quite alarmed.

"Yeah."

"Do I have to sing?" he said, to much mirth.

"No. It's all in your head." I stretched to my full height and pretended to talk into a microphone I was holding in my right hand. "For forty years, the football world has trembled at the sound of my cannonballs. Now, it will tremble at the sound of your silence." I paused. "Nothing?" Sigh. "Anyone who wants to play for Chester next season needs to watch *The Hunt for Red October.* Youngster, don't stress. I'll help you. Glenn and Sam will help you. Together, we'll set the tempo. Listen to the music—it rises and falls. We attack, we defend. We press, we relax, we go wide, we play central. We do whatever the fuck we want! With no formation change. No substitutions. Right, I made some notes about the song."

I turned to the next page, where I'd made some bullet points.

- First 30 secs, pump. Up up up!
- Vocals = thought
- Transitions—slows it down; brings it up (masterful)

- Church organ!
- 1:45—so chill
- Skips, but it's intentional (*cojones!!*), transition out so satisfying
- 2:40—builds. We're on one.
- 5:05—got 'em by the throat!
- 6:14—D-Day
- 7:02—all in

Seeing D-Day's name intrigued everyone. They really wanted to know what that meant. Especially him. I think it made a few people pay a lot more attention.

I played the first thirty seconds. There was a brief sort of blare, then right into pumping action music. I paused it. "Whoo!" I said. "Up! Fast start. Every team we play starts fast and furious, and so do we, because if we don't, we can lose in the first five minutes. If we *play* like this *sounds*, we're winning our duels, mate. We're pushing *them* back."

The next section. "The vocals. Forget the lyrics, apart from the title! There's two kinds of vocals in this song. The first, this one now, you can think whatever you want. Maybe you think of it as me, reminding you to let it happen. The second is like a stream of consciousness. To me, that's the sound of us scanning, thinking, calculating. It's never very intense, never very loud or quiet. It's us calmly thinking things through. Where are they trying to hurt us? Do I need to shuffle across for a minute? That voice is the sound of our brains at work. Yeah?"

The next section. "Kind of weird, distorted stuff. That's us going against what the crowd wants. They want nonstop action. This kind of extreme control is boring. But five minutes of control buys us five minutes of nonstop attack later on. We're telling a story. Some bits are boring so the end is exciting. Right?"

Next. "Now he brings the mood up again. Step by step. Gradually increasing the pressure. Come on! And did that sound like a church organ to you, Youngster? This song was written for you."

Next. "Here it gets so chill. It's such a vibe. We're controlling the match and we know it."

Then came a part that sounded like an old CD was skipping back and back and back. The first time I heard it, it was extremely aggravating. "This is where Youngster drops deep and plays short passes to

Glenn and Gerald. Pass pass pass pass. The other team has to come and do something. They *have* to move up the pitch, because this is so annoying. And when they come, the transition is so smooth. It's glorious. Look at all the space we've created. Can you feel it, lads? This isn't a song. It's a football match. Come on!"

I let the song play a few minutes without pausing. I felt like a lot of people were on the verge of understanding my basic concept now. If I'd had more time, we could have done interesting things with it. Broken the mass into small groups. Let them come up with their own ways to extend the concept. Maybe even let them find their own songs to turn into match commentary.

At the five-minute mark, the song entered yet another new phase. I paused where I could. "Synths, full drums, awesome, uplifting. I see the part before this as us inviting pressure at the start of the second half. They've been hyped up, come out blazing. We've weathered it—piece of piss—and now we're pushing them back up the pitch, easy as you like. Taking the match by the fucking throat, lads. Our ball. Our tempo. Our decisions."

At 6:10, I paused. "Guys? Are you ready for the greatest transition in musical history? You'd better be. Because this is the sound of D-Day busting out moves on the left wing. Nutmegs. Feints. Dragbacks. Trick overlapping. Low cross, happy slapping. *Bum bu BOM bowow!*" I mimed slapping a bass guitar as I mimicked the funky notes. I let the bass do its thing, then paused. "Talk about the Art of Slapping! It's fucking sick, that bit. Now shut up. You thought that bit was top? It gets better. How does it keep getting *better?*"

From the seven-minute mark, every element previously heard comes back. I talked over it. "How fucking satisfying is this? We're slapping left, right, and centre. We've taken such control of the pitch we can do whatever we want, wherever we want. There's D-Day! The up-voice, the down-voice. Our brain, still ticking over. There's the synths, the drums! Let's fucking gooooo!"

The song finished. I was still biting my bottom lip, bopping my shoulders, hand claps to the left, jabbed fingers to the right. "Three points. They don't know what hit them. Fans want to rewind and press play. Yeah, you can, next Saturday. For ten pounds. Buy a pie while you're at it." I burst into a smile. Full set of teeth. "Welcome to Chester."

Everyone had a different look on his or her face. Some bewilderment, some excitement.

Aff was more in the former camp. "Is that how you think about football?" If I had to choose a word that described his mood, I'd probably plump for *dismayed*.

"Yep," I said, still shaking my head to the beat.

Henri had stood. He came towards me and offered me a handshake. I accepted, and he burst into a grin. He wandered away, admiring his hand the way he normally admired mirrors.

From where he was sitting, Sam raised his hand just over his head. "Max." He licked his lips. For once, he was uncertain. "I . . . I sort of get what you're saying here. Sort of. The speed of play. When to press. Being relaxed. Letting the ball do the work. Don't get me wrong, the idea's great. But . . . it's not really something we can actually do. Like, on the pitch. Right?"

I smiled. "What, you think I'm just going to talk a load of shit and send you home to write an essay about it?" I pulled off my hoodie. Underneath I was wearing a Chester FC home kit. I turned around so they could see *Best* 77 on the back. I stuck my tongue out. "This lesson has a practical component."

Dear Jackie,

Vimsy here. I know what hozzies are like. Dead boring. When I was in with me ticker a mate wrote me a couple times a week and it cheered me right up. Proper letters, like. On paper. We used to do that. So's I thought I'd drop you a little note, cheer you up. And maybe this is for me, too, because I can't get my head round what I've just seen.

It's that bloody Max Best again, like I'm sure you've guessed.

Try and picture the scene.

Instead of proper training, he gets us all in the meeting room and does a speech. First part, big fan. Tells the players what he likes about them. Pretty basic, but they were eating it up. He's right. Not been anywhere near enough of that. Then it turns south. He says he's got a song to teach us football from. A song! I'm dreading it. Jill's dreading it. Speccy's excited.

We go on the pitch (at last!) but he's got more talking to do first. And then he plays the song. The magic song what'll turn us into champions! And it's dire. Zero stars. Most of it's just noise. Max says the song takes you on a journey. What's wrong with a tune you can hum? Jill was on my side. Speccy hated it, too, I think, but was too loyal to let it show. Half the players are curling their toes. How did I end up at this club with this madman running it? To be fair, Joe likes it, and he's a DJ at them clubs.

Then Max goes through the song again, yelling, "This bit's the offside trap!" and "This bit is D-Day doing megs!" and madness like that. Trust me, it's all just noise! At this point, I'm wondering if I can stick two weeks of this.

So Sam says, "I don't get it" (speak for England!) and Max is happy because he was hoping someone would say just that. You know how he is. And he strips off and he's in full Chester kit. Players run inside to get changed, run back to the pitch. First team lines up in 4-1-4-1, Max as DM. No opposition.

Spectrum's on the side holding up the speaker, hits play, Max moves around like it's a match. He shouts that Wisey should jump for a header. They shuffle right. Slide left. Max is calling out things that are happening in the match. But get this, Jack, there's no ball. He's making it all up!

At this point, I'm worried. Proper worried. Jill looks a bit sick, like, do we have to section our boss or what?! I'm thinking yes for the good of society, but then I'll have to run the line on Saturday and so society can look after itself, if it's all the same to society.

The song's about seven minutes and Max is dancing almost the whole time, slapping his hands and doing air guitar and all that. While pretending to pass the ball, demanding the team squash up, fan out, move left, whatever craziness he hears when he listens to that song. When it gets to the slappy bass bit (which is good in fairness), he rushes over and says, "Bagsy D-Day!" and gets a ball and does skills. He really lets rip. He whizzes down the left doing something, no clue what, feet are moving too fast. Actually, you know what it was? That thing roller bladers do where they cross their legs really fast. Max is doing it with a ball, left right left, and at the byline he yells, "Defend that, bitches!" Then he runs back to DM. He pushes the team up. "Up up up!" And for the last minute of the song, it's two centre backs on the halfway line, Max in front, and the rest of the team up around the penalty box. All-out attack.

Jackie, you should have seen it. You know little girls having a tea party, pouring imaginary tea for their imaginary friends? He's doing that with pros on a full-sized pitch.

So then we start again, with a ball, and with an opposition. Max stays as DM. Spectrum plays the song again. It's a normal match, normal rules, but with one player dancing around, spinning, clapping, shouting "I love this bit," and all the while doing a flawless impression of a defensive midfielder! The other team chose Pascal to mark him, and you know how fast that little guy is. How relentless. He couldn't lay a glove on Max. He's not doing his skills, either. It's no-frills, clean, simple passes. He's doing what Youngster can do, and not more.

Max slows things down, speeds them up. When the music gets faster, he sprints forward ten yards and the rest of the team match him. When it slows, he dribbles backwards and demands the team fall back with him. When he does air guitar it means Sam and Trick should push on and join up with D-Day, and when it breaks down and the ball is cleared, Max recovers it in seconds and puts it back into the zone so they can have another go. Fuck but he's a good player.

And the last push, the big finish, the all-out attack. It's not so funny now. It works! The reserves try to absorb it, try to keep bodies up the pitch for counters. They're working so hard to resist. But Max intercepts or clears every single bloody break and gets the ball forward and it's like he keeps saying: pressure, pressure, more pressure.

All the coaches are standing around, thinking, *What the hell is going on here?*

Song ends, Max swaps himself out with Youngster. Max wants him to play DM against Chorley. Youngster tries, struggles. Max skips to a certain part of the song and does a little dance. Spectrum joins in. One of the two looks like a fucking idiot. The music and the dancing help the kid. He tackles, he intercepts, he zips around connecting the play according to the tempo Max is dancing at. Youngster's moving the team up and down. Up makes sense to everyone. Everyone's fine with that. But Max wants the team to retreat. Glenn and the defenders are not happy about it. But the more we drop back, the more space opens up. Henri's got six players near him. A few passes later, there's only two! Youngster passes to D-Day, who lays it off to Sam, and that's how simple it is. There's gaps everywhere.

Max wants to swap some players around, give more players a try. But Sam doesn't want to leave! He's into it! So's D-Day. They hate Best. But they love this.

The ball's zipping around. Triangles, zigzags. It's getting faster and faster. Even when Youngster's slowing things down, the passes are fast. The reserves start to give up. They've lost a bit of spirit. They can't get near the ball!

Aff gets a go on the left. Talk about duck to water. I didn't have him down as the poetic type. The Max type. I can't remember seeing him play with swagger. He plays with swagger. He bursts into space like Angel di Maria. He doesn't wait for Trick to come and help—he plays long one-twos with Henri. It's so good, Jackie.

Just as I'm starting to get into it, starting to understand it, Max calls everyone in. He's away with the fairies, I think, but he sighs and says, "Yeah, not bad. We can work on it." Not bad! We've practiced a new formation, new philosophy, in one session, the lads pick it up pretty good, and he's not happy. "Tomorrow we'll work on components. Final third entries, AKA the Art of Slapping. Overloads." He says he wants crazy, four-man overloads. He wants whirlwinds. Spectrum and Jude will do those. Says he didn't like the defensive spacing. Asks me to have a think about that. The rest defence was pretty sloppy. If Trick goes and Carl goes, then one of Sam or Wisey needs to stay. What are the triggers for that?, Can Jill come up with a few ideas? He's gone from wild man of the woods to mild-mannered egghead. He reels off lists of drills and how many minutes they'll take, runs the numbers, and then comes the strangest part of all. He says, "Double session tomorrow," and instead of groaning, like always follows those words, there's more than a few guys who look pleased. That's when I realise I'm on the wrong side of all this. Yeah, I don't get it. Yeah, it's borderline unprofessional. But if Sam's into it, and so's Aff, maybe I need to lighten up.

Yeah. I'll do that. Try to be more positive. I'll let it happen.

I just wish he'd picked a better song. Has he never heard of John Denver?

Thinking of you, buddy,
Vimsy

12

CHORLEY YOU CAN'T BE SERIOUS

Friday, March 24.

I was pleased with the reaction to my first proper training session, but once the adrenaline wore off, I started to have doubts. Had I asked for too much too soon? Was there a risk that by putting an advanced concept into their heads, they'd fixate on that and forget the basics?

On Friday morning, we did lots of small drills with the various coaches I'd corralled, culminating in a big sesh where we focused on overloads. MD came to watch, then joined us for lunch. He caught me being introspective.

"What's wrong?" he said.

Vimsy, Jill, and Jude paused eating. I frowned. "This morning was good, overall, but my grand concept doesn't work. We don't have enough left-footed players. There's Trick, Aff, and Doug, and only one will be on the pitch for the first half. Here's what happens on the right. A right-footed player passes to a right-footed player while a right-footed player zooms to the goal line. Right? If we do it properly, someone like Carl ends up alone with the ball, hitting it on his favoured foot towards Henri. Every pass is pretty easy, actually, in terms of technique. It's all hard when there's thousands of people screaming at you, but the actual skill is easy. Does that make sense?"

"Course, yeah. It's easier to pass from the right-hand side of the pitch with your right foot."

"Invert it. From the other side of the goal, a player needs to use his left foot to achieve the same effect. Look around. Almost everyone's left foot is fucking abysmal."

"Oh," said MD. Panic set in. "Are we going to get relegated because of it?"

I exhaled. "Yep." I held up a finger, turned it upside down, and whistled as I crashed it into my plate.

"That's not funny, Max."

"Vimsy, what do you think? Can we go asymmetrical with it?"

"Maybe. Remind me what asymmetrical means."

"Different on each side."

"Oh. You mean we only do overloads on the right? What about the left?"

"Standard overlaps. Let D-Day do tricks."

"I don't see why not."

"Top. Will we tell them now or let them enjoy their food?"

Vimsy hesitated. There were pros and cons. "I'll talk to Sam." That made sense. Sam was the left-sided of the two central midfielders. He'd be the one combining with D-Day and Trick.

I turned my plate into a tactical map while I imagined how the match would play out. "Makes us even more solid if he doesn't push on as much, and if they're closer together, Sam can talk Youngster through the match. Fuck, I like a symmetrical team, though."

"Raffi's two-footed," said Jill.

"Yeah. So when we've got Aff, Trick, and Raffi in the team, we can have balance. But we're not going to get that this week. Maybe next Saturday."

MD smiled. "I like that you plan ahead."

I scoffed. "It's a two-match timetable. It's not planning *ahead*."

"I heard you told Ben he'd play the last match of the season if we were safe. That's planning ahead."

"That's basic," I said. "That's squad building. Anyway, I shouldn't have done that. Jackie will be picking that team."

"I'm sure he'll listen to you about that kind of thing." MD dabbed his lips with his napkin. "Couple of things. First, I know you're busy now, but it would be great if you could rewrite the manager notes," he looked at his watch, "before two o'clock."

"Why?"

"That's the deadline from the printers. The text you sent yesterday was a bit . . . unserious."

"Nah it was top. I'm busy today, Mike. Sorry if you're used to something more boring."

Jill was interested. "What does unserious mean, in the context of a *match programme*?"

MD's eyes widened as he remembered it. There was a sort of horrified quality to the way he stared into nothingness. "I suppose you'll see. But Max, if you could be a little bit more reverential the week after, I'd appreciate it."

"I pwomise," I said, as I shovelled some chicken into my mouth.

MD tutted. "And tonight. The optics would be better if you didn't manage the women's team."

Jill frowned. Like most outsiders who spent time with MD, she was learning that he wasn't the cold, hapless penny-pincher he appeared to be from a distance. But she didn't like *that*. "Why?"

MD squirmed. "Some people—"

"Gammons," I said, helpfully, though it did result in a bit of spillage from my overladen mouth.

"Some paying fans, members of all political persuasions, do tend to think we should prioritise the men's team and Max should maybe be resting himself for the big match tomorrow. If we lose against Chorley, they'll blame the women's team. Don't look at me like that, Jill. Don't shoot the messenger."

"Jill, it's all right," I said. "MD's right." I patted him on the back. "I won't go anywhere near the women's team this evening, mate. I pwomise."

After lunch, the squad did a firsts-versus-reserves session on the full pitch. Half-pace, just getting used to the positions, the spacing, watching for Youngster's signals to determine the tempo, our attacking vectors, and, yes, trying the tactic where we dropped really deep to make the other team spread out.

It was pretty rough, in my opinion. Trying this in an important match near the end of a bruising season was folly.

My doubts intensified.

There was a slightly unpleasant incident before the women's match. I got out of my car about twenty minutes before kickoff. Jill knew the formation and lineup and was happy to let me arrive late in case MD had spies in the area.

So I was pretty chill, walking without any particular hurry from the car park to the pitches, when a woman emerged from behind a tree and stood in my path. It triggered a fear response—I turned round, heart suddenly racing, expecting a blow to land. I kept looking in a wide circle, sure I was about to be attacked, when finally a bit of common sense kicked in. I had a clear view for fifty yards in every direction.

I took a proper look at the woman—girl, really—and it clicked. She was the sixteen-year-old PA 53 striker that Playdar had led me to the day after I found Pippa. In retrospect, she'd have been an amazing signing, but she had a much older hooligan or hooligan-adjacent boyfriend. When he'd challenged me about turning his club into Snow-flake FC, I'd wound him up by saying I was just getting started and soon enough the entire club would be vegan.

I hadn't thought about her since.

"Julie?" I said.

"Yeah," she whispered, and again I spun around, looking for danger. "He's not here. I broke up with him."

We were absurdly far apart to have any sort of conversation, so I took a couple of steps closer. "Yeah? Good for you. Listen, I've got a match in a minute."

"I know." She rubbed her arm. "I was waiting to talk to you. I thought maybe you weren't coming."

Quick scan of the area. "What do you want to talk about?"

She looked down at her feet. "Just, like, maybe I could try for the team. Like you said."

Another scan, and then the heart pounding came all the way back. Terror sweat. I realised why I'd gone from nought to sixty so fast—I'd *seen* the boyfriend in a parked car. Just a fraction of a glimpse, but my brain must have processed it on some level. There was a crack of a twig, and he was emerging from behind a tree, coming towards me, with his equally sinister mate.

"No!" shouted the girl. "Welly, no! Leave me alone!"

The guys kept coming. They were ready to rumble. I saw the flash of something metal. "I knew it!" cried Welly. "Knew it was coz o' him!"

Now, I had the physical ability to jump high, run fast, and yeah, maybe slip in the odd cheeky backheel nutmeg here and there. But fighting? Give me a football and I could knock one guy's head off, but the other would then beat me to a pulp. I'd never been in a fight my entire life.

Nevertheless, aggression 20 kicked in. I could probably land one good shot. One of the two would regret this forever. I found myself hunched, fists curled, snarling.

"Oi!" came a shout. A mini thunder of footsteps from diagonally behind the ex-boyfriend. I couldn't believe it—Sam, Tony, and Len. The ex made a run for it. His mate was a step behind.

"Best," said Sam, panting as he sprinted to me. "What the fuck was that?"

I leaned over, hands on knees, as the fear came flooding back. I put my trembling hands behind my head while I tried to turn shaky, shallow breaths into deep, calm ones. One side of my mouth lifted of its own accord. "Chester fans. I think they don't want us going to a flat back four." I closed my eyes and swallowed. My throat felt swollen. "You should have let them batter me, Sam."

"Why?"

"Then you'd be player-manager." He didn't think that was funny. I held my hand out. "Thanks, mate."

He shook it and looked around. When he saw there was no danger, he said, "Player-manager? I'm not that stupid. Not many are."

"Fuck," I said, as another surge of fear rippled through me. My imagination was running wild. I looked around. "Where's the girl?"

"She ran off," said Len. "Should we go and get her? Or . . . or what?"

I blew air out of my lungs. "I don't know. This is all a bit out of my skillset, if you know what I mean." I had enough presence of mind to realise I was still in danger. "Are you lads going to stick around the whole match?"

They looked at each other. Sam put his hand on my shoulder, turned me, and got my feet walking in the direction of the pitches. "We were just going to do the first half then go eat. Wanted to see your Dani in person." My Dani. Unfortunate phrasing given that the idea of an inappropriate relationship is what had just caused the scene. "Didn't think you'd be here. But we'll stay. Make sure you get to your car. Right, lads?"

"We'll get a pizza," said Tony.

"What, to the side of the pitch?"

"Why not?"

I laughed. "Can I have one?"

"Course!"

Safety and pizza. Cheered me all the way up. "If someone's going to attack me, they could at least wait till tomorrow night. We need a result against Chorley, but any muppet could beat Southport."

Sam side-eyed me. "Got a lot of enemies, do you, Best?"

I side-eyed him *all* the way back. "Not as many as I used to."

Chester Women versus Accrington Stanley Women.

I was in a bit of a state when I got to the side of the pitch. The women immediately gathered round and saw me all sweaty and manic, flanked by three of the men's team who were monitoring the area like Secret Service agents. So, a standard Friday.

I didn't have time to worry about Dani's crush on me—if she even had one. Which was helpful, because I'd thought about ignoring her until I remembered Emma saying ignoring her made her like me more. Which was tricky, because giving her attention seemed to make her like me more, too. What a world.

I named the team, raced through the formation and tactics—4-5-1, fast start, hit 'em before they knew what to expect—then stopped dead. I'd finally caught a proper look at the Accrington lot.

We hadn't added much in the way of CA since the Wrexham match. I was starting to get a bit of a feel for how it worked. Growth was steady most of the time, but when there was a big match or big incident, there could either be a big jump or nothing. We'd come out mostly on the nothing side. That was fine; at some point in the near future, the women would have a double jump, or two great weeks in a row. The gap where nothing happened was the time needed to process the drama, the emotion, the learning.

We'd added Bonnie to the lineup, whose CA had started at 1 and was now 2. So our average CA was under 7. Our average PA, though, was an amazing 56! Some of that was Lucy, who would probably not get anywhere close to hers, but it was still great to see. The team was really starting to take shape. Long-term.

Accrington Stanley were an ambitious tier-six team. Their average CA was 25.

That was sobering.

Yes, we were progressing nicely, but not fast enough to realistically compete with tier-six teams. Not this early in our development. Especially since I hadn't been able to do much scouting recently. A few more high-potential players like Dani would have done wonders. But then again, she hadn't improved as quickly as hoped. She was still only CA 9.

"New plan," I said, and the mood changed. Everyone was instantly alert. "They're good. Better than Wrexham."

"Whoa," said Jill. "New plan? When did you decide that?"

Cooking up excuses to explain my sudden acts of caprice was getting easier and easier. "Just now," I said, pointing to the other team's number 7. "I thought she was injured. Apparently not. Now, that number seven is different gravy. That changes things. Okay? We're lucky she plays on the right and we're strong down that side. Lucy, you'll need your wits about you. Bonnie, you're left centre back today. Between you, you'll be all right. But guys, you know I hate saying this, we're going to have to defend. Put a shift in. Yeah? Look out for your spacing. Press a few yards, then back to your lines, like we've been telling you. Lines, spacing, workrate, togetherness. You with me?"

"Hold on," said Sam. I'd have said he looked amused, but he almost never smiled. On match days, he was very serious. "Who are you and what have you done with Max Best?"

"What?"

"You're gonna keep it tight first half, make the game scrappy, be hard to beat?"

I lip-shrugged. "What else?"

Sam decided he'd said enough, but Len had less to lose. "We thought you was, like, only into attacking. How many shots. How many overloads. Slapping."

Eyes wide with astonishment, I stood tall, made eye contact with many of the women. "Did you hear that, ladies? These guys don't think you can defend. Don't think you've learned to shuffle and slide! You gonna just stand there and let them talk shit about you? Get out there and show them what 'one for all, all for one' actually looks like! Come on!"

The women roared and ran onto the pitch, followed a few seconds later by Dani, once she'd caught up with the reading. As she stepped on the pitch, she turned to scowl at Len.

"You're in trouble now, mate," said Jill.

"What'd I do?" said Len, pointing to himself.

The three men settled into a spot behind halfway. There wasn't much of a turnout for this match. The club had agreed not to promote it. Let the drama settle down. Get back to normal. "Best," called Sam, inviting me over. He nodded. "That? That was good." High praise! "What do you want?"

"Oh. Er . . ." I faced the pitch. "Competition for goalie. Midfielder. Striker. Oh, and a DM. Yeah, DM would be very nice."

"Pizza."

"Right! Ham and mushroom."

"They've got vegan stuff."

"Is ham and mushroom vegan?"

"Don't think so."

"I don't want vegan, then, do I?"

Len coughed. "Max. Can I have a word?" We stepped away, and he told me he'd decided to leave in the summer. He'd thought we were getting relegated, he wasn't getting playing time, and he admitted he thought I was a liability. He knew better now, but he'd already agreed a contract. I told him he was right to leave, because next season I'd be available to play, so there would be one less attacking spot in the team. Plus, I'd be bringing my mate from FC United over and while Len was a better all-round player, Ziggy was more suited to this 4-1-4-1 system. So it was absolutely fine if he left. He deserved to play regular football, and I knew I could count on him for the final matches if I needed him.

So that was easy. One low CA, low PA player out. Nice big space open for a new star striker. With Henri heading to tier three or four, I'd be able to bring in two, maybe even three hot talents. Or put all the wages into one really, really hot prospect.

Still, it was a shame, in a way. Len was a wholehearted player. I'd gotten used to having him around the club, and ever since he'd saved my life ten minutes before, I'd realised that I really liked him.

We shook hands. Awkward little man-smiles.

The match kicked off and I went back to my technical area.

There was nothing for me to do except look for ways we could try to hurt Accrington in the second half. Nothing really came to mind. Put Bonnie as striker and punt long balls at her? Nah.

"Jill," I said. "Next week there's no match, right? The week after it's Redcar. They're tier five, so probably even better than this lot. Then it's FC United, tier four. Then the PitchWreck Cup."

"Right."

"We can't just defend non-stop for a month. We've got to give them some fun. And hard as it is, this match is the best chance to do any attacking this season."

Jill sucked air through her teeth. "We can't string passes together. Accrington's press is really good. It's going to be hard to do our moves."

"We've messed up. It was a nice concept, but the progression was much too steep."

"Okay, I agree. But they're learning to be professional players. All this defending, all this shape work, it's good for them. Not everyone's like you; they won't throw a tantrum if they don't score two goals every game. And three years from now when they're in a tough league campaign, they'll remember these nights."

She was right. I had to let it happen, and I hated it. "Ugh. Tell you what. Fine. We'll take our medicine in matches. But then training needs to be extra fun. Good?"

"Good."

I stood at the side and shared my pizza with the subs, watched the match ratings go up and down, and thought about what I could do against Accrington if I had different tools.

"Best," said Sam, who'd snuck up on me. Bad idea, given my earlier fright.

"Jesus, mate."

"Sorry. That girl there, Pippa."

"Woman."

"Right. Right. Pippa. She's good."

I eyed him. Pippa wasn't playing well, and didn't look like a player. Without the curse, I'd never have looked twice at her. But Sam had seen something. "She's got all the raw material."

Sam nodded a few times, then slunk away. I wondered if I needed to worry about that. But he came back five minutes later. "You're going to make us help the young players, you said. What if I helped *her*?"

I sighed. "No one has to do anything they don't want to. And you signed your contract before I was here. If anyone gets a pass next season, it's you. You and Tony both, I suppose. You didn't sign up to my way of doing things."

His eyes were locked onto midfield, sliding left and right. "If I'm here, I'm here. Know what I mean? There's agents after me. Telling me I could get a good move. But if I'm here, I'm here. So, Pippa."

I lowered my voice. "I have to ask this, mate, but is this a football thing now?"

Hint of anger. "I'm married, lad. Got a kid."

"All right. What's the first lesson?"

Eyes flicked away from the pitch for a second, checking out my expression. "Her pressing's shit. Pointless, what she's doing."

"She mostly played five-a-side."

"Yeah," he said, slowly. "Yeah. I can fix that."

"They train Mondays, Wednesdays, and Fridays when there isn't a game. Talk to Jill. Spectrum. They'll help you design a drill."

"Nah, I can just show her."

"I've got five midfielders out there, mate."

"Fair point. All right. You want it a bit more serious. All right."

"Hey, tell you what. Do it at halftime."

"What?" said Sam and Jill, together.

"Yeah. Show her, with the others watching. Jill, you'll take it and turn it into a drill. We'll do the drill on Monday or Wednesday. Sam, you'll be there, and you'll refine it. Add levels. Tailor it to different match situations. All that fun stuff. We'll take what's in your head, we'll make it into something. Sound good?"

"Yeah, but, Max. This isn't how it's done."

I smiled at him. "I've never had a pizza delivered to the side of a field." I picked up my last slice and let the box fall. "This isn't how it's done. But I'm enjoying it."

We lost, as expected. We clung on for seventy minutes, then buckled. Buckled but didn't break, thanks to the defensive solidity and leadership provided by Lucy and Bonnie. Three–nil wasn't fun, but the abiding memory was Sam Topps giving an impromptu on-pitch lesson in how to boss a midfield. He was raw. Not a natural coach, didn't explain most of what he was showing, sometimes spoke the opposite direction from where his audience was facing. But they were rapt.

This wasn't the sterile positional play taught by the real coaches. This wasn't Sun Tzu placing arrows on a map. This was how it really went, down in the trenches. How to block a runner without the referee getting involved. Why he normally jumped for headers sideways (so he could track back faster). How he'd learned to use his first touch to move away from danger and the pros and cons that came with that. And most of all, how to press like Sam Topps.

When the second half kicked off, the three first teamers hung around the technical area. The women had insisted.

I was pretty emotional. Sam had all this knowledge, all these tricks, and I'd somehow been able to convince him to share. I felt proud. Excited. But also, burning with curiosity. Why? Why *now*? Me going all-out with my "Let It Happen" drill? The *Daily Mail* story, maybe? The abysmal contract terms the FA had emailed? I wanted to bottle it up, pretend it didn't affect me, but I had to ask.

"Sam. Why did you do that? I mean, why did you offer? You've never done anything like this before."

He gave me a strange look. "No one's ever asked me before."

I sighed. He wasn't telling the truth. There was more to it. I guessed I'd never know. "Will you do it again? With the boys?"

"Do I get paid extra?"

"No."

"Not much of an incentive."

"It's worse than that. You'll be teaching the kid who'll take your place in the team."

"Oh, will I? Why would I do that?"

I locked eyes with him. Got more and more animated as I replied. "Because that's the standard. Because it's obvious that it's a requirement. And because if you're scared of some sixteen-year-old taking your place, maybe it's time to move to a veterans' league. In Italy. Where you can still hack it."

He looked away.

And just for a second, the edges of his lips twitched.

Saturday, March 25. Match 42 of 46: Chester versus Chorley.

From Chester's match day programme, "The Cestrian."
Page 5, the manager notes, AKA "In the Dugout."

Hi, everyone!

Max Best here, filling in for your boy JR, the J-Man, Jackie Reaper, who is dangling upside down on a custom-made inversion table, quote, waiting for the next full moon to manifest and awaken my full power, end quote. I'm helping out for this Saturday's match, and Southport next week, too. Then for Farsley we'll all be singing "Return of the Jack."

How do these manager notes usually go? I'm supposed to welcome our visitors. Well, I won't do that. I don't like London and never have. (Chorley's in Lancashire. –Ed.) And they come here, swanning around with their two Champions League wins (What? –Ed.) and spending £600,000,000 in a year (Oh, God. He thinks it's Chelsea. Someone get Max on the phone! –Ed.) and they want me to roll out the red carpet? No, mate. We'll see you on the pitch!

What else? Managers normally talk about recent results. I asked Jackie what he thought about our 2–0 win over Blyth and he said, and I quote, and he won't mind me repeating this, "Whoo, baby! That's how you do it! That's how you do it! You feel me, dawg?" I asked him who he thought our man of the match was, and he swung his arm around like a lasso singing "Ride on Time" by Black Box, except with new lyrics. "Cos it's Ryder time. Ryder time!" I think that was his way of praising yet another dominant defensive performance from Glenn Ryder, but he refused to answer any clarifying questions. He also praised Joe Anka's gorgeous cross that Henri Lyons nodded home. "Max, pick up that plate. Yeah? Now put that apple on it. You've put that apple on a plate. And that's what Joe did for Henri. Do you get me, Max? Do you get me?"

I said yes but he kept explaining it.

Later, he texted me saying the apple was a metaphor for the power the full moon could give mankind if only we knew how to harness it. (Can we fact check all this, please? Doesn't really sound like Jackie. –Ed.)

Then we popped down to Kettering for a routine win: 25 shots, 70% possession, no big deal, barely worth mentioning.

I will mention, though, our recent debutants. Youngster came on against Blyth in his favoured defensive midfield slot and did quite well. We did, however, get some complaints from both OFCOM and air traffic control. Apparently Youngster's goofy smile was bouncing off the ionosphere and causing interference with their instruments. In the Kettering game, I was delighted to hand a debut to Pascal Bochum, whose speed was a constant nuisance and gave Kettering a lot of problems.

Together, they represent the tip of the iceberg. A lot of talent is coming up through the ranks at this club. I'm deliriously happy with the progress we've made on that front, and so is Jackie. In fact, he said, and he won't mind me repeating this, "The universal ego is the individual unfettered by limitations and boundaries. Young minds are cosmic droplets of individual universality." Which I think we can all agree with. But then he added, "And their youthful essence can be harvested to power dark rituals." (I'm not printing this. Rewrite! –Ed.)

All right, let's land this plane. Whatever happens today, get yourself back to the Deva next Saturday against Southport. I'm not the sort of person to make rash promises, but I promise to win at least 9–0. If I'm wrong, I'll be in the Blues Bar, buying drinks for (*checks wallet*) up to twenty people.

To close, I'll leave you with Jackie's famous rallying cry, the one he screams into the faces of the players before every match: "Seals do have ears. Seals DO have ears! Remember that today, boys!"

Come on, you Seals.
Max

One hour before kickoff.

I handed in the team sheet, had a nice chat with the referee, then went out onto the pitch to watch the players do their first jogs.

Chorley's average CA was 43, and the curse told me they'd start with 4-4-2. They were decent. Solid outfit, with their strengths being a good goalkeeper, their two central midfielders, one of the strikers, and a very fast left back. Their main weakness was their right back. He was old and slow. Surely D-Day would destroy him. Or would the guy's experience allow him to play better than his attributes suggested?

The players went back inside, and I stayed out for a minute to soak up the atmosphere. I wasn't the centre of attention; I was merely filling in for Jackie. But holy shit, I was into it. I turned full circle and the stands filled before my eyes, the noise dialling up by tiny fractions. We were a struggling team in a small city, yeah, but I was the ringleader, and soon enough I'd bring out my elephants, trapeze artists, sword swallowers, and, in the case of Trick Williams, deeply unfunny clowns.

I'd worked hard to get here. Very, very hard. I could have made it a lot easier for myself by going with a basic 4-4-2 or even 4-1-4-1 without the "here's how I think about football" nonsense. But there was the easy way. And there was the right way.

I found myself striding past the early-bird fans, glaring, scaring kids with my intensity. I burst into the dressing room and asked for everybody's attention.

"I know I already told you the lineup on Thursday, but I made a late change. I had to. It was only logical." All eyes wide open. Some from panic, some from hope. "I spent the morning with Spectrum. He's got one of those AI computers. We were thinking . . . if Henri scores one goal when he plays forty-five minutes, would he score two goals if he only played half an hour?" I smiled broadly and stretched out my arms. "Computer says yes."

"But Max," said Joe Anka, "wouldn't that mean if he only played fifteen minutes, he'd score *three* goals?"

"Fuck," I said, pacing around. "I think *so!*"

Henri got to his feet, clomped towards the door, and paused with his fingers on the handle. He turned back. "I do *not* respond," he said, and seconds later Glenn was grabbing him by the shoulders, Joe was pulling him back to his part of the bench, and we were all laughing. Henri glowed—my joke had made him the centre of attention, as he deserved.

Ten minutes before kickoff.

After pretending to be doing important things in the manager's room for a while, I crashed back into the dressing room and the general hubbub died down. Everyone turned to look at me. I'd say the mood was one of cautious excitement. We were going to use our new formation, with a teenager in the key role. We were going to try to dance our way to victory. Do things the Max Best way. It could be amazing. Or, more likely, it could blow up in our faces and we'd all be humiliated. I didn't let those doubts show on my face.

The lads knew the team—I'd told them on Thursday. Robbo in goal. Back four: Trick, Glenn, Gerald May, Carl. Youngster as DM. Midfield: D-Day, Sam, Wisey, Joe Anka. Henri as the lone striker. Average CA: 40.8. Ben as the reserve goalie, plus Magnus, Tony, Pascal, and Aff, who was up to CA 48, close to gold standard. Decent coverage for different parts of the pitch, there, but still no place for Raffi. I hoped I wasn't wrecking his confidence.

This time, shortly before kickoff, was the part where most managers yelled and shouted and tried to get the guys hyped up.

Not me.

"Lads, people are mad at me. My programme notes, they say, are not sufficiently reverential. Training has been strange. Things just aren't serious around here. If we lose today, I'll be hauled over the coals. So, let's get serious. Fuck it, let's get *sombre*. Eyes looking sadly at the floor, please. Youngster, I'm serious. Eyes down. Look vaguely sad." I took a breath. "Now, what people on the outside can't see is how fucking hard you've all been working. It's not just with Jackie. With Ian, too." A few heads snapped up, not least Sam's. "We weren't soulmates or anything, but I know you were putting it all in for him, for the team, for the club. I know that. I saw it." I let out a long breath. "It's different with Jackie. It's a joy to come to work. You all know how to shuffle and slide, how to defend a corner, how to get stuck in when you need. All teams need that as a base. My women's team, I've maybe neglected some of that. I've been all giddy about the fun stuff. The combos, the overlaps, the slapping. But with you fucks, I can do it. You know the levels. You've never let anybody down with your workrate and effort. And Jackie's taken all that and honed it. So when I come in and say, let's get fucking weird with it, I know I can do it because the foundation is rock solid. I know you all know that. And I know you've indulged me in my mad football fantasy these past couple of days because no matter how messy it gets, we're not going to get dicked, because you look around and you see grown men who know their business." I looked up, then down again. Nodded a few times. "I'm deadly serious, what I say next." I pushed my lips into and away from each other so hard it made a clicking noise. "We're going to slap today."

"Yeah!" said someone. I was being so solemn I didn't register who.

"Yeah," I agreed. "But I've got one, like, bit of bad news." That really lowered the energy. I think people started worrying about Jackie. Like they'd half-expected me to save some bad Jackie news for just this moment so I could manipulate them into playing their hearts out. Let's just say it had occurred to me. "You probably know I got into trouble for the whole fake Jackie thing, even though it was legendary." At this point I was so solemn I could have presented a royal funeral. "And I've been formally reprimanded and instructed, in no uncertain terms, not to bring a fake Jackie to the touchline again." I sighed. "But they didn't say anything about *two* fake Jackies!"

Two bald men in Chester FC coats with the letters *JR* next to the club badge burst into the room. They started dicking about, slapping guys on the tops of their heads, doing moronic Ibiza dances.

The room erupted. Even Henri, who thought these pranks were a bit *too* British, was up and laughing.

I launched myself onto the nearest bench and started a chant:

Jackie One!

Jackie Two!

We've got more Jackies than you!

Jackie One!

Jackie Two!

We've got more Jackies than you!

The bell rang to signal one minute until kickoff, and we all rushed out, a joyous mass, seeping past the Chorley players like a pressurised liquid. The shock alone was worth a goal.

You think I can't get serious?

Sit the fuck down.

Thirty seconds until kickoff.

I placed everyone in the split dugouts. I had Physio Dean, Magnus, and Pascal in the shelter nearest the halfway line. I didn't expect them to respond to any provocation. The hotheads got pushed farther away—Vimsy, Jill, and the rest of the subs. They did not like it. Fuck 'em.

Jackie One and Jackie Two stood on the touchline next to me. Their secondary job was to help me communicate with the players through the medium of dance. Their primary job was to be funny.

The referee counted the players and was getting very close to blowing his whistle. I did the Fast Start dance. This was based on the first thirty seconds of "Let It Happen." When I heard it, my body wanted to do a kind of speed-walking dance, which according to an infographic called "White Man Dance Moves" is my very remedial version of something called *the Running Man.*

The Jackies (one was our temporary medical assistant, as in Kettering; the other our kit man for the day) were being paid a hundred pounds each (by me) to copy my moves (subject to not speaking to the referee, ever), and they did so now. There was much derision from the Chorley bench, but I didn't give a shit. Sam saw me, and did his own version. Youngster nodded. Trick clapped his hands together. Glenn roared.

Kickoff.

The ball started moving. Instantly, my players thundered around. Tackles, headers, clearances. We matched Chorley stride for stride, effort for effort. After thirty seconds, the ball broke into midfield. Youngster hared after it and kicked it high into the stands.

I jumped and clapped. Game on!

"I thought he was, like, a Rolls Royce player," said Jackie Two, the prick. He was—you'd never guess—a Liverpool fan.

"Give it a couple of years," I said, "and he'll turn those rushed clearances into calm passes to someone who's in space. But is it all right with you, J2, if he fucking learns his trade maybe in the meantime?"

J2 grinned. "All right by me, yeah. I didn't mean nuthin' by it."

J1 piped up. "This is why I won the Jackie vote first time round, Max. J2's a dick. He doesn't even look like Jackie."

"I do an' all. My head tapers. Yours is like St. Paul's."

"I've got an *empathetic* face."

"I've got the right accent."

"Guys, shut up," I said. "I'm trying to slap."

Another thirty seconds, another clearance from Youngster. I didn't mind the scrappy start. It just proved my team were up for it. They were proving that they would match Chorley for intensity, and that would probably be enough to get us a point. Sure, Chorley had slightly higher CA, but they were wasting it on futile efforts. Blasting the ball long towards their striker? Glenn ate it all up. Trying to overrun midfield? Sam and Wisey were too good, plus Youngster would get in there and help out.

Five minutes in, and according to the match ratings we were already slightly on top. Henri had barely touched the ball, so he was stuck on 6 out of 10. D-Day and Joe were on 6, too. But the guys in the centre—Glenn, May, Sam, Wisey, and Youngster—had all eased to 7. From the centre, we would slowly start to dominate the sides.

Right?

I felt the tempo slipping. We had defaulted to the standard sixth-tier patterns of play. No!

"Air dancers!" I demanded.

"Back or forward?" asked J1.

"They're always back," I said.

We reached up and swayed, allowing our bodies thand arms to flow back towards Robbo in the goal. Wisey called it out. Sam and Youngster caught on. "What's going on?" yelled Glenn.

"Fall back," yelled Sam.

"What?" he couldn't hear with all the noise. So Sam did the dance himself. Glenn's fist clenched. He'd need to be on his toes for the next few minutes.

Youngster took a pass, feinted to play it out to D-Day, then turned and rolled it to Trick. He bounced it back to Youngster. He bounced it to Glenn, and scampered more or less sideways, starting his epic journey across the width of the pitch. Youngster, May, Youngster, Carl. All the time, Glenn sank, and the others in the back four followed him.

Chorley couldn't believe their luck. They pressed forward, chasing after the inexperienced idiot who was passing the wrong way, hoping to recover the ball close to our goal. Instead, Youngster waited, waited, then passed to May. He pushed it to Glenn. The idea from there was that Youngster would zoom into space for the return pass, but Chorley's lines had become so disrupted that Glenn had a better idea. He struck a long pass to left mid. D-Day played it square and burst forward. Sam played it square and burst forward. Wisey touched it to Joe, checked who was behind him, and burst forward.

Joe got the ball and tried to dribble past the left back. The defender missed his first swipe but was fast enough to recover and desperately bundle the ball out of play. The slightest mistake and we would have had five attackers against three defenders.

During this entire sequence, I was jockey-jumping, increasingly excited as my brain predicted the next moves. When the defender had gotten lucky—very lucky—we had five in attack and five in defence. Four midfielders surging forward to create something for Henri to finish, safe in the knowledge that five outfield players were behind them.

All we got for our efforts was a harmless throw-in.

So it must have been pretty weird for the fans to see me celebrate like we'd scored. I punched the air. I jogged inelegantly down the touchline. I pumped both fists. And if you think that was just me losing my mind, get this: Vimsy burst out of his prison and leapt onto me. Leapt! At his age! We bounced around, joined by Jill, who understood what had just happened, and the Jackies, who didn't.

"Fucking get in!" I screamed.

The Chorley manager reacted with nothing short of panic—they went Men Behind Ball. After eight minutes!

When I calmed down enough for rational thought to kick back in, I sent the Jackies to the nearest shelter and the coaches back to the farthest one.

I spent the rest of the half grinding my teeth, furiously calculating. Every move, every pass, every mistake, it was all fodder for what would surely be a legendary halftime team talk.

In the meantime, though, I had to let the players get on with it. I had to let Youngster feel the music in him, if it was there. I wasn't sure that it was—the most exciting music he listened to, as far as I could tell, was by nineties Christian temptress Amy Grant.

He had support, though. When he started to look lost, Sam or Glenn would put an arm around him and give him a pep talk. Once, and I almost snapped out of my brooding intensity because it was so funny, both Glenn and Sam tried to give advice at the same time. Sam was doing a clockwise gesture to indicate that Youngster should increase the tempo, push the team up the pitch. Meanwhile, Glenn was doing a counterclockwise one to suggest Youngster should slow the game down, give the defence a breather.

Our attacks down the left focused on D-Day's battle with his full-back, which was weighted slightly in favour of the wily old defender. Trick hadn't been able to get forward to create overlaps, owing to a general lack of security in knowing how his role intersected with those of others. Understandable; a lot of people like Trick struggled to understand intersectionality.

On the right, we were getting the overloads I wanted, but there would always be one pass too hard, one run that was made just too early, causing Carl or Joe to be caught offside, or something. Just a tiny miscalibration. Tiny, but persistent.

I nearly burst from the effort of not intervening, but I restrained myself. These were teething problems, nothing more. The frustration was part of the learning process. Just like when the Darlo players and I had been frustrated with each other. Just like when I'd banned Tyson from shooting and he'd had to relearn how to play.

At half-time, the Chorley lot tried to get in my face, tried to start some aggro. "What's all this acid house shit? Are you taking the piss?" And so on. I think one of them had read my manager notes and felt disrespected. Poor bunnies. I let it wash over me, but idly noted that my players all zipped past the scene, straight to the dressing room.

Exactly as I wanted.

I gave my rival manager one last, utterly blank look, then went in to give the *Raft of the Medusa* of halftime speeches. My magnum opus. Everything I'd ever learned packed into one tiny bundle of vowels, consonants, and, if the spirit moved me, animalistic grunts.

"Guys," I said. "That was mint. You're winning your duels. We're in total control of all parts of the pitch. But listen. The song is called 'Let It Happen.' I know it's a mindfuck, but do everything you're doing, and right at the end, switch your brain off. Just let what needs to happen, happen. Seeya."

Exit stage left.

I signed match programmes. I posed for selfies. I peered up at the director's box to see if I could spot Emma. As far as I knew, David Cutter hadn't accepted my invitation. I checked the time. Still eight minutes of halftime left. Eight minutes! I popped my AirPods in, pressed play on the song of the moment, got Kian to send me a ball, and did tekkers on a slow circuit.

The plan had been to bring Pascal on at halftime, but I decided to hold off for ten minutes. I wanted to give Joe Anka time to have a go, now that he'd seen our defence was holding up and he could take more risks. Now that he'd had a little break to understand that yes, this was really happening. And yes, this was really how we were going to play.

I made my way back to the technical area, and just when I was wondering if I needed to do the Fast Start dance, Henri and D-Day, the players who everyone was looking at, did it for me.

My snarl was back.

I'd created something. Created a beast that would devour all in its path. Blood pumped and my lips pulled back into a savage grin. I prowled the touchline like a panther, hyper aware of every detail from the pitch, and nothing off it.

Time passed. I found I was much less interested in the raw stats, the possession, the shots on goal, than trying to interpret the *mood* of it all.

The vibe. Who was feeling funky? Who was ready to slap? The short answer? They all were.

I didn't make any subs. I was in absolute football heaven. Yeah, it was raw. Yeah, there were a lot of fucking rough edges. But holy shit, I hadn't seen anything like this . . . ever? We were *smashing* a team slightly above our level, and it wasn't because of Bench Boosts or Triple Captains. It was because I'd empowered the players to take the skills they had and combine them in the construction of a single narrative. A team of Max Bests! Taking the fans on a journey. On an adventure.

The last remaining brain cell that hadn't been sucked into my own narrative was screaming, "Push! Push! Tell them to push!"

At that point, a guy from Chorley was inches away from me, jostling me, shouting I don't know what, but it barely registered. He felt emboldened to do that because the referee was over by an injured player. I decided I had to step forward. Much as I wanted to let the players find their own ways through this adventure, we also really, really needed the three points if we could get them. So I brushed past my aggressor and inhaled, but then slowly let the air out.

To my astonishment and delight, Youngster started doing a kind of skipping dance. When Sam saw it, he went crazy, yelling at D-Day and Wisey. I had this absolute certainty that Youngster was in the "Got 'Em by the Throat" section of the song, the bit where we started applying more and more pressure, taking more and more risks, the part that preceded the awesome D-Day solo.

"Yes, mate!" I shouted, nodding, laughing, spinning, doing a funky little shuffle. The little maestro got it. He really got it! "YeeeeEEESSSSSS."

Five minutes of high pressure followed. I scanned and scanned and knew I'd need a massage and a sauna if I ever wanted my muscles to untense. The overloads kept coming on the right—Chorley had no clue how to defend with four players in one small attacking zone. And the quality rose. The passes were more relaxed. Wisey, Joe, and Carl started letting the ball do the work. We finally, finally, started getting to the byline and hitting low balls towards Henri. The first: cleared. The second: blocked. The third: agonisingly ahead of Henri's outstretched foot.

Time for a change. I replaced Joe with Pascal.

More pace. More directness. Pascal was an intelligent player. He knew what I wanted, and this kind of intricate combination work would be meat and drink for him. I cackled.

But . . . it bombed.

The left back was fast, negating one of Pascal's big strengths. Against Kettering, Pascal had usually found himself in acres of space, able to run at the opposition, or able to play long passes to Henri or Wisey. But here, with Chorley sitting deep, crowding the space, Pascal seemed tiny, weak, and feeble. Our attacks on the right instantly became insipid. They fizzled out.

Chorley's manager sensed blood and unlocked the Men Behind Ball instruction. Suddenly, they were pushing us back. Youngster was called into defensive duties, making interceptions, slowing down breaks, picking up second balls. It wasn't serious pressure, then, but my entire strategy had come to naught.

"Vimsy," I called. He raced forward. "The fuck is this?"

"What?"

"Pascal. Four out of ten. He was so good against Kettering."

"Can I speak freely?"

I grabbed the old coot by the coat. Two clumps. "We're fighting relegation, mate! Get the fuck on with it!"

"He's just a kid!" Vimsy yelled back, trying and failing to push me off. "He's just a kid! You can't have two teenagers on in this kind of game."

"Course I can," I hissed. "That's not it." I released him. "Cut that dinosaur shit out. What is it?"

Vimsy gave me the stink eye. All the tension building up since an hour before kickoff, all the tension I wouldn't let him release by beefing with his opposite number, came out. "It's fucking *you*! While you were showing off in training, that poor bastard was trying to mark you. You didn't let him get a touch. Made him think he was rubbish. Broke his spirit. Now you want him to play in the most important match of the season?"

I lost my shit. "And you're only telling me this *now*?"

"Oh, Mr. Perfect, Mr. Know-It-All is human, is he?"

"Fucking hell, mate! We can't go down because you're too chickenshit to tell me when I'm making a mistake!"

"Fine!" he yelled. "You're making a mistake! You're making a mistake!"

We snarled and hissed at each other like, I don't know, alligators. I walked away, head in hands. This had the potential to be the biggest disaster since my mate "invested" a thousand pounds buying digital "art" from a guy whose Twitter bio read, "Here's three reasons why this is NOT a Ponzi scheme." Maybe if I'd been able to afford the Morale perk, I'd have known that Pascal's head had gone. I really needed that perk—football squads were just too big to notice every player's mood swings.

I paced back towards him. "We sub him for Aff, put D-Day on the right."

Vimsy's rage died instantly, and he thought it through. "Bad for the kid." Subbing off a substitute was generally considered to be humiliating.

"The kid'll get over it. With your help. Right?"

Vimsy glanced at the pitch. He wasn't a big fan of the Pascal signing. Didn't see what I saw in him. Didn't see the point. He sighed, but some steel came into his look. "Right."

"Aff," I called, and made the change.

Pascal slunk from the pitch, his seven-minute cameo an object lesson in failure.

I thought about giving him a hug or whatever, but Vimsy was there first. He wrapped his arms around the German, then Jill was there to help him into a big coat—or a medium coat, as it was for Pascal. The other subs made a big show of getting off the bench to give him high-fives or hugs, or slaps on the butt or whatever.

I couldn't worry too much about it now. With Aff on the left, and D-Day on the right, our average CA had shot up to 41.9. Virtually neck and neck with Chorley.

They had a few chances in this period. Some of their attacks were snuffed out by Youngster. Some crashed into the rock that was Glenn Ryder. But those channelled through Gerald May were more productive: shot off target, shot on target, shot hit the post!

Sam screamed and went over to demand something of Youngster.

And that was the last we saw of Chorley's attackers.

I mean, spoiler alert, but we just took complete control. Youngster didn't do a dance, but slipped back into the pass-and-move groove that most closely matched the "Got 'Em by the Throat" parts of the song. A few minutes of that, with Chorley retreating and retreating, not because they'd been set to Men Behind Ball, but because that's all they could do, and then, the single greatest moment of my life (possible slight exaggeration): James Yalley, Youngster, putting his foot on the ball at the edge of the centre circle and miming a slappy bass guitar.

I jumped for joy. Punched the air. Paced up and down. By now I was sweating from the mental exertion. From the hopes and fears. Wait, fears? Not much of that, to be fair. Almost as soon as the match had kicked off, fear, doubt, uncertainty had gone. This was fearless football—of a sort.

And now there was Youngster, this goofy little Manc, putting his foot on the ball. On the ball! So that he could play air bass. Air bass! In a professional football match! To signal to his colleagues that it was time to get *funky.*

My pulse went bonkers. Scattergun heartbeats. Dizzy spells. Neck sweats. Spine rivers. Don't ask about my armpits.

But on the pitch, it was serene. Serene as the day is long.

Youngster intercepts. His sixth of the match—a new high in the National League North this season.

He pauses.

He plays it forward to Wisey.

He lays it off square to Topps.

Topps touches it to Aff, who feints to dribble.

He waits for the overlap from Trick.

The pass is nicely into Trick's path.

He plays a 1-2 with Sam. Chester are in a great position!

There's a defender blocking the cross.

Trick turns and feeds the ball back to Aff.

He needs no second invitation to cross.

Lyons and Brown compete at the far post.

GOOOAAAALLLL!!!!

Brown was no match for Lyons.

He rose like a salmon and powered the ball down and in!

I was so woozy, in such a dreamlike state, that I collapsed to one knee.

I literally couldn't believe what I'd seen. We'd created almost nothing for Henri, and he'd made so many runs to the near post that had come to nothing that I thought he would get angry and stop trying. I suspect that's what I would have done. But the Frenchman had kept going, kept making the runs, and had started to do the same when Trick had shaped to cross. But Henri, that magnificent bastard, had realised, somehow, that Trick's cross would never come, so he ran in a loop, and when the ball was passed to Aff in such a delicious position, Henri's eyes must have lit up.

It was all just so, so beautiful.

I realised I was crying.

Someone lifted me to my feet, made me stand up before crushing me with a hug.

"You did it, mate. You did it, lad! Argh! Haha! HAA!"

Vimsy, euphoric. Then the Jackies. And Jill, and the subs.

I started to get a grip until, wiping the last tear away, I saw that most of the players on the pitch hadn't run to celebrate with Henri, but with Youngster.

And then it was waterworks, all over again.

I hid in the shelter for a while. Sat next to Pascal. When I was finally back in control, I slapped him on the knee. "You all right?"

"Yes, Max. I was shit. You took me off. You were right to." He was disconsolate, to say the least.

Again, I was struck by the thought that this was good for him. He needed moments like this to reach his full potential. "Yeah. You were shit." I laughed. "But that's my fault. This wasn't the right game for you. All right? It's on me. I'll take the blame."

"No!" he said, as angry as I'd ever seen him, I think. "You will not! I am responsible for my performance."

"Fuck that. I know what I did. Now, listen. Learn from today, beat yourself up if you want. But I need half an hour of fast, progressive forward play from you next Saturday. Think you can do that for me?"

His face went on a journey, I can tell you. By the end, he couldn't even speak. He nodded.

"Talk it through with Vimsy. Good?"

I got back to my feet and resumed my prowling.

With ten minutes to go, Chorley's manager decided he had to do something. Take a bit of a swing at us. He switched to 3-5-2. Bear in mind most of these guys hadn't played 3-5-2 for years, if ever, and had only started practising it in training because word on the street was that's how you messed Jackie Reaper up.

I went fucking feral. I didn't dance. I didn't shout. I was so angry I couldn't form words.

Sam Topps saw my rage, jogged next to Youngster. Glenn went over to add his tuppence. Youngster pointed—he'd seen the formation switch. All that World Cup studying had paid off. Sam spat an expletive. Glenn nodded furiously. The huddle lasted no more than ten seconds, but Sam looked over at me and did a Maxy Two-Thumbs.

When play resumed, Sam sprinted like a maniac to get the ball, passed it to Youngster, and Sam, Youngster, and Glenn did the dance that meant all-out attack. A shuffle step, a head bob, and a handclap.

The rest of the team reacted like they'd been given a mild electric shock.

I put my hands behind my head.

My heart was pounding so hard it was alarming, but I realised I'd wound this toy up as far as it could go.

If I let it loose, it would zoom off in wild, unpredictable ways.

Almost all of which would be extremely entertaining.

All I needed to do . . . was let it happen.

D-Day feints to drive forward.

He sweeps his leg over the ball.

The left back isn't amused. He swipes out!

Surely a foul?

But D-Day, from his prone position, manages to clip the ball to Wisey.

Carl has made a lung-busting run forward.

A simple 1-2.

Now Carl is by the corner flag. He shapes to cross . . .

But he passes sideways.

To himself! He's free in the box.

He slows down . . . zips the ball low and hard into the danger zone.

GOOOAAAALLLL!!!!

Lyons was completely unmarked.

He couldn't miss!

I fell to my haunches. This was staggering. Four of the twenty best moves I'd seen in National League North matches had happened *today*. Carried out by Chester. By *my* team.

I punched the turf in triumphant fury, and realised, with a helluva shock, that Sam Topps was thundering towards me. I stood, braced, and let him collide into me. But he wasn't the only one. Soon I was being crushed at the bottom of a pile. The fifteen-second celebration was more painful than my entire rugby career.

The players got up, did stupid Ibiza dances with the Jackies, and ran back onto the pitch with a series of whoops and "get ins," leaving me about three centimetres buried. I flapped my arms and legs like a snow angel, partly out of joy, and partly to check my limbs still worked.

Vimsy loomed over me. "You all right? Anything hurt?"

"Nothing serious."

13

GOOD MATCH

Chester 2, Chorley 0. Full time.

The results from our rivals were a mixed bag. Bradford got a good win, and Blyth picked up a point. But we were now only a point behind eighteenth-placed Farsley, who we would play soon, and three behind Buxton. All those other teams had games in hand, but we were on a winning streak and they weren't. We were more likely to finish seventeenth than be relegated.

My players did a tiny tour of the centre circle, applauding the fans in the various stands. The fans, in turn, gave the lads a standing ovation and launched into a throaty rendition of "We Are Staying Up."

The hospitality volunteer grabbed me and said I had to talk to the media after the match. I said I didn't want to, but she said the club would get a fine if I didn't. While I was trying to work out how to get someone else to do it, Sam, Len, and Tony came to get me. They dragged me in front of a section of the main stand where most of the women's team were still cheering and yelling things.

"What's up?" I said.

"Dani's trying to sign something to us," said Sam. "I wish I understood it. How do you do it?"

I shielded my eyes from the floodlights, already needed in the fading evening, and scanned upwards until I found Dani. I gave her a little thumbs-up, the go-ahead to repeat her sign, and she did things with her hands that I actually recognised. I replied by miming *me or Sam?*

Sam.

"Well, bro. You've got a new fan."

"What did she say?"

"Done good job, mate. Done good job."

Sam Topps fucking *beamed*.

I wanted to get my team into the dressing room, express my feelings, and do some planning. I wanted to think about my XP and the direction of my skills. To trigger Playdar and find a new talent. To grab Emma and find the nearest fireplace with a sheepskin rug.

Instead, moronically, with my head an absolute maelstrom, full of the sound and the fury, thinking of Youngster, Trick, and Emma (the good, the bad, and the snuggly), I was plunked in front of the world's media.

The world's media was Gary, a reporter from *Cheshire Live*, the local newspaper. He had short hair (decent cut), stubble (nicely trimmed), and a checked shirt (looked itchy). He recorded the interview on his phone (Android). I'd read some of his match reports. They were always about how shit the refs were, all the injustices Chester had suffered, and if Chester lost, fixated on some scapegoat. At one point, he must have felt he'd landed his dream job. But now he was jaded. Complacent and lazy. In his own way, he was as much a dinosaur as Ian Evans, and he was hurting our brand.

He was *deeply* annoying, though to be fair, anyone would annoy me if they kept me from my players and my perfect woman and my lifelong dream of finding a backup goalie for the women's team. I was feeling combative and my responses might have reflected that.

"Max," said Gary. "Great win! How do you feel about that?"

"Neutral."

"Sorry?"

"You know people who like their steaks done medium, which is objectively pointless? I feel like one of those people. I feel medium."

His smile wobbled. "That's the third win in a row since you appeared on the touchline."

"Just as accurately, it's the third win in a row since Joe Anka changed his toothpaste."

"I don't quite follow you."

"Okay."

"Max! You've just won your second match as caretaker manager. Chester are flying up the table! I thought you'd be happier."

"I want to go celebrate with the lads. Why am I here? I'm not being paid enough for this. Ask me some questions so I can get going."

"Yes. I understand. So, er . . . the referee was bad, wasn't he?"

"No."

"We should have had two penalties. There was a clear handball in the first half, and James Wise was hauled to the turf from a corner."

I sighed and pinched the bridge of my nose. "What's your question?"

"Don't you think the referee was bad?"

"The referee refereed the game to the best of his ability."

"You subbed Bochum off after seven minutes."

"So?"

"So people are saying he's too small for the hurly-burly of professional football."

"Hurly-burly? How many people have ever said that out loud? You just said it, and so did I. That makes two out of seven billion. Pretty low percentage."

"People are saying he's too small."

"You're really bad at asking questions."

"Do you think he's too small?"

"No. That's why I *signed* him and why I put him in the squad *two matches in a row.*"

"Then why did you take him off?"

"Injury."

"Injury? He didn't look injured. What's the injury?"

"His head fell off."

"Max, be serious. I have to write a match report."

"Okay. Check this out. Here's your report. Sure that's recording? Three, two . . . Jackie Reaper's Chester Football Club worked hard, competed, and showed moments of true quality against a feisty Chorley team who had been on a good run. Are you getting this? Big hero photo. Then a description of the goals and all that. Then you go: Chester's ambitious attacking play bore all the hallmarks of a Jackie Reaper team, while being built on a clearly identifiable foundation of Ian Evans solidity. Reporters who obsess over insignificant refereeing decisions or a young player being mishandled by an inexperienced stand-in are missing the stupendously more interesting bigger picture, which is that Chester are back, Chester are staying up, and a lot of people have worked very hard to get us to this point."

"Right. But what did you say at halftime? You were out on the pitch for most of it."

"I said, would you like me to sign your match programme? Would you like a selfie?"

"What did you say *in the dressing room*?"

"I said, 'Do you need me to tell you how to play football?' and they said 'No, Max, we're all experienced professionals; we know our jobs we'll be fine.' So I left them to it."

"You were very excited to win a throw-in early in the first half. It was like we'd scored a goal."

"That was exactly the time I got a text saying I'd won third place in a beauty contest."

"Who was man of the match, in your eyes?"

"Pascal Bochum."

Gary let out an exasperated noise. "What's wrong, Max? I'm just doing my job."

"All right, let me help you. Couple of juicy nuggets for you and your readers to think about. Things that are actually interesting and not the same old stuff. One. The focus on our training was attacking the near post. Near-post run, near-post cross. So why did our two goals come from far-post finishes? If you know the answer, send me your CV. Two. Which player in today's game set a new National League North record for a certain key metric, and why is that important? Best answer gets to do the post-match interview next Saturday. I'm off to talk to my players, then hit the Blues Bar for some drinks."

"Are you really going to buy drinks for fans next week?"

"Ah! A question people want to know the answer to. Yes. Whatever happens, I will buy some beers. If we win, I might have a couple myself."

I rushed into the dressing room, where most of the lads had already had their freezing-cold showers and were towelling themselves off, half-dressed, or blow-drying their hair.

"Quiet," I said, dashing to the flipchart and tactics board. Vimsy helped get everyone's attention. "Everyone here?"

"Henri's still in the shower."

"Magnus, will you get him, please?"

"He doesn't like being interrupted, Max."

I sighed. "Just say something nebulous like, 'The hour of Odin is at hand.'" I looked around. "Where's Jill?"

"In the manager's room," said Vimsy. "Because of all the naked men," he added, when I pulled a face.

"Why are there naked men in the manager's room?"

Vimsy smiled. "Because of the naked men *in here*," he said.

"Come on," I said. "It's not like she's never seen a man's body before. Er . . ." I pointed to Robbo. "Maybe she's never seen one of those. Anyway, will you get her, please? I've got things to do."

When Henri and Jill were in, I said my piece. "Right. That was good. Some rough edges for the coaches to work on this week. No match on Tuesday, so double training. Vimsy, Tuesday morning or afternoon is yours. Defensive shit. Shuffles, slides, set pieces. Go full dinosaur. The rest is skills and formation practice."

"Are you not coming?" said Spectrum.

"I'll be there for some of it and up in the office for some of it. Watching. Always watching." This was a tissue of lies; I didn't plan to return to Chester until the next match. "I might take Friday off and take Emma somewhere romantic, like . . ." I tried to think of the funniest place. "Leeds."

A few people snickered, but not many. Henri tilted his head. "Emma would love Leeds, Max. I think you were joking but it's a good idea."

"Really?"

"Yes. Great food, great shopping, great nightlife. Investigate that. May I return to my shower now?"

"No. I want to prepare you for next Saturday's match." I flipped to the next clean page and sketched out the team, again in the 4-1-4-1 formation. "Robbo, Glenn, Gerald. For the fullbacks, two of Trick, Magnus, and Carl. I'll almost certainly use you all."

Henri spoke again. "You're telling us the team *now*?"

"Yes, mate, yes. What's the problem?"

"No problem. It is unconventional. Why not Monday morning?"

"I played Southport. I know every little thing about them. I'll text individual things to look out for, but if we play our game, it's game over. Midfield, we'll start with Aff, so it's D-Day and Joe for the spot on the right. I might let Vimsy decide based on who trains the best. In the middle, Sam and Raffi. Wisey, you've been fucking mint, seriously. But Raffi's two-footedness is going to help us with our left-sided attacks. I'm sure Jackie will have you back in for the last three matches. Henri up front. Pascal and Tony, you prepare yourselves properly for this one, because if we change the formation, we're going four-two-four and there will be goals and assists for days. Right? And Len, I need you sharp in case one of the others gets a knock or dies from only having a twenty-minute shower. Chad, Doug, same with you. And by the way, if results go our way on Tuesday, and we win on Saturday, we could be sitting pretty. I'm going to ask Jackie to give everyone a runout in the last three matches, so keep yourselves fit, keep yourselves sharp. Any questions?"

"What if Youngster hurts himself? Do we still play with a DM?"

"Yep. Magnus."

"Er . . . Max, I've never played there."

"Sure you have. In my trial. But yeah, good point. Let's make sure Magnus gets practice time as DM. Youngster, teach him what you've learned. Right, I'm off."

MD wanted me to go up to the executive lounge to talk to some sponsors, but I made him bring them down to the Blues Bar so the normal fans could see us. There were about twenty more people in than the week before, and the atmosphere was even better. It was fun for a while, but then fatigue set in. I'd expended a lot of energy during the match, even though I had very little to actually do.

Emma drove me home, and we spent a cosy night watching trashy shows and a lazy Sunday pottering around a damp Darlington.

A perfect weekend.

Tuesday was all about Ziggy.

Emma took a half-day off work so I could show her around Manchester. Some of the places that were important to me as a kid, plus a bit of culture at The Lowry Centre. We lingered, as everyone did, at L.S. Lowry's most famous work, *Going to the Match*, depicting his idiosyncratic mobs of matchstick men heading towards a Bolton Wanderers match.

I overheard a teacher telling some schoolkids that it was a feature of Lowry's football paintings that they showed very little of the football and were all about the flows of people outside the stadiums.

"So it's a piece of content that claims to be about football but there's virtually no football in it," said some smart aleck. "Does that make it the *Ted Lasso* of its day?"

The teacher mumbled something about threading the needle of what audiences can tolerate from an unfamiliar sport and led her flock away, leaving the painting to me and Emma.

"Is this your favourite? Because it's got football in it?" said Emma, as her eyes swept around the canvas. Top-left, the Burnden Park stadium; top-right, mills and gas holders; bottom half, hundreds of olden-days people streaming towards the turnstiles.

"I prefer Vermeer," I said, which got a smile because she wasn't sure if I was joking or not, and she liked that about me. "This one is fun. I don't know that a lot of artists were trying to capture moments like these. Northern industrial scenes. Dark satanic mills and all that." I leaned closer. "Maybe this is what match day looked like when this was painted." I checked the label. "1953. But see, there's no kids."

Emma peered closer, too. "Huh."

"There are dogs. People bringing their dogs to the game. That's weird. But one of the best things in football is when there's a mum or dad bringing their kid to the match. I always wonder if that's their first time and how excited they must be. I really hope there are some first-timers next week. I'm going to make them fall in love with Chester, whether they like it or not."

"Did your dad take you to a match?"

Once in a while, Emma tried to ask about my, like, backstory or whatever. I wasn't into it. "No."

"Your mum?"

"No. I started at Sunday League. There were fields near where I grew up. Hough End—we drove past last time we were here. I used to walk down and watch twenty minutes. It was always absolute shit. I don't know why I went. Watched some of my school matches when a mate was playing."

"You didn't play?"

"I got picked once. Didn't throw myself into a dangerous tackle, so I got subbed off. That was the end of that."

"Jesus."

"We went up to Carlisle one weekend, for some reason. I went to watch a match there while Mum was doing whatever she was doing. I think that was the first proper match I saw."

"On your own."

"Yeah."

"Do you want to go to Man United's stadium? It's just across the road. If we're doing a tour of important places in the life of Max Best, like."

I checked my phone. "No. We've got time for one more stop. I want to go somewhere more important than Old Trafford. The place where my life finally got good." Tiny smile, tiny frown as she tried to guess what it would be. "A little deli in Didsbury," I explained. Where I met her that day after Ziggy's trial and told her why I liked football. Emma gave me the happiest, most genuine smile I'd ever seen.

Ziggy got us into the VIP section for FC United's Tuesday night home match against Bamber Bridge (known to themselves as "Brig," I learned).

While waiting for things to get going, I told Emma about the situation at the top of tier seven.

South Shields were well ahead in first, the only place guaranteed promotion. In the first of the four playoff spots sat Warrington Town. Warrington was in Cheshire, so I supposed they'd be big rivals for Chester. If they got promoted, we'd have local derbies. Lots of buzz for those games, then. On balance, that would be better for my club. But as a Mancunian and a Ziggy fan, FC United making it through the playoffs would be awesome.

FCU were third in the league, hoping for a win to cement their place in the playoffs. Bamber Bridge were fourth, so this was a real promotion six-pointer.

I explained all this to Emma, who pretended to give a shit. She was good like that.

"Is Ziggy playing?"

"He's a sub," I said, even though we hadn't heard the teams being announced. Emma was rarely suspicious about how I knew things.

"Lame," she said, and went to get drinks.

I took stock of my XP.

XP balance: 518

Debt repaid: 1,411/3,000

Getting 4 XP per minute from managing the first team was nice, but all the thinking and the preparation and the commuting meant I was actually earning less XP per *week* than when I had freedom to attend any old game I wanted. And being hunched over laptops every evening was terrible in terms of having the ways and means to use Playdar.

That was one of the reasons I'd decided to let Vimsy and our collection of coaches do most of the training sessions without me. I hoped to find a balance between making sure the first team won on Saturday and continuing my own development.

My development. There was the match tonight, which was only going to get me 90 XP, all told, because it was tier seven. Then I planned to hit London on Wednesday night to watch Arsenal Women's Champions League tie against Bayern Munich. I expected 7 XP per minute for that one. Then I'd stay overnight in London (urgh) and watch another Champions League match: Chelsea Women versus the famous Lyon Women team. Then a day off on Friday, and do something nice with Emma on Friday evening.

Another reason to stay away from training was that, while doing my crazy session had lit a fire under Sam's arse—and, I was told, Aff's—it had been bad for Pascal and maybe some others. A normal week of training would let things settle down. No pluses from me, but no minuses, either. And two days in, I'd already been rewarded with some green CAs and attribute pops.

So that was the plan. Give my employees space. Let it happen. At some point over the weekend, I'd have enough to buy the Morale perk for 2,000 XP, or with another few hours of grinding, 3-5-2 (for 2,200). That formation would help me step into Jackie's shoes with less disruption, but I'd only need it if his knees really had turned to sand. Which they hadn't. Doctor Sanj had three-finger promised.

FC United against Bamber, then. Good match!

The first half was real blood-and-thunder stuff. Two teams going at each other hell for leather, trying to land knock-out blows, but with first and second blood going to the home team. Brig pulled one back, then conceded. Halftime came and went. Around the hour mark, Brig scored to get back into the match. Three–two to FC United, and the first hint of nerves around the stadium.

From the stand across, behind the goal to my right, came an unfamiliar chant, one that made Emma's head snap in its direction. She actually giggled.

"What?" I said.

"They're singing the Spice Girls!" she said, amazed.

"No," I said, dismissively. Loads of burly, beer-bellied big boys singing about girl power? No chance.

"She's right," said a guy in front of us. He shifted so he could explain. "I'll tell you what I want, what I really really want. Ziggy Zig-a-zig-ahh!"

"Ziggy's got a chant?" I said in disbelief.

"He's got two."

"What? You're having me on."

He smirked at Emma and rearranged his face into football song mode. "Zigginho oh oh! Zigginho. He used to be a blue, but now he loves Man U!"

Emma did her charming, relaxed giggle again. "What!"

"He used to be a Man City fan, now he likes United," I explained.

Emma looked around. "Is this Manchester United?"

I'd explained this about eight times, but with Emma my patience was boundless. "This is FC United. It's all Man United fans who are sick of the owners. They made their own club, to have it the way it was when they were still fans and not customers."

"Damn right," said the guy, nodding as he turned to face the pitch again.

"So when Man United is sold, they'll close this one down?"

"No. The new owners will be just as bad. Or worse." I looked around. Great stadium, great atmosphere. "Why would you ever give this up to go back to being some rich guy's plaything?" I wasn't really in the mood to talk about ownership models. "So Ziggy's popular. Didn't expect that." I shook my head. It was fantastic, but how? He had "scored" and celebrated wildly in a heavy loss; it was later credited as an own goal. And he'd scored an equaliser against Hyde. Total career goals, then: one. "Last time I was here, everyone was saying he was shit."

The guy twisted his neck so he could have the last word. "Grafts, dunnee? Puts a shift in, never gives up, leaves it all on the pitch, and he's a goalscorer. Proper poacher. Top lad on the club socials, too. He's been winning us over, one at a time."

This was all really unexpected. When FC United were desperate for a striker, Ziggy had started two matches with CA 11—totally unprepared. Then there had been a huge gap where he hadn't played a minute. But he'd kept plugging away in training, and as his CA had crept up, so had his proximity to the first team. Last time I'd seen him, about ten weeks ago, he'd been on CA 24. And now . . .

BARRETT "ZIGGY" GRAVES		
Born 13.1.1999	(Age 24)	English
Acceleration 6		
	Handling 1	Stamina 8
	Heading 8	Strength 8
		Tackling 4
	Jumping 7	Teamwork 16
Bravery 4		Technique 8
	Pace 6	Preferred foot R
	Passing 8	
Dribbling 5	Positioning 6	
Finishing 17		
CA 29	PA 58	
Striker		

So he'd added 5 CA, and improved his stamina. Not tremendous. Had he hit a wall on all his other attributes? Surely not.

I doubted he would add much more CA in the rest of the season, but when he moved to Chester in the summer, with Jackie coaching him again and with his teammates and opponents at a higher level, he'd kick on again.

With those attributes, we'd have to ease him into the team. He could be the pure finisher my 4-1-4-1 needed, but with other formations he'd struggle. We'd lose a lot of tactical flexibility with him in the team. He was exceptional at one thing: finishing. But he couldn't hold the ball up and wasn't fast enough to disrupt enemy lines. How many games would he actually play for us? Could he hit CA 40 by the new year? What would his end-of-season profile look like?

"What are you thinking?" said Emma.

"Planning," I said.

"Oh, great. So we can plan our holiday."

I stuck my tongue out the side of my mouth. Emma had been trying to get me to commit to a summer trip to Spain for a while. I'd applied for and got a passport, but that had been before I knew Jackie's knees were made of balsa wood. "Babes," I said, but then a huge cheer erupted. The guy in the seat in front turned and nodded.

Ziggy was coming on! He was on the touchline, wiggling his hips, pulling his soles up to his bottom, then sprinting towards the Brig goal.

"Whoo Ziggy!" yelled Emma, shooting off her seat.

When we sat back down, I started thinking about the summer. "April, we've got three Saturday matches. Jackie might want me around to annoy the other teams. The kids have Easter tournaments I'd like to attend. Then the playoffs start, and I'll want to watch as much of that as poss. Especially the tier-seven matches, because I'll be scouting one of next year's opponents, but also the teams that *don't* get promoted might have ambitious players I can poach. May there's still loads of footy, plus the exit trials. I'm so excited about those! Hoping to *really* stock up on older teenagers, maybe even some lads we can put in the first-team squad. I'll need to sit down with the entire men's first team, renew contracts and all that. It's a chance to get rid of some baddies, but the more I cut, the harder I have to work to replace them in the squad. To me, it's worth the time. Fix the culture and improve the squad in one fell swoop. Yes, please! I should talk to the coaches and physios and so on and see if they want to stay. I need to find a coach of Jackie's calibre in case his knee stops him from taking training again in the future. Maybe an old guy who could come out of retirement for a few weeks here and there. I need to sign some of the women onto proper contracts, and I really, really, need to bring in at least five new players before the season starts. June there will be thousands of out-of-contract players looking for a club. No way I can leave the country in June. July, same. July and August is the women's World Cup."

"Oh! Don't tell me you're doing another of your online courses."

"I hope not!" I said, with a slight shudder. Emma gave me a strange look, because why would I choose to do something I didn't want to do? I pressed on. "I'll want to watch the matches, though. But not, like, all of them."

"They have TVs in Ibiza."

"Okay, and that's another thing. I'm not exactly loaded, and I need to find a place to live in Chester. Henri's been so generous, but . . . Ugh! Henri. We haven't sorted *his* future. Though all these goals he's slapping in will add another few hundred to his wages."

Emma blew air through her lips and a shimmer of annoyance crossed her face. She lowered her voice. "I said I'd pay for it. I want a summer holiday, babes. With you."

I knew there was no real difference between Henri letting me live in his house for free and Emma taking me on holiday, but it *felt* like there was. I couldn't get past it. "It makes me feel weird. Look," I added quickly before she got too frustrated, "if we beat Southport next week we'll be pretty much safe, and if Jackie's knee is okay and he's back for the Farsley game . . . I'll try. I'll really try. Maybe . . . the end of July. I'll grind to get things done before. But," I added, "I need a place to live. That's more important than a bit of sun."

She stuck her tongue into her lower cheek. "And when are you going to start looking for a place to live, Max?"

"On Saturday at seven p.m., when we hit fifty points with three games left."

We sat in vaguely grumpy silence for a while, until Emma and I looked at each other and smiled. We were a good match.

We focused on the football for a while. FC United increased the tempo, then increased it *again*, creating chance after chance.

Finally, one fell to Ziggy, and he passed the ball first-time into the bottom corner. Goal! Absolutely nerveless. Very cool, calm finish, followed by a demented celebration.

A few minutes later, he was sharp and brave from a corner, stooping to flick a bouncing ball into the net. His celebration this time was a lot more sensible. Two goals in ten minutes for Zigginho, and a rampant 5–2 win against their promotion rivals for FC United.

Ziggy applauded the fans as he went into the tunnel, pausing to listen to his Zigginho song with a big smile on his face.

We went into the Main Bar, FC United's equivalent of the Blues Bar, which was pretty rammed. We saw a few people wearing Ziggy 33 shirts. The man himself appeared, and we made small talk, but not for long. Ziggy had important topics to discuss.

"Max, listen," he said, scanning the room as though he thought he might be attacked by someone he had wronged. "There was this agent guy trying to get me to leave you and go with him. Said he'd make it worth my while."

"Yeah? Was his name Brad?"

"Yes! He's the guy who was dicking you around, right? I think he doesn't realise we're top mates." Ziggy licked his lips, got very dark, very intense. "I was thinking we could string him along. Get him to talk shit about you, whatever. Do something against the rules, yeah? But we'd be recording it."

I tried to keep a straight face, but the laugh burst out of me. "Ziggy! Are you offering to wear a wire?"

"Yes," he said, still with that intensity. But then his features softened. "You think it's ridiculous."

I explained it to Emma. "Ziggy's named after a guy from *The Wire*. The TV series. He never wanted to be a player. He wants to be a *gangster*."

"But do you want me to do it? These guys are coming for you!"

"No," I said. "They took their best shot. It was decent, to be fair. But they can't hurt me anymore."

"Okay. If that's what you want. I didn't think about *The Wire*. That's funny," he said, trying to suppress a grin. It faded for real. "But Max, I need to tell you something." He sucked in a breath. "I know you want to bring me to Chester and that." He looked around at all the FC United fans. "But I love it here. I want to stay. You've found your home, and so have I."

He was doing his quiet determination thing. I smiled. "You think I'd try to stop you?"

"It's just . . . I know you've been counting on me. I don't want to let you down."

"You and United are a good match." It was fascinating how quickly I pivoted from having Ziggy as my backup striker next season to accepting that he wouldn't be coming. Maybe I'd listened to "Let It Happen" a few dozen times too many. But then again, what was the point of trying to persuade him? He was happy and there were hundreds of strikers I could sign. "Am I still your agent?"

"Course!"

"Have they *said* they want you to stay?"

He looked embarrassed. Guilty. "Sort of." That meant yes.

"So let's get you a proper contract and all that."

"Okay! I'll talk to Neil and set something up."

"Fuck that," I said. "He's over there. Let's get it sorted. No point clogging up my summer with meetings I can do now. Right, Emma?"

Got a great smile for that one. "Right."

We negotiated Ziggy a two-year deal and a pay raise. From £300 a week to £450, plus an improved goal bonus (£250, up from £200). Emma got stuck in, too, shocking Neil by demanding a signing-on fee and image rights. It helped that there was a guy in a Ziggy 33 shirt who was more than happy to let Emma drag him across the bar to the negotiating table. She got Ziggy a three-grand bonus! Three hundred pounds for me, which she ordered me to put towards my Cerveza Fund.

We had some more drinks together, and then there was one last hug before Emma drove me back to Darlo.

I would keep an eye on him, of course, and try to get him some sponsorships and whatnot. But basically, the Ziggy story was on pause. Or was it over? By the time his FC United contract ran out, Chester would have moved up two divisions. Ziggy wouldn't be able to follow. Most likely, he'd do well where he was, get an extension, and have that season I'd told him about. Twenty league goals and a hat trick against a big team in the cup.

"I was lucky with him," I said, in a sudden wave of nostalgia. Ziggy had been with me almost from the start. His journey had been mine.

"Ziggy?"

"Yeah. He's talented, sure, but when I think about it, I really needed the first player I scouted to make it. And he's got that determination. That willingness to learn, to graft. Not every player has that."

"Right. But *he* needed an agent who believed in him. Who'd do crazy things to get him a chance. You were lucky to find each other. That's the definition of a good match."

"Ha," I said.

"What?"

"If they get promoted, I'll play against him next season."

"Ooh! Make sure you get me tickets to that one."

"Absolutely. But that won't be a good match. I would absolutely destroy them. Oh!" I'd totally forgotten that our rival teams were playing. I checked the scores. "Wow."

"What?"

"Blyth, Leamington, and Bradford lost. Buxton and Farsley drew."

"Is that good?"

"We. Are. Staying up. Said we are staying up!"

"I'll take that as a yes."

	TEAM	P	GD	PTS
17	Buxton	41	-13	51
18	Farsley	42	-8	49
19	Chester	42	-10	47
20	Bradford	41	-26	45
21	Blyth Spartans	42	-36	45
22	Leamington	41	-23	39
23	Kettering	42	-40	33
24	AFC Telford	42	-45	28

On Wednesday, it was off to the capital, where I was one of 20,000 who watched Arsenal win, and on the following night, one of 15,000 who watched Chelsea lose, but win on penalties after extra time. That was a long, late drive home, I can tell you.

But it achieved my goal of blasting my XP to levels where I could nearly buy something useful. And it pushed me past the halfway point on my debt repayments. All downhill from here!

XP balance: 1,733

Debt repaid: 1,546/3,000

On Thursday, while pottering around random parks and triggering Playdar—I found a tiny genius only to discover he'd already been snapped up by Crystal Palace—I started thinking about the manager notes I would write for Saturday's programme.

I'd done a funny one, but since it would be my last go at managing the men's team for a long, long time, I thought I'd get a bit more real with this one. It would be my last chance to talk to the fans from a position they understood and respected. Sure, as DoF I could always go back on *Seals Live* and talk to Boggy about what was going on behind the scenes, but a lot of people didn't really understand the director of football role. The first-team manager would always be the club's true figurehead.

April 1 match day programme. Chester versus Southport.
Page 5, "In the Dugout"

Hey, everyone, Max Best here.

It's my last day as Jackie Reaper's locum, which sounds dirty but isn't. If we get a win against Southport, we'll move on to 50 points with three games to go. No room for complacency, of course, but we'd all allow ourselves to breathe out some of the tension we've been holding in. We'd finally be able to start planning—really planning—for next season.

But first I want to look back at how far we've come and how well I've kept my promises. I've been director of football at Chester for three months, and it's been pretty hectic. When I appeared on *Seals Live* on Boxing Day, I made some rash promises, not least that I would invent a time machine and that my first passenger would be Boggy. I promised I would scour Cheshire looking for players, and I've done that. You've seen me on Sunday League pitches, at five-a-side centres, and climbing over fences to get to your work's lunchtime games. We've found and signed boys of all ages and started a women's team. I promised a better atmosphere in the ground, which was stupid of me because I'm not the one singing. You are. But the more you've seen us play attacking football, the more you've responded, and my buddy Crackers said last week's win over Chorley was as noisy as the Deva's been for a long time.

I promised young players would come into the team, and we recently handed two debuts to seventeen-year-olds. They didn't come through the Chester academy, but I'm sure you'll understand that *that* will take more than a few weeks! But it shows our willingness to use young players, which will motivate those in the age groups, plus help us attract even more talent.

I've done my part, then.

But it wouldn't mean a thing if the rest of the staff hadn't done their part, too. The medical staff, without extra resources, have had to cover one more high-intensity match per week. The ground staff were happy to accommodate our entertaining women's match against Wrexham, but were less happy when I added the PitchWreck Cup to our end-of-season schedule. I know that secretly they love a challenge. Inga, our office stalwart, assisted me with all sorts of weird and wonderful tasks. I can't thank her enough. Most of all, the coaches have been put under real pressure. More sessions, more complexity, more demands, more mixing and matching of responsibilities. The results are there to see: young players starting to impress scouts from other clubs; wonderful team goals; a sense of togetherness that is so infectious it's even having an effect on the cold, dead hearts of the men's first team. All that extra coaching, all those sessions, for no extra salary. Vimsy, Terry, Spectrum, and Jill, you've put a shift in and you will get your rewards—that's another promise.

So, money. Soon MD will press the big red button on his desk that unleashes the yearly Boost the Budget campaign, which decides whether Chester can survive another season. I know you'll give generously, as always.

But it is my intention that this will be the last year the button is pressed. Ever. The last time we ask for extra help. This time next year, we *will* have increased ticket income, sponsorships, Don't Mess with Chesters merch, Dani 7 replica kits, prize money, and player sales. We will be self-sufficient. And that's a promise, too.

So if you can afford it, give me your money. I won't need it next year; I need it now. I will use it to bring in fullbacks and strikers. To sign top young talents like Youngster to long-term contracts. And if you're not sure you trust me with your cash, stick around for halftime, when I'll be taking free kicks against goalkeepers from the JM Goalkeeper Academy. Imagine the team on the pitch today, playing with the same purpose and unity, plus me firing in free kicks. That's what's on offer next season if you support us financially. And if Jackie picks me.

And since I've drifted onto the topic of the future . . . Don't you think it's about time this club went on a cup run?

Come on, you Seals,
Max

14

SAFETY

Saturday, April 1.

Emma left after breakfast to help her dad with something. I didn't mind—it left me free to do whatever preparation came into my head. For some reason, I thought it would bring me luck to talk through my plans for the match with Henri's crab apple tree. Its leaves had come in and it was starting to grow buds. I was really keen to see what it got up to in the coming weeks.

Then I drove to Chester and parked on a quiet side street far from the stadium. From there I slowly made my way through the city centre, trying to get a sense of the mood.

The weather was abysmal—cold, overcast, windy—but there were a few people in Chester kits walking around. Nervous. Hopeful.

I didn't see what I wanted to see, which was a parent and kid who were obviously going to the match. I hoped to find a little dude who was being taken to his first match. Ah, well. Can't have everything.

Spectrum: I've been invited onto Seals Live to do co-comms and analysis. MD thinks it will be good for fundraising. Is it okay with you?

Me: Go for it, bro! You'd be good at that. You're allowed to slag me off. Give the fans what they want!

Ziggy: Good luck, Max!

Me: You, too, fellow United fan.

When I got to the stadium, I found a couple of obstacles. First, a large batch of hooligan types were loitering around one part of the car park, as they always did. They were all dressed like Welly, the guy who had wanted to attack me the previous Friday. Welly wasn't there, as far as I could see, but I just didn't need that kind of aggro. So I gave them a wide berth, only to see a few Southport players and staff hanging around their team bus. One was a left back I'd humiliated out of the team when Darlo played them in December. I was sure he would have things to say to me—things that should be said with a referee watching.

So I went even farther around, wondering how I was going to get inside. It didn't take long: The Blues Bar exit, down the creepy side alley. I tested my stadium master key in its lock—great success!

I locked the door behind me, did my first tour of the nearly empty stadium, then went up to my office to have a bit of a lie down. Saving my strength.

I pretended to check on the players as they did their first light jogs on the pitch, though of course I had access to their player profiles. In the past week, with lots of coaches chipping in, we'd had some attribute pops and a small amount of CA growth. About the same amount we got in pre-Jackie times. Better than nothing, but it really showed the difference one Scouser could make. Without him, we wouldn't be able to coach our way out of this division.

There were no injuries, no knocks, so I filled in the team sheet and gave it to the ref early. We had six bronze players in the first eleven, the lowest being Youngster on CA 30. We had two silvers, Carl and Aff, and three golds, Glenn, Sam, and Henri. Our average CA was 41.3.

Southport's average was 39, so even though we had Youngster and Raffi pushing our numbers down, we were slight favourites. Add home advantage and we were looking good. But we also had Wisey and Tony on the bench, so we could take off the inexperienced young guys, stick the old hands on, and bump our average up to 43.6. Southport didn't have any such luxury, though it looked like they had options on the bench so they could switch from 4-4-2 to 3-5-2. Hadn't they got the memo that that particular gimmick no longer worked?

I let Vimsy, Jill, and Angles (back from the flu) lead the players through the pre-match rituals, promising to be back to hype them up ten minutes before kickoff.

Satisfied that all was in order, I went on what I was already thinking of as my farewell tour. I'd fucking grafted for three months injecting some life into this club. Some life, some new blood, a new way of thinking. And it was paying off in hundreds of ways that were invisible to the fans. They'd see it on the pitch today, though, that was for sure.

My victory tour would take me along the main stand, up a short flight of stairs into the director's box and Legends Lounge, then down through the inner sanctums and back into the dressing room. But I almost abandoned it after a few strides. On the last row of seats behind the home team dugout, perhaps fifteen metres behind where I would stand the whole match, were Old Nick's imps. Though they were dressed as business boys again, they looked as different as every other time I'd laid eyes on them. One was reading the match programme. One was asleep. One was writing on a little notepad. The last was sending business texts, double-thumbing it, very serious. Or perhaps he was texting Nick.

What did Old Nick want? I hadn't played. I was managing the women's team, and this would be my third go at the men's team, too. And I'd been grinding, so if it was true that he earned XP when I did, he should have been delighted.

Although, I *had* sort of publicly announced I'd be doing a free kick masterclass at halftime. And recently I had been doing loads of tekkers to entertain the fans. Would a bit of harmless showing off get Nick into trouble with the curse police?

I closed my eyes, pointed my eyelids at the ominous clouds above, and exhaled. I couldn't do anything about it.

Or could I?

Nick wasn't around. Maybe I could try talking to the imps instead of spending my whole life guessing. I went through the little gate and up the steps. They didn't spot me coming, so the fact that I was suddenly looming over them came as a shock. First, though, I was able to get a closer look at what they were doing. The one on his phone wasn't sending texts. He had an old Nokia and was playing Snake. The one reading the match programme was doodling formations in the margins. A real Tommy Tactics! And the one with the notebook wasn't writing, he was sketching. His work-in-progress showed the rough outline of a house, complete with chimney and smoke, and a matchstick family, except there was no mummy, daddy, children, and pet. Instead, there was a clearly identifiable Nick, four imps, and a little dog thing with about twenty legs. The imp was presently adding a few lemon trees to balance out the composition.

I rubbed my forehead. I think I preferred my life the way it was, before I'd seen all that. "What are you *doing?*" I said.

To say my question startled them would be something of an understatement. They reacted with various forms of panic. The sleeper leapt up and sprinted away.

I sighed. "Why don't you leave me alone?"

The Nokia imp was closest to me, frozen. With terror, maybe. Next to him, the tactics imp grabbed his mate's notepad, scribbled on it, and held it up to me with a pen. "Autograph."

"I'm not signing anything from *you* fucks. Are you fucking mental?"

"Autographhhh," he whined, and I had this unexpected little moment of empathy for the bunch of them. They were victims of Nick, too. So I took the notepad and pen. I brought it closer. In the shaky, uncertain handwriting you'd normally associate with a small boy, he had written *GET WIBWOB.*

Again I looked up at the dark clouds, pregnant with rain. "Is this to help me or hurt me?"

"Max wins. Everyone wins," said the tactics imp.

"Right. Top. But this Wibwob thing isn't in the shop. So either sort that out or stop going on about it. Do you know what I mean?"

"Not in shop?"

"Not in shop."

The three imps who were still there became animated, and had a rapid-fire chat in various languages. They seemed to cycle through about six different ones without even realising it, so I only caught fragments of what they were saying, including "system too old" and "post-season update."

They finished, and the tactics one said, "Get Wibwob."

"What *is* it?" I said, clenching my fist so hard part of the pen broke off. They shrunk in their seats. I looked around to see if Nick was approaching, but no. Clearly, they weren't allowed to get specific. I had one last try. "I need to buy Morale. Staff Search. Contracts."

Tactics Imp shook his head. He was quite annoyed with me for not getting the importance of this amazing thing he was talking about. He reached out to get the notepad and pen back. "Conserve. Wait. Buy Wibwob. You go now."

I stood there for a minute, tapping the back of one of the blue plastic chairs, but the scene felt pretty well over. Demons, imps, curses. I murmured, "Bloody hell," and got on with the tour.

I changed my plan and decided to do a complete lap of the stadium. I turned left and walked past the away fans. People from Southport were known as Sandgrounders, which was one of the more colourful demonyms I'd heard. The away fans had come in good numbers. But as I walked past them, I stopped. There was a guy there in a heavy coat, big woolly hat, and dark glasses, and for a second I swore it was Ian Evans in disguise. I looked again and he was gone. Weird.

Then in the Centurion Stand, I saw Vivek with his family. I charmed his mum for a while until I spotted most of the Chester Knights not all that far away. I popped up to shake hands and take some selfies and whatnot. Terry was with them, and he was very happy I'd taken the time. Then another nice surprise—Mr. and Mrs. Yalley, along with Pastor Yaw. I promised him a ninety-minute sermon on the theme of pounding your enemy into dust. He laughed and said he would prefer one about forgiveness.

"But where's Kisi?"

Mrs. Yalley answered, "She's coming with her friends from Manchester City. Coach Sandra. Some of her teammates. Meghan."

"Top," I said, smiling. "I always enjoy seeing the Butcher of Burnage. I'll come over at halftime if I can. After the match my head will be wrecked."

Next, I saw Raffi's wife Shona, and her father-in-law, Moss. When he saw I was heading their way, Moss got up and walked down the stairs that led to the toilet. I would have said the timing was a coincidence, but Shona confirmed he was mad at me. First, for the jerk/yellow card incident at the World Cup dinner party. And second, because from his point of view I'd dropped Raffi from the team. Bit annoying, especially as I'd put him back in as soon as I could! Some people just wanted to be angry with me whether I deserved it or not.

The next stand was the Harry McNally Terrace with capacity for just over a thousand fans. Having to be on their feet the whole match meant they skewed younger and more boisterous than in the main stand. I didn't expect to see anyone I knew in there, but I was quite wrong. Most of the women's team had taken up residence, along with the Bulldog brothers, Tyson, and Benny. Dani was the glue that bound those groups. Mr. and Mrs. Smith-Smithe looked very out of place, and I suggested I could take them up to the director's box instead. Bulldog assured them he'd keep Dani safe.

In the director's box, I handed the Smith-Smithes off to Ruth, who was more than delighted to take care of them—she wanted their daughter to join "her" agency. Dahveed was there, looking well-packaged as always. He was deep in conversation with Crackers, who was tapping his walking stick against the floor in an unusual release of nervous energy. Sumo was chatting excitedly to Barnesy, the board member who used to be in the army. I think Sumo was talking about how realistic the new *Call of Duty* game was. Inga and Secretary Joe were there with a guy I sort of vaguely recognised. Then a little kid came into view—Steven Watson, the nine-year-old prodigy I'd scouted when I took Jackie to Liverpool. I made a big fuss of him and his dad. I had planned to end the tour there, but I decided to do one last sweep of the main stand to see if Future and his gran were around. I felt like Future and Steven would get on. They were both DMs, after all.

And that's when things got super, super weird.

First, I brushed past someone as I headed back pitchside. I apologised, then realised I was talking to none other than Beth. She was cuddled into some rando. I said hi and all that. I *think* Beth introduced him as something like "Mick Bairstow," but I know for a fact that I looked at him funny, because Beth sent me a text complaining about it. Problem was, it was like looking in a mirror, if mirrors could make you, like, forty-five percent less attractive. In the interests of balance, he was in a much nicer hoodie.

So I was weirded out when I bumped into even more unexpected spectators: Bradley Rymarquis and Richard Carling. The agents I was at war with. I moved past them in silence. They had been chatting a mile a minute until they saw me. They shut their gobs, then when I was far enough away, started whispering.

And the hits just kept coming. Next was Sean and Ollie, the board members I despised. I wasn't sure why they weren't with the rest of the board upstairs. Nothing to do with me, I thought. Last time I'd talked to them, it had all been quite civil. They shot me dirty looks anyway. All I could imagine was that they thought I was trying to usurp Jackie. Not guilty!

And then a brief respite from the unpleasantness, or so I thought. Eve, the hot manager of Wrexham Women, dashed down to the front of the stand to have a flirty little chat with me. But then she said, "And I think you've met Smackface." Obviously she used the guy's real name as she pointed up the stand to where he was sitting. We managed a fake smile and tiny nod just so Eve wouldn't get suspish, but holy shit it was the Wrexham youth team coach I'd been a dick to at Das Tournament. He was now immortalised as a villain for the ages in Beth's "Wizard of Us" article. She hadn't used his name, but word had got back to me that he was on very, very thin ice. Damaging the club's slick new branding. So when Eve turned away from him, he gave me absolute daggers. If looks could kill. All that was going on while Eve playfully suggested I ask Southport to weaken their team.

"They already did," I said, checking to see where the nearest match stewards and police were. Once I looked for them, I saw about fifty in the main stand alone. I relaxed. "I demolished their best left back in December. The new guy's, like, thirty-seven."

"I'm thirty-seven," she said.

"But *you've* still got great legs," I said, but then Smackface gave me one too many dirty looks and I decided to leave before I got aggressive.

So, yeah. It wasn't like everyone I'd ever met was in the stadium, but it did feel like everyone I'd ever *upset* was there.

My pulse added a couple of beats per minute. Winning wouldn't just guarantee safety. It would piss off a lot of people who I liked pissing off. I jogged back to the dressing room to demand a fast start.

Match 43 of 46: Chester versus Southport. The first half.

The whistle went, and my players were straight off the blocks. The usual two minutes of competing, winning duels. Footballers and football fans place a disproportionate value on things like tackling the ball out for a throw-in, winning midfield headers, and blocking defensive clearances. I was much more relaxed about such things; they barely impacted the overall flow of the match. But in the first two minutes, I wanted my teams to do all that caveman shit. Because when the other team's cavemen see that they can't beat you on the basics, they really don't have much else to work with.

And sure enough, over the rest of the first ten minutes, we got a grip of the match.

Normally, the home team tries to do a lot of attacking in the early stages of a match, when the crowd is primed for action. Youngster, though, had absorbed my way of thinking—that a match was like a story and it got more exciting, more action-packed towards the end. So he was happy to keep the ball in our defensive third, passing around to the defenders.

This had the added benefit of wearing out Southport's strikers. They were fine, nothing special, but they'd been brought up to chase defenders, to close down the ball when it came near them; essentially, to waste their energy.

It was risky, of course. If Youngster had hit a stray pass, one of the strikers might have pounced on it and had a relatively easy route to goal. But the passes we played were very basic, and the pressure was almost nonexistent. So we passed, passed, passed, conserving our energy while Southport burned theirs.

Everything was going to plan.

After a quarter of an hour, the crowd started to get restless. They wanted to see us try to make something happen. The change in mood filtered through to Youngster, and he led the team farther up the pitch, a few yards at a time.

That's when the match got chaotic. We started to do our overloads and overlaps, with plenty of players in defensive positions in the unlikely event of a good counterattack. And every time our moves broke down, Southport hit us with a good counterattack!

I had my hands on my head for a while. On the one hand, I wanted to stop these breaks from happening. On the other, if I went defensive for a while and shut it down, I would lose an opportunity to learn something new about football.

It took three minutes from realising something strange was happening to working out the cause. A lifetime, given all my advantages.

My first clue was the match ratings. Most Chester players had moved from 6 out of 10 to 7 (the notable exceptions being our goalie and Henri, neither of whom had been involved much). Southport were generally stuck on 6s, except their moronic strikers, who were on 5s. Their goalie was on 7, which always worried me. No more super keepers, please!

But the outstanding players on the pitch, according to the curse, were Youngster and Southport's elderly left back, both on 8 out of 10. So I focused on the Southport number 3, who'd been brought in to replace the guy I'd dribbled to distraction. And yes, this number 3 was old, and his legs had gone. He was so slow even the one-paced D-Day had the edge over him, but he had positioning 14, so we couldn't really take advantage. But most of all, he had passing 20.

Passing 20! On a random left back in nonleague!

And Southport's manager wasn't shy in using it. In fact, he made it his entire game plan.

Diving into parts of the tactics screens I didn't need to check all that often, I found that the left back had been set as playmaker. A left back as playmaker! In the sixth tier! My respect for Southport's manager increased fivefold.

What it all meant in practice was a sequence that would go something like this:

Raffi, Aff, and Trick would combine on our left, forming a triangle of players passing to themselves, trying to force a gap in Southport's lines. If we couldn't get it to work, Sam Topps would drift over to be a fourth passing option. And with four men in one relatively small part of the pitch, we had great success in getting the ball behind the offside trap, into a position where one of the left-footed guys could thrash the ball across the face of the goal, where Henri was working hard to get on the end of those moves.

But when it broke down—and it normally did; football is hard—Southport would quickly cycle the ball out to their left back, and he'd send an outstanding pass through our wide-open midfield, or even ping a long pass out to their right midfielder. *That* was deadly, since our left-sided players had all been attacking seconds before and were unable to help defend.

I'd seen enough. The guy needed to be shut down. I waved my arms like an air dancer, and in our possession, Youngster retreated back to our goal. We had a few minutes to catch our breath, let me reorganise, and yeah, wear out their strikers even more.

"Vimsy," I called. He came over from the naughty corner—I still didn't trust him not to lose his shit when we were inevitably provoked. The players had started teasing him about it, which actually helped because the theme wasn't me excluding him, but me not letting his passion get the better of him. "I would like to use Pascal today. Do you have anything to say on the subject?"

He stuck his tongue in his cheek and inhaled. "If I did, Max, I'd have said before you handed in the team sheet."

"Good to know! Let's warm him up."

"You're going to change it already?"

"I'll see if I can wait till halftime. I already know what I want to do, though."

So Pascal got up and jogged around for a bit. On the pitch, the match continued to be uneventful. More accurately, boring. Sam looked over at me. *Attack?* I gave him a big thumbs-down. "This!" I shouted. Then I got Pascal, and asked if he was willing to do the shittest job in the history of jobs.

His eyes lit up, the weirdo. "Yes, Max!"

"Right. See that left back? He's killing us on counters."

"You want me to press him?"

That would involve Pascal playing a normal right-midfield role and then sprinting towards the left back every time he got the ball, to give him less time to pick out the right pass. Bit like blitzing the quarterback. "No. I want you to mark him."

"Mark him?" Pascal was surprised. I'd never asked a Chester player to mark an opponent, ever. My theory was, if we played our game well, what the other team did barely mattered. But I had to be pragmatic today.

"Yeah. Don't join attacks. Don't overlap. I don't want you involved in the game at all. Just stay on him like a barnacle."

"Barnacle?"

"Stay on him like a koala."

"Oh." He pulled a face. "Make null their biggest weapon."

Top football brain, this lad. "I told you it'd be shitty."

He nodded. "I'll do it. I owe you for last week."

I shook my head and told him he'd start the second half. I didn't blame him for his poor performance against Chorley, but he wouldn't believe me.

Anyway, now I had a dilemma. Did I keep things conservative for the first half and make sure Southport didn't get a goal? Or did I slug things out and hope our ten percent chances outperformed their five percent ones?

I thought of Jackie, listening from Livia's living room. If I won this match, he'd be able to come back with three games to play, win at least two, and get his confidence up. If I lost just because I wanted to show off in front of my many enemies, it would make Jackie's life so much harder. And sure, maybe he'd come through and this triumph over adversity would be the thing that kickstarted his management career.

I waved my arms around like an air dancer. Keep things tight!

The crowd's discontent grew. Lots of moans when we played the ball back towards our own goal. Some angry shouts. Some rude gestures. The usual output from a football fan with a few pints in him. But mostly people were simply anxious. Towards the end of the season, fans watch the match and at every break in play check the scores from the other games. The two teams below us, Blyth Spartans and Bradford (Park Avenue) were playing against each other. That made the calculations even more convoluted, but everyone in the stadium knew one thing: Despair lurked around every corner.

If Blyth beat Bradford, and on Tuesday night Bradford won their game in hand, both teams would go to 48 points. As it stood, Chester would finish the day on 48 points. It was far, far too tight.

Tight. We kept things tight. A modern version, involving lots of short, safe passes, but still, not the fearless football I'd promised Emma. Then again, it wasn't the fearful football Ian Evans had punished the city with for so long. This was a pragmatic balance, and in the second half, we'd push. And we'd be able to push even harder knowing that Southport's strikers had run themselves into the ground chasing lost causes.

The fucking idiots.

Talking of idiots . . . The angst from the crowd made D-Day snap and go against my instructions and the on-pitch vibe set by Youngster.

He took a pass from Sam Topps. Youngster had rolled into position for the backwards pass and was already on the half-turn, clearly intending to move the ball to Carl Carlile. But D-Day decided he needed to make something happen. So instead of passing, he went on a dribble. Seeing that, Carl sprinted forward to support his mate. In any other circumstance, a wonderfully selfless piece of play.

Perhaps D-Day thought the old left back was there for the taking, but all that happened was he handed the ball to his wily old opponent, and now we had no cover on the right of the pitch. The left back played a neat, curving pass that one of the strikers ran onto. Suddenly, all Southport's midfielders streamed forward. The striker drove forward, waited for Gerald May to move out of position to engage him, and then cut back inside onto his right foot. He looked for an option and found he had four targets, with only Glenn and Youngster defending.

The cross was shanked, somewhat—tired legs helping us—but was collected by the other striker. He feinted to shoot, taking Youngster out of the picture. Instead, their number 9 chipped the ball towards the back post, where Glenn heroically rose between two Southport players and headed the ball away.

But it only got as far as another midfielder, and he absolutely pummelled it towards Robbo's goal. Sam Topps appeared out of nowhere and flung himself into the path of the ball. It hit his head and spun away for a corner.

"Dean!" I screamed, and our physio sprinted onto the pitch. Sam's technique, passing, and stamina had turned red. Not good. "Pascal, you ready?"

"Yes, Max."

Vimsy dashed over. "You're going to put him on instead of D-Day, right? You're not taking Sam off. Max, come on. Please. Please, mate."

I smiled at him. "See that? That was Southport's last shot. If they get another shot today, I'll give you—" I closed my eyes and calculated how much I could afford to commit. I'd promised to buy drinks in the Blues Bar after the match. "A trillion pounds. Er . . . doesn't include this corner."

"I don't want a trillion pounds. I want three points. I want Sam on the pitch."

"Sam's concussed, mate. We don't dick around with head injuries."

He sucked in a breath to stop himself saying something he'd regret. "It's a young team you want to use. Not much power. Know what I mean?"

I did. Replacing Sam with Pascal would bring our average CA down to a pitiful 39. "Power is nothing without control. I learned that from a car commercial." Before I could get Pascal on the pitch, I had to deal with the all-too-predictable farce of Sam saying he was fine to keep playing, and Dean enabling him. Fucking Dean. I pointed to Sam's head. "Concussion. One day, no activity. Get him somewhere nice and quiet. My office has a bed, if that helps. But if you don't get this guy off the pitch in the next five seconds, you'll be the first physio to be fired mid-match since Mourinho fired that one who didn't let him cheat the way he wanted."

"Gaffer, I'm fine," said Sam, calling me by the title he'd used for Ian Evans. What more proof did Dean need?

"This drama is costing the team, mate. Get fucked before I lose my temper."

Dean supported Sam down the tunnel, with the nearby fans applauding them. Pascal zipped onto the pitch, taking up his usual position near the edge of the box, ready for a fast break. But the corner was pretty good, and a caveman centre back got his head on it. It went a couple of feet over the bar.

One day, my luck would run out.

As the team reset, with D-Day now playing Sam's central midfield role and Pascal marking the left back, I gave D-Day a quick blast. A long-distance hairdryer. Then I told Wisey to warm up. The slightest hint that D-Day wasn't doing exactly as he was told would be the end of his Chester career.

But something galvanised him. Either it was the horror of his shitty decision-making leading to his teammate getting his head nearly caved in, or the fact that I'd taken the handbrake off and he was allowed to attack. He not only did a good job in an unfamiliar position, he gave us an extra attacking option through the centre. That was needed, because I'd abandoned the right-hand side.

I tweaked all the settings—attack down left, lock Carl into place, Raffi playmaker—did my "attack" dance, and Youngster, Raffi, and D-Day took control of the midfield. We pushed Southport back, then started to do terrible things to them on the left-hand side.

Until . . .

Transcript from Seals Live, 3:39 p.m.

Boggy: If you're just joining us, a reminder that it's still nil–nil here in the Deva. Bit of a circumspect start from Chester, and Southport have had the two best chances. Sam Topps has gone off injured, and young Pascal Bochum is playing on the right. The latest is that Blyth are beating Bradford, so that's the nightmare scenario all set up. With me is Chester coach, Spectrum. Spectrum, what do you make of Bochum's performance so far? He hasn't been involved much.

Spectrum: Well, it's true he hasn't affected play very much. I . . . I can't quite get my head around the change. But Max had Pascal warming up for a long time. It seemed like he wanted to get Pascal on as soon as he could. And since then, we've been much better. But why?

Boggy: If *you* don't know, then at least I have an excuse! I would have put James Wise on instead of Sam. Like-for-like swap. Keep things simple.

Spectrum: [Sighs.] I mean, yeah. That's what I'd have done, too.

Boggy: D-Day isn't quite up for the physical side of playing in the centre. I feel safe saying that.

Spectrum: He's not the player you associate with tackles and interceptions, no. But he's moving the ball around nicely. I think as long as we have most of the possession, he'll do all right there.

Boggy: You're nervous, Spectrum.

Spectrum: Look, you've got to be nervous given the situation in the league. It's been a strange start. I know Max intended to be on the front foot today.

Boggy: Southport haven't let us.

Spectrum: No.

Boggy: Well, let's see what happens here. It's Trick Williams with the ball in the left-back slot. He passes to Youngster. Little noise from Spectrum, there.

Spectrum: The way he turned away from danger. That was slick.

Boggy: I didn't notice, to be honest. But it's with D-Day now. He lends it to Pascal. Again, that bounce pass. It's like he can't work out his feet. Oh, what's this? Message on the chat. "Here comes the blunderkind?" What does that mean? Oh, blunderkind. That's not nice. The ball's back with Youngster. I have to say, Chester look like a team from a few divisions higher. You coaches have done great work.

Fans: [Excitement.]

Boggy: Now Aff's on the run. He dribbles past one. Holds the ball up. Simple for Brown. Brown holds off a challenge. Passes to Trick. Aff. Brown. Trick. Aff. Brown. Trick and Aff both dart forward! Raffi passes, no! He turns inside, feeds D-Day. Now Brown goes wide. Trick and Aff are back onside. Aff lays it off to Brown. One–two with Trick. This is wonderful football!

Fans: [Excitement increases.]

Boggy: Back to D-Day again. He chips it first-time, outside of the foot, cheeky. It spins into the path of Aff. In the six-yard box, Lyons checks his run, wants it cut back. Aff—shoots! There's a huge noise. Fans are screaming for handball! So is Aff! The ref's given it! [High-pitched] Penalty to Chester! Penalty to Chester! Southport are furious.

Spectrum: That's a clear pen. He'll be lucky not to get a red card for that. He stopped a goal!

Boggy: Who's going to take it?

Spectrum: Henri.

Boggy: D-Day has picked the ball up.

Spectrum: Max will kill him.

Boggy: Max will have to get in the queue. We all remember what Donny did last time he took a penalty in a big match. D-Day's got the ball, standing over the penalty spot to stop the Southport players from scuffing it up. The ref needs to get a grip, here. Lots of mind games going on. Ah, now D-Day is handing the ball over. That's a relief.

Spectrum: He was taking the aggro on himself. Letting Henri clear his head.

Boggy: Are you confident?

Spectrum: [Squeakily] Yes.

Boggy: Lyons is ready. The keeper is dancing around, trying to put him off. The French hitman is shooting towards the Hipkiss stand where all the away fans are. They're bouncing around, too. Lyons . . . scores! [High-pitched] He scores!

Spectrum: Great penalty!

Boggy: Struck it low and hard to the keeper's right. Keeper guessed the right way. No problem! Right in the corner. Chester lead! And now the fans come alive.

Spectrum: And there goes Max.

Boggy: There goes Max? What do you mean?

Spectrum: It's on. It's happening. [Mild shriek.] We're going to win, Boggy!

Boggy: Great enthusiasm, there! Er . . . all I see is Max Best walking up and down the touchline. Seems normal, to be completely honest.

Spectrum: That's his shark walk. He smells blood. Trust me. Ah, look, he's ordering them back. He does this. Doesn't want managers seeing all of what we can do in the first half because they've got fifteen minutes to try to work it out. Second half he'll do whatever he's got planned, and they won't have any answers.

Boggy: I'd be tempted to say you were kidding yourself, but we've already seen it three times. Message from the chat. This from do_ what_thou_wilt_666. "Bin JR. Max Best for manager!" Now, Spectrum, be honest. Since Max Best has been on the touchline, we've won three in a row. If we hold on here, that's twelve points from twelve. He's single-handedly dragging the club out of the muck. Message from Nigel in Cotton Edmunds: "Evans good, Jackie better, Max best."

Spectrum: [Pause.] Look, Max would say three of those four wins were at home and all were against teams near the bottom of the table. Teams Jackie would have beat on his own. Matches we should be winning. And he's right. I wouldn't let him hear you talking like that, Boggy. Max has a high opinion of himself, we all know that, so now imagine how high his opinion of Jackie is. If you put it to Max we should sack Jackie, he'd probably quit on the spot to shut you up. He won't have it. He's in absolute awe of Jackie's training and man management. Max wants to find players like Youngster and let Jackie turn them into stars. Max and Jackie—it's the dream team.

Boggy: The referee's blown for halftime. Max is storming towards the tunnel. Vimsy has intercepted him, reminding him of his promise to take free kicks for the Boost the Budget campaign. Young goalkeepers from all around Cheshire have come to try to save them. Spectrum, what are your plans?

Spectrum: I'm going to find out what he's up to with Pascal and if I'm allowed to say it here.

Boggy: Okay. See you in fifteen. [Click.] Off air.

Boggy: [Huge exhale.] [Sound of a man slapping himself on the cheeks with his mouth slightly open.]

Boggy: Christ, I can't take this.

Halftime.

I was in a mental fury, thoughts travelling through my tunnel vision, replaying the match, checking the stats, plotting, anticipating moves, and preparing countermoves. I absentmindedly put on my football boots and was led out onto the pitch by two men. They had microphones and were talking a lot of shit. They paused, expectant, with me two yards away from a football. Twenty-five yards away, a lanky goalie was slightly bent over, on his toes, ready for action.

"Shoot?" I said.

Vaguely affirmatory noises penetrated the whirlwind. I took all my fears, worries, and stress, turned them into a ball of heat, sent it down through my leg, into my right foot, and then I twatted the ball like it was to blame.

"Holy shit, Max," said someone.

"Steady on," said another.

I snapped out of it. Smasho and Nice One were emceeing the half-time entertainment. The fans behind the goal were either cowering or had scattered. The goalie was exactly where he had started, but now with an added knee-knocking sound effect.

I reached out for the nearest mic. "Soz," I said. "Just needed to vent."

That got some laughs, and so did the rest of the exhibition. It was part thrilling exhibition of pure ball striking, part clowning. They gave me tasks like facing two goalies, long walls of mannequins, whatever they could think of. The *pièce de résistance* was the final shot. They'd collected three of those large circus hoops spanned with paper—think dolphin tricks—and famous former players held them up. I was allowed to move the guys around a little bit, but basically, I had to really rip a curved shot through all three hoops and into the net.

I moved the first guy as far right of goal as I thought I could manage, and when I was ready, Nice One stopped. Pretending to be talking to me and not into the microphone, he said, "Max, seriously, this is crazy. Save something for next year."

I pretended to think about it. "You know what, you're right. The paper might take some of the spin off the ball anyway." So I moved the guy a foot to the left. It was still absurd looking, but a bit more realistic.

I cleared my mind. For a half a second I was back in Moss Side, Manchester, where I'd gained my powers. I counted to five, listening to the murmur of the crowd. It ceased when I rocked back slightly to begin my run-up.

My shot tore through the first hoop, dead centre. It hit the next left of centre. The third was way left. The shot smacked against the left-hand post and rebounded with a loud *clang*.

The away fans let out a snide, mocking "Aaaah!" which made me laugh. But as the ball came to a rest, the first drops of rain fell. I looked up at the dark clouds. "Oh, that's ominous," said Nice One, as he and the other former players scampered off the pitch.

I ambled to the dressing room to check on things. Vimsy mumbled that I didn't need to do anything about D-Day. I took it to mean the rest of the team had laid into him and the matter was closed.

"How's Sam?"

Physio Dean had left Sam alone while he checked the other players. Magnus was also going round looking into his teammates' small knocks and complaints. That was kind of ludicrous, since he was our left back, but at a small team you needed to accept some weirdness. Dean came over. "Concussion, like you said. He's fine. Should be all right for next Saturday. The hardest thing was stopping him from trying to get back out to watch."

"No stimuli," I said, starting to get hot.

"I know, Max," said Dean in an unusually soothing way. "I know. I'm doing it your way."

"What way's that?" I said. Little bit snarky.

Dean did a weird little grin. "The right way."

Vimsy put his hand on my arm. "Max. Trust your staff, now. Come on. It's been a bumpy ride, but you know what we all say."

This was such an obvious set up, but I was curious. "What do you all say?"

"Max knows best."

I counted to five as I breathed in, then shoved it all out of me. "Bunch of nutjobs," I said, walking to the tactics board and flipchart. I was still smiling when I picked up the nearest marker pen, which signalled everyone to shut up.

Spectrum burst in with a burger, eliciting tons of complaints from the hungry players. "Sorry! I need to know why Pascal's playing right mid and not doing anything. No offence, mate," he added, talking to the German.

"None taken," I said, because he was actually offending me, if anyone. I slapped the board. "Right. Pascal's there to cut that left back out of the match. You've noticed they've done absolutely nothing since Pascal came on. Now you know why. We're playing great. Keep it up. They don't have much on the bench. They can change to three-five-two and switch one of their strikers. We keep making them run. Easy. They're already blowing, did you notice? Yeah. It's just more of the same, please. Any questions?"

Henri stood. "Can we discuss the tactics?"

"Course."

He looked down, inhaled, then spoke. "It's very clever, what you're doing. And we're winning. It might be enough. But it's such an important game for the club. If the scores are still close near the end, I should like to see our experienced players on the pitch with me."

I nodded. "I understand that. But the way things are, Youngster and Pascal are shutting down most of their attacks."

"Perhaps James Wise instead of Donny. A more natural fit in the centre."

"I expect to use Wisey in the second half."

"Their centre backs are good. They are not giving me much. A second striker would help." He was anxious! Funny. For all his bluster and as much as he tried to act aloof, he cared. He cared about the club.

"Henri," I said, my smile reshaping my cheeks. "You know I love getting ideas. You know I'm not too proud to ask for help." He nodded. "But I've got this." I shuffled around the dressing room looking into the eyes of my soldiers. "You know if I was even slightly worried, I'd wind Henri up, get him ready for battle. Listen to this: Henri, mate? I like French wine. French cheese is top. French movies are . . . Well, let's just say I like France." The biggest laugh came from Youngster. "All right? No extra motivation needed today." I continued my tour. "The Southport manager is all right. For this level. But he's got the same eleven out there who started on Tuesday. You've run them ragged already, and the rain's coming down. Their legs are getting heavier and heavier. We've barely broken a sweat! We're playing great and we've got loads in reserve. This war is *won*, lads. We're already ahead of where I thought we'd be. We've got our hands on their balls and we're going to squeeeeeeze. I've got plans B, C, and D that we won't ever need. I'm not going to tell you what they are because you'll get too excited. I want you calm, like you've *been*. Calm. Steady. Let it happen!"

The players went back onto the pitch, but Vimsy held me back, with Jill hovering behind him.

"What's the plan? What have you got up your sleeve?"

A worried look crossed my face. "I was lying. I don't know *what* to do."

"Fuck," said Jill, then as she sometimes did when she swore, added, "Sorry."

Vimsy nodded, trying to look positive, but some blood had drained from his face. "Right. You got them hyped up, though. It's not what I'm used to, but it worked."

I frowned at them. "Guys. I'm fucking with you. I've got so many tricks up my sleeve I can't even feel my hands. Now will you fucking relax? We're at home to Southport. It's a routine win. Jesus."

The second half.

Southport came out fired up, competing hard, snapping into tackles, sprinting for their lives. The sense was that if they could find a quick equaliser, I'd panic and start making mistakes.

I asked for a ball from the nearest ball boy and did some kick-ups. Nothing fancy. It was just to send a message—*I've got this.*

A few minutes in and Youngster took a pass and retreated back towards Carl. I burst into a laugh; it was the absolute perfect move! I felt Southport's hardworking strikers get demoralised. And after ten minutes of calm, controlled play, I was feeling good. If it had been the fifth game of the season or something relatively unimportant like that, I wouldn't have thought twice about it. The only jeopardy came from our position in the league and the series of events that could mean we went into the final three games level on points with Blyth and Bradford.

I rolled the ball towards the dugout and stretched.

Physio Dean came out of the tunnel. "Sam's good. His wife's with him. She won't let him do anything daft. We'll keep him here for a while, then take him home later when it's dark."

I looked up. "Pretty dark now, Dean."

"When it's even darker," he said, pulling his coat around his neck. "Top stuff. Get in the shelter, mate."

"What about you?"

I pulled my hood over my head. "Comes with in-built protection."

"Right. But you're not using it."

I laughed and pushed the hood off me. I leaned back and let the rain smash into my face. It felt awesome.

He shuffled away, trying to move in a way that stopped water getting inside his clothes. But he came straight back. "MD said to look at the box." Then he rushed off.

So I turned and shielded my eyes from the rain and the floodlights. The director's box wasn't all that far away, but the light reflecting on the glass meant I couldn't see anything from my angle. I did an exaggerated shrug to show I couldn't see. In my peripheral vision, I saw movement. A flash of blonde hair. But I couldn't move my eyes. I'd just locked on to the menacing, smug visage of Old Nick. The waves of power emanating from him crashed into me.

I'd felt this before, almost exactly like this, when he'd tried to stop me taking the free kick against Alfreton.

But that time, it was hostile. A warning. A threat. This wave crashing into me was . . . pleasant.

I scowled at him for some time, then turned away. Started pacing up and down.

What was his plan?

I took another quick glance. He was in the middle of his little patch, with two imps either side of him. Nokia and the tactics imp were wearing earphones and tapping away on laptops.

What did he want?

He wanted me to manage football matches. The imp had said when I won a match, everyone won. Everyone meaning Nick. So he didn't only want me to manage, he wanted me to manage well. So why would he distract me? Make me doubt my plan?

I bit my lip and stared at the pitch. Everything was going great . . . wasn't it?

Selected match ratings:

Robbo 6 (not much work for our goalie to do)

Glenn 6 (the curse didn't reward him for organising the back line, only for his individual contributions like blocks and tackles)

Youngster 8 (mopping up all the second balls and loose passes; with *this* rain he'd need a bigger mop)

Raffi 6 (doing fine)

Pascal 4 (he had touched the ball maybe four times since he'd come on)

Henri 7 (barely any involvement, but everything he'd done had been neat and tidy and he'd scored the pen)

Minute 70.

The rain eased off. For some reason, I turned to Nick and when he saw me looking, his head tipped backwards and he did the most cartoonish evil laugh I'd ever seen on a real face. What the . . . ?

All the hairs on my neck stood up, which was some achievement given how soggy I was.

Transcript from Seals Live, 4:26 p.m.

Boggy: So just over half of the second half gone. It's still Chester having the lion's share of possession, and Southport still not really threatening. I'm very happy to report the rain has eased off. I can finally hear myself think again!

Spectrum: I'm fascinated that neither manager has made a change yet.

Boggy: What would you normally expect in this situation?

Spectrum: Well, the older managers like to pressure inexperienced managers with sudden formations shifts or dramatic substitutions. Southport do probably need to do something like that, to be honest. At one–nil, they're still in the game, and they could get a goal from a corner or set piece, but they aren't creating much.

Boggy: Why doesn't he change it, then?

Spectrum: Maybe he's heard that stuff doesn't work on Max Best.

Boggy: Don't mess with Chesters!

Spectrum: Right. But I'm sure Max isn't happy with one–nil. He's got great options on the bench. I wonder what he's thinking.

Boggy: He's thinking *if it isn't broke, don't fix it.*

Spectrum: Extremely sure he never thinks that. Ah, here we go.

Boggy: What?

Spectrum: Overload coming on the left.

Boggy: Chester sticking to their four-one-four-one formation, playing from left to right, attacking the Harry McNally Terrace. Hasn't been much goalmouth action this half. But now here's Raffi Brown. He's been at the heart of things for Chester. Exchanges a few passes with D-Day. Oh, they don't like that! Nichols tries to barge Brown off the ball, but Brown resists. He plays it away to Youngster, who encourages Trick forward. Trick pushes it to Aff, who takes a touch and waits. The defender isn't sure if he should dive in—nothing's really worked for him today. Aff plays the ball inside to Brown. Yes, the overload is happening now. I can see it! Three players moving to the edge of the penalty box, the left side, calm as you like.

Spectrum: Four. Watch D-Day get closer.

Boggy: Spectrum calls it! There he goes now. He's on the ball. Shapes to pass to Trick, but no!

Fans: [Roar of approval.]

Boggy: D-Day's forward pass, long one, Aff's burst forward! Aff to cross! Lyons in the middle. Cross doesn't come. We go again. Trick. Aff. Trick. Brown. Trick. D-Day.

Fans: [Loud roar of approval.]

Boggy: Southport player slips. Aff takes full advantage. He's in miles of space. Here comes the cross. Lyons! [Shrieks.]

Fans: [Explosive cheer.]

[Microphone rattles.]

Boggy: It's there! Lyons has [inaudible]. Ches [unintelligible].

Spectrum: Aaaaaargh!

Boggy: My word! It's deafening here. The Deva stadium is bouncing. The atmosphere is *unreal*. Haha! I can't believe this. Two–nil! What a goal! Lyons can't stop scoring!

Spectrum: This formation and way of playing is a dream for a player like him.

Boggy: It's a dream for me, too. It's like watching Brazil! Never thought I'd be able to say that and mean it. Now, what's this?

Spectrum: What?

Boggy: Unless my eyes deceive me, Max Best is angry.

Spectrum: Oh, shit.

Boggy: He's incan*descent* with rage. One of the fans has really wound him up. Spectrum, can you work out what's going on?

Spectrum: Uh.

Boggy: Southport kick off. They've got a mountain to climb now. They try to work it to number three, but Bochum is right in his face! All he can do is pass back to his goalie. Well, you were right, Spectrum. That tactic was unconventional, and Bochum hasn't contributed much with the ball, but he's completely shut down that line of attack. Oh! Oh my word! What's happening now? Max Best is storming off. Where's he going? I— Oh! I thought he was going to complain to the assistant referee but he's gone right past him. Where's he going? The corner flag?

Spectrum: Hear the fans?

Main Stand Fans (some): Max Best's Blue-and-White Army!

Spectrum: That was started there. There's five guys there, they've got Max Best scarves.

Boggy: I've never seen one of those.

Spectrum: Me neither. I would have said they didn't exist. Anyway, there's five guys there, and they've stood and started chanting "Max Best's Blue-and-White Army," and loads of people have joined in.

Boggy: And Max does *not* like that. He's halfway round the McNally now. Harry was another manager who did crazy things sometimes, as older listeners will remember. There's nothing happening in the game, by the way—the Chester players seem stunned by what's happening, as are we all. Okay he's stopped. He's at the Community Stand opposite us, near the halfway line. He's waving for them to be quiet. They seem to be obeying him. And now he seems to be chanting something. Oh!

Community Stand: Jackie Reaper's Blue-and-White Army! Jackie Reaper's Blue-and-White Army!

Boggy: That's lifted the players! Here they come again! Aff's powering forward. Will he cross? He *shoots*! It's just over. Oh, it's kicking off, here. Max Best is back at the McNally Terrace. He turns to the Community Stand. What's he doing?

Spectrum: Telling them to shush!

Boggy: He is! He's going to conduct the fans! Conduct the stadium! This is wild. [Cackles.] This is *wild*.

Harry McNally Terrace fans: Jackie Reaper's Blue-and-White Army! Jackie Reaper's Blue-and-White Army!

Boggy: It's ear-splitting! Now he's sprinting back to the main stand. He's at the first section. He's demanding they chant and they're responding! He's still absolutely incensed. Have you ever seen him like this?

Spectrum: Once when I put sugar in his tea.

Boggy: Er . . . Brown heads. D-Day cushions it to [inaudible].

All Home Fans: Jackie Reaper's Blue-and-White Army! Jackie Reaper's Blue-and-White Army! We. Are. Staying Up! Said we are staying up!

Boggy: Pandemonium here at the Deva. It's bedlam. The very soil is shaking.

Spectrum: Southport subs.

Boggy: Okay. Let's look.

Spectrum: They'll go three-five-two now.

Boggy: How do you know?

Spectrum: Max said that was the only explanation for who they had on the bench.

Boggy: Wait. Is he a wizard? Is he actually a wizard, though? Ah, that left back is going off. That's a relief.

Spectrum: Chester subs now.

Boggy: Ah! Southport blinked first. Who's coming on?

Spectrum: Er . . . James Wise and Tony Hetherington.

Boggy: And it looks like he's bringing off . . . Youngster. That's a surprise. And—oh!—Pascal Bochum. That's harsh.

Spectrum: He's done his job.

Boggy: That's a hell of a shift he's put in. Talk about thankless tasks. I hope he gets a nice reception. So . . . I'm trying to work out how this changes the shape. There's two strikers now. And, er . . . Wow. I have no clue.

Spectrum: [Nervous laugh.] Four-two-four.

Boggy: You're joking.

Spectrum: [Sigh.] The midfield is Raffi and Wisey. Aff left, D-Day right. Henri and Tony up top. He's going for it. Death or glory. [Deep sigh.]

Boggy: What about Southport? They've got five in midfield. They'll dominate possession.

Spectrum: I know what Max will say. He'll say, "So what?"

Boggy: Spectrum, mate, I can't take it. My heart.

Spectrum: This is Chester, now.

Boggy: Southport's manager did one thing well, there. He calmed the crowd down.

Spectrum: Yeah. Good luck with that.

I paced up and down the touchline, still raging about Nick's ham-fisted attempt to get Jackie sacked and me put in his place.

Fuck that.

I glared at the pitch. Southport were enjoying a rare spell of possession, and they had a striker who was fresh, hungry, keen to impress. I set Glenn Ryder to mark him and that was the last I ever thought about him.

Aff and D-Day were loitering on the wings, completely unmarked. The Southport manager was staring at the pitch in horror. They'd practised this move to 3–5–2. Probably been very diligent about it, very professional. But they hadn't worked on what to do if someone used 4–2–4 against it.

Because they *still* didn't know I was a floating megabrain. Did no one in this league ever do their homework? Well, bad students get punished.

The keeper punts the ball forward.

Ryder steps in front of his man and uses his strength to hold him off.

He plays a simple pass wide to Carlile.

Carlile has licence to run forward for the first time in the second half.

He knocks it forward to D-Day and surges after it.

Carlile overlaps. D-Day hits a long pass across the pitch and runs forward.

Aff controls the pass. He's in acres of space!

He drives forward and looks up.

He's got four targets to aim at!

He fires it low.

The ball skids across the wet turf.

Bodies fly everywhere! The keeper gets nowhere near it.

Carlile is at the back post.

GOOOOAAAALLLL!!!!

He couldn't miss!

I continued to prowl up and down. I tuned everything and everybody out, and when my players came over to celebrate, I pushed them away, shouting, "We're not done! We're not done!"

When the match resumed, Southport dragged their wide players back, so they were in a 5-3-2 formation. Which they hadn't practised. I set Trick and Carl to make forward runs. I switched Aff to playmaker. I wanted the rest of the match to be nonstop attacks while the fans chanted for Jackie.

And that's what I got.

The ball is played out to Aff.

He has so many options!

He shapes to cross, but checks and plays a simple square ball to Brown.

Brown looks to pass wide, but unleashes a surprise shot.

It goes through the massed defence, splashes off the surface, and nestles into the corner of the net.

GOOOOAAAALLLL!!!!

His first for the club!

Now I let the tension leave me. Four–nil, and Chester were safe. The fans were orgasmic. The rain came pouring down again. I turned and saw five empty seats behind me, and the end of a blue-and-white scarf, abandoned by its former owner.

As Southport retreated even more, I switched to a defensive 4-4-2. We would let the clock run down, and I'd hand the team back to Jackie, virtually injury-free, morale high, even more of a united, functional team than the one he'd given me.

At the final whistle, I shook hands with the Southport guy, then sprinted down the tunnel to get changed into some dry clothes.

I did my media duties for the last time in a long time. I'm pretty sure I said nothing of interest.

I went into the dressing room and bathed in the noise of our celebrations. But after a couple of minutes, I got the lads to quiet down. My last speech to them.

"Guys, we've had ups and downs. Like in a good book, we're ending on a high. I'll take a little wedge of the credit, but more goes to Jackie, and yeah, some to Ian Evans. But you guys, bloody hell. The crowd were going nuts today. I lost my head a couple of times, but you kept cool. Kept playing. The teamwork's great. The togetherness is good. The football has been absolutely sensational. Some of the passing, some of the movement, hiss!" I mimed touching a hot stove. "So enjoy yourselves. Jackie's back next week. Finish strong, because next season we're going to fuck some shit up." A cheer. "Contract talks begin Monday." An even bigger cheer.

Henri grabbed my shoulders and stared into my eyes, then pulled me close and hugged me. "Thank you, Max Best."

"Thank you, bro."

"I will be outside your office at nine a.m.," he said. His jokes were so weird sometimes.

"Hey, Max." Raffi.

"Sup?"

"That was amazing. I'm glad I know you."

"The feeling's mutual. Maybe you can get your dad off my case? I don't need more enemies."

"It's not serious. He really liked Ian Evans, is all."

I rubbed the back of my head. I'd expended so much psychic energy I was starting to get dizzy. "I'm allowed to make a few mistakes, right? That's . . . that's part of learning, isn't it? Part of growing up?"

He gave me a trademark lopsided grin. "You don't make that many. That's why they stand out."

Finally, I said goodbye to Pascal and Youngster. "You guys were fantastic," I said. "I'm really proud of you. Two teenagers helped bring us to safety. And next year, you'll help us win the league."

"And the cup," said Youngster. "I read your match programme."

"Let's just win every match we ever play. What do you think?"

"Yes, Max," said Pascal. Most of the outside world wouldn't know what he'd done today. They'd call him names, laugh at him, call him a waste of money. But everyone in this dressing room knew what he'd done. What he'd sacrificed, how he'd contributed. Vimsy was looking at him with new eyes. The dinosaur had finally seen the space invader for what he was: the ultimate team player. Fast, diligent, a man you could *trust*.

"Dean," I said, before I headed to the bar. "I'd like to say bye to Sam. Should I leave it?"

"If you can leave it, leave it."

I nodded. Smiled. "I'll see him Monday morning."

Dean hesitated. "Max . . . I went past your office to check it out. For Sam, like. Er . . . I think you deserve a bigger space."

"Ha. I hadn't thought about it. Maybe I'll get them to give me the boardroom."

"If you asked *now*, I think they'd say yes."

I grinned. He was probably right. I stepped into the manager's office to take a minute. I closed my eyes and concentrated on my breathing until my head stopped spinning, until the ringing in my ears quietened.

I had kept a lot of promises. Now I needed to keep one more.

I headed towards the Blues Bar, where I would buy drinks until my cash ran out.

The room was as noisy and chaotic as the last twenty minutes of the match. I ploughed into the mass of bodies, through the limbs and the dancing men and the singing women. I got to the bar, elevated myself, and held up a twenty-pound note.

"Drinks on me!" I yelled.

To a stony, frosty silence. One massive, hulking brute jabbed a sausagey finger at me. "Your money's no good here, Max Best. You don't buy drinks in this city. This city buys drinks for you."

"Come on," I said. "I promised."

"BEST!" yelled one of the guy's mates. "Best will tear you apart! Again!"

And then they were off. No reasoning with them. Someone handed me a beer. I took a sip. And then I saw the one thing that had been missing. The last piece in the puzzle. I scrambled across the room, through the ecstatic fans, in the direction of a young boy with large, wide-open eyes.

But on the way there was even more shit to deal with. First, I saw Sullivan, the only boy I'd cut from the youth system. Or, more accurately, the only boy I'd cut who I hadn't let back in. He should have been there with us at Das Tournament. His name should have been in Beth's article, alongside Tyson's and Benny's. His dad was there, too. Of course—they were Chester fans. But no. Not "of course." In their shoes, I'd never have set foot in the stadium again. Had they come just to scowl at me? Because that's what they were doing.

And, even more crazily, when a certain group of dancers moved left, and another few people moved right, I spotted, in the far corner of the bar, a surly, grumpy-faced couple. I'd never seen the man before, but he'd been cast in the same mould as the guy who wouldn't let me pay for drinks: oversized, massive neck folds, huge hands. Such men were ten a penny.

But in the seat next to him was the referee. Not the cheerful, almost-competent ref from tonight's game. No, the one who had yellow-carded Dani for being deaf. Who had been humiliated in the *Daily Mail*. My cheeks blazed with righteous indignation.

I had a choice: talk to the boy or berate the woman and make her leave?

The woman had suffered enough, possibly. But the boy. I made my way over to him, and he tugged at a man's jacket. The guy turned, saw me, and beamed. For once I had no hesitation in shaking a stranger's hand. "Max Best! What on Earth are you doing in here?"

"Promised to buy drinks," I said, having to all but shout because we were so close to a speaker. "Who's this little guy?"

"He's called Max! Would you believe it?"

"Not really."

"He is! It's his first match. What a first match to come to!"

First match! It had really happened! I felt my knees go weak, but I managed to keep things together. Just. "Do you think you'll come back, Max?"

He nodded. "Dad likes Chester, but Mum likes United. I saw you do free kicks. Are you a player and a manager?"

"Sort of," I confessed. "I'll play next season. But only if you come and watch. Otherwise there's no point."

He looked up at his dad with that *Is he joking now?* face kids are so good at. "Okay!"

I bent down. "Hey, Max. Can I have a selfie with you?"

"*You* with *me*? Ye-ah!"

We took two. One with my phone, one with Max's dad's.

And that was it. I'd done it. Brought Chester to safety *and* started on my stretch goal of making this club the place local kids wanted to come.

I floated away, but then reality hit once more, as it does. MD was rushing around the Blues Bar, trying to find me. I watched from above as he put his hands on my shoulders. "Max," he said, from a stretchy distance away. I snapped back into my body. "Max," he repeated.

"What?"

"First of all, I want to thank you for the most amazing evening of my life. It was better than *Les Miserables*, and I mean that. You're . . . you're incredible. God, I just want to get hammered and flirt with women you think are out of my league. Thing is, Jackie just called. He wants you to be first-team manager."

"What?"

"He thinks you should take over. He wants me to announce it, like, now."

The dizzy, spinning sensation returned with a vengeance. This was Old Nick's doing! Somehow he'd planted this insane idea in Jackie's head, and the madman had gone with it. "No."

MD was confused. "Max, he's going to quit. He's going to force us."

"No one tells me what to do," I said, getting steamed up. "We need him. If you let him go, I'll never forgive you. You know what? Fuck that. I'm going to talk to him right now. Right now. You hear me? Get back on the phone, and you tell him I'm coming. And if *he* quits, I quit. Are we a hundred percent clear about that?"

"Max, no. It's . . . he's—"

But I was already storming out. Out of the stadium into the alley. Into the torrential rain. All I could hear was rain. I took three purposeful steps towards the car park, then hesitated. At the end of the alley was a guy wearing a black balaclava. I suddenly remembered that I'd entered the stadium by this door to bypass some potential threats. And the stadium had been full of people who hated me. They were packed in like sardines.

Terror coursed through me like a bolt of lightning, but then I relaxed. Idiot, Max! It wasn't a guy in a balaclava. It was someone I knew. Someone wonderful. I stepped forward again, foot splashing in a hidden puddle, and the man was suddenly running towards me, hand raised.

What?

Under the sound of the rain and the streams of water running along the sides of the alley, I heard something else. Steps. Movement. The hand waved harder, trying to signal—trying to warn. Too late, I tried to throw myself forward, or sideways, or something.

I didn't feel the blow. Everything went black. It was like falling asleep.

A well-earned rest after a long, hard season.

15

EPILOGUE

Chester Live, April 1
Soccer star, 22, in A&E after brutal attack

Chester FC's director of football, Max Best, has been rushed to Countess of Chester Hospital with massive head injuries after being attacked outside the Deva Stadium. Best, who had just led the team to its fourth win in a row, was struck with a blunt object, apparently on his way to the car park. His injuries are described as very serious, though his condition is not thought to be immediately life-threatening.

A Ghanaian man has been detained in connection with the incident. Police are not looking for other suspects.

More on this story as it develops.

BBC North West Tonight, April 2
Police hunt Best attacker

Police have appealed for witnesses and clues in connection with the savage assault on Chester FC star Max Best after Saturday's match. Best left the stadium through the Blues Bar at around 5:30 p.m. If you have information, please use the contact details above.

The police had initially arrested a foreign national, but their case collapsed almost instantly. The suspect's lawyer, one Sebastian Weaver, laid into the arresting officer, claiming the officer's actions were prosecutable in themselves, and he had allowed Best's assailant to flee the scene and merge into the nearby crowds with impunity.

Cheshire Police declined to comment.

Best remains in critical condition in Countess of Chester's intensive care unit.

April 3
Excerpt from transcript of the UK's number one football podcast

Mark: And that's when Gary realised he'd soiled himself again.
All: [Laughter.]

Mark: But on a serious note, horrible, shocking news from nonleague football, where Max Best, a young manager, was attacked after a game. He's still in hospital with serious head injuries, but it seems the blow wasn't as bad as initially feared. One of his own player's fathers witnessed the attack and rushed to stop it and get help. His bravery and quick thinking are thought to have saved Best from more serious injuries and loss of blood, though the father was then detained by local police.

Gary: Jesus, Mary, and Joseph.

Mark: Best is said to be improving, and doctors are optimistic he'll be out of intensive care very soon. Jean-Jacques, you wanted to comment on this.

JJ: Yes, Mark, thank you. As it happens, I have a friend who knows Max Best very well, and he called me in absolute bits. It's not quite correct to call him a manager, not in the sense you mean. He was care-taker manager of the men's team while the usual manager rested after surgery, but in fact he is Chester's director of football and is by all ac-counts very good at it. And he's also a player, and from the footage I've seen, an extraordinary one. I hope very much he makes a full recovery, because the stories I've been hearing speak of a rare talent.

Mark: Wait. It's just clicked. He's the winger who turned down a big move to . . . Yes, I remember the name now. But he's *amazing*.

Gary: Hang on. Isn't he the one who took his team off the pitch be-cause the referee booked a deaf player?

JJ: That's him.

Mark: He sounds like quite the character. I'm sure we all wish him a speedy recovery. Jean-Jacques, will you keep us updated?

JJ: Will do, Mark.

Mark: Final question today comes from Pete in Eavesham. Would you rather fight one gigantic Easter bunny, or a thousand small ones?

Chester Live, April 8
Emotional Seals thrash Farsley

Taking to the pitch wearing Best 77 shirts, in-form Chester wept before and after the match, and spent the ninety minutes in between marauding all around West Yorkshire. The 5–0 scoreline suggests a one-sided match, but in truth, the contest was so uneven a boxing referee would have ended the bout within sixty seconds.

Manager Jackie Reaper batted away questions about Chester mathematically securing their National League North status for another year, and focused on Max Best, whose recovery from assault continues apace.

News Item from Chester FC's Website, April 15
Boost the Budget a "massive success"

Ahead of Chester's final home game of the season, managing director Mike Dean has announced that the club's fundraising efforts have smashed all previous efforts. "The club is financially stable for another year, thanks to the incredible generosity of the community. It feels like the city is uniting behind the club and is keen to see us succeed next season. We all know why it has happened. Not a penny will be spent until he's back at the wheel."

Cheshire Independent, April 22
Double joy for Chester

Chester have two reasons to celebrate tonight, as the men's first team beat Peterborough Sports 3–2 in an entertaining game to finish the season in an improbable fourteenth place. Six wins in the last seven games, plus a creditable draw against playoff hopefuls Scarborough, propelled Chester close to the halfway point in the league, after seeming certain to be relegated.

Much of the credit for their unlikely turnaround has been attributed to the impressive director of football, Max Best, who was hospitalised after being struck outside the stadium. The other good news is that Best has declared himself well enough to see visitors.

Manager Jackie Reaper, visibly emotional on hearing the news, told reporters he was chuffed. "The next match is August, so he's got the whole summer to rest and recover. Knowing him, he'll want to be back in work tomorrow. Wow. Now I'm wondering who he'll see first. I mean, I know who'll be first. But who'll be second?"

April 23
@ChesterFC

We are delighted to announce that Henri Lyons has been named National League North Player of the Month for April! His seven goals, including a hat trick against Farsley Celtic, made him a shoo-in for the award. He leaves the club on a high. *Merci*, Henri!

April 24
Transcript from Deva Victrix, the unofficial Chester podcast

Huey: So Player of the Season, we've got two votes for Glenn Ryder, one vote for Sam Topps. Sounds about right, to be fair.

Dewey: Let's move onto Goal of the Season.

Louie: Hold up a second. I've got stats.

Others: [Groans.]

Louie: So. National League North goalscorers. Guy from Fylde was top with twenty-six. Haughton. This is league goals only, by the way. Taylor from Spennymoor is second on twenty-three. Eighth on the list with sixteen league goals: Henri Lyons. But when you look at goals per minute, Haughton scored a goal every 137 minutes. Taylor, every 160 minutes. Lyons? Goal for Chester every 105 minutes.

Huey: Not bad.

Louie: Not bad? He didn't score for four games. Cut them out and the numbers would start to get silly. But you know what else is silly?

Dewey: You're gonna tell us about Max Best.

Louie: Nine goals in the league, doesn't put him in the top twenty, so you can't see his stats easily. But I went through the match reports and worked it out. He played in six league games for Darlington.

Huey: Only six?

Louie: Two hundred ninety minutes total, give or take. Nine goals.

Dewey: I'm on my third pale ale, so don't be asking us to do maths.

Louie: A goal every thirty-two minutes.

Others: [Disbelieving jeers.]

Louie: I worked it out! I wasn't even drunk!

Huey: Get stuffed. That's three goals a game. Shut up. Right, Goal of the Season. For me, question is, best goal or goal I enjoyed most. So if we go back to the Oldham match . . .

Undated

Dear Max Best,

I hope you won't be sick for long because you are such a good person.

You were so nice to me, and my dad says you are very brave.

I liked it when you made us sing the army song. I am a Chester fan now.

My mum was not happy, but Dad said I did it right. He said I am one of us.

Max

Max Best Playing Stats

Darlington FC 22/23

Squad Number: 77

Appearances: 5 starts, 2 subs

Goals: 9

Assists: 3

Man of the Match Awards: 4

Yellow Cards: 0

Red Cards: 0

Average Rating out of 10 (as estimated by Max Best): 11

Max Best Manager Stats

Chester Men

National League North

Played 3, Won 3 (Goals For 7, Goals Against 0)

Manager Points: 135

Chester Women

Friendlies

Played 5, Won 2 (Goals For 11, Goals Against 17)

Manager Points: n/a

ABOUT THE AUTHOR

Ted Steel is the author of the Player Manager series, which features a charming but secretive main character. He also wrote Nerves of Steel, a LitRPG featuring a charming but secretive main character. When asked to provide a bit of color for his biography, Steel was charming but . . . secretive. Learn more at www.ted-steel.com.

Podium